PRAISE FOR
Paperback Original
by Will Rhode

"Far from joining the ranks of Post-Modern literary tricksters chasing a new definition of authorship, Rhode has written a rollicking Anglo-Indian thriller with a twist. . . . It becomes really engrossing . . . descriptive passages of real skill and beauty . . . real and moving insight. . . . Rhode has a wickedly ironic sense of humor. His hero is wonderfully self-deprecating and this truly puts the Anglo into the Anglo-Indian: think Kipling's *Plain Tales* told by a twenty-first-century P. G. Wodehouse. . . . His version not only of India, but of what it is like to be privileged and unhappy, traveling but trapped, is convincing and astute." —*The Times* (London)

"The opening of Rhode's first novel certainly hooks you in. . . . Will it be a bestseller? We wouldn't be surprised."
—*In Style* (UK)

"A devious thriller . . . entertaining." —*Independent on Sunday* (UK)

"Should appeal to fans of *The Beach*." —*Glamour* (UK)

"Rhode has skillfully put together a good novel that has the intelligence of a classic without losing the contemporary cutting edge. . . . Few events are more thrilling than finding a novel that takes storytelling in a new direction. The witty, provocative and ultimately wise [*Paperback Original*] is a novel a new generation has been waiting for." —*Asian Times*

"[A] crazy tale of drugs, dreams and a Viagra overdose that the literary in-crowd are calling this year's answer to *The Beach*."
—*Marie Claire* (UK)

"A confident, energetically written, cheekily ironic and mordantly funny companion to stuff into the backpack." —*Daily Mail* (UK)

continued . . .

"A fresh spin on the Generation-X story."   —*Eve* (UK)

"Reads like a James Bond script . . . an entertaining package."
—*Heat* (UK)

"This funny and gripping tale shuns the 'Delhi Belly' depictions of India, showing instead a far more interesting side of the country."
—*New Woman* (UK)

"A heavy dose of backpacking lad lit."   —*Mirror* (UK)

"Like a spicy Pot Noodle—tasty, seductive."   —*TNT* (UK)

"Wacky."   —*Scotland on Sunday*

"Will Rhode's first novel is about being dazed, confused, and minus a passport in India's 'travelers' underground.' . . . A lively tale with an obvious appeal for twenty-something readers of *The Beach*. The story starts with an amusing if improbable premise . . . and the plot thickens from there. Zestful writing, fresh characters, black comedy, and an unself-consciously authentic grasp of the backdrop—seedy nightclubs and drug-fueled parties—make [*Paperback Original*] an entertaining read. [It] is also very much about the chronic insecurities that go with the territory of being in one's twenties."   —*The Bookseller* (UK)

"A word of warning if you are heading off on your gap year to India: this is not a travel guide. Heavier than *Are You Experienced?* and set in a schizophrenic world of poverty and prosperity . . . [it] is a mind-blowing tale of corruption and suspicion showing how far you'll go when desperation is your guide."
—*The List* (Glasgow & Edinburgh)

"Fantastical, provocative and world-wise jape."   —*Belfast Telegraph*

PAPERBACK ORIGINAL

WILL RHODE

Riverhead Books
New York

Riverhead Books
Published by The Berkley Publishing Group
A division of Penguin Group (USA) Inc.
375 Hudson Street
New York, New York 10014

First published in Great Britain as *Paperback Raita* by Simon & Schuster UK Ltd. in 2002
First Riverhead trade paperback edition: April 2003

Visit our website at www.penguinputnam.com

Library of Congress Cataloging-in-Publication Data

Rhode, Will, 1972–
[Paperback raita]
Paperback original / Will Rhode.— 1st Riverhead trade pbk. ed.
p.   cm.
First published in Great Britain as Paperback raita by Simon & Schuster in 2002.
ISBN 1-57322-980-6
1. Inheritance and succession—Fiction.   2. Fiction—Authorship—Fiction.
3. Fathers and sons—Fiction.   4. British—India—Fiction.   5. Journalists—Fiction.
I. Title.

PR6118.H47P36   2003
823'.914—dc21
2002037191

10   9   8   7   6   5   4   3   2   1

For Mob

ACKNOWLEDGMENTS

Many thanks to Shân Millie, Shai Hill, Pari Gray, and Martha Lowe for their insight and support.

Dear Josh,

By the time you read this letter I'll be dead and you'll be cursing me because it is the only thing I have left you. I know you won't expect me to make any apologies. Like I've always told you: Life's a bitch and then you die.

But I do owe you an explanation.

The first thing you should know is that you have no right to my money. Just because you are my son does not mean that you are entitled to it.

More importantly, I'm worried that you are wasting your life. You seem incapable of sticking to anything. I didn't invest all that money in your education just to watch you flit from one career to the next and spend the intervals on a beach or in some drug-induced fantasyland. By leaving you with nothing, I hope to give you something you've never had before. I'm giving you single-mindedness of purpose.

For what, you might ask?

It's quite simple, really. I want you to write a book—with me in it.

As you know, I've always thought that literature holds the key to immortality. Characters in books are the only people that go on living. They get revitalized with every read. And in a funny way, that's part of the reason for killing myself. I'm hoping that my death will inspire you. I'm killing myself so that I can live longer.

I know what you're thinking. If it means that much to me, why don't I write a book myself? The answer is, I don't have Time. My number's up, at least that's what the antiaging doctors tell me. They totally screwed things up and now I'm getting old very fast. Something to do with my testosterone-replacement therapy—an overdose—and now my body's on fast-forward. The real bitch is, I don't think I was more than a generation or two away from eternal youth. So I figure, if I'm the guinea pig for all the experiments that will help you live forever, the least you can do is write me into the future.

So here's the deal: Write a book with me in it (you know what I mean, a significant part, nothing major, just . . . significant) and I'll give you £5 million. Fail and you get nothing. And it's got to be a bestseller (I won't be very immortal if no one bothers to imagine me). I'll give you five years.

I know that may seem mercenary, but let's face it: I'm doing you a favor. It's about time you focused on your writing. I know that, deep down, that's really what you want to do. And just think—you could be rich. On top of the five mill I give you, there'll be book sales. You can spend the rest of your life pissing about after that for all I care.

Good luck. You're going to need it.

Love, Dad

P.S.: In case you don't already know, I am leaving the rest of my money to Morag. I know that will upset you, since you don't like her very much. But, in all fairness, she deserves it. After all, she did help me make a lot of it, whereas you, Josh, have done nothing to earn your share. Don't try and contest the will. I've had a mental evaluation and there is a medical report stating that I am in full control of my senses. This idea to kill myself is simply a logical decision to end my life how and when I want to. You'll probably never know it, but when you're close, the prospect of growing old becomes far worse than the idea of dying.

PART ONE

THE GREEN

It isn't unusual for the police to raid the Green Guesthouse. It's all part of the deal. The fat twins that run the place are ex-cops. Everyone knows that. And if you don't, chances are they are coming for you.

The Green is essentially a box within a box: four walls with four more walls running parallel inside. The guest-house rooms are built between the ten-foot gap that separates them. The building is five stories high and is tucked into the corner of a small, shoulder-shaped cul-de-sac off the main bazaar. There is no roof and each floor looks down the gaping rectangular hole that plunges through the center of the building. When it rains, like it is doing on this muggy monsoon night, the lower rooms flood. Maybe that's why people call its rectangular gut "the well." But I think that is just a euphemism.

The fact is, the Green looks like a jail and the gaping hole in the middle is its exercise enclosure. The rooms don't have windows and each landing is lined with six-foot bars to prevent people falling down the well. The only air and the only light come in from the open roof.

I'll admit I've found it scary living here these past six months. The raids always make me nervous. You can never be totally sure that some junkie—and there are lots of them in the Green—hasn't set you up. And if the police do decide to raid your room, there is no guarantee that they will accept a bribe to let you off.

Of course, they almost always do—after all, that's the whole point. The fat proprietors tip off their old friends about a guest they don't like or who looks too green for the Green, and one midnight trip and a few scare tactics later, they split the winnings.

That's the worst thing about the raids—the fact that they always come at night. It's usually two or three in the morning, when sleep is deepest and the shock factor is greatest. They know that their newcomers are naked then, panicked and vulnerable with a flashlight in their faces and the crack of the door still echoing in their ears.

But sometimes, and for unknown reasons, it does happen, they won't accept *baksheesh*. It doesn't matter whether the person has hash in their room or not. If they decide you are going down, that's it: ten years. Ten years in an Indian prison.

And in that sense, I suppose, the Green is like a halfway house that goes the wrong way. It looks like a prison, and for some unlucky people, it's an acclimatization chamber that leads there. It always freaks everyone out when they wake up to find there's one less guest, one more empty room. A lot of people check out then.

But I never do. For me, it's better than staying in any of the other places on Pahar Ganj—the first stop for every budget traveler arriving in Delhi. For starters, I feel marginally protected at the Green. I know that one of the twins, Ashok, the one with the betel-nut-stained teeth and greasy black mustache, likes me.

He's a Space Invader. Whenever a raid is in the cards, he always warns me in advance, pressing himself against my body till I feel the heat of his breath against my face. I don't mind flirting with him. It seems like a small price to pay for staying safe. And at least he's predictable. I can't be sure that the other hotel owners will afford me the same security.

But the real reason I stay at the Green is because it is *the* place to meet travelers. Its prison design is perfect for it. Hardly anyone stays in their stuffy little rooms during the day and the landings frequently turn into layers of social activity.

And by travelers, I mean the travelers who count, the ones who have sold their passports and have lived in India for ten, fifteen, twenty years. Most of them aren't even travelers anymore. They're just criminals, on the make and eking out existences on drug runs and other dodgy deals.

They are also the ones who know how to find Baba.

TRUSTAFARIAN

To say that I was angry with my father after reading his suicide note, his will, his final testament—whatever you want to call it— would be an understatement of the highest order. In the months immediately after he killed himself, when people asked me how I felt, I would spit the words out.

Most people thought I was angry because he didn't leave me any money. One or two of my closest friends, the only other people who saw his letter, thought that maybe I was angry because his final words to me had been so harsh.

But the reality was that I was angry with my father because, well, how can I put this? . . . He didn't leave me any money. Of course it was because of that.

And as for the so-called favor he was doing me. Focus on being a writer? I didn't want to be a writer. Not in the way he made out, anyway. I think I may have mentioned it—*once*—but I said it in the same way a six-year-old says he wants to be a fireman when he grows up, and even then it was only really intended to please him. I knew his feelings on the the subject. I suppose I should have been more careful.

My father wrote two novels before selling out to go into property development. He never showed them to anyone, so I have no idea what they were about. All I know is that they didn't pass the

"Who Cares?" test, so he locked them away in a chest never to be seen again.

I thought I was off the hook. I should have known that my flirtations with his own youthful aspirations would eventually come back to haunt me. Now I was screwed. By the time of his death, the only thing I did know was that I didn't want to be poor. I'd just spent the previous five years, with the odd working interlude, very happily taking my place as a directionless member of the downwardly mobile middle class.

The closest I had actually come to writing anything were a couple of articles for an Indian newspaper called the *Hindu Week*. And that was six years before. Forgive the initiative on my part. It was just after college and I was caught up in posteducation panic. Everyone else seemed to be running around, finding something "to do with their lives," and I guess I just didn't want to be left out—or behind.

But that didn't last. The only reason I ever worked after that was because Dad offered to match my salary with a monthly allowance. We'd first come to the arrangement when I was sixteen. He'd wanted me to spend a school holiday working as a laborer on one of his building sites for "experience." Really it was just to get me out of his hair while he and Morag got married and honeymooned. I know he paid me double because he still felt guilty about Mum leaving with my two siblings, "to start her own family," as she called it. And I would have gone with her if I'd known Morag was sticking around. Dad had to bribe me to get out of a betrayal that big. He'd sworn he'd never stay with her.

Which is partly why I was especially angry with him after I got his letter. It was abandonment, pure and simple. Our long-standing arrangement was suddenly at an abrupt end. The last thing I needed was to "focus." I was far too busy already: traveling, taking drugs, growing my hair.

I blamed Morag, of course. For everything. For his death, inasmuch as her youth made my father feel older than he really was. Dad was only sixty-four when he killed himself, and he probably could have lived for at least another twenty years—had he not embarked on all that antiaging madness. Who wants to live forever anyway? Just being with her made him want to be thirty all over again. And she didn't exactly make a lot of effort to stop his attempts at rejuvenating himself.

And then, of course, there was the fact that he left everything— which included three houses, six cars, a yacht, two speedboats, and a small plane (as well as my five million should I fail to fulfill his final wish within five years)—to her.

In the end, though, I didn't bother contesting the will, even though one lawyer I saw said I had a good chance of winning if I did. I guess I couldn't bear to go through the whole legal proceedings, especially since it would probably have meant even more media attention.

The newspapers couldn't get enough of my father's suicide. And I have to admit, I can't really blame them. Of all the Viagra scandals that hit the nineties—from cardiac arrests to lawsuits— my father's death was the most sensational. Why he couldn't just drive his six-series Mercedes into the Mediterranean without taking all his clothes off and without the overdose was beyond me. Most papers tactfully placed one of those black stars over his erection, but a couple didn't.

I decided that my life had already turned into something out of an episode of *Dynasty*, without the added drama of a legal battle over his will. I just wanted the whole thing to be over. And besides, he hadn't exactly left me with much choice. So, in accordance with his wishes, I set about writing the Bestseller.

And what a joke that turned out to be. Before starting, I did some research to figure out my chances of success, only to discover that more than five thousand books get published each month, and of them, only ten or so each year go on to become massive hits.

There were other problems too. Like . . . I couldn't come up with a decent story. I thought about doing something on Dad and the Viagra Sensation, or how my father had made his fortune, or perhaps his penchant for life-threatening outdoor activities, but I couldn't see any of those ideas really selling. I even entertained the idea of buying up half a million copies in advance, but even with the five million, the math didn't look great. And knowing Dad, there would have been some clause in his will against that sort of thing anyway.

And so, after six months of so-called writing that actually involved working in a gay bar, I finally swallowed my pride and went to Morag-darling-sweetie-so-gorgeous-to-see-you for money. I should have known better. She said that she'd help me get a job instead.

AN UNINVITED GUEST

It is a ferociously hot night, maybe 120 degrees plus. The fans have been cutting out all night, as they always do when the rains first arrive, and I'm not really sleeping. I'm just lying on my bed, my pores popping beads of sweat—turning my skin into bubble-wrap.

There's a knock on my door.

"Who is it?" I can hear footsteps in the well. "Who is it?"—a little louder. I am answered by another brief, urgent rap. I tie a lunghi around my waist and press my eye up against the crack in the saloon-style door. I can hear breathing, but the person is out of my one-inch line of sight. I open the door.

I see the flashlights first. My room is on the fifth floor and I can see them bouncing up and down the well, carving up the night and arresting the rainfall in cylindrical freeze frames. Ashok hadn't told me that there would be a raid tonight.

Then she just forces her way past me into my room.

"Please, you have to help me." Her voice sounds European, but it is laced with traces of an American accent. She is breathing heavily, presumably from running up the stairs.

I turn on the lights before she suddenly lunges and turns them back off again. Call me a sucker, but in that one, brief stroboscopic moment I decide that I am not going to throw her out. That's all it takes. That, and her smell.

"Please, leave the lights off," she whispers desperately.

"What do you want?"

"Let me stay here for a while."

"Why?"

"The police."

"What about them?"

"They're questioning my boyfriend."

For a while, I just listen to her breathing in the dark. Her breath is slowing down, gradually. "What for?"

"I don't know," she says urgently, almost angrily.

"If you want me to help . . ."

"Honestly, I don't know. All I know is, I went to the toilet, and when I came back they were in our room, searching him. That's when I ran up here. Your door was the first one I came to."

"Will they find anything?"

"We've got some *charas*—a tiny bit—and a couple of *chillums,* that's all."

"That's enough."

"What are they going to do?" she asks.

"I dunno. I'm sure it will be fine. Your boyfriend will just have to pay some *baksheesh* and they'll let him off. They'll be gone in half an hour."

"Do you mind if I stay here?"

I pause to double-check with myself. "No, I suppose not."

"Thank you."

I am naturally clumsy. Not just clumsy in a "he'll knock the glass over" type way but clumsy in every sense. Physically speaking,

I'm lanky. I'm six foot two and I slouch. People think I'm five eleven, max. My friends call me "No Neck." I'm also very mal-coordinated. I look gawky and awkward. I lumber. My hands and feet are too big for me. In fact, I blame my feet. They were the first things to start growing when the hormones kicked in. I've got the same size feet today as I did when I was twelve. I was five foot two with size-thirteen feet. They're also very flat. Exceedingly flat, in fact—archless. My feet made me crap at sports. People laughed at me. It made me nervous. Ever since then I've blundered. I'm tactless. I bungle. I always manage to make exactly the wrong move at exactly the wrong time. How else can I put it? I'm Homer Simpson clumsy.

That's the only explanation I have for why I decide to sneak a quick look outside to see what's going on. A flashlight catches me full in the face. I jerk myself out of its beam and pull my head in behind the doors, but I know it's too late.

"Doh."

"What happened?" the girl asks, nervously.

"I think you'd better hide," I say, biting my lip.

We listen to the footsteps pounding their way across the landing and then up the stairs. By my reckoning we have two flights to do something. I look around the room. The only decent place to hide is in the en suite bathroom, which is essentially a shower and a hole in the floor for the toilet separated by a heavy metal door covered in rust. She suggests hiding under the bed.

CURRICULUM VITAE

Name: Joshua King
Born: 13 March 1972
Home address: c/o Mrs. M. King, 29 Holland Villas Rd., London
   W14
Nationality: British
Status: Single
Languages: English, French (basic)
Driver's license: Clean

EDUCATION

1992–1993: St. Christopher's Secretarial College, Oxford 1st Class
Advanced Word Processing

September 1991–December 1991: Art foundation, St. Martin's
College, London

1988–1990: Lensfield Sixth Form College, Cambridge 2 "A" levels:
English, Art

1985–1988: Westminster College 9 "O" levels

1979–1985: Essex House Preparatory School, London

WORK EXPERIENCE

August 1998–present: Associate Manager, The Gardens, London

August 1997–July 1998: Manager, Antiques Anonymous, Portobello Road

October 1994–June 1995: Correspondent, *Hindu Week,* Delhi, India

June 1988–September 1988: Construction Worker

September 1987–June 1988: Editor, school newspaper

INTERESTS

Travel, music, reading, meditation, film, the arts, acting, football, and boxing (watching)

REFERENCES

Supplied upon request

THE INTERVIEW

"Are you married?"

"No."

"Would you be prepared to go into dangerous situations?"

The Reuters newsroom buzzed outside. I had been in the offices all day, getting the guided tour and shaking hands with all the big cheeses. Rodney Pinter and Harold Brisbane were big cheeses. And here they were, asking me if I was prepared to go into dangerous situations. The interview was going well, I thought.

"Absolutely."

Morag had felt that journalism was as good a place as any for me to start. After all, there was my "experience" at the *Hindu Week,* which, she said, "was sure to help," and, for me, well, it seemed like a logical stepping-stone. Didn't a lot of wannabe authors become journalists instead? For all I knew, this might be the solution to my lack-of-material dilemma. I might end up writing a political thriller with Dad as the heroic president.

"That's great, Joshua. We're glad you came in to visit us today. Now, are there any questions you would like to ask us?"

My mind raced. I knew that I had to ask them something, but I had spent so much energy making sure I had answers to their questions, coming up with a question of my own escaped me.

"Er. Yes. I'd just like to know what Reuters thinks of me."

Looking back on it now, it's easy to see what a silly question that was. Sometimes I wonder whether things might have turned out differently had I asked something else. "How did you come to be so successful, Mr. Pinter?" Or, "What's the secret to your amazing talent, Mr. Brisbane?" Put it down to the clumsy in me. Of all the questions I could have asked, this was among the most blundering of them all.

"Not much." It was Pinter talking. He was a small man with an Edinburgh accent. He had fat fingers and receding orange hair and he only seemed to come alive when he was insulting people. I can't even really remember what he said. It all became a big orange blur. "Think you can waltz in 'ere . . . fockin' public-school boys with yer rich daddies and fancy accents . . . so fockin' presumptuous . . . Mummy knows someone, does she? Well, I couldn't give a fock . . ."

After a while Brisbane stepped in. Pinter was losing the plot. "Look, Joshua, the point is, you don't have anything to offer us." Brisbane's words were harder to swallow and they have been harder to forget. In contrast to Pinter, Brisbane was tall and dashing, dressed in a pair of chinos and a green checkered shirt. And when he spoke he did so almost sympathetically, lifting his thin eyebrows understandingly and turning his head gently to emphasize each insult with caring concern. It was a ruthless combination and I almost broke down in front of him. He managed to make me regret myself completely. "You can't speak any languages . . ."

"Yes, I can," I muttered.

"What?" he asked, picking up my CV and squinting at it through a pair of half-moon glasses. "French?"

"Er, yes."

"Go on, then."

"Go on what?"

"Parlez-moi en français."

"I can't think of anything to say."

"Oh, for fock's—" Pinter was back.

Brisbane put his hand up to stop him. "Look, Joshua. Take my advice. Try and find something you want to do. We don't care who your mother—"

"Stepmother."

"—who your stepmother knows. We're never going to give someone like you a job. There are people that have worked hard all their lives to get where they are at this company. I don't know what you think you've been doing with your life so far, but taking a typing course and writing a couple of stories for an Indian newspaper doesn't make you a journalist. And if I was you, next time you go for an interview, try and think up some way to justify these enormous gaps in your life. Just out of interest, what exactly were you doing between 1995 and 1997?"

"Traveling."

Pinter and Brisbane looked at each other. Pinter laid into me for a while longer, Brisbane came back in with his good-cop routine before, eventually, I had had enough.

"It's all right, gentlemen," I finally said, being sure to look them in the eye. "I get the message. I can see myself out." And I did. It seemed strange that two men at the top of their profession would choose to dedicate so much energy to putting me down. If life in an office did that to you, then I wanted no part of it, I thought to myself as I handed my visitor badge back to the security man at the main entrance. At least that was the consolation I came up with to fight back the despair. So much for nepotism.

STAGE FRIGHT

"Open up!"

"Who is it?"

"Poh-leese! Open up!"

"Hang on a second."

I haven't bolted the door, so when they kick it open the two sides just bounce back off the walls and shut beautifully into place. There is a small pause, as if they are trying to figure out whether this is some cunning design on my part, before they actually step into the room. I am sitting on the edge of my bed.

"Get up," the policeman says, shining the light in my face. I turn and reach for the light switch beside me. The beam of the flashlight is drowned out. He keeps shining it at me anyway. He is wearing a brown beret and a safari shirt with a white plastic name tag on the breast pocket. It's written in Sanskrit, so I don't get the name. He is also carrying a waist-high length of bamboo, which he presumably uses for beating people. Apart from his mustache, he has no other uniform to speak of. Another policeman walks in behind him. They look identical. I get up. "Passport."

"Yes, sir." I reach under my pillow for my money belt and hand it to him.

"British?" he says, flicking through its pages.

"Yes."

He puts the passport in his pocket and starts looking around the room before saying, "Please step outside."

"Why?"

"Please, outside. We want to search the room."

"But I haven't done anything wrong."

"Please, outside."

For a few seconds I just stand there. Then I need the toilet.

"Do you mind if I go to the bathroom first?"

The policeman looks at me. "Go."

I can feel the girl trapped behind the rusty metal door as I squeeze my way in. I am careful not to let the shadow of her feet show. When I close the door she stays pressed against the wall. She looks at me as if to ask me what the hell it is I think I'm doing. I can see that she is trying hard to control her breathing. The situation suddenly seems to have become far too serious. I don't know what this girl is running from, but I am sure that if the policemen find her, we're both finished.

I turn my back and steady myself over the hole in the floor, but I can't go. I can feel her staring at the back of my head. I try to relax, but when, after thirty seconds, still nothing happens I start to become desperate. A hot flush comes over me as the panic sets in. I start pushing, begging my bladder to work, but if anything, it has the opposite effect.

The policeman bangs on the door with his fist. "What is happening?"

I turn to look at the girl. Her face is asking the same question.

"Er, just one more minute."

I can hear them searching my room. The bathroom starts to shrink and I can feel my head going light. I have to get out, the heat of the night is overwhelming. I take one desperate last look to see if there is any way of escape, even though I know there isn't.

I unbolt the door, and stumble back into the bedroom sweating. I remember that I didn't flush the toilet.

The policeman doesn't seem to care. He grabs me by the arm and leads me out into the corridor. As soon as he touches me, my bladder releases and I can feel hot urine splash against the inside of my legs. Somehow I manage not to let go completely.

I know that it won't be long before they find the lump of hash I hurriedly stuffed into the small hole above the door. I don't know why I didn't just throw it down the loo. Panic, I guess. I was too busy trying to figure out where to hide the girl. I wonder if they will find her before they find the dope. I briefly consider making a run for it, but then I remember that they have my passport. I have to think of something quickly, but there is only the sound of my heart thumping in my head.

I'm too late. The policemen step out of my room looking triumphant but serious, the quiet one holding the hash between thumb and forefinger.

"You are under arrest, Mr. King," the other one says. "Do you know the penalty in India for drugs?" He doesn't wait to see if I answer. "It is very serious. Ten years in prison."

A friend of mine, Chris, who used to do drug runs to support a work-free existence, once told me that real danger does not produce fear, it produces fearlessness. At least that's the only explanation I have for how I manage to whisper, "Do you know who I am?" He ignores me. I grab his arm, "I said, do you know who I am?"

The policeman double-takes briefly. "What?"

"Keep your voice down," I say angrily. I wait a second, then indicate that we should talk in my room. I close the doors behind me. "Did Ashok tell you who I am?" They just look at me. "I work for Mani Shankar Aiyar, the editor at the *Hindu Week*." The policeman holding the hash frowns and lets "Exhibit A" drop to his side in a closed fist. "That's right, I am working undercover. And you, gentlemen, have just blown everything." They don't look very convinced. I decide to keep talking. I tap my chin with a clenched fist as if in deep and anxious thought. "If you arrest me, we're all finished. The operation will be over and I'll have to explain why. Mani has spent a lot of money setting this up. We are this close"—I hold my fingers up an inch apart to stress the point—"to blowing the lid on one of the biggest drug-smuggling operations in Delhi." I pause for effect. "You know that he is friendly with Police Commissioner Sanghvi, don't you? We could all lose our jobs over this."

"You are journalist?" the one giving the orders says incredulously.

"Yes, didn't Ashok tell you? Look, here's my ID." I rummage around in one of the drawers in my bedside table and pull out a business card with *Hindu Week* embossed in black letters across the top.

Anyone could have a visitor card like this made up at the photocopying shop in Connaught Place, but they are suitably impressed. The fact is, the card is just a copy of the one I had from my days at the paper all those years ago. I had a new batch made up for fun more than anything else.

The policeman starts flicking through my passport. Before he has a chance to find the valid tourist visa, I point him to the page showing my old work visa from before. He is so amazed by the red stamp with PROFESSION: *journalist* written on it that he fails to notice that it is out-of-date.

"We have to think of a way to make this look normal," I say, maintaining the initiative. I pat my face down with a flustered palm. "What are we going to do, what are we going to do?" I mutter. "That's it!" I snap suddenly, clicking my fingers together and flashing my eyes at them. "If anyone asks you, tell them I paid you *baksheesh*. That way, my cover will be even more believable to every drug smuggler in this hotel and you will keep your jobs."

"We cannot do that," the lead policeman answers.

"Why not?"

"We have been told to make arrests, we are below quota for the month."

"Well, arrest someone else," I snap. "And preferably not here. Now give me back my passport and go before you ruin everything."

They look at me. It's late and they want to go home. It would be easier to arrest me than find another hotel and another suspect. Even if they set someone up, it will take another hour at least. It will be dawn by then.

But then again, I've been enough trouble already. The lead policeman slips my business card into his pocket, hands me back my passport, and says, "We did not find anything in this room. Sorry to trouble you."

Even more unbelievably, the quiet one gives me back my hash. We shake hands.

As I listen to them walking down the stairs, I take out a cigarette and light it—a Wills. It tastes bitter and the tobacco is dry. After four drags I am through to the butt. They are always stale. I promise myself that I will splash out on a packet of Chestertons or Marlboros in the morning. A wave of sickness breaks in the back of my throat. When I am sure that they have gone I announce, "It's all right, you can come out now."

ANYTHING IS POSSIBLE

To say that I displayed absolutely no potential of becoming a writer wouldn't have been, strictly speaking, true. I was always making up stuff and telling stories. I never actually *wrote* anything, but still, the potential was there.

Invariably, my stories were simply very exaggerated versions of the truth. Typically, I'd start with some strange experience worth retelling. Then, slowly, incrementally, I'd add bits here and there—you know, for dramatic effect.

It seemed fair enough—at first. As far as I could figure, *actual* experience—however shocking, frightening, funny, or humiliating—always got lost in the telling. All great authors bitch about the inadequacy of language as a medium for relating experience. My solution to the conundrum was simply to make the daredevil moments that much more extreme, the pain ten times more intense, the farce that little bit more ridiculous. As far as I was concerned, I was simply re-creating the *experience* I had had for the benefit of my listener. If the facts had to be, well, readjusted slightly, then so be it. Everything was relative, after all.

And I didn't just reinvent the events. I sometimes, maybe more than sometimes, tended to reinvent myself as well, you know, in terms of the role I might play. I may as well just come out with it: I had a hero complex.

I know it sounds stupid, but I loved the idea of being a good guy, someone who saved the day, someone who was—and there isn't a better way to put this—*different*. I don't know why. I guess I just felt . . . psychologically compelled.

Morag's shrink, whom she bribed me to go and see in the weeks after Dad died, told me I suffered from low self-esteem. He said it was common for people with a low sense of self-worth to fantasize, pretend that they might be something more than they really were. I could see something in that—after all, it was true that I didn't have a very high opinion of my real-life self.

But I think the problem predated my psychological molding.

I think it was genetic, something I inherited from my father. Truth was, Dad and I were very similar in a lot of ways. He wanted to live forever because he wanted his life to amount to something. He thought he was different, special. And so did I. I didn't want to live forever (even if it did become possible one day), but I certainly thought that my life would amount to more than it was, to something spectacular.

The fact that I only ever achieved average grades, was average (poor really) at sports, only averagely liked, enjoyed average success with women—was average in just about everything I put my hand to, didn't shake this sense within me. If anything, it only made it worse.

I quite literally saw myself as the hero in one of those frustrating movies where only *he* knows the Truth and no one else believes him. Still, it was only a matter of time. Just like the hero in the movie, my day would come. I would be vindicated. Soon, everyone was going to realize how really very special I was.

In the meantime, of course, it meant that I spent a lot of my life being disappointed.

And that's part of the reason, perhaps, for why I kept on creating this parallel universe, this fantasyland, this *other place,* where everything that happened was super-exciting and thrilling and tragic and comic and fast and fantastic and where, obviously, I was the principal agent. The one that made *that* universe tick, the one that kept order, the one who battled evil and righted wrongs— in other words, the *hero*.

The fact that I'd also started taking very large quantities of recreational drugs didn't help much either.

Which is part of the reason I decided, even after the Reuters debacle, to give journalism another go. I badly needed a reality check. If I was going to write a book I was going to need some training in the Truth—or at least how to tell it. I had to step out of my fantasyland and into the real world. If I could just get back on track, if I could just inject one small measure of accuracy into my perception of reality, then the possibilities were, dare I say it, unimaginable.

And then, of course, there was the *information* I had gathered on Baba.

Which, on sum, made the *Hindu Week* the perfect place to return to. Most importantly, because it was the only place I could think of that might give me a job. But there was another consideration in the back of my mind as well. If, and it was a very big "if" by this stage, I was going to earn myself the credibility necessary for writing a novel, then it seemed to me that India would be the perfect backdrop.

Not only is it fertile storytelling ground, it is also such an extreme and ridiculous place, almost anything I wrote about it could probably be passed off as believable. I wouldn't need to worry *too much* about overstepping the mark. Anything dubious I might mention about life in India would likely be accepted. It seemed the perfect halfway house between my fantasyland and the real world.

I figured if things got too out of hand, well, readers would pass it off like the Indian adage (picture: happy head nods and smiling faces): *Anything is possible, anything is possible.* Because, in India, just like in my mind, pretty much anything is possible even, and especially, when it is absolutely clear that it is not possible, not possible at all.

YASMIN

I suppose it is the way she carries herself that makes her stand out.

She is petite, but she walks tall with her head high, turning between the gaps in the crowd as if she is looking for something more important than a restaurant or a rickshaw ride. Somehow she manages to glide through the melee untouched, the beggars choosing not to badger her, the hawkers hassling the next guy, the stream of people parting just in time to make way for her graceful stride.

Maybe it's her sexy beauty, an air of confidence that she carries around her like a protective force field, things and people and traffic and events respectfully moving aside because, well, a girl like her—she doesn't need the grief. She deserves better and she gets it—just because of the way she looks. I imagine jealous friends might call her arrogant—or something worse.

She has hazelnut hair in the truest sense—there's several shades of brown in it, with reds and almost blondish strands too— wrapped tight and high and in on itself in a thick, lustrous swirl at the back of her head.

She has breasts. They swell and then curl like two waves breaking against her chest into the slim wash of a stomach that ripples below, naked and exposed by the brightly colored patchwork blouse cut short at the ribs. Mirrored sunglasses wrap around her eyes and sunlight bounces off small mirrors sewn into the red miniskirt she's wearing. It's almost as if she intends people to see themselves in her.

I watch her take a seat outside one of the cafés that spill onto the street. A sign advertising international telephone calls says STD in big red letters above her head. I decide to eat at the restaurant across the road, partly because it does the best breakfast and partly because I want to watch her for a while.

As I order my toast and milk coffee (which is just that, no water) I catch glimpses of her amid the chaos of the street between us . . .

. . . A rickshaw wallah, draping himself dramatically over the handlebars of his bicycle, drags a customer to his destination. The sun catches the remnants of a highlight in the ends of her dark hair. An enlightened-looking cow ambles toward some rotting vegetation in the gutter and stoops down to chew it. She puts a cigarette between a pair of peach-pink lips and draws tensely on it. A blue Bajaj scooter doubling as the family car splutters, teeters, and weaves precariously down the road. She scratches a thick eyebrow with a slender finger. A man with gray hair and dirty, loose-fitting clothes runs across the street shouting at the cow, which has now found its way to his fruit cart. She is looking directly at me, pushing the glasses that are slipping off her head back in their place . . .

I am startled. She doesn't wave or acknowledge me. She just keeps looking at me, piercingly, almost accusingly. A hot flush spreads through me. I feel as if I have been caught doing something wrong, caught spying on her. After what seems like an agonizingly long moment she turns back to talk to one of the adolescent waiters. It takes me a few minutes before I summon the courage to cross the street.

"Do you mind if I join you?" I manage casually. She looks at me cursorily with emerald eyes and, moving her metal chair to one side of the table, indicates a space for me to take. "How's it going?" I say, knowing already that I've taken up too much of this nonconversation, that there are too many words attributed to me.

"They arrested James," she delivers, without looking at me. If she's trying to stun me, it works.

"What?" I say, sort of meaning "Who?" but then, as I quickly figure that James must be the boyfriend she referred to last night, I realize that "What?" is the appropriate question after all. I am genuinely amazed that the police went back downstairs to arrest him after my little diversion. Not so much because I was so convincing in my deterrence, but really because an arrest had actually been made at the Green. I say that the guest house is scary and that raids happen "all the time," but if I'm being truly honest, I've only ever witnessed one.

After all, those are just the kinds of things I exaggerate, things like the Green and how dangerous it is. How else do I adequately translate that night, that terrible first night, newly arrived, fresh, frightened, and wide-eyed, when I really did witness a drug raid? It's not enough to say: *I'm staying in a guest house where I witnessed a junkie get arrested once a couple of years ago.* That doesn't mean anything. Arrests have to happen all the time if the Green and all its horrors are to come across properly. Of course I get a kick out of this kind of internal narrative. Thinking, imagining, believing I am living this exciting life, tracking down an international drug smuggler I'm not even sure exists. On the outside, I'm simply doing the same as everyone else: economizing unnecessarily below my means. But inside my head: I'm undercover and heroic in a seedy guest house surrounded by junkies and living on the edge of the law. And when the police came around last night, even though I wet my pants, I felt vindicated, my imaginary life was vindicated. It meant that the Green really is a scary place to stay. It meant that I really have been living life dangerously, that I am someone, a traveler, an underworld adventurer in some sort of heroin-infested Hades. And when I woke up this morning I was worried that it had been a dream. I wasn't sure if it had actually happened or if I was twisting things again. But now that I know that her boyfriend has been arrested, I know it's not a dream. It's real. And the excitement is back. I try to remain sympathetic.

"Last night."

"How? I don't understand."

"When I got back to my room he was gone."

"Really? But I was sure that after they came to my room they left the hotel."

She draws the dark glasses down to hide the shine in her eyes. "I've just seen him. I went to the police. He is in jail." It feels as if she is blaming me in some way, as if it should have been me who was arrested, not James. I ignore the thought. It doesn't make any sense.

"Just because of a little piece of hash?" I ask.

She nods her head and sniffs. "Yup."

"That's bad news." I know it's an inane comment and she doesn't say anything. I try to think of something else, something to reassure her. "Listen, I'm sure it will be okay. Have they charged him yet?"

"Yes. He goes to court next week."

"Jesus, they're not messing around." There's another uncomfortable pause. "Have you been to the embassy?"

"I'm going this afternoon."

"Do you want me to come with you?" And that's the straw that breaks the camel's back, the last sympathetic question she can bear. Two tears race to reach the ends of her face from under her glasses. She wipes them away before they are even halfway to the finish line. Seeing her cry shocks me a little. The reality of the situation is hitting me. While I'm getting excited with my scary life, this girl is suffering. I feel genuinely sad for her. But partly because I sense that she'd hate the pity. Watching her walk down the road like she just did—you'd never have known that something so terrible had just occurred in her life. She looked so cool, so hard, so beautiful, so untouchable.

But now, seeing her break like this, so suddenly, unexpectedly, and yet so understandably, makes her seem particularly vulnerable. More vulnerable than most. I find myself rubbing her back softly with my hand. I wouldn't have dared if I'd actually thought about it. It just happens. It feels as if there's a sudden intimacy between us, a privileged confidentiality that comes from—I don't know where. Perhaps from a bizarre mutual experience like the one we shared last night. I mean, this girl has seen me trying to pee, and I don't even know her name.

"It's going to be okay," I say. "Don't worry, it will all be okay."

We spend the next few minutes like that. I relish the tactility of it all. Like I'm getting through. I keep rubbing her back. Softly, firmly, with the palm of my hand, not my fingers. I'm not fondling her. I'm holding her. I can feel myself bypassing all her hardness, overcoming her proud attitude, breaking down the defensive barriers, because I know her, she's letting me know her, and now she needs me—as a friend.

After a while, with a small, childlike shiver to mark the end of the tears, she says, "Thank you, er . . ."

"Josh," I say quickly, catching the falling end of her question. It's all part of the me-being-there role I've stumbled into. I've got the answers. I'm the only one here who can make her feel better.

"Thank you, Josh. For everything."

You're very welcome, I think to myself, trying not to look up at the guy staring at us from the next-door table and wondering for a moment what she means by "everything," before being beguiled by the more appealing notion that the guy next door might think that this girl and I are a couple. Maybe he thinks I'm dumping her. Maybe he thinks that's why she's crying. That would certainly make me pretty cool—to be breaking *this* girl's heart.

"What's your name?" I say, throwing the fantasy away. They're just the kind of mind trips that get me into trouble. I remind myself that this is actually quite a serious situation.

"Yasmin." Her voice sounds hoarse when she says it, sexy like a sore-throat voice. Hyasmeen.

"Try not to worry," I say, part of me wanting to believe that Yasmin can't really be true. She's so beautiful. I find her looks haunting. I notice that her top lip is slightly thicker than the lower one. And that name, her name. I don't think I've met anyone called Yasmin before. Jasmine, yes. But Yasmin—it's so hot. Like Jasmine with a lisp.

I suddenly realize I am staring at her and immediately force my gaze away to the salt and pepper pots on the table. I try to think of something else to say, but I'm lost for answers. I vaguely mumble something along the lines of being there for her, but it's not me talking. Eventually I manage to string together: "You're sure that you don't want me to come with you to the embassy?"

"No. I'll be fine," she says, stabbing out the last of her cigarette and pushing back her chair quite suddenly. A small falling feeling in my stomach tells me that I've lost her. Somewhere in the midst of my idiotic fantasizing, Yasmin—the real Yasmin—pulled herself together. And now she's the sexy, hard chick again, a million miles aloof and completely out of my fucking league. Forget the privileged intimacy—the moment's snapped.

She gets up to leave.

"Where are you going?" I stammer.

"For a walk."

"But your breakfast . . ." I say, looking around for the waiter. By the time I turn back around, she's gone.

THE PITCH

Most of the Indian newspapers have offices in the same building. It's like anywhere else. Journalists seem to like sticking together. Cordoning off a section of the city for themselves, an area where they can plan out their media blitzes and garner intelligence in a single hive—like giant war rooms.

And the Chandra Patrika Bazar building looks like it has been bombed several times. Huge slabs of plaster hang off the front of the building, and for some unknown reason, a stack of splitting sandbags lines the wall and spills out onto the street.

Inside isn't any better. The ceilings are falling down, square slabs of asbestos hanging precariously from thin aluminum rafters. Strip lights line the blood-brown halls and flicker painfully. Looking at them is like having a pin driven repeatedly into the back of the eye. Water drips and spills from unknown places.

I walk into the *Hindu Week* office. It's been several weeks since I was last here. The journalists look battle-weary, slouched in front of plastic crap computers. Everything looks the same—the computers, the enamel desks, the swivel-around chairs. They all have the same color, the same hue, like smoke-stained teeth.

I wish someone would open the blinds.

"Hi, everybody," I say too cheerfully. No one looks up. They all hate me. I can't really blame them. I'm far too eager, always have been. From the very first moment I stumbled into their office by mistake, I naively assumed I could make friends. Truth was, when Mani did eventually give me a job, I must have come across like a teacher's pet, only worse.

For starters, everyone knows Mani only employs me because I'm white. It titillates him to hire a Britisher. I think it appeals to his sense of irony. Whatever. It's still one less job for an Indian. But to make matters worse, it's so obvious that I'm not really a journalist. I don't really deserve to be here, earning the same wage as them. Like the employees at Reuters, these journalists have worked hard to get where they are.

Me? I'm just another English guy who came to India on his year off and then kept coming back. The only difference between me and the other slummers is that I'm not here for the drugs or the raves or the gurus (not ostensibly, anyway). I'm here in search of a career. And somehow that minimum of initiative has earned me an automatic passport for employment. That and my skin.

I tip my head to hide my embarrassment and search out the colonel. He's sitting in the corner as usual, in his red leather-bound chair—the only decent piece of furniture in the whole office. The colonel is Mani's second-in-command. Not so much a hard-assed hack, more of a manager, a people man. He's the one who smoothes out the ruffled feathers, irons out the creases, keeps the operation in order. If it were just Mani running the show, there would be chaos, a crazed competition for his whimsical attentions. No one would actually do any work, they'd just spend their whole time bitching.

But the colonel keeps everyone happy. He doesn't look up when I stand next to him. Part of keeping everyone else happy involves disliking me. He can't keep it up for long though. At the end of the day, he knows I'm just a boy.

"Hi, Josh." He sighs gently before looking up at me. He has gray-blue eyes, thinning hair, and a trimmed beard. The beard is going white. He says it makes him look stately, more dignified. It really just makes him look old. No one can believe that he's younger than Mani. He looks old enough to be his father. "What's happening?"

"Is Mani coming in today?"

"Says so."

That doesn't mean anything. Mani often says he's coming in then shocks everyone by calling in rebelliously from the Taj in Mumbai. He thrives on the attention, the disruption he can cause. "Mani's in Mumbai, Mani's in Mumbai, why, why, why?" Then, of course, there are the entrances. "Mani's coming, Mani's coming, he's in the hall." People are practically applauding by the time the door swings open.

"Well, do you know where he is?"

"Nope."

"Is he at the studio?" Among other things, Mani's an anchor on a TV program called *Politics and the Nation*. That's where I met him, at the Doordarshan studios. The first story I wrote was about an outbreak of the bubonic plague in Surat. I took it to the *Hindu Week,* and instead of publishing it, the colonel suggested I go on Mani's next show to discuss the topic "Is India becoming a pariah nation?"

"I don't know."

"Oh, okay, then. I'll just wait, I guess."

"Suit yourself."

Three hours later, Mani arrives. The transformation is magnificent, like sunshine. Lyla, a dumpy girl with eyes too close together and a face like a rat, finally stops scowling at old fashion magazines and suddenly becomes a bubbly scurry of giggles, flashing her eyes and encouraging Mani to pinch the folds in her waist flirtatiously. She almost looks pretty. Lakshmi, who wears thick bands of black eyeliner and who is probably the only genuine hack in the whole office, can't help but puff up with pride when Mani nods his respectful hello. Jitender, the six-foot photographer, and his dim-witted assistant, Nitin, manage to give up endlessly rearranging their collection of slides and films, and slip on identical pocket-lined combat jackets, ready for action. The colonel calls order and announces a long-awaited editorial meeting for the excited troops. People pull up chairs, peons are sent out for tea, Lakshmi lights up a cigarette while Lyla dips into a sachet of *pan*.

I sit on the fringes.

"Right, then," Mani eventually says, smoothing his balding hair with two hands. In contrast to the colonel, he dyes it black, and wears it long and sleeked and gelled, his beard dark and dashing. "What have we got?" There's a shuffle of feet and Lakshmi eventually comes through with a tip she's received about the election commissioner accepting bribes. Lyla says she's managed to get an interview with a Delhi socialite and Jitender says something random about doing some photographs for a new book on India. "What about you, Josh?" Mani asks suddenly, turning to face me.

He's caught me off guard, but I know I have to say something, anything. "I'm still working undercover on that drug-ring thing," I say too quietly, without conviction. I can't help it. I feel humble all of a sudden, in front of Mani's bombastic enthusiasm. Maybe it's the social ostracism finally getting to me. Or maybe it's the fact that, really, I know that I don't have a story. All I've got is a few anecdotes of life as a budget traveler living in Pahar Ganj. I say I've found a trail leading to Baba, but all I'm really doing is betraying my conversations with other travelers and using their existences as evidence of something far more sinister. But I have to say something. I have to wing it.

"What?" Mani booms back.

"I said," a little too loudly now, "I'm still working on that undercover drug-ring story."

Lyla sniggers and slams a palm across her mouth, tipping her head in toward Lakshmi's breasts in mock shame. Ever serious, Lakshmi tries hard to contain a smirk. What a pair of bitches. Right, I think to myself, I'll show them.

"Go on, then, give us an update," Mani continues.

"Okay," I start with a draw of breath, preparing the crowd for the full bullshit treatment. If there's one thing I've learned in all my years of talking crap, it's how to work the sense of anticipation. "I'm trying to track down someone the travelers call Baba. I think he's an out-of-work Bollywood actor that spends a lot of his time doing drug runs for the Mafia, but I'm not sure." It's always good never to sound too sure of your own lies. That way you hedge yourself from being hauled up on something and you make the audience feel as if they are involved in some way, almost as if you're working the problem *with* them. "What I do know is that each month he travels to Jaisalmer, the old fortress town near the Pakistan border, to pick up a consignment of heroin and gems. Some of the heroin is sold in Bombay, but most of it is shipped abroad. The gems are also exported, mainly to the Middle East, and while the Mafia makes some money dealing in them, it primarily trades the diamonds to help launder the profits from the heroin operation. Each of Baba's trips is specifically designed to kill two birds with one stone: he buys the heroin for the following month's worth of business and enough gemstones to launder the profits from the previous month. Simple, really."

"Go on. Good. I like this."

"According to my sources," I say, sitting up a little straighter, rising to the journalistic moment, "Baba has set up a small international trading operation of his own. Each month, he takes a minor detour to visit Pushkar, the tourist town near Ajmer, and meets with three Westerners. He sells them whatever he has to spare—heroin and semiprecious stones mainly—and they, in turn, sell on the stuff to other travelers. I hear that it has become such big business for these three individuals that they now have an extensive network of salesmen spanning most of the country."

"Who are these Westerners? Do you know them?"

"No."

"Do they operate together?"

"I don't know. All I do know is that they have lived in India a very long time and are very high up in this weird hierarchy of underworld travelers. Apparently, one of them made his name organizing raves in Goa, but apart from that, I don't know much else."

"So, what leads do you have?"

"Well, I'm working on two. I've spent the last four months in Delhi, putting out my feelers for the three Westerners to see if I can buy some heroin from them or maybe even get a job as one of their salespeople. I was thinking about going to Pushkar and just hanging out there to see if I came across Baba. But I was worried that even if I found him, I'd still need an introduction. I think I have a better chance here because so many more travelers pass through these parts and it's easy to meet them."

"Four months?" Lyla jumps in. "It's taken you four months just to find that out?"

"It's not easy, Lyla," I say, being sure to look at her. "You wouldn't believe how hierarchical these people are. It's like trying to get into a Masonic lodge or something. If you haven't lived in

India for at least two years or been a member of one of the big ashrams for at least six months, they won't even talk to you. And it's also very dangerous. Whenever I try to broach the subject of Baba's trading operation with the junkies, they get very twitchy. And last night I almost got arrested." It feels good to say that, to report a real event, something that actually happened.

"Really?" Mani says. "How did you get out of that?"

"Well, I hope you don't mind, but I had to mention your name to get myself out of trouble. So, if anyone from the police calls, can you say that I still work here?"

"Okay, sure, no problem. What's your second lead?"

"The other thing I'm working on seems more promising. I have a friend working in Bollywood at the moment. I'm much keener on this idea. We go back a long way and I'm tempted to just go straight to the source without having to go through this travelers' network. There's a strong chance that he knows who this Bollywood actor is and maybe he could get me an introduction from that angle. I spoke to him a couple of days ago and he said that he's planning to come up to Delhi, so I'll talk to him about it then."

"Interesting, very interesting. An international drug ring, a Bollywood scandal, a secret travelers' network—I like this story. I want you to go with it."

"Anything you say, Mani," I say, loving the limelight. A total ride, if ever there was one. I'm almost starting to believe it myself. I can feel Lyla glaring. I decide it's time to convert my initiative. "But . . ." I begin.

"Yes?"

"I may need some money."

"How much?"

"I don't know. Twenty-five thousand rupees?" I venture. The room virtually convulses.

"Twenty-five thousand rupees!" Lyla shouts. "That's nearly six months' bloody salary. You must be joking."

Mani is smiling at me, listening to the ruckus. After a few minutes, the colonel manages to quiet everyone down.

"Well, Josh," Mani says. "You certainly think highly of yourself."

"Yeah, but you haven't paid me for four months so—"

"THAT'S BECAUSE YOU HAVEN'T WORKED HERE FOR FOUR MONTHS, YOU ARROGANT PIECE OF SHIT!" Mani suddenly screams at me.

I jump. My bladder twitches. Maybe I've pushed it. "Yes, I know but—" I try, weakly.

"NO! THAT'S ENOUGH." Silence. I can feel all their eyes on me. I hate coming into this office. It reminds me of school. Lyla is beaming maliciously at me. I don't say anything. Eventually, Mani says, "Okay. You can have your twenty-five thousand." The room gasps. "But . . ."

"Yes, Mani."

"You'd better infiltrate this thing and have an exclusive for me within the next three months, otherwise . . ." We look at each other. "Otherwise, you, me, and this whole game we're playing with your life is over."

"What game? What do you mean?"

"I think you know." There's a brief pause as he looks meaningfully at me. Then he snaps suddenly out of it. "Right, Lyla, Lakshmi, you're taking me out to lunch."

QUENTIN

If I didn't know Quentin for as long as I have, I probably wouldn't like him very much. For starters, he's too good-looking—and he knows it. He has all those classic dark features that somehow translate into real beauty: high cheekbones, a slender nose, clear olive skin, and full dark lips. His hair is thick and black and his eyes are a walnut brown. He's one of those rare examples of a man that other men can appreciate has good looks.

But in a funny way, his beauty is his own worst enemy. He is incredibly vain. I don't think he's ever walked past a car or shop front without stealing a glance at his own reflection in the window. And even though there is a lot to him, he somehow manages to come across as being very superficial. When he opens his mouth, most women end up cringing. His lingering gazes are almost always mistimed and his moves always fall flat.

And as I watch him arrive at New Delhi station, I realize that in the fifteen years I've known him, he hasn't changed a bit. As soon as he throws his duffel bag off the slowing train and jumps onto the platform with the kind of affected casualness only he is capable of, I can't stop myself from smiling. I know that he is thinking: Hey, I'm so cool I think I'm just going to throw my bag off the train and then I'm going to throw myself off after it—

crazy! I also know that he has already seen me, but that doesn't stop him from pretending that he hasn't.

"QUENTIN!" I call out.

With all the overacting of a Bollywood musical moment, Quentin searches the crowd, squints in my direction, and pretends to be surprised.

"JOSH," he calls back, and runs to hug me. It is one of those few moments spent in Quentin's company when I feel he isn't being pretentious in any way. I relish it. It's also good to see an old face again after so long in India. "How are you, buddy?" he says, giving me a squeeze.

"Pretty good. It's good to see you. How's Bollywood?"

"Oh, Josh, the babes. The bay-hey-hey-hey-bies in Bollywood are sooo fine."

"So you're still not getting any sex, then."

"No," he replies with uncharacteristically deadpan humor. We both laugh.

"Let me help you with your bag."

Quentin is in "India mode" at the moment. He still has the kiss-curled hair, designer stubble, white T-shirt, blue Levi's, and comb-in-the-back-pocket look—which became his trademark image on the King's Road during his adolescent years—but now he's also wearing sandals and a Nehru cap. And, despite the fact that like a lot of NRIs (Non-Resident Indians) he can barely speak Hindi, he insists on engaging every beggar, tout, and rickshaw driver in conversation as we walk out of the station.

Eventually, we find a rickshaw that agrees to take us back to the Green for a decent price. But it's only after we climb into the black-and-yellow screaming three-wheeler that we realize there's a catch: the driver is a complete psycho. He insists on going head-to-head with every kind of oncoming traffic—from elephants to enormous belching trucks—and then swerving back into his own lane at the last second. We fly through the traffic like an angry bumblebee. After fifteen stomach-turning minutes we make it back to the Green safely.

"Fuck me, what a shithole," Quentin says, looking at the Home from Home sign above the entrance.

"Just come in and keep quiet, will you."

As we walk in, I see Yasmin crossing the bottom of the well. She's wearing another sexy outfit, a simple blue-black dress this time—short, of course, to show off her slender legs. She doesn't see us at first, because she's busy slipping something, a travel document or a traveler's check, into the bulging bumbag that sits on her hips. But then, just as I'm trying to figure out whether I should say hello or pretend I haven't seen her, she suddenly looks up and flashes me a sunny smile, sweet and genuine and just for me.

"Hi," she says, pausing.

"Hey, Yasmin, how's it going?" I say, not wanting to get drawn in too quickly by her charm. Last time I did that, she left me sitting cold.

"Okay," she says, nodding her head slightly as if she's still processing the question and discovering, to her own mild surprise, that yes, she does feel okay today. "Okay." She smiles again, half of the sunny smile she just gave me but just as lovely.

"Any word?"

"No, not yet," she says, biting her lower lip with relaxed intent, as if she's trying to scrape something off it with her pearly teeth. I find myself wondering if she knows how attractive these casual mannerisms make her.

"Did you go to the embassy?"

"They say I should wait."

I nod slowly at her. "Well, I suppose they would."

There's a small pause and I suddenly notice that Quentin is buzzing behind me. "Hello," he says, seizing the opportunity to butt in by quickly thrusting a hand over my shoulder. "I'm Sanjay."

Yasmin shifts her glance and shakes hands with Quentin, smiling, slightly surprised. I am caught sandwiched and confused between them. Sanjay?

"Hello," she says coolly. My heart secretly leaps when I see that she doesn't seem to be taking much notice of Quentin's good looks.

"Sanjay is visiting from Mumbai," I recover quickly, picking up my part.

"I see," Yasmin says, nodding without expression. I can't help resenting Quentin for muscling in on my act. I feel as if I'm having to carry him now. There's not just me now, there's an "us," "a Josh and a Sanjay." We're a pair.

"Sooooo," Quentin says clapping his hands and shuffling his way beside me, sealing our union. "How do you two know each other?"

I groan silently. It's getting worse. I feel like the shamed half of a Siamese twin. Suddenly fused at the hip with someone utterly intolerable. "We just met," Yasmin answers, smiling so platonically it's hard to believe there was any chemistry between us a few moments ago. Everything has gone sterile.

"Yeah, a couple of days ago," I confirm, wading my way through the sentence like it's mud.

"Great," Quentin says, grinning. "That's just great."

This is what I mean when I talk about Quentin and girls. He's so incredibly and insensitively thick-skinned when it comes to the Vibe, the Energy that carries a relationship into bed. He thinks it's all about chat-up lines he gets from the movies. If he had any idea he would have noticed the small glances and the warm smiles of a few moments ago and flown low. I mean, where's his goddamned tact? Why didn't he just sidle off conveniently for a couple of minutes? Because he's a tosser, that's why. I mean, he must have known I would have introduced him eventually. Or maybe, on second thought, he knew that, actually, I wouldn't have. I guess that explains things. That's when I realize. The fucker is spoiling my turf deliberately. And he calls himself a friend.

"Are you staying in Delhi for long?" Yasmin asks politely, softening the silence.

"No." Quentin leaps. "Just a few days."

"Oh." Yasmin nods again.

The next pause is like standing on hot coals. I don't know why Quentin can't just leave well enough alone. What did I ever do to him? I shift on my feet uncomfortably. And what is it with this Sanjay thing? "Well, Quent—I mean Sanjay. We should probably get you checked in." I smile with bright, cheerful eyes, desperate to bring the whole unfortunate meeting to an end.

"Yes, yes, definitely. I definitely want to check in," he says finally, beaming at Yasmin. I try not to look. Part of me feels like crying. The other part wants to kill Quentin.

"Well"—Yasmin wraps it up—"it was nice to meet you." She smiles one last time. "See you around," she says, more to me than to "us." That's something at least.

"How about tonight?" Quentin suddenly blurts out as Yasmin starts her first step. Arrrrgggh! Why can't he just fucking well seize up and die? Does he have to mess up every moment, however tiny? She stops. "I mean, won't you join us for dinner tonight? Josh knows this fantastic restaurant he's been promising to take me to for months. It would be great if you could come." The prick is just rambling now. Blabbering like some salivating, lecherous troll.

Yasmin looks at me as I stare at Quentin. The whole world seems to be moving in slow motion. I am picturing my hands gripping his slender neck. I want to feel his bones breaking. It's just a matter of time, I tell myself with pathological calm. In a few more minutes we'll be alone. Then I will kill him. "Yes, all right. Why not?" I hear her saying.

"Fantastic." I see Quentin's lips moving without really hearing the words. "We'll meet you here at around . . . hmmm . . . six?"

"Fine," she agrees quickly, and then, before I have a chance to realize that it's happened, she disappears again. All I can do is stare at Quentin. I'm shaking slightly.

"What?" he says, throwing his hands up in the air.

"All right, come on, what's the deal with the name change, then?" I ask as Quentin unpacks his things. Somehow I've mustered the charity to forgive him. The fact is, I'm looking forward to seeing Yasmin myself and I can't help giving him some of the credit for arranging the date in the first place. I know that I would never have had the guts. Far too scared by the possibility of rejection for that. Maybe there's something to be said for Quentin's thick skin after all.

"What do you mean?" he says as he refolds his clothes in color-coordinated piles on the spare bed. I'd forgotten how anal he could be.

"You know exactly what I mean."

"It's no big deal. I just need an Indian name for Bollywood. And, besides," he says, refolding a pair of trousers along the crease, "it is my real name."

"I'm sorry?"

"Mum said I should call myself Quentin in England. She thought it sounded upper class. Like Joshooarrrr."

"Very funny," I say as he presses a shirt with his hands. "So your real name is Sanjay?"

"Actually it's Sanjay Shahid Bhagat Jones, but you can call me Sanj for short if you like."

"You're being weird."

"Not really. In case you hadn't noticed, we are in India and I *am* Indian. Why shouldn't I use my Indian name?"

"No reason, it's just confusing, that's all. I'm still getting used to calling Bombay Mumbai."

"Personally, I think it's a relief to finally get rid of all those colonial misnomers," Sanjay says, taking a tangent. "All those names we used: Arthur and Dougall, Cruickshank and Bruce, Sandhurst and Victoria—fucking ridiculous. Why should Indian streets be named after stuffy army colonels and fat British queens?"

"But it's not just the British names, is it? The Mumbai government has got rid of a lot of Muslim and Parsi street names as well."

"So?"

"Well, it's not exactly secular, is it?"

"Look, there's nothing wrong with being proud of your country."

"What's that got to do with it? In case you hadn't noticed," I say, deliberately mimicking him, "India isn't just a Hindu country."

"You don't understand," he says, sneering and shuffling past me into the bathroom. He tips the contents of his washbag into the sink and starts arranging three different aftershaves in order of height along the shelf.

I don't let him off the hook. I decide that this will be my revenge for his behavior downstairs. "Jesus, next thing you'll be saying how clever India is for developing the bomb."

"Well," he says, shrugging his shoulders, "why shouldn't we have the bomb?"

"Fuck off, Quentin."

He stops fiddling with his stuff and looks Bollywood-menacing at me. "Don't ever call me that again. Do you understand?"

"Now I'm scared."

"Look, the thing is, right," he says, breathing heavily, "you've got no fucking idea what it's like to be an Indian. The Paki fundos breathing down on top of us, the Chinese picking up the tab—we've got a right to defend ourselves, you know. No one else would just sit there and take it. So you can shove your nuclear nonproliferation crap back up your ignorant ass."

This is depressing. Quentin has clearly got something to prove. Maybe it's because he's half white that he's acting so fanatical. Caught between two identities with neither side really accepting him. Maybe he figures he'll always be more Indian than white, so he'd better start acting it. Either way, I'm not going to get any closer to discovering Baba's identity this way. I back off.

"Whatever you say, Sanjay."

THE RESTAURANT WITH NO NAME

Walking through Old Delhi is like going back in time. Most of the streets are narrow, cobbled pathways that twist and turn like a maze, and unless you know exactly where you are going, it's very easy to get lost. Which is why, after thirty-four turns, double-backing on ourselves once and walking through three different people's low-ceiling houses in order to reach the restaurant, I am convinced that we are being followed.

"There, over there," I am whispering at Yasmin and Sanjay urgently. The restaurant is throbbing around us. Sweaty cooks bob over charcoal fires, waiters negotiate their way around the tables at Grand Prix speeds, aluminum cups and paper plates swim over oily blue heads of hair. "Five o'clock."

True to the form I've come to expect only of myself, Sanjay wheels around, looks in the direction of the only other white man sitting in the restaurant, and shouts, "WHERE? Oh yeah, I see him," before turning back to face me.

"Did you have to do that?"

"What?" he asks innocently.

I just glare at him.

"I'm sure you're not the only tourist who knows about this place, Josh," Yasmin interjects. "I mean is it . . . what's it called again?"

"It doesn't have a name," I reply.

"How ridiculous," Sanjay says.

"Well, I just thought that with all the confusion over names lately, we'd be better off eating somewhere anonymous." I sneer back at him. I can't help it. He's pressing all my buttons. I tell myself to be nice.

"Well, is it really such a big secret?" Yasmin says, filling the tense pause.

"Yes. Hardly anyone knows about this place. That's the whole point."

"Aren't you just being precious?" Yasmin says with a hint of condescension.

"It's not about the fucking restaurant," I suddenly snap. Yasmin and Sanjay both jump a little. "Look, I couldn't give a shit if some guy eats at the same place as us. It's just that I saw that guy in Pahar Ganj when we were leaving and he was trailing us on our way here. Didn't either of you notice?"

"No," they say together.

A waiter arrives and throws an assortment of deeply colored condiments and three cups of water in front of us. He takes our order. There's only one thing left on the menu—lamb kabobs. But they are the best lamb kabobs in the world, he reassures us. The interlude gives me a minute to gather my thoughts. I had hoped to discuss Baba in private with Sanjay, but now I feel as if I owe Yasmin an explanation. I briefly consider the wisdom of letting another traveler in on the secret, but after the police episode, she knows half of it already. Besides, she has other, more important things to worry about. And when I see the young man I believe has been following us get up and leave before eating anything, it confirms all my worst fears. Suddenly I have an urgent need to share my story.

"The reason I'm worried about being followed is because I'm up to my eyeballs in something that could, potentially, be quite dangerous," I start. They both look at me. "You may find this hard to believe, but I'm working as an undercover journalist infiltrating an international drug-smuggling ring." Sanjay snorts sarcastically. I manage to ignore him. If there was ever a time for conviction it is now. After all, this is how I convert fantasy into reality. I tell people the story. "And the reason I've asked you to come and stay with me, Sanjay, is because I want you to help me."

"Sure, mate, whatever you say." He looks around the rest of the restaurant, acting bored.

"I'm serious. I want you to introduce me to someone."

He turns and looks at me through a pair of thick, skeptical, half-closed eyelids. "All right, I'll play. Who?"

"Someone in Bollywood."

"Can you be more specific?"

"No. I don't know who he is yet."

"Well, that makes life easier."

"Look, do you want me to explain or not?"

"Go on, then." He sighs wearily, extending an arm salaciously over the back of Yasmin's seat. I swallow the urge to break his nose and start the story. That's the best way to win Yasmin, I reckon. Just tell her a story. It's one of the few charming traits I possess.

"When I first came to India three years ago I went to Jaisalmer to do a camel trek. You know, the usual tourist thing. One night, by the fire, my camel driver told me a story about smuggling heroin in from Pakistan. He was leaping around the fire, mimicking the chase he had had with Indian customs on their camels. It was very funny."

Neither of them seems interested. I press on.

"Anyway, a few days later I met these two travelers, Will and Darren. Darren was into smack. He kept going on and on about a Baba and his source. I told him that he should go and see my camel driver. I just thought Baba was a generic name for anyone that dealt dope. I thought the camel driver would probably know where to find a Baba. So I showed Will and Darren where to find the guide. I even introduced them to one another. Two days after that, Darren died of an overdose in his hotel room and Will disappeared. The police came to see me about it. They said that I had been seen wandering around town with this Darren guy and asked, did I know anything about him, who he was, so on and so forth. Of course I didn't say anything. I told them that I'd seen him around once or twice, but apart from that, I knew nothing. They didn't believe me and I spent a day in jail because of it."

"What for?" Sanjay finally bites.

"They don't need a reason," Yasmin answers for me, a little bitterly.

"Exactly. Anyway, they eventually let me go. I left town. Three days later, I saw a newspaper article. It was about Will. It turned out that he was the son of the right-hand man to the British ambassador. The army had found him, with the camel driver, way out in the middle of the desert. Their feet had been cut off."

"Er, gross," Sanjay says as Yasmin grimaces. "Were they dead?"

"No, they just needed a glass of water. Of course they were fucking dead. The army patrol that found them said they left a trail of blood stretching more than a hundred meters."

Our lamb kabobs turn up. "I'm not very hungry," Yasmin says, pushing her plate aside.

Sanjay, on the other hand, plows in. He starts by sectioning off portions of rice with his fingers, kneading and squeezing them with his kabob into parcels, adding chutneys and chilies, then using his thumb to push each parcel into his mouth. He eats quickly without a single grain of rice falling from his fingers. After three mouthfuls he grabs his water, throws his head back, and drinks the entire glass in one gulp. I know he's only doing it to show off, thinking he can impress the travelers with his local eating skills. And, actually, in a funny way he does. I'm impressed in any case.

"Hmm, these are great. Do you mind?" he says to Yasmin as he pulls her plate toward him.

"Go ahead."

"Carry on," Sanjay says eagerly. I can see the food at various stages of mastication between his words.

"Are you sure you don't mind, Yasmin?" I ask. She shakes her head. I briefly wonder if it's a good idea that she is hearing this, but I move on. I've started now so I may as well finish. And besides, I'm aware that my narrative is keeping her focused on me. When push comes to shove, that's really all I want from the moment: Yasmin's gaze. Forget the consequence. "Well, it didn't take me long to figure out that if it hadn't been for the police, I probably would have ended up joining them. I had a lucky escape. Still, I wasn't risking anything. I got as far away from Jaisalmer as I possibly could. I think I went to Kathmandu after that. I didn't even want to be in India anymore. I was completely freaked."

"I'm not surprised," Yasmin says sympathetically.

"Well, nothing happened for a while. I eventually finished my trip and went back to England and forgot about the whole episode. It was only when I came back the following year that I heard the name Baba again. I was in Pushkar and I met these travelers talking about him like he was some sort of guru. They were saying stuff like, 'If it weren't for Baba there'd be no underground traveler's movement,' and stuff like that. They said he was a legend in his own time. No one ever saw him and no one knew his real name, but they said he was responsible for 'making it all happen'—whatever that meant. At first, I didn't think it had anything to do with my Baba. I just thought they were spouting off the usual bullshit traveling myths. It was only when I started working for the *Hindu Week* that I found out about the drug routes from Pakistan into India, the links with the Bombay Mafia, and all that stuff. It got me wondering. After some snooping around I eventually figured out that Baba wasn't a myth. He's a real person. Ever since then, I've been piecing things together. I know roughly where he lives, what he does, what his system is, where the drugs go—pretty much everything. Except who he is. And that's where you come in, Sanjay."

"You think this Baba character is someone in Bollywood?"

"Yes. Someone with links to the Mafia there."

"That hardly narrows the search."

"But you know people in Bollywood, don't you? I mean doesn't your mum have loads of connections and stuff?"

"Yeah, but so what? Why are you getting involved with all this? Even if there is a Baba, which I'm sure there is in every country that's hot enough to grow dope, why do you want to meet him?"

"Because I'm a journalist and I'm chasing down my story."

"Now I've heard it all," Sanjay says cynically. "Mr. Joshua King, BBC correspondent, I don't think. Are you mad? All you've done is write a couple of soppy stories for the *Hindu Week.* You're hardly an experienced investigative journalist, and even if you were, do you really think a journalist would be stupid enough to go messing around with some drug-running ring?"

"Yes, I do. And, I may not have had much experience in journalism, but this is my chance to make it. This is My Big Story."

"Yeah, yeah," he replies tiredly.

"What's that supposed to mean?"

"Look, Josh, just ask yourself this: If it were a bunch of hard-core British yardies or New York dons—would you be so keen to blow the lid on their operations? I think you are making a big mistake if you think the Indian Mafia isn't as serious. You may find India a funny place to hang out and get stoned, man," he says, flashing a peace sign and a dopey expression at me, "but the gangsters here are no nicer than they are anywhere else. Trust me."

"But I'm not taking on the whole Mafia," I press, trying very hard not to let my confidence go. I don't want Yasmin to sense what's stale in my relationship with Sanjay. I want her to see me as fresh and reasonable and able to take the grief. I'm even hoping to make Sanjay look bad—the cynical piss-taker. Now that would be nice. "I'm just investigating this one guy, Baba. He's just some courier who's made a name for himself by doing deals on the side with the traveling community here. I'm sure that once the Mafia hears about that, they'll be far more concerned with dealing with him than me. And besides, I'll be out of the country before it comes to that."

Sanjay turns to face Yasmin, shaking his head. "Can you believe how naive this guy is being?" I try not to watch her reaction. I'm worried she might agree. Then he turns back to me. "Wake up, Josh, and read my lips. I'M NOT GOING TO HELP YOU," he half shouts. "As far as I can see, this so-called solution to your career dilemma can only lead to one of two places—absolutely nowhere or, worse, with both of us in the desert without our shoes. Now, I love you, Josh. I've known you a long time. But I'm not about to help you go off on some wild-goose chase after the Mafia, least of all for some stupid newspaper. I just don't want any part of it. It's as simple as that. Now," he says with a fresh tone and pointing at my plate, "are you going to eat your kabobs or am I?"

I have to admit Sanjay does have a point. After all, he does know me. He knows the kind of school I went to—one where the kids were too rich to ever get physical. He knows I'm not hard. I don't even know how to fight. How am I—a clumsy white boy, a pants-wetter no less—meant to take on the Mob?

And that's when I realize.

If I am going to write a Bestseller, I might have to do things—scary things, dangerous things—just to get the story. *Am I prepared to go into dangerous situations?* For a moment, I'm not so sure anymore. His reality check has infected me with self-doubt. What do all my words mean? Where am I hoping to go with these speeches—to Sanjay, to Mani? Sanjay *is* right. Poor is one thing, but hurt, or even dead, is quite another. What is it, exactly, that I am doing?

A hollow, sick feeling nuzzles its way into the pit of my stomach. I can sense failure. After all, this plan is my only solution. If it really is as unrealistic as Sanjay makes out, what other choices do I have left? Very few. I'm suddenly depressed. I see Sanjay turning to talk to Yasmin and I decide I'll just have to think about it later. While I sit here deliberating he's getting a head start.

"So where are you from, Yasmin?"

"Holland," she replies.

"How did you end up in India?" I hear his slimy voice slipping through my foggy thoughts.

"Huh," Yasmin says with a small snort. "That's a good question. I don't know. I've been here so many times now, I can't really remember why I came the first time."

"Why do you come so often, then?"

"For Osho," she says conclusively.

"Who?" Sanjay says.

"Bhagwan Rajneesh," I interject—it's my turn to show off a little. If there's one thing I've learned while trying to infiltrate the underground traveler scene (well, while living in a guest house on Pahar Ganj in any case), it's to be well versed in the various ashrams and the most popular gurus of the time. I know all about Osho, though I've never been to the ashram. "I didn't know you were a sannyasin, Yasmin."

She smiles at me. "You never asked."

"Oh, you mean the guy in Pune," Sanjay recovers. "Yeah, my mum was into him for a while. Isn't he the free-sex guy?"

"It's not just about that," Yasmin says, almost as if "free sex" is passé, for the tourists

"Yeah, but doesn't everyone have to take an AIDS test before they join?" he pushes.

"Yes, but—"

"And isn't there a room, like a padded cell in the dark, where anything goes?" Sanjay interrupts eagerly. I can see that Yasmin is getting irritated. I let him dig his own grave. "Fuck, man, we should go there one day," he says, flashing a grin and throwing a nudge-nudge-wink-wink expression my way.

I leave him stranded with a cursory shrug of the shoulders, as if I've heard it all before and am completely unimpressed. "So have you been going there for long?" I say, looking softly at her.

"A few years," she says, only talking to me now, completely shutting out Sanjay.

"Did you ever meet him? Osho, I mean?"

"Once, just before he died, very briefly," she says. "He initiated me."

"Wow," I say with suitable adulation. "What was he like? Was it amazing?"

She smiles at me, her pink lips sealed gently together, and nods without saying anything. I smile back at her, as if we're both caught in a moment of mutual spiritual ecstasy, as if the very fact that Yasmin has met Osho—once and many years ago—now enables me to viscerally absorb his wondrous powers. I'm not even faking it that much. Yasmin is so beautiful, there's a part of all this that really does feel spiritual, in a way. Sexy spiritual, if you know what I mean. After all, isn't that what Osho is all about?

"So is Yasmin your real name, then?" Sanjay blunders his way back into the conversation with all the sensitivity of a bulldozer. "'Coz I heard that, like, all the disciples—"

"Sannyasins," Yasmin corrects, still looking at me.

"Sorry, sannyasins. I heard that all the sannyasins change their names once they're initiated."

"Not everyone has a compulsive need to change their name, you know, Saaaannjaaay," I dig at him again. I get a sick pleasure from ripping him this way, like I'm punching a bruise.

"No, he's right," Yasmin says, to my dismay and Sanjay's visible relief. "A lot of people do change their names. But I didn't."

"Why not?" Sanjay asks.

"Because Osho said my name already reflected my inner beauty. He said I didn't need to change my name to shed my ego. It was already pure."

"Wowwww." Sanjay and I gasp simultaneously. Yasmin smiles with quiet pride back at us. I smile at her but then feel it fade as

I remember, from somewhere, that Osho went into silence in the years before he died. How could he have conveyed all this to Yasmin without saying anything? Bit weird.

"So," I hear Sanjay continuing, obviously determined not to let his own recovery slip away from him, "how did you get into it? I mean, how did you hear about Osho in the first place?"

"My boyfriend introduced me. His parents were sannyasins. He was practically born into it."

I enjoy watching Sanjay's face falter. "Oh, right," he says, eyebrows raised as if in interest, really to hide the dismay that yes, of course, how couldn't there be a boyfriend on the scene. After all, she is hot. She's clearly the kind of girl that somehow seamlessly slips from one relationship to the next, far too attractive to ever be left in limbo like the rest of us. "Is he here, your boyfriend? In Delhi, I mean," he recovers, quite well.

"Yes."

Sanjay can't help himself from frowning then. "So why didn't he come out with us tonight? It would have been nice to meet him." At least he tries to say it cheerfully.

"He's in prison."

If only Sanjay could actually act as genuinely gob-smacked as he looks at this moment, he probably would make it as a movie star, I think to myself.

"Oh. Shit. Sorry. Why? I mean. That's. Pretty. Heavy."

"Hmm." Yasmin nods, sucking her lips in. "If it hadn't been for Josh, I'd probably be in prison too," she adds, vaguely smiling at me.

Sanjay looks between us. "Yeah? How so?"

Yasmin recounts our first encounter and flatteringly describes my handling of the police. It feels good to hear her describe how my journalistic status saved her, how my professionalism caught the police off guard. Partly because she makes me feel like I really am a journalist and partly because her take on that night is so different from mine. Like she can't believe I knew the name of the police commissioner. I don't even remember how I know that—probably from some interview he did with the *Hindu Week*. But it completely wows the traveler in her. It's as if she expects herself to know everything about India because she's spent so long here, and she is stunned to discover that, actually, she doesn't know everything. In fact, she knows very little. Like a lot of other travelers, Yasmin only knows about things like Hinduism and how to haggle. She doesn't know anything about the daily reality of life in India: about its politics, its middle classes, its police commissioners. And for my part, I thought I was just bullshitting my way through things. She says that I'm an expert in charm. That's news to me.

"Wow," Sanjay says, disappointed. "That's quite a story. Your boyfriend, though. Will he get off?"

"I don't know. It does not look good. Unless . . ." She lingers.

"Unless what?" Sanjay and I say together.

"Oh, nothing," she says, drawing in the line a little.

Like the little fish that we are, Sanjay and I take the bait eagerly. "What?" I say.

"Yeah, come on," Sanjay encourages.

"Well"—she drags it out—"one of the officers told me that they could help James escape."

"You're kidding," I say. "What do you have to do in return?"

"What do you think?" she says, looking at me directly.

"Oh, God, he wants you to sleep with him," Sanjay jumps in.

"No, no, nothing like that," she says with a small snort. I love the way Sanjay is portraying himself, rather accurately I might add, as a sex-obsessed adolescent. "No. He wants money."

"How much?" I ask.

"It's not even worth thinking about."

"Go on, tell us," Sanjay presses.

"He wants"—she pauses and draws air in between her teeth—"one crore."

"How much is that?" I ask. "A hundred thousand?"

"No, that's a lakh," Sanjay answers.

"So how much is a crore, then? I can never remember."

"Ten million rupees," Yasmin says.

"Oh."

"Oh."

"Yes, oh," Yasmin confirms.

We all do the mental calculations. I figure it out last: one crore is £200,000.

I scratch my chin and look at Sanjay. We both wish we'd stuck to the original line.

"So when's his court case?" Sanjay says for us.

"Next week."

"Maybe he'll get off," Sanjay tries.

"I do not think so. It is only a preliminary hearing. The embassy says it could take years before his case actually comes to trial."

"Look, I'm sure it won't take as long as that," Sanjay says, before adding, "Do you have family, you know, that could help out? Maybe lend you the money."

"No," she snaps, tetchily. There's a small pause as Sanjay and I absorb this unexpected energy. Family is clearly a touchy subject for Yasmin. I can see the muscles pulling on the corners of her mouth. I think she is about to cry and I pass her one of the paper napkins, but then, quite suddenly, she doesn't seem to need it. She takes the paper and simply folds it in one hand before saying: "No, none that I can depend on anyway."

For some reason her stoicism—I'm not sure whether it's in the face of talking about James or her family—makes me feel proud. Neither Sanjay nor I digs deeper. I think we both see that Yasmin deserves to be alone with her thoughts. The restaurant is practically empty now. I look at my watch. It's eight, but most of Delhi is already in bed. I look at Sanjay and nod my head toward the waiter, who is hovering just a few tables away.

"Yeah, sure. I'll just go settle the bill."

"Thanks, mate," I say, and turn to rub Yasmin's arm. "It's going to be okay, Yasmin. I promise," I say while he's gone.

She looks at me with burning eyes. "You should not make promises you cannot keep."

A BRAZILIAN DRUMMER AND A
SINGAPOREAN DRAGON

I have some real coffee, a kerosene stove, and an Italian percolator back at the Green, so I suggest going onto the roof for a cup. Yasmin declines, kisses me on the cheek (but not Sanjay), and returns to her room for the night. When we reach the top we see two silhouettes sitting in the corner, the glow of a burning *chillum* floating between them. Sanjay suggests that we say hello.

As we get closer I recognize one of them. He is a rakishly thin Singaporean I've seen hanging around in the well. He's a long-termer—a heroin addict who sold his passport years ago. I remember him chasing the dragon in front of me once. He was spinning around on his haunches like a windup toy frog, gathering his equipment for the task: matches, foil ripped from a cigarette packet, a short straw, a coin, and the sugar of course. I remember the most interesting thing was the coin. He put it inside his O-shaped mouth to cool the smoke, he explained.

He's on his haunches now. Long black hair loosely covers the shaven sides of his head. Wispy hairs sprout from his chin and crawl between the hollow pits in his waxy yellow cheeks. The sight of him, in the pair of black Thai fisherman's trousers he always wears, depresses me. For some reason, he makes me feel like I'll never leave India. I'll just be stuck here, like him, wasting my life away in some half-horrific dream state that everyone calls traveling.

I don't know what I'd do if I had to sell my passport and actually live that kind of life. Half the attraction of coming to India is the ability to leave it.

I've never seen the other guy before, but he is more cheering. He has mad, frizzy hair that springs from his head in a random Afro. Every time he moves, it bounces. And it turns out that he does a lot of moving. He introduces himself, gesticulating madly, as a Brazilian drummer. But after Sanjay and I pick up on his Australian accent we discover that he's actually a taxi driver living in Sydney. He makes me smile when we find that out. I find it reassuring that like me, a lot of other people have two versions of themselves.

After politely accepting Sanjay's paltry contribution of hash, the Australian/Brazilian drummer prepares the mix. He shakes a Wills out of a crumpled hard pack and puts it behind his ear while he lights a match. Then he cups the cigarette in his hand and glides the long, yellow flame across the paper until it is charred black and the tobacco inside is roasted and dry. He drops the match and breaks the contents of the cigarette into his palm. Then he starts picking at the hash. He doesn't heat it or crumble it. He just picks pieces off the lump and rubs his fingers together until the resin comes unstuck and falls into the pile of tobacco. After a few minutes the mix is coated. He sets aside the *charas* with religious deliberation and starts grinding and rubbing the mix together with his free hand. Then he pulls the *chillum* out of its ethnic cloth case. It looks like a hollow pestle. He does some silly circular sweeps with the phallic-looking pipe over the mix and chants a few words as if he's casting a spell. Then he starts driving the fat end of the pipe into his palm, shoveling and packing the tobacco in until it's all inside.

The Singaporean dragon pulls out a yellow rag with red Sanskrit letters inked on it and tears a square piece off the end. He reaches for the half-empty bottle of mineral water beside him, unscrews the top, sticks the piece of cloth in the end, and tips the bottle upside down until water starts dripping through his fingers and onto the hot brick roof. He puts the bottle back and squeezes the excess moisture out of the cloth. Then he flicks it open, spraying more water, and hands the small sheet to the Brazilian. The drummer wraps the wet cloth around the small end of the pipe and ties it in on itself so that it stays. It will cool the smoke. He hands it to Sanjay.

Sanjay grins, shifts on his feet, then slides the *chillum* so that it stands between two fingers and his thumb, with a small gap left open at the bottom. He takes his left hand, flat, and wraps it around the two fingers holding the pipe, forming a seal. The Brazilian lights another match.

Sanjay touches the pipe to his forehead, flaps his elbows till his hands are holding the pipe just right, and shouts out the Shiva salutation: "BOOM SHANKAR!"—another "Holy Smoking" ritual that travelers have picked up on in the name of ethnic authenticity, the Indian equivalent of Jah Rastafari. I don't know if he does it because he's in India mode or to impress the travelers, but either way, none of us gives him the kudos I know he wants for it.

"Keep your voice down, mate," the Brazilian urges as his voice echoes down the well. "The police might still be hanging around."

"Sorry."

Sanjay tips his head to one side and pulls the *chillum* to his mouth. The Brazilian holds the match over the mix and lets it shrink and flame, shrink and flame, as Sanjay draws on the end like it's a big cigar. After five puffs the mix is glowing orange, like a comet burning up in the atmosphere. Sanjay performs one last puff and then sucks hard, so that the hash fizzes and the glow goes red. He snaps the *chillum* away just as he comes to the end of his breath and lets in some air to cool the smoke.

It doesn't work. Sanjay flashes me a panicked glance to tell me that he's taken too much and I can see his throat twitching as the smoke fights its way back out. Sanjay quickly hands me the *chillum,* catches six rapid-fire sneezes in the back of his throat, and releases an enormous, five-second stream of smoke like steam from a pressure cooker. Then he starts coughing. Huge, gut-wrenching heaves that make his cheeks puff out, his lips turn purple, and his throat issues noises that sound like notices of imminent death.

We all laugh at him. He looks at me. Tears stream from his eyes. For a second I think he's crying.

"Your turn," he manages to splutter.

I cup the *chillum* the same way, give it a couple of puffs to get it going, and heave, half praying that I won't be as greedy as Sanjay. I let the smoke cascade down my throat and feel it filling my lungs like a bath. It tastes of flowers, a sweet smell like nectar. I pull it away just as my lungs tell me I'm reaching full capacity and suck in some oxygen. I hold before releasing, watching the smoke pour out of my mouth like a satisfied superhuman porn star.

For a second I don't feel anything. Then it starts. First there is the deep rumbling sound, welling up from inside my lungs and exploding in my ears like a mushroom cloud. I pass the pipe to the Singaporean dragon, who says something, but I can't hear what he says because the sound of the explosion in my heart and lungs and ears just rumbles on and on and on. I find myself grinning.

And then the rumbling sound starts fading into the distance somewhere. I suddenly feel incredibly light. My head is clear and—there's no other way to describe it—I just feel wonderfully alive, content, and calm. Everything makes sense and I just let myself enjoy the flowery taste still lingering in my throat.

Next thing I know, I'm rolling around the floor with laughter and I don't know why. I vaguely remember hearing Sanjay burp and watching a small cloud of smoke come out and think that maybe that's what I find so funny.

The *chillum* goes around two more times, rumbling and giggling until we all feel as if we just fell out of the sky and can't believe where we've found ourselves except to say that it's extremely funny and doesn't seem very serious at all.

Eventually, we get it together enough to start talking. Or at least I get it together, because I only notice the fact that we're having a conversation halfway through someone else's sentence. The Brazilian is busy tipping out the burned remains of the *chillum* onto the roof and slamming the end of the pipe against his palm until the stone that's inside it pops out. He lets it drop like a hot rock.

The Singaporean is busy tearing another strip from the cloth, not square, but long and thin this time. He rolls it against his thigh until it wraps up inside itself and looks like a piece of string. He hands it to the Brazilian, who threads the string through the fat end of the pipe. After a couple of tries, the string pops through the other side. The Singaporean grabs one end while the Brazilian holds the other and then he starts vigorously rubbing the inside of the pipe until the cloth turns black with tar. When he's finished, he peers through the pipe into the night sky like it's a telescope.

"That looks clean to me," he says, giving the stone a quick rubdown before dropping it back into the fat end of the *chillum*.

"It might be a hassle but it sure gets you fucked," Sanjay says, still coughing gently.

"Yeah," we all agree dopily.

"So, anyways, like I was saying, the whole fackin' world's a bloody con. You might as well screw it before it screws you—thas what I say," the Brazilian restarts. He says screw like kangaroo—*scurroo*.

"Yeah," the Singaporean smackhead offers. "I did insurance scam once. Two-thousand dollar. Easy. I travel six months in India. Thank you, insurance man. All my life, I give insurance company money. Time they give back."

"I just wish I could think of a scam that would make me enough money so that I'd never have to work again," Sanjay says. "That's the biggest con. Working all our lives in jobs we hate, just for some fucking pension fifty years down the line when we're too old to really enjoy it."

"Yeah," we all agree again.

"I don't wanna be rich," the Brazilian says waving his hands in front of our faces. "I jus' wanna have enough money so that I can live life on my own terms. I'll be honest. I've been playing the drums for ten years. I'll probably never make a living out of it. I'm not good enuf. So what 'ave I gotta do instead? Drive a fackin' taxi all my life. Ballox."

"I can relate to that," I say.

The Singaporean is slouched against the wall, fucked up on smack. "I betta take 'im down," the Brazilian says, quietly. "I need another hit anyways." He stands up and pulls the Singaporean to his feet. His legs look like they are going to snap under the effort.

MONEY

After they leave, Sanjay and I lie on our backs and try to look for stars. All we can see is the pink neon of the city reflected in brown clouds. I'm feeling mellow now. The tension between us seems to have dissipated a little. I'm hoping to make a new start.

"Sanj?"

"Yeah."

"Do you remember when my father died?"

"Yeah."

"Did I ever show you the letter he wrote to me?"

"No. You told me about it once, though. I seem to remember you saying there was a lot of stuff about immortality and coming back from the dead. Poor bloke. He must have been pretty mad by the end."

"Yeah. It was all those weird drugs he was taking."

"I'm surprised you never sued. By the sounds of things, those doctors really fucked up."

"The doctors didn't have anything to do with it. Not that I could prove, anyway. Dad had this mad notion in his head that he'd rather die first than grow old, so he boshed fifty-six Viagra, thirteen Es, and a couple of wraps of speed before going for a drive off the Estérel cliffs. They never figured out exactly what killed him first."

"Jesus. Good way to go, though . . . I guess."

"Maybe."

I pause, letting the moment sink in, allowing the intimacy opener to do its work, unlock doors, prize open his defenses.

"Anyway," I restart. "Did I ever tell you that his dying wish was that I write a book?"

"No. Really? What about?"

"Oh, nothing in particular," I lie. I don't know why. Maybe I'm just going slowly, building up to the task. "He said that he just wanted to see me get my life together. You know, focus on something."

"That's just what you need, isn't it? A lecture from the grave."

"Well, the funny thing is, I think I'm coming around to the idea."

"Really?"

"Yeah. I think I'm getting to a point where I'd like to do something with my life, you know, something meaningful."

"Nothing wrong with that," Sanjay says.

So far so good.

"Trouble is . . ." I lure him.

"What?"

"Well, getting published, you know, it's not exactly easy and, well, there's the cash-flow problem."

"You need some money?"

"No, no. Nothing like that. I'm still managing on my savings from work." I love that. "Work." As if I actually *do* something. Not like I've been living on my dead father's charity at all. "It's just, well, how can I put this? If I write a book and don't get published, then I won't have any means of supporting myself."

"True."

"And I don't exactly like the idea of being a starving artist."

"I can understand that. Most starving artists have starved to death, or, at least, sold out their talent to some job they hate."

"So . . . what would you suggest I do?"

"I dunno. Get a job and write in your spare time, I guess."

"Exactly."

"Exactly what?"

"That's exactly what I thought."

"And?"

"Well, I've got a job . . . sort of."

"Oh, oh. We're not back to this *Hindu Week* thing again, are we?"

I hear the good vibes suddenly twang.

"Listen," I continue quickly, desperate to explain myself before the barriers go up again, "if I do this story for the *Hindu Week* right, I get to kill two birds with one stone. They'll pay me and I'll get published. It could be just the start I'm looking for. Don't you see? It makes so much sense."

"Okay. Stop right there. Let's just get this straight, shall we? So you say that the *Hindu Week* is going to pay you."

"Yeah."

"How much?"

I don't answer. I knew he'd be this way.

"Come on, how much?" he presses.

"Twenty-five thousand rupees," I mutter under my breath.

"How much! Twenty-five thousand? That's only five hundred quid, Josh. Jesus. That's even less than I thought. I can't believe you sometimes. You wouldn't last a month on that money—even in India."

"I know, but at least I'll get published."

"Woop, woop. Some shitty little article. That's brilliant, that is."

"Well, it's better than nothing."

"It's not better than being dead." I don't have an answer for that one. He marches on mercilessly. He knows when he's got the upper hand. "Listen, pal, the only really good reason to go fucking with the Mob is if it were going to make you so much money you could afford to never have to work again. Five hundred quid isn't going to get you very far. And if you think a news article is going to help you get a book published then you've got another think coming."

"Yeah, but the adventure might give me the material I need to write a book."

"You really are something, you know that, Josh. I mean, here you are, trying to convince me to help you infiltrate the Mafia so that *you,* Mr. Wannabe Writer, can get the material for a book. After all these years, you still amaze me. Don't you think it's just a little presumptuous to assume that I might want to risk my life for you?"

I don't say anything. He's on a roll and there's no point in standing in his way. I know that I've failed. There's nothing I can do now. I've failed before I've even begun. And there's a big part of me that agrees with Sanjay. I don't have the right to ask him to help me on this. I even feel slightly embarrassed by my audacity.

"If you're really that into the idea of writing a book on the Mafia in India, why don't you just make it up like everyone else?"

"I'm worried that it might not be believable," I say meekly.

"So what? Fiction's just fiction," he counters bombastically.

"It won't work if it's not believable. I need to do this for . . . research." That's the word I'm giving to experience these days. It has a professional ring. After all, I know that I can't just make stuff up. That's far too dangerous. I'm too susceptible to the unbelievable, I have to at least have a thread of reality I can bend. I have to actually meet the Indian Mafia to write a book.

"Write about something else, then."

"I can't think of anything else to write about." I sound pathetic now and I know it. This is the last resort. I'm trying to solicit his pity. Get him to feel so sorry for me that he concedes.

"You're sad. Writing a book isn't about doing dangerous things and going on adventures, you know. It's about good writing. If you really want to do something meaningful with your life, then you should learn how to write well. Stop wasting your time with this ridiculous idea. It's just so stupid."

"Well, what would you suggest I write about?"

"Anything you like. Why not write about your father?"

"I could, I guess. It's just that . . ."

"What?"

"I have to—" I know this is going to sound stupid but I say it anyway. "I have to write a bestseller." I don't know why I don't just come clean with Sanjay about my father's challenge. I guess I'm embarrassed now. I sort of wish I'd never even mentioned any of this. Then, of course, there's the seed of greed—still growing— in the back of my mind. If I tell Sanjay about the £5 million, there's a chance—a strong chance—that he'll want a cut. Not that I'm totally averse to sharing some of it with him. I just don't want to get his hopes up. I don't want to make out that by helping me I'll definitely, one day, give him a couple of million. There's no guarantee, no guarantee at all, of that. No. There's no point in getting his hopes up. Better to test his charity and then reward him, out of the blue and gloriously. Maybe that's what I'm doing. Testing him, testing our friendship. He doesn't know it, but if he helps, he might end up rich . . . *might* being the operative word, of course. Because I'm still hedging. For all I know, I might yet turn out to be a really greedy, stingy, traitorous bastard. It all depends. There are so many variables. The jury is still out on me. Am I nice guy? Let's think about that once the £5 million is in the bag. That's my point. That's why I'm not saying anything. Because nothing is certain. Not the bestseller, not the money, not even me.

Sanjay doesn't say anything for a while. There's a part of me that thinks things are probably better this way. I don't like feeling greedy. Five million pounds—it's a lot of money. My head spins whenever I think about it. It's like a disease. I don't think I'm a greedy person. I just think the thought of all that money infects me with avarice. It's a powerful motive. Some of me believes I'd be best not to touch the idea. Better to lead a normal, dull life and stay pure, keep my soul clean. I should just go home and get a job like everyone else. That's when I feel guilty. I feel bad for asking Sanjay at all. I hope he doesn't hold it against me. I hope he doesn't mention this episode to any of our other friends. That would be embarrassing. People will think I've really lost it.

Then, just as I'm coming around to his way of thinking and am on the verge of letting it all go, he goes and launches into a whole new speech. I don't know where it comes from. "You know what I think?" he starts with patronizing omniscience. "I don't think this has anything to do with 'doing something meaningful' at all. I think you're just looking for a shortcut to being rich and famous. I'm right, aren't I? You think that chasing the Mob will somehow make you famous. You don't even want to be a writer that much. You just like the idea of having your name up in lights. Well? Am I right?"

"Why do you say that?"

"Maybe because this is the first time I've ever heard you express an interest in writing a book. It all seems so random. And the fact that you insist on it being a bestseller. That's a giveaway."

"I told you, my father said I should do it."

"So what? What's so meaningful about writing a book, anyway? I certainly don't see how writing a book about the Mafia in India is that meaningful. Unless of course you're hoping that it might make you rich and famous and, in that sense, make your existence meaningful."

"I think that's your bag, not mine." He's irritating me now with this new diatribe. Why can't he just quit when he's ahead? He has to harp on. I'm glad I didn't mention the £5 million now.

"What do you mean by that?"

"Well, why do you want to be a Bollywood superstar? If that's not for money and fame then I don't know what is," I bite back.

"Oh, why don't you just go and fuck yourself?"

I don't say anything. I knew that last comment would strike at the heart. I'm not even trying to convince him of anything anymore. We're just fighting. And I'm firing arrows at his weak heel. I know his story. I know how to hurt him.

Truth is Sanjay has come to work in Bollywood because he's sold out. He originally wanted to be an actor—"a real actor" as he says—in London. But despite a long and extended career in school plays, Sanjay just couldn't cut it on the professional circuit.

That's why he has all those preprepared quips about "starving artists" vs. "working in jobs we hate" = "pointless." He knows what it is to be on the dole as well as on the gray-suit commute. He's done just about everything to avoid this eventuality. Starved and done the office job—filing, mainly.

But he's finally given in. I guess, after a while, all those rejections, all those "Don't call us, we'll call yous," wore him down. It's probably also got something to do with five years of persistent badgering from an overbearing mother who has employed a rather intelligent strategy of simultaneously putting him down as a "boy with limited talents who should know his limits" while also reassuring him of the "fantastic acting career" waiting for him in India (primarily in order to woo her only son back home).

Whatever the reason, Sanjay has finally conceded. He's packed in his dreams and returned home where he's been promised work. This is his compromise. This way, he gets to "act" and make good money. The worst thing about his situation is that Sanjay can't stand India, he despises Bollywood, and he hates his mother. Nevertheless, he can't handle the two life choices waiting for him back in London. So he's finally returned home, where he has been promised work. Call it a colonial hangover, but apparently nepotism still works here. At least, I would have said so, and so would Sanjay, I presume. The amusing thing for anyone watching is that Sanjay's been here six months so far and he hasn't even been asked to take one screen test. All he's been doing is lounging around his mother's apartment being nagged at, getting stoned, and trying to reintroduce himself to the Mumbai social scene. I know all this from our telephone calls. For the last few weeks I've been his only sympathetic ear. But now I'm using his own confessions as weapons against him. Why shouldn't I? It's not as if he hasn't been giving me a good old go.

"Well, at least I'm not risking my life over it," Sanjay eventually restarts weakly, then he stops, as if he's thinking better of the whole situation. I can tell then that I have managed to hurt his feelings. He's very sensitive, our Sanjay—about certain things at least. Thick-skinned and inept with the chicks, but one little dig in the right place and he's cowing meekly. Maybe he feels betrayed. There's a part of me that feels bad. I don't want to attack him. Sanjay's my mate. And this isn't about fighting. It's about trying to convince him to help me. I realize then that I've fucked up. I try and think of something to say, something to smooth things over. At the very least, we should stick together, Sanjay and I. We're all we've got over here, in India, all by ourselves.

"Sanjay," I start.

He doesn't respond.

"Sanjay, listen. I'm sorry, really, Sanjay—"

Then he just cuts in, quite fey, all stormy, nose in the air, and says, "You know what? This is just stupid. I've had enough of this conversation. I'm going to bed."

"Oh, come on, buddy . . ."

"No." He pouts. "I don't want to talk to you anymore."

"Suit yourself." Actors. So bloody tempestuous.

"Good night," he says, getting up to leave.

" 'Night."

Shit.

DÉJÀ VU

Yasmin is in my room.

"Come on, Josh, hurry, hurry."

"Are you sure they are coming for me?"

"Does it matter?" she hisses, flicking nervous glances through the crack of the door. I figure that she is probably right. Better safe than sorry. I grab a T-shirt and pad barefoot out into the stairwell, dressing as we go. I resist the temptation to look down for flashlights.

We trot down the first set of stairs two at a time before I remember Sanjay. I grab Yasmin's shoulder. "Sanjay, we can't leave him," I say, and before she has a chance to answer, I run back up the stairs to his room. It's locked. I can't bear to knock and make a noise. Sanjay, Sanjay, Sanj—" I am half growling through his wire-meshed window. I can see his silhouette, curled up with his hands prayerlike between his thighs. "Quentin, wake up. Fuck, man, get up." He doesn't even stir. "Shit."

Yasmin is halfway back up the staircase, flapping her hands at me like an impatient air-traffic controller. Her green eyes, catlike, scream at me in the dark. I press my hand against the wire mesh, a sort of good-luck gesture, before scampering after her. We skip down two flights of stairs to the third floor. "Quick, in here,"

Yasmin calls hoarsely to me, then pulls me by my wrist into an empty room, three doors away from hers.

She slips the door shut and we stand, breathing in the dark. For a while, everything, except for us, seems quiet. My ears strain for clues. This doesn't seem like a police raid. It's all far too quiet. The whole guest house should be awake and scrambling with panic by now. At least, it was that one time I saw a raid.

"Are you sure—" I start before Yasmin cuts me off with a *shush*. That's when I hear them. There are whispers. I can't make out what they are saying. Yasmin's thoughts are telepathically drowning out their words. All I can hear in my head is her voice: "THERE, THAT. NOW DO YOU BELIEVE ME?"

A shadow manages to glance through the night, past the crack in our door. It doesn't see us. Then a pair of rubber-soled shoes squeak their way up the stairs.

"Come on," Yasmin whispers. She snatches a quick look into the stairwell before leading me, like a blind man, into the unknown. I don't ask questions, I stop looking for clues. My mind is filled only with commands to move my body. I am following some primordial instinct to escape. Fight or flight. Move leg, tiptoe, don't fall. The feeling is strangely meditative, calm. Take away the voice, there's just the void. The oh-so-bearable-emptiness-of-being.

Having dodged the cops, the rest is easy. We shudder past reception unseen, and scramble outside into the half-tarmacked cul-de-sac. We start running, my senses on full alert for cowpats and dog shit. My oversized feet suddenly don't feel so clumpy when I think of them—the prospect of slipping into worm-ridden crap has the profound effect of making me coordinated. I almost enjoy skipping through the black street with all its ominous shapes and shadows. Feeling my body react to my command is an alien, but deeply fulfilling feeling.

A few yards down the main road, a tick-ridden dog—its coat half scratched away to reveal raw patches of skin covered in bloody welts—suddenly springs out at us from the shadows and snaps at our feet. The shock makes us jump into a sprint that we keep up until well past its territory. My heartbeat is throbbing painfully in my teeth and I can taste blood in my throat.

I call to Yasmin to stop. "Where are we going?" I pant, stooping down, holding my weak knees firm by pressing my hands against them and locking my arms.

"I don't know," she heaves back. "I just thought we should get the hell out of there."

"You're sure it was the police?"

"Yes, I'm sure. I do not enjoy running around Delhi in the middle of the night half naked, you know." It's only then that I notice how little Yasmin is wearing. Just a pair of gray cotton shorts, which look more like underwear than shorts, a matching gray vest with flimsy shoulder straps, and a pair of flip-flops. I want her.

"We should find somewhere to stay," I say, before adding quickly, "It's not safe."

She agrees and we step into the nearest alleyway we can find. It isn't long before we come upon a pink neon sign and a white-tiled reception. I fail to notice the name. I am too busy counting the hairs stroking the back of Yasmin's neck.

She wakes the teenage boy behind the counter, who sleepwalks us to a room. A double bed, with clean white sheets, stands gloriously alone in the center of the floor. There is even air-conditioning, and towels hang freshly under a sign boasting the mechanics of the hot-water system. It's strange to be in a normal guest house. It's clean and comfortable and not intimidating. It suddenly strikes me that not everyone comes to India to take drugs, flirt with the police, and meet freaks. Some people come here and stay in normal guest houses and do normal things like see the Taj Mahal and worry about the food. I notice Yasmin hand a small stack of rupees to the kid and I briefly wonder if I should offer to chip in. Then I realize I don't have any money with me and kind of ask myself how on earth Yasmin had the foresight to bring some with her. Maybe she always carries her money belt on her. I can't see a bulge in her skimpy clothes. But just as I am starting to wonder if that's strange, the door clicks behind us and we are suddenly alone.

"It seemed too complicated to ask for separate rooms," Yasmin says, turning to face me. "Do you mind?"

I try not to fall over my reply. "No, not at all, no worries. This is great." I know I have failed.

"I'm going to have a shower," she announces, looking down at her feet, which are filthy from the street. She disappears with one of the towels.

"After you," I call, far too excitedly. I tell myself to stay cool but instead find myself sitting on the edge of the bed, shaking my right leg maniacally. I suddenly remember someone telling me that people who shake their legs in public are really simulating masturbation. I stop shaking my leg and look around the room, desperate for something to do. I listen to the water crashing against the floor next door, then being muted by her naked shape, then crashing, then muting, then crashing, mixed with the sound of soap lathering. I look down to find both of my legs bouncing like horny hounds.

I get up and read the instructions for the air-conditioning unit. First in English, then German, then Sanskrit. I turn it on. Level

1, 2, 3, 4, 5. Arctic air blasts through my hair. I go back down again. 5, 4, 3, 2, 1. Then up again, down again. The water stops. I settle for mark 2 and scramble for something to do. The room is empty. Where's a newspaper when you need one? I lie on the bed, and force a pair of imaginary gravity boots onto my feet, clamping them to the floor. "Don't shake, don't shake." I try not to imagine exactly which part of her body she is rubbing with the towel. I wonder if I'll be able to use the same one in the morning. Will it smell of her or of soap?

The bathroom door opens.

I suppose there have been times, moments really, when I discover that the woman I am with doesn't quite fit the necessary requirements. It doesn't matter who, I always manage to find some flaw, some inadequacy that dampens the excitement of the initial vision. Legs too short, ass slightly too big, breasts too small—whatever. The fact is, most people aren't perfect, and for some reason, I manage to let my preoccupation with these failings grow until they become a turnoff. The inadequacies I find myself forgiving in the beginning become the reasons for ending things in the end.

But Yasmin is perfect. There is nothing wrong with her. Nothing. There are no nasty moles or other obscene protrusions. No hidden repellents like a pair of unshaved armpits. No cellulite dimples, no mannish hands, no purple scars. That's when I know. I could love Yasmin forever.

She stands there briefly, blocking out the yellow glow of the bathroom lightbulb perfectly with the shape of her head. I can see a halo. The towel is holding itself tightly against her more-than-a-handful breasts and stretching around the curve of her hips and across the tops of her thighs. She is still dripping, holding her clothes in one hand.

"Your turn," she says, squeezing the excess water from the ends of her hair and flashing me a smile.

I try to be nonchalant but suddenly realize that I have literally raced to the door, and I catch her, one leg still in the doorway, as I pass. The moment is uncomfortable and we don't say anything. Just before I finish my shower, which takes me all of five minutes, it suddenly occurs to me that I should thank Yasmin for saving my skin. It might make a good start.

By the time I walk back into the bedroom, she is in bed with her clothes on, the sheet taking over from the towel as it stretches itself across her chest and the pillow, darkening as it drinks itself damp on her hair. Her arms are folded and she is looking blankly into the distance.

"Yasmin," I say gently, being sure to keep my stomach tense. I learned that trick in a physiotherapy class I took to help me stop slouching. Standing up straight is all in the stomach.

She snaps out of her daydream and focuses sleepily on me before smiling. "Yuh."

I walk around to the side of the bed and sit next to her. She is looking right back at me, into my eyes. She doesn't seem in the least bit vulnerable. Not even perturbed. Butterflies are crashing against my stomach wall. I consider taking her hand, but decide against it. I know that my palms will feel sweaty and twitch.

"I just wanted to say thanks."

"What for?"

"For helping me just now, with the police and everything."

"Don't be silly."

"No, seriously," I say, flashing her the kindest eyes my mother ever gave me. "I could be in a lot of trouble now if it wasn't for you."

"The last thing I need is to see more friends go to jail in India. And besides . . ."

"What?"

"Oh, nothing."

The air-conditioning unit hums in the silence. I wonder whether I should ask if I can kiss her and the thought spins the swarm of butterflies into a blind panic. Then I remember the rule: if you have to ask, it's not going to happen.

"How did you hear them, anyway?" I ask, settling the massacre. "I mean, the police. They were being so quiet."

"I was awake and I heard someone say your name. That's how I figured they were coming for you."

"You did? Shit. You don't suppose they found out my work visa expired, do you?"

"Maybe. Who knows? It doesn't matter now, anyway. You're safe, that's all that matters."

"I hope Sanjay's okay."

"He'll be fine," she replies confidently, before sinking down into the mattress. "Now let's get some sleep. It's late."

"Yeah, you're right," I say, pulling my T-shirt over my face as I take it off, to hide the rejection, and walking around the bed before hitting the lights and climbing in next to her. A cool clean chasm separates us, but I dare not move closer for warmth. There's been enough excitement for one night.

IN AT THE DEEP END

I can just make out the tops of his thighs above the water. My arms are getting tired. The chlorine from the pool is making my eyes burn and I can taste it in my mouth. When the water isn't lapping against my ears and the sound of splashing isn't too loud, I can hear him calling me.

"Come on, Josh, you can do it. You can do it. Swim to Daddy."

My legs are getting heavier and heavier. I can't seem to hold myself above the water. My legs are dragging me down. I wiggle and point my toes, desperately trying to feel for the bottom of the pool, but there's nothing but water. I pout my lips and strain my neck, reaching out for air as my head starts to sink beneath the surface. I paddle as hard as I can, the muscles in my shoulders burning, but it's no use. I can feel the water creeping into my mouth and catching in my throat. I am drowning, I think to myself. Fear overwhelms me, and sorrow too. Even in the warm water I can feel the heat of my tears as I blink with the concentration of trying to stay alive.

How can he do this to me? Why is Daddy letting me drown? "Help, Daddy. Daddy, help. Please." I know he can't hear me. The muffled sound of my own heartbeat pumps in my ears and fire rages in my lungs.

Then I hear him. He is calling out to me. I open my eyes and see that he is standing almost beside me. If I can just reach out. I claw at the surface of the water. He is saying something. I can see him, standing like a giant, his arms outstretched to me. I am so close. The water falls away for a split second and I gasp for air. My ears empty with a *glug, glug, glug*.

"Kick, Josh. Kick. Look, I have the money. Here's the five million. Swim for it. Come on, swim!"

I thrash my legs and pump my feet and start to feel myself rising. I realize that I am going to make it. He's so close now. Joy propels me and I start kicking and paddling with all I have left. My lungs need air but it will all be over soon, I think to myself. I am so happy that I am not going to drown. His blue nylon shorts waft before me and I reach out to grab them. I feel the cloth on the ends of my fingertips. I've made it. I've made it.

Then suddenly he's gone. I snatch at the water, but he's not there. I open my eyes again and see him, miles away. At the last second, he stepped away. For a moment I am overwhelmed by the injustice of it all. I am never going to reach him. Each time I get close, he'll just walk away. I can feel hope slipping out of my mind, down my body, and into my feet. The weight of despair starts to drag me down again. Everything slows down, and as I sink beneath the surface of the water once more, I can hear him say, "Come on, Josh. Kick! Think of the money."

I stop paddling and feel myself falling deeper and deeper. The weight of the water presses against my eyes and I can feel my cheeks filling with my dying breath. There's only a few more seconds left and it will all be over. In the final moments, all he could say to me was: "Think of the money." He left me to drown and all he could say was: "Think of the money."

One second left now. A fist of dead air is punching its way from out of my lungs and into my throat, forcing my mouth to open. I can feel my lips bruising blue as I hold them tight against it. It starts pushing its way up, into my brain and behind my eyes. It starts expanding. My head is exploding. Something has to give. I open my mouth and the air rushes around me in a confusion of bubbles. My lungs instinctively reverse the engines and the push becomes a pull. I try to drink the water instead of breathing it, but it is hopeless. I feel the flow of the water between my teeth. It tickles my throat and starts to fill me.

Suddenly a hand grabs me from under my armpit, and with a great whoosh, I am flying to the surface of the water. Freedom and light and air are everywhere. The release is rapturous. Then comes the pain. My lungs heave. I start gagging and retching. Water mixed with sticky thick strands of saliva and sick trickle over my father's freckled shoulder. I can feel the reassuring pat of his huge hands across my back and under my bum where he is holding me.

"I'm sorry, son. I'm sorry. I didn't mean to push you so hard. It's all over now. It's all over."

Eventually, the spasms in my gut subside and give way to dry sobs. All my limbs ache and I feel sleepy with shock. My lower lip quivers with cold and disbelief at what has just happened.

"Why, Daddy?" I manage to splutter. "Why did you do it?"

"I was testing you, son," he says, his hand still patting me. "I wanted to see what you were made of. I wanted to see how badly you wanted the money."

"But I nearly died, Daddy."

"I know, son, I know. I'm sorry."

I wipe sick from my chin and the thought suddenly occurs to me.

"Daddy?"

"Yes."

"Can I have the money now?"

There is a small pause and I can feel him shifting his hands so that they are around my chest. He squeezes me tight and I can feel him picking me off his shoulder to face him. My soft cheek brushes against the sandpaper stubble of his face and I wonder why he hasn't shaved. Then I see his face. It blurs before me and I can't make out any features, but I know who it is. It is Baba!

I scream and thrash wildly with my arms and legs, but he is holding me outstretched before him and I only connect with the air and the hard bone of his forearm. Spit flies from his twisting mouth as he shouts: "No, you can't, because you didn't make it. Look at yourself, little boy. You're weak. You're nothing. You'll always be nothing!"

His head tips back as he starts cackling his throaty, wicked laugh. I feel his hands tightening around my chest and crushing my ribs as he tips his head back to face me. Hate trickles in from the corner of his eyes and fills his stare.

"Stop it. Help. I can't breathe."

And with that he plunges me back, deep down into the water. Air rushes out of my lungs once more and water races in. Twisting and turning, I thrash and punch and scream. I pound my fist against his arms, but the bones are so hard. My knuckles ache with pain. Just as I reach the threshold of death, I wake up.

FEARED CONFESSIONS

I am sitting bolt upright in my bed. I am breathing hard. I reach over and turn on the light. The sheets are everywhere, soaked in sweat. My right hand is throbbing with pain. I look at it. The skin on the knuckles is shredded and my little finger feels like it is broken. I look around and see where I have been punching the wooden headboard. It is splintered. I look around the rest of the room. Yasmin is crouched in the corner, sobbing.

"I tried waking you, I tried," she says, the tears streaming down her face, her mouth twisting. "You were attacking me. You scared me. I'm sorry, I tried, I tried . . ."

I am shaking, terrorized. "Hold me."

She scrambles over the end of the bed and throws herself onto me. We hold each other like disturbed children, rocking, patting, panting, squeezing, stroking, kissing. Eyes, ears, hair, sweat, tears, blood, breath, lips, tongues. Affection, tenderness—balms to the destruction.

Then the swellings start. Twisting, turning, a writhing contortion of limbs, we wrestle blindly into nakedness. I grab hard bones and soft flesh. She pinches skin and feels forbidden places. I eat her neck and she lets me. We don't wait. Suddenly I am inside her, wet warmth grinding against me, pumping deeply. She pushes up, taking me deeper, and I feel myself kicking against the sheets like I'm still learning how to swim. She starts calling my name. I slide my hands under her. She twists her legs in mine, locking us together. And then we're joined completely, as close as we can be. Something rubs on the end of me and I know that it's the beginning of her. She starts quivering and shaking her head against mine, telling me to fuck her. We drown in each other's screams. I release. She twitches and spasms and then she says something deep in my ear, "I can't, I can't, I can't . . ." before we finally collapse into each other, like two deflated balloons.

It takes a long time before we unshackle ourselves. We lie there listening to our breathing, watching the sweat dry off each other. She strokes my face. I can feel the dawn stretching itself outside. After a long while, she says, "What's happening, Josh?" I don't say anything. I want to tell her about Dad. I feel I should explain. That's when I realize. I jump off the bed and am dressed by the time I run into the corridor.

THE TALISMAN

Sanjay is squatting outside my door when I arrive.

"Where the fucking hell have you been?"

I don't answer. I can feel him watching me as I scramble through the debris. Half of my room is strewn around the stairwell. The other half is gone. Yasmin arrives behind me, panting from the run.

"Oh no," she says.

Money, passport, plane tickets, traveler's checks—everything is gone. They have even taken my penknife and Walkman. It doesn't seem to matter.

"The letter, where's the fucking letter?" I can't seem to focus before Sanjay stops me, holding up a tattered piece of paper.

"I think I managed to save it," he says nervously.

"Give it to me," I snap, before sinking to the ground. I can feel them looking at me. I turn to face Yasmin and say disjointedly, "My father, this is my father's letter." She nods her head gently at me and smiles with her eyes, following the non sequitur.

STRANDED

In the end it is Yasmin's idea to rip off Baba. We are in the bank, standing amid a pressing mass of bodies and arms, people piling against their respective booths from all sides. Yasmin is waiting to cash some traveler's checks. She says she can lend me some money to get by.

I am only just starting to realize how much trouble I am in. At first, I didn't think anything the cops took mattered to me: I had my father's letter. But now I can see that I am stranded. Like all the other criminals, junkies, and lost souls in the Green, I'm stuck in India with no means of escape. If I ever needed a reality check, I certainly got one.

"Yasmin?"

"Yuh."

"How the fuck am I going to get out of this country without a passport?"

"Don't worry. We will think of something."

"You're sure that it was the police, aren't you? You're sure I wasn't just robbed?"

"We have talked about this already. You know I'm sure."

"Maybe you were mistaken. I mean, maybe I should take my chances and go to the embassy for a new passport."

Yasmin suddenly swings round to face me. "No, Josh. It's too dangerous. They might report you."

"But—"

"No *buts*. The police will have given your name to the embassy by now and the officials will have to report you if you show up there. I saw a whole bunch of wanted posters for Dutch people when I went to get help for James."

"I just can't believe it. I just can't believe Mani let me down like that. Why didn't he cover for me?"

"Well, you said it yourself. Anyone could have picked up the phone at your newspaper. What about that Lyla girl? Maybe she said something."

"I have to admit, that is extremely likely." Depression overwhelms me. I am so fucked. I don't even feel scared now. I just feel resigned. This is my fate, I think to myself. My worst nightmare is coming true. This is what I deserve for . . . for what, I'm not sure. Being an asshole, embarking on this stupid idea, not really loving my dad, for being so selfish, only thinking about the money. I feel full of self-loathing. This is where it's got me—the same place as the Singaporean dragon.

I look at an armed guard, who is propping up his chin on the end of a double-barrel shotgun, ogling Yasmin. I give him the evil eye, willing his gun to go off, picturing his brains flying against the air-conditioning unit in the wall behind him. I hate the Indian men for staring at Yasmin all the time, though I know I do it a lot myself. "I wonder if I can still count on Mani for the twenty-five thousand."

"I doubt it."

"Why not?"

"Well, his word has not been very reliable so far, has it?"

"No, I guess not," I say despondently. "Maybe I should go and see him."

"It might be a risk."

"It might help."

"Well, you should go, then." She maneuvers her head around to look directly into my downcast eyes and lifts her eyebrows. "Cheer up. Look, everything is going to be fine. We'll figure something out. Okay?"

"Yup, 'course it is."

She twists her fingers through mine. I smile at her. And that's when she says it.

"Hey, you know what we should do? We should steal the money from your Mr. Baba!" Then she starts laughing, a wonderful laugh, full of honest spontaneity.

The funny thing is, when she says it, it seems so obvious. I suddenly feel exhilarated, though I'm not sure whether it's because of Yasmin's brain wave or because she is holding my hand. All I know is, the whole world suddenly seems to make sense. I know exactly what it is I have to do. I suddenly realize that, all this time, I've been wasting time. I don't need to risk my life for a newspaper article. Sanjay was right. I always knew, deep down, that he was right. This whole idea has been totally ridiculous. The real answer to what I want has been staring me full in the face all along.

If I'm going to tangle with the Mafia, I might as well make it worth my while. After all, what is it that I really want? I just want to have the money, right? Why go about things the long way? Why piss the Mafia off for the sake of a story that may or may not make me millions—especially when there is the opportunity to just take the money directly? The risks are the same but the rewards are much greater. And besides, I know that I don't want to be an author. Not really. I'm too lazy and incapable. Writing a bestseller takes hard work and talent—two things I'm in short supply of. All I really want is to drop out and not work. I don't want to participate. I'm a nothing and I'll always be a nothing. Participation opens the door to failure. I can't handle the rejection it takes to write a book. The last thing I need is a reminder that I'm a loser. I know I'm a loser. I don't need to get tricked into getting involved in life, in society, in attempted success. I don't want to make anything of my life. I just want to chill.

And I don't need Dad's money to do that. I don't need his carrot on a stick, reinstating his wayward son in the ways of the world. Fuck that. I can get my own money. Outside the norm, outside the confines of protocol and the system. I can become a criminal. Even better than that. I can be a criminal ripping off the criminals. I'm not a bad bloke. I don't want to be the bad guy it usually takes to outwit the system. This way I get to be a good guy, too. A rich hero. Yes, yes, yes, yes. It all makes sense. This is me. This is a role tailor-made for my mentality. I don't need Dad anymore. Fuck him. He tried to change me. This way I get what I want and stay myself. Finally, yes thank God, fuck him and his immortality. It's time he died and stayed dead. Who needs his resurrection?

At last, life makes sense. I feel that I've found myself. I look back into Yasmin's eyes. They seem extremely green. Maybe it's the extra moisture. I notice a small black fleck in her right iris, her only imperfection. Somehow it manages to make her appear more perfect.

"Yasmin, you're a genius," I finally manage.

She doesn't hear me at first. I sink into thought for a second. Then she says, "I am sorry. What did you say?"

"What?" I reemerge, grinning. "I said you're a fucking genius,

Yasmin, a fucking genius." Inspired, I pick her up and squeeze her.

She squeals. "Put me down. Fuck, you're crazy."

I can feel the whole bank watching us but I don't care. I can't stop smiling at her. "Don't you see?" I whisper excitedly. "It would be the answer to all our problems," I say, stretching out the *all* to include everything in our long list. "We could make enough money to take care of you, me, James, all of us. Fuck, I can't believe we hadn't thought of it before."

A small woman wearing a sari covered in red and yellow flowers twisting themselves in vines around her body turns around and says randomly, "We are all waiting for money, maddhum. You must wait. I must wait."

Yasmin ignores her. "What are you talking about?"

"We're going to rip off Baba."

"What?"

"We are going to steal the money from Baba."

"Rip off Baba?" she says.

"Yes."

"How?"

Sanjay takes to the idea surprisingly well. He's on the roof, watching the kids fly kites as they stand on the white, pink, and redbrick rooftops shifting against the skyline. We haven't really talked since our argument, but after the raid, I feel there's been an implicit mutual apology in the air—a refreshed solidarity between us. That's why I'm so nervous broaching the subject for a third time with him. I don't want to completely destroy the unspoken armistice.

"You'll never believe what these kids are up to," he says when he sees us coming. "It's kite hijacking. See this guy here," he says, pointing to a teenage boy with a shaved head on the roof next door to the hotel, "he just nicked that boy's kite." He points to another small boy, who is screaming on a rooftop two houses away. "He used a piece of string with a stone attached to it and then threw it over the string the other boy was using to fly the kite. Then he pulled the kite toward himself, cut the little boy's string, tied on a new one, and that was that. It's mad." We look at the teenage boy proudly flying his stolen kite, occasionally looking across at his helpless victim to gloat. "Quite ingenious," he says. Eventually he turns around and sees our smiles. "What happened?" he asks.

"We've got some news, or rather an idea, for you," I say carefully.

"This doesn't sound good."

"Why do you say that?" I ask, my smile and enthusiasm faltering slightly.

"Because last time you had a good idea, Josh, it involved eating dodgy kabobs and chasing drug couriers for the Mafia."

At least he's joking about it. I press on. "It's not my idea," I say, a little too defensively. Then quickly add, with pride, "It's Yasmin's." He looks between us. I can see that he is jealous. Probably not a good idea to rub his nose in that. I know he knows that something happened between Yasmin and me the other night, but we've kept it low-profile. Besides, my secret excitement with the conquest has been muted quite considerably ever since the raid marooned me.

After she tells him the plan Sanjay doesn't say anything for a while. He just looks at the teenager flying his kite and scratches his stubble. We wait. After a while, he simply nods. It's as if, like me in the bank, everything seems to make sense to Sanjay for once. At least, the idea of chasing the Mafia starts to finally make some sense. He doesn't say anything, but it's obvious that he's thinking about the money we might make and, more importantly, the freedom he could buy with it. It's not about me and my book anymore. No, it's about Sanjay and his dreams now. It's about escaping his mother and his developed, expatriate dread of India. It's about aspiring to more than Bollywood. It's never having to work in an office again. It's about everything I've been thinking and saying and trying to do—but it's all in his context now.

Or maybe he's thinking that the whole adventure is still too far away to get hurt by. No harm in taking one step closer, for a better look, perhaps. Who knows what's going on in Sanjay's head?

For all I know, he read the letter my father wrote to me and now he finally understands why I am doing all of this. Maybe he's taking a punt. Maybe he thinks that at the very least, I will get material for a book and claim my £5 million. He certainly doesn't mention it. He certainly doesn't demand a piece of that pie. Or maybe he just fancies Yasmin. Thinks getting involved will help him get her. All I care is that he finally blurts out the five words I've spent the last two years of my life waiting to hear.

"I know who he is," he says—still without turning to face us. I don't say anything. Standing with him watching the kite fliers seems like the only sensible thing to do for the time being. The pastel-colored kites bob against a Delhi skyline turning pink on pollution and dusk. They go up and down and occasionally spin out of control as the string pullers dare the wind. Sometimes they crash and burn. That's the risk you run when you go out in search of cheap thrills, I suppose.

PART TWO

ELEVATE YOUR MIND

It's early. I am awake. I am staying in the Jesuit hostel near the red-light district of Mumbai. My room is opposite the bathroom and I can hear men coughing up phlegm and going through their morning ablutions. They always wake me up, five-thirty, six in the morning. I don't mind. Life doesn't get more beautiful than this.

This is the moment when life stops. No, it's even better than that. This is the moment before life has even begun. Dawn in the city. Before the horns and the exhaust, before the heat and the sticky sweat, before the hellos and the grimy smiles, before the hunger and the money, before the stench of daily survival really sets in.

I lie, propped up slightly on a solid sponge pillow, and look out my window onto the small garden outside. There isn't much, just a couple of palm trees and some bougainvillea, but it's enough to give me a sense of nature in this running sewer of a city. Sixteen hundred kilometers south of Delhi, the north-moving monsoon has passed, so the air is as cool and fresh as the dew on the lawn. Golden sunlight drips off fronds like brilliant jewelry. A blackbird caws.

Many are meditating now. Clearing their minds, emptying their loads, breathing for the sake of breathing.

I close my eyes. My view, the last freeze-frame of the outside world burned on the back of my eyelids, starts to slowly fall away, piece by piece, as if the world itself is disintegrating. First the desk in my room, and then the window frame; the blackbird flies away and the palm tree suddenly disappears. Piece by piece, the world is removed for me to see what stands behind. The void—a benevolent blue blackness filling the cardboard-cutout spaces, like the Truth revealed.

"AAAARRRRRGGGGHHHHH!   CHARTARRRRRRRR! WHOCH! WHOCH! PHLOOP!"

Phlegm hits the basin with a dull thud and the fat fucking Indian (I can only imagine) that's doing the purging sighs with satisfied relief. The illusion is suddenly over (or suddenly restarts, depending on which way you want to look at it) and I am back in the real world. And that's that. My daily dose of enlightenment is over.

So I decide to think about Yasmin instead. Or at least I try to. Picturing her before me is almost as hard as meditating. All I see are other people's faces disrupting the reception. I try focusing on select parts of her face and body, features that I'm sure of, starting points from which to get my bearings.

But even that doesn't help. I see a sticking-out belly button, a red-tipped ear, a small tongue licking a pair of lips, but none of the pieces seem to want to glue together into a single image. It is very frustrating. I simply cannot see her in my mind's eye. I curse myself for never taking any pictures. I should have known this would be a problem. I've always suffered from mental block when it comes to remembering new loves.

So, even though I've done it a hundred times already, I decide to go over the plan in my mind one more time. It's not as if I have anything better to do.

AND IN THE RED CORNER

Here's the spread. We know that Baba is dealing in heroin and diamonds. At least I say we do. Really, I only have my suspicions, pieces I've put together in a coherent fashion because they seem to fit. I don't have any real, hard evidence to illustrate his methods, but Yasmin and Sanjay have never pressed me for proof. I think I've swept them up in my own conviction. At least one of us has to pretend they know what they are doing.

We all agree that we're not interested in stealing heroin from Baba. For some reason, getting involved in heroin seems heavy. Maybe it's all those eighties ads—the ones that made out that the mere sight of smack was enough to get hooked and lead to a life of loserdom. I don't know. Heroin just seems scary. And, for my part, there's still a sense that if this plan doesn't work out, I might just end up having to write a book about it after all. In which case, I'll need to be a hero, not a heroin dealer. Maybe I just haven't managed to shed my hero complex yet. Or maybe I'm just hedging, making sure that whichever way this plan turns there's a bag of cash waiting for me at the end of the line. For some reason the idea of entirely throwing away the prospect of becoming a novelist just doesn't seem . . . *prudent*. Not yet. Either way, it doesn't really matter. We all agree that none of us would know what to do with a bagful of smack once we'd nicked it anyway.

So that's that. Heroin is out of the picture. The alternative we've come up with instead is to steal the money and gems Baba uses to finance his operation. And we plan to do it in just two suitcase switches. Simple. Clean. Nice.

The key to the scam is trust. For some reason, I conclude that Baba has been dealing with his Pakistani counterparts for so long now that there'll be a trust between them. That means if, and it is an enormous if, we get the opportunity to swap the money he uses to buy the smack for fake bills, the Pakistanis won't check.

And that's crucial. We figure that Baba isn't dealing in enough heroin on a single trip for us to only swap the money. I estimate (though don't ask me how I came up with these figures) that Baba is buying a quarter, half at the most—half a million quid's worth of gear each time he travels to Jaisalmer. And even that's pushing it. We all agree that half a million pounds isn't enough to make a risky scheme like this worthwhile. The scam has to make enough to set us all up for life—as well as the money we need to get James out of prison.

So we have to set it up so that Baba comes out of his next deal alive. Just enough time for us to do the second suitcase switch for the diamonds. This is where we figure the real money is to be made. We all reckon that Baba is getting diamonds from Pakistan at an enormous discount. The markup on diamonds in the black market could be two, three times at least. We don't know it, but that doesn't seem unrealistic.

And there's a very good chance that the profit from each of Baba's trips far exceeds a million quid. If Baba buys a quarter of a million in heroin and sells it at six, seven times the price, he'll be buying at least one to two million in diamonds to launder the profits. Even at a conservative estimate, one and a half million in diamonds at the border will fetch, easy, three million on the black market.

And there's the math. A quarter of a million in cash, three million minimum in diamonds and other stones. That means, not including James's bailout fund, we all get a million each. More than enough, we agree, to live on for the rest of our lives without lifting a finger ever again.

We've divided the tasks between us. Yasmin says she thinks she knows a place in Amsterdam that can arrange fake bills and we agree that while she's back home, she might as well enroll in a gemstone course. If we're going to swap the diamonds for fakes, we'd better make sure that at least one of us knows the difference between a real diamond and a fake one, and, even better, the difference between a good fake and a bad fake.

Because, even more crucial than Baba coming out of his border deal alive is us getting out of India alive before he smells a rat. We're aware that we may need to hang around in India for a while even after we've done the scam. We can't just jump on a plane and run. After all, it will take at least a couple of weeks to negotiate James's exit from prison. So it has to be smooth. We have to make sure the alarm bells don't ring too soon. And, to avoid that, we've got to make sure that the stones we exchange are convincing enough for him not to notice anything fishy until it's too late. Sanjay believes the Mafia, or the Pakistanis, will knock Baba off fairly quickly once they discover the true quality of their respective goods.

Which suits all of us down to the ground. With Baba out of the picture once the scam is complete, there'll be nothing linking us to the robbery. The theory is that the bad guys will simply blame Baba. And we'll be off, scot-free. At least, that's the theory. For my part, I kind of like the idea of the Robin Hood twist to the plot. Ripping off the bad guys in a web of their own intrigue appeals to me. I like the idea of them bumping off their own guy. Turning the bad guy into the victim. I don't know how I'll feel about the reality of it, should it occur, but hell, Baba is meant to be the bad guy. Isn't he meant to have it coming to him? That's how it works in the bestsellers, I tell myself. At the very least, his death will sit well with that.

Sanjay's primary responsibility is introducing us to Baba. He still hasn't revealed who he is yet—says he needs time to make triple sure he's got the right guy—but this seems responsibility enough for Sanj to earn his share. Without him, we've got nothing. Yasmin and I know it. And from everything that Sanjay has told us, there's enough history between Baba and his family to make his introduction a strong one.

It's all got something to do with Sanjay's mum, who has some-how developed extensive links with the Mumbai Mafia. She seems to know all the right people. It could be by virtue of her second marriage to a guy that Sanjay hates so vehemently he can barely manage to repeat his name, which happens to be Sunil Dutt, just like the famous film director turned politician—if you can believe that.

In any case, Baba and Sanjay go back a few years. I think they may have even gone to the same kindergarten, though they weren't in the same year. He's not been entirely clear about the association. It doesn't really matter to Yasmin or me. As long as he can deliver an introduction. That means he gets his mil.

Like I say, the key to this scam is trust. If we don't get near Baba, we don't get near the suitcases. Earning his trust is every-thing. Without it, there's no scam, no money, no prison break, no escaping the system, no nothing. And, for some reason, that's the task that's been assigned to me. I am the one who has to earn

Baba's trust. And that's why I'm here, biding my time and lying low in a Jesuit hostel in the red-light district of Mumbai.

I am the one who has to get near enough to do the suitcase switch. Sanjay insists he doesn't know Baba well enough to pull it off. He could just be scared. He could figure that there's only so far he's prepared to stick his neck out for this madcap caper. And frankly, I can't blame him. Because I'm scared and I don't even know the guy. Still, someone has to do it, and seeing as this whole thing got started by me in the first place, it only seems fair that I be the one to take on the task, to take on Baba.

And that's partly why I've been trying to meditate. Clearing my mind with clean breaths before the ring of the bell sounds the next round. It's also why I'm going over the plan one more time. I'm gathering my thoughts, focusing my inner abilities, trying to stay calm. Getting ready to take on the bad guy. So, this is it. I look at myself in the mirror. I'm on my own now. Yasmin left for Amsterdam a week ago. Sanjay says once he's made his introductions, he'll have to stay in the background. Baba is too close to home for him to get deeply involved.

I've only got me to depend on. This is where I face my fears and fight my good fight. This is the part where it all kicks off. Do I have it in me? This is no time for self-doubt, I tell myself. This is where I test my mettle. I'm getting ready to go into a dangerous situation. Wrong. I'm ready already. I curl my mouth and pump out five *oo-oo-oos,* shadowboxing with my own reflection. I look good. Blue eyes, blond hair, a vague show of pectorals against my skinny frame. I'm not a bad-looking guy. Fuck that. I'm goddamn beautiful. Say it out loud. Come on, Josh—punch, punch, one, two, dummy, nip, tuck—say it out loud, you're Josh and you're proud.

"You are the man," I say to myself too quietly, not too convincingly. Come on, Josh, better than that. You are the mother-fucking man. Let's hear it, louder. "You are the finest looking mudderfucker," I try, still too gently. Come on, buddy, if you're going to take on Baba you have to believe. "COME ON, BABA! LETTTTT'S GETTTTT REAAAADYYY TO RUUUUMBLE!" I yell.

There's a bang on my door.

"Will you please be keeping it down in there! There are guests sleeping."

"Er, yeah, sure. Sorry."

"Thank you."

I look back at myself, embarrassed cheeks flushing red. "Yeah, come on, Baba. I'm ready to rumble . . . I think."

BABA

Baba's real name is Faizad Gerstad. He is a Parsi, which means he is rich. Most Parsis in Mumbai are rich. They first made their money because the colonial British favored them for their fair Persian skins. Then when the British left the subcontinent they bought up Bombay properties on the cheap. They're worth millions today.

I am in one of these properties with Sanjay. It is a high-rise built on Malabar Hill, overlooking the ocean. His mother's flat is on the fourteenth floor. There are only three bedrooms, but compared to my humble dwellings at the Shiv Niketan, it feels like a palace. Yellow light from a low-hanging sun fills each room, while a latticed terrace spreads a gentle shadow over the wooden floor in the sitting room. Red and orange folk paintings from Rajasthan cover the walls and a patchwork hanging spills over the end of the long white sofa we are sitting on.

In front of us, a low, ornately carved walnut coffee table is covered with books about healing and herbal recipes for making Ayurvedic medicine. It's Sanjay's mum's latest spiritual craze, apparently. After venturing into every other religion from Scientology to voodoo, she's going back to her roots now, focusing on the Indian mystics in her search for the Truth.

We are bent over the table drinking milky cardamom-flavored

tea. Sanjay is showing me a fashion-magazine interview Faizad once agreed to do to promote a film he was making for Channel 4. It is about four years old. He is posing naked, but you can't see his genitals. Most of the shots are in black-and-white and are of him squatting and bending his head down so that a set of ratty-looking dreadlocks covers the naughty bits.

He is young, about our age—late twenties—in the photos, with a thin long nose and slightly pitted skin. A thick pair of pointed sideburns dart down from his hairline and across his cheeks. For some reason they make him look a little like the devil. In one photo he is screaming at the camera, his face distorted in pain, his mouth and long tongue stretching to expose his tonsils.

"So he's not an actor, then?"

"No, he produces and directs," Sanjay explains. "At least he used to."

"Does he have anything to do with Bollywood?"

"Very little. Since he started working for Dowdy Ibrahim he's hardly done any filmmaking."

"Who's Dowdy Ibrahim?"

"Oh, come on, Josh," Sanjay says, shaking his head and lifting his eyes to the skies. "Fine journalist you'll make. Dowdy Ibrahim is probably the biggest don in Mumbai. He runs everything. The film industry, the drug industry, the terrorists, everyone. Even the fucking police answer to Dowdy at the end of the day. This is his town and, some people say, it's his state too."

"Yeah, okay, okay. Dowdy Ibrahim. Sure. I've heard of him," I say, rushing to cover my ignorance. "He's the guy that organized all those bomb blasts, the ones that led up to the Bombay riots," I venture.

"Yup. That's him. He's fucking hard-core. You don't ever, ever want to be caught crossing his path. He'll chew you up and spit you out. It's as simple as that."

"So how do you know this guy Faizad Gerstad?" I say, changing the subject slightly. I really don't want to be reminded—for the ninth time—just how incredibly hard the Indian Mafia really is.

"I told you, we went to school together once. A long time ago."

"And he'll remember you, will he?"

"I see him around still. We kind of mix in the same social circles."

"What, you make a habit of hanging out with Mafia couriers, do you?"

"No, but Mumbai isn't exactly a big town. If you've got money, there's only so many places to go and hang out. So, like I say, we see each other around."

"How can you be sure he's Baba?"

"Because he's dodgy as fuck."

"That's not exactly solid proof. Are you absolutely certain?"

"Yes."

"How?"

"Trust me. Faizad is Baba."

"I want to know how you know."

"I can't tell you that."

Just then a servant comes in through the door. He looks like half the man he should be, skinny, shriveled, and bent double. He's dressed in a white button-down coat that's too big for him. It looks like he's the one that got shrunk in the wash.

Sanjay snaps at him in Hindi when he tries to clear the empty teacups. The old man swivels on his heels and exits as meekly as he came. Poor sod, I think to myself when I see that. Eighty going on eight hundred and still running around after Sanjay.

"Why not?" I say, as if the conversation had never been interrupted.

"Because I can't. You'll just have to trust me."

I think about that one for a moment. There's no real reason why I shouldn't trust Sanjay on this. Maybe he's being secretive because of his own family connection with the Mob. Seems likely. I decide not to press him on it.

"As long as you can get me an introduction."

"I'll try. I know where he hangs out. I'll take you there tonight."

"Good."

THE CELLAR

Of all the nightclubs I've ever been to in my life, the Cellar ranks among the worst. By the time Sanjay and I arrive at around eleven, the place is packed. It takes us fifteen minutes to get through the five meters that separate the entrance from the bar, and the drinks cost more than two unpleasant weeks at the Shiv Niketan.

The music rattling the speakers, which sound like they have been made out of two toilet-paper rolls and a cardboard box, is a bizarre mixture of heavy metal, house, soft rock, hip-hop, and pop. "Walk Like an Egyptian" by the Bangles is presently being followed with "Back in Black" by AC/DC. For a while, a group of varsity-looking types on the small dance floor at the back nod their heads back and forth like chickens, which I presume to be "walking like an Egyptian," but then they ease more comfortably into a straightforward head bang as AC/DC progresses.

The only other distinguishable feature is the graffiti on the walls. The whole club is covered in offensive humor written with different-colored marker pens. After finding a small corner with limited jostling, Sanjay explains to me above the music how, on the club's opening night, kids were invited to write whatever they liked on the walls. Most of the limericks and gags are sexist, but without fail they are all bad. The only half-decent one I notice is: "Experience is the name people give to their mistakes."

But in spite of its village disco feel, the Cellar still manages to make me feel totally uncool. Sanjay warned me earlier that I should make an effort, but I only have my "traveling clothes" with me, which basically consist of all the things from my home wardrobe I've been prepared to lose or ruin. And after nearly six months here, and several beatings from the *dhobis,* they look decidedly worse for wear. Half the buttons on my "best" shirt are smashed and the cuffs are disintegrating. I've also lost so much weight that my jeans, the only comfortable semblance of the West I've managed to preserve, are practically falling off me. I've had to do my belt up so tight there's now an embarrassing crease in my ass where all the extra material seems to be collecting and folding in on itself. I look like an obese person that's had the fat artificially removed and my jeans are like the loose skin left over, stretch marks and all.

Sanjay by contrast looks gorgeous. He's wearing a black cotton shirt that hangs like silk, black jeans, and black motorbike boots with a silver buckle around the ankle. They all seem to be of a perfect cut, accentuating his slim build in all the right places, so that he looks like he has muscles where he really doesn't and curving his hips and shoulders in just the right way that even I want to slide my arms around him.

I wonder why 501s seem to fit him just like the guy in the ad, while mine, even on a good day, are too tight around the ankle (exaggerating my large feet), too tight around the thighs (revealing my skinny legs), and too loose in the groin (doing nothing for my nothing-butt).

Sanjay also has the sense to add the necessary personal touch too, to get away from the cardboard-cutout image and display himself as individually beautiful. Bit like a supermodel with a mole on her face, I guess. Sanjay's touch tonight is to allow a small show of dark hair at the top of his shirt while also wearing a black leather necklace threaded through small yellow, red, and blue Fimo beads. The necklace sits tight around his neck like a choker. This combination of hair and unassuming jewelry works perfectly. He looks both manly and effeminately sexy at the same time, hunky and yet infinitely approachable.

And approached he is.

Girls stream to meet Sanjay, some of whom he already knows, some who literally hang around shamelessly batting their eyes at him until he finally gets too embarrassed to not do anything about it. He's kind enough to introduce me to most of them, but the imbalance is just too much for me to bear after a while. I'm all too aware that we must look like the male equivalent of the fat girl with the bad teeth and the beautiful friend. People must think he hangs out with me because he's too beautiful to have any real character or real friends, and I hang out with him because I'm sex-starved and hope to pick up the scraps that he leaves behind on the flirt circuit.

Trouble is, I don't manage to pick up any leftovers, and eventually Sanjay starts talking to a real stunner, sweeping his hand through Brylcreemed hair every five seconds and laughing cheesily, while I'm left hovering behind him chain-smoking cigarettes.

Eight drinks later and the nightmare continues. Faizad is still nowhere to be seen. It's just gone 1:30 A.M. The club is only slightly less crowded, but things have deteriorated considerably. Almost all the lights have been turned off and there are couples in every corner making out like teenagers. "Voodoo Ray" by A Guy Called Gerald is playing. Sanjay and his girl are standing so close I could be accused of voyeurism if I hung around much longer, so I rashly decide that house music is my music and that I'm drunk, and incognito enough, to start dancing on my own.

It turns out to be a bad move. It takes me a few minutes of strutting my funky stuff (which takes no small amount of concentration on my part) before I realize that I am surrounded by gyrating silhouettes. I catch flashes of hands and thighlike flesh, and on more than one occasion, I definitely see out-and-out hip pumping. I can't believe that people are shagging around me. I beat a hasty retreat, deciding that I'll just have to barge my way back into conversation with Sanjay if I want something to do. I know it's rude and it will probably be embarrassing, but, frankly, anything's better than looking like the bored, lonely loser on the fuck floor.

"Are those people doing what I think they're doing?" I shout at Sanjay, lunging toward his ear, pointing at the crowd and ignoring the dark beauty busy being beautiful next to him.

He looks over my shoulder briefly before saying simply, "Yes."

"That's disgusting," I say, with drunken morality.

"Why? What's wrong with screwing?"

"Yes, but on the dance floor," I slur. "It's just not right."

"Most people in Mumbai live with their parents because it's too expensive for them to get places of their own," he explains, a little impatiently and far too soberly. I wonder how Sanjay can be so *compos mentis*. He can't have drunk as much as me. Too busy chatting up the hot tart that's still hovering around, no doubt. Can't she tell when she's not wanted? "So if a girl has a boyfriend there's nowhere for them to shag. Except here."

"Shouldn't they be a bit more subtle about it?"

"What do you mean? There's no better place. It's dark, and even better, everyone is too busy doing their own thing to worry about what everyone else is up to. It's no different from a lovers' lane."

"What about virgin brides and all that stuff?" I say, slinging one arm around his shoulder and being sure to look accusingly at the babe.

"A lot of women in the city don't get married until well into their twenties these days. No one can expect to remain a virgin for that long," Sanjay says, being sure to smile at the chick.

Much to my annoyance, she smiles back at him and says, "That's right. So when are you going to ask *me* to dance, Sanjay?"

"Right now," he says, leaning over and kissing her while my arm remains somehow stuck to his neck. I watch her put her tongue in his mouth and drag him blindly backward out of my grip and into the copulating crowd.

"That's disgusting," I shout drunkenly at them as they disappear, then turn around to hide my embarrassment at being so easily upped by the sexpot.

For a while I scan the crowd and watch all the faces melt into one another before thinking to myself how drunk I am. I decide that I should probably go home because Faizad's never going to show and I even take a step toward the exit when, suddenly, out of the blue and from nowhere, I spot him.

He's smaller than I had imagined him to be from my days in Delhi, where he took on a larger-than-life quality in my mind's eye. At least he looks small as he hugs the enormous round bouncer at the door. I notice that he has cut his dreads off. His hair is short now and sleeked back. The gel looks like it's dripping onto the designer suit he is wearing. But he still has the devilish sideburns. Three girls, one of whom is dressed in a miniskirt shockingly short for India, trail prettily in his wake. I watch the bouncer pick a few people up by the scruff of their necks and place them firmly to one side, clearing a path to the bar. Faizad is clearly in his element. He shakes hands in a variety of ways with the barman, who then proceeds to throw his hand in the air when Faizad tries to pass him a wad of money. Faizad puts a cigarette in his mouth and lets it hang coolly off the edge of his lips. The bouncer lights it for him.

"A real Mumbai homeboy," I mutter. I look around to see if I can spot Sanjay, but he's long gone. All I can see are hunched shoulders and working limbs and rolling heads of dark hair. Sanjay could be any one of them.

I don't know whether it's just the alcohol emboldening me, but I decide I'd rather face Faizad on my own than work my way back through the fuck floor, tapping men on the shoulder in their moment of triumph until I find Sanjay, who'll no doubt be otherwise distracted himself. I just can't face the further humiliation.

"How hard can it be to say hello?" I say out loud and to myself. Two teenage girls standing nearby give me a weird look. Then before I know what I am really doing, I find myself walking toward Baba, the Baba I've been looking for all this time.

As I reach him, a small area clears for him and his entourage near the bar, so in an attempt to be subtle, I veer toward the back of them as if I am making my way toward the exit. I see him glance at me momentarily.

"I preferred you with dreads," I say quickly as our eyes meet, but by the time I've finished the sentence he isn't looking at me anymore and the words either dissolve into the terrible music or are ignored. My alcohol mask slips briefly then and I suddenly don't feel so brave. I wish Sanjay were with me. But he isn't. I take a deep breath and work my way around the entourage until I am close enough to put my mouth inches away from his ear. "I said," with slightly irritated emphasis, "I preferred you with dreads."

He turns around to look at me. I see the round bouncer moving toward me out of the corner of my eye. "Do I know you?" he asks, his thin lips tightening at the corners.

"Not yet," I reply. His eyes are black and lifeless. They narrow on me before exchanging glances with the bouncer, who is now standing behind me. "I'm a journalist from London," I start nonchalantly but trying not to slur, "and I'd like to do an article on you as part of a series my paper is doing on Indian filmmakers. Are you interested?"

The right side of his lip twitches into a sneer. There is a brief pause before he nods at the bouncer. The next thing I know, I am being hauled through the crowd by a thick hand around my upper arm.

I don't have time to protest. I vaguely notice heads turning in my direction and I scan the crowd for Sanjay, but, of course, he is nowhere to be seen. My bladder twitches threateningly. Next thing I know, we are outside in the warm night. The bouncer drags me into a dark parking lot at the back of the nightclub and throws me up against the wall and presses his elbow into my neck. He leans against my jugular vein, forcing tears into my eyes. It's hard to breathe. I start to feel dizzy. Then Faizad's face swims into my view, his features blurred. Suddenly I am back in my dream, back with Baba in the swimming pool.

"Why don't you do some research next time you decide to go writing articles?" I can smell the nicotine in his breath. "Fucking journalists," he spits. The bouncer presses harder against my neck. I am close to fainting.

"I can't . . ." I try.

"You should know that I don't make films anymore."

". . . breathe. I can't . . ."

He punches me in the stomach, catching me in the solar plexus as the bouncer holds me firm against the wall. What little air there is in my lungs flies out with a gurgling sound. Then, as I draw for breath, I double-take when nothing happens. It feels like someone has just thrown me in an ice-cold pond—my lungs are heaving in short, involuntary snatches. I lurch forward as the bouncer loosens his grip and I hold my diaphragm. I can feel it spasm but there's no air being drawn into my lungs. The bouncer lets go of me completely. I try to take a few paces forward, gulping at the air like a goldfish. There is no room in my mind for calm. My lungs aren't working, and for one horrible moment, I believe that I am going to die. I collapse on the ground, wheezing and tucking my knees into my chest like an embryo. I am staring into the tarmac when everything goes quiet.

The next thing I know, the bouncer is pulling me off the ground and stretching my arms above my head. "Standup, mun, standup, mun," he is saying. My testicles are burning with pain. Every part of my body is telling me to crouch down into a ball.

I can vaguely hear Sanjay in the background. "Oh, my ber-luddy God, Faizad. What have you done, yaar?"

"He's just winded." I can hear the bouncer breathing heavily. "He'll be ohh-kay."

"I didn't know he was a friend of yours," Faizad is saying. "You should tell him to be more careful about what he says to strangers in the future."

"Oh yes, of course, Faizad. I'll tell him, don't you worry."

"Good. Then you can take over from here, can't you? Come on, Khan, we're going back inside."

Somehow I manage to stay on my feet when the bouncer lets go of me. Sanjay runs to grab me by the waist and steadies me before I collapse again. There is some air in my lungs now and I manage to use what little there is to say, "You still haven't answered my question."

Faizad swings around on his heels. I can hear Sanjay urging me to shut up and then pleading with Faizad to ignore me. I manage to push Sanjay off and stand as straight as possible, so that I am towering above Faizad by the time he gets near. He looks nasty. He might be small but I reckon he could take me, easy. He's like the small guy with the chip on his shoulder. I try not to let my fear show. He's the type that can smell fear.

"Jesus Christ, Josh, shut up . . . Pulease, Faizad," Sanjay is volleying.

"No, you shut the fuck up, Sanjay," I snap. "Just one drink, Faizad, thassall. I'll buy." Faizad is looking at me as Khan steps in front of him to take over. "I just wanna talk. Off the record."

Faizad holds Khan's arm and squints at me. He pauses before saying, "What about?"

"Anything you like. You, the film industry, whatever."

He pauses again. "If I see my name in any newspaper, I'll come looking for you."

"Like I said, off the record, Faizad. Just a chat."

After what seems like a very long time, he finally says, "Fine. The Taj, tomorrow night, nine o'clock," before turning to leave. As soon as they have gone I stoop down and try to breathe as deeply as possible.

"Jesus, Josh, have you completely lost your mind?" Sanjay says after I've caught my breath.

"No, Sanjay. I'm just taking a few risks," I say, smiling at him and throwing my arm around his neck for support. "After all, you've got to have balls to make money."

"You're bloody lucky you've got any balls at all," he says, half laughing.

I wince when I try to laugh with him. "Just put me in a taxi home, will you?"

There are three yellow-topped Premiers waiting outside the club. Before I climb into one, I turn to face him, propping myself up on an open door. "Thanks, Sanjay. If it hadn't been for you— well, I'd be fucked now, I think."

He smiles at me, nodding slightly. "Sure. And if wasn't for you I'd be *getting* fucked now, I think."

"Yeah, sorry about that. How did you know to come looking for me?"

"Call it my sixth sense."

"Apologize to the honey for me."

"I will, if I can find her. Now go home and remember not to be obnoxious to every criminal we meet from now on, all right?"

"It's a promise," I say before falling into the seat.

"Byculla, boss," Sanjay tells the taxi driver as he leans through the front window. The taxi driver slams the gears into first and careens out into the street without looking.

BRASS BARS, FAST CARS

The Shiv Niketan is locked when I get back. I groan when I see the accordion-style brass bars and the chunky brass lock. This is the last thing I need. I rattle on the gate and press my mouth against it so that my lips are poking through one of the diamond-shape gaps.

"Hullohh! Is anybody there?" I shout. My voice echoes in the hall and bounces back into the street. I become painfully aware of the sound. Out of the corner of my eye I spy what I had thought to be a pile of sacks stirring in the gutter. "Hullohh," I half call again. I notice a prostitute at the end of the block smoking a cigarette. For some reason, her presence reassures me slightly. Maybe it's because she's a woman. I rattle the gates again. Still no answer. I see that there is a man talking to the prostitute now. I wonder whether it is her pimp or a client. I look to the left. The six-lane highway stretches darkly into the distance. There isn't a car to be seen but exhaust still seems to fill the air. The night is brown.

I sit on the steps and weigh my options. I can't go to Sanjay's house without waking his mum. I don't want to go to one of the hotels in Colaba. After all, the main reason I am staying at the Shiv Niketan is to avoid other travelers.

And that's when I notice that I am being watched. For a while I don't look up. I just sit there, head bowed, but I can see him looking at me from across the street. I flick my eyes to the right. The prostitute isn't there anymore. My heartbeat starts to pulse in my teeth. Even the sound of my breathing seems too loud.

I try to get up and turn around to rattle the gate without making eye contact. If I don't look at him, maybe he'll disappear, I reason irrationally with myself. I close my eyes and press my head against the gate, whispering a small prayer. "Please answer the door. Someone please wake up." I shake the bars and take a breath before calling out boldly, "Hello. Wake up, it's me, the Englishman. Open up!"

I wince again when I hear my voice bouncing around the street. I notice that my hands are shaking. I can feel his eyes boring into the back of my head. I turn around with the same stupid compulsion of someone tiptoeing down the cellar stairs in a horror movie. It's too dark to see if it's the same person who was following me in Delhi.

Before I know what I am doing, I hear myself shouting at him across the street, "What do you want? Why are you following me?" Even the echo sounds shaky. He doesn't answer.

Suddenly the hum of a car coming toward us fills the horizon. Its lights betray the night as it tilts over the crest of the overpass. We are both looking at it as it picks up speed on the downhill; then, when its headlights bounce back up on the horizontal flat, I see his face. He's still too far away to know if it's the same guy who followed me in Delhi, but he is white, which makes me assume that he must be. He looks tall but thickset, as if he lifted weights once. He has brown hair, parted, and it looks like he is smiling.

The car passes before I can make out any more. I briefly entertain the idea of walking across the road to face him, but then I hear the brass bars rattle behind me. I swing around to see a young boy, his eyes still closed with sleep as he fumbles with the lock.

"Thank you, God," I say. He slides the gate open just enough for me to squeeze through. I turn around to check the street as the boy slams the bars shut. A pink neon light on the concrete island separating the two sides of the road flickers briefly. But apart from that, there is nothing else to see.

THE AKANKSHA FOUNDATION

Sanjay doesn't believe me when I tell him that I am being watched. We are lying on the grass by the pool at Breach Candy Club— another relic of colonial history that only recently opened to allow Indians in. I can still see the red warning under the whitewash on the wall behind us: NO INDIANS ALLOWED. It amazes me to think that the policy lasted so long after the end of the empire. Even now, the Indians who seek solitude within its peaceful confines are as white as any Westerner. Fat balding men with upper-class English accents shout at children eating ice cream while women in jeans sunbathe.

"Why would somebody be following you?"

"I don't know. I think it might have something to do with this secret travelers' network. Maybe they're on to me after I started snooping around in Delhi."

"Do you have any idea how paranoid you sound?"

I don't say anything. I have to admit it does feel like a dream now. For all I know it could be my imagination playing tricks on me again—throwing the mysterious white man into the mix for the benefit of the narrative. I try to remember how much of my memory is true. Was it the alcohol? Was it a dream? Was it fear illuminating things that weren't there? Maybe I spotted a figure across the street and turned him into a spy, a nightmare in the night. After all, why would someone be following me? Why would anyone hang around on a highway waiting for me to show up only to disappear back into the night once I arrived? To scare me? To make sure I got home safely? It all seems too unlikely. I can't trust myself anymore. My head hurts from the hangover and the heat isn't making it any better. I think about taking a swim, but then I notice a pretty, overweight girl watching us from the other side of the pool. Even from this distance I can see her breasts fighting their way out of her white T-shirt and her ample hips straining the buttons on a black pair of Levi's 501s.

"Is that her?"

Sanjay pulls himself off his elbows and looks across briefly before jumping to his feet quickly and brushing mown grass off the backs of his legs. "Yup." He walks briskly for a couple of steps before turning around and urging, "Come on, then." By the time I catch up, I can hear him cooing. "Rumanaaaah, my darling. So serwheat of you to come, yaar. So berluddy good to see you again. Oh my God! How long? How long has it been?" I can't blame Sanjay for putting on a Mumbai accent. After all, he is meant to be from here.

I can see her smiling sweetly up at him as he hugs her and tells her how well she looks. Sanjay lets me hover behind him uncomfortably for a few seconds before introducing me. "Now, Rumana, I want you to meet a veddy, veddy good friend of mine. He is very intarrested in the Akanksha Foundeshan and he would love to meet you. Rumana, this is my old friend, Joshooarr."

"Hi, Rumana, I've heard a lot about you," I say, extending my hand and meeting her gaze. She has kind, doey eyes. A thin film of dark hair covers her cheeks, giving her face a soft-focus look.

"Hello, Joshooarr."

"Please, call me Josh."

She smiles a big white smile that separates slightly from her gums. In the three seconds that I have met her, Rumana seems to be sweetness itself. I am finding it hard to believe that she used to go out with Faizad. Sanjay offers to get ice cream as Rumana and I sit back down on the grass. A small boy in tiny blue Speedo swimming trunks runs past us, quickly followed by two small girls with braids.

"It won't be that way for long," I joke as we both laugh at them.

"Ohhh, I don't know about that. We Bombay girls like chasing the boys."

I feel like saying that she's got that right—I'm still a little hung up on Sanjay's success last night—but I resist. "Really? I wouldn't imagine that you'd have to do any chasing," I say instead, being smarmy, but Rumana doesn't giggle coyly or blush. She just looks at me with sad eyes, and for a moment, I think she is about to cry. "I'm sorry, that was meant to be a compliment," I say, genuinely concerned.

She smiles weakly at me. "I know, you are very kind, yaar. But, unfortunately, ever since I split up with my boyfriend, that's all I seem to be doing nowadays."

I can't help feeling pleased with myself. Sanjay said that it wouldn't take much to get Rumana talking about Faizad, but I am amazed at just how quickly she wants to.

"How long has it been?"

"Two yeas."

"That's a long time."

"I know. Pathetic, isn't it?" Her eyes are still glistening. I feel sorry for her and find myself feeling guilty that we are using her like this. But the wannabe journalist in me doesn't let it last long.

"What happened?"

"Ohhhhh," she sighs with the weight of the world, "it is a very, very long story. But if you really want to know . . ."

She is right. It does turn out to be a very long story. At least the way she tells it. But three ice creams and two hours later, I know all that I need to know for the purposes of my meeting with Faizad tonight. By the end, I don't even feel too bad about deceiving her. It's clear that she is still desperately in love with him, in spite of the way he treated her, and that talking about him somehow seems to make her pain more manageable. And despite my dwindling funds, I even give a small donation to the Akanksha Foundation, which buys me the privilege of sponsoring a Mumbai street kid for a year.

It doesn't take me long to figure out that Faizad is off his head on coke by the time he turns up at the Taj Mahal Hotel, forty-five minutes late. He is sniffing incessantly and his fish eyes have dilated into those of a shark's. He doesn't even acknowledge my presence when he sits down opposite me, orders a rum and Coke, squeezes the waitress's backside, gets slapped in the face, and calls her a fat bitch.

"Come on, let's go, whitey," are his only words to me. A stretch limousine with tinted windows is waiting for us outside, and as we climb into the backseat, we are swarmed by street kids. Faizad literally spits at them before several doormen rush to shoo them away. "Drive," he barks at the chauffeur before pulling a small panel from out of the door and tipping a pile of coke onto it.

"Where to, sir?"

"Just drive," he says, chopping up the coke with a credit card. The limousine is too long for the small entrance outside the hotel and it takes us several farcical minutes to negotiate our way out of the driveway. Faizad is cursing incessantly as the driver reverses and inches forward to the directions of fifteen shouting doormen. Amused street kids are sticking to the windows to watch the new zoo attraction. "Here," he says, handing me a rolled-up hundred-dollar bill. I look down and see that he has racked up six lines. I don't argue, but I gag when I come up and see a melted limb rapping on the window beside me.

"Not used to it, hey?" Faizad sneers when he sees me holding down the sick lurching at the back of my throat. For a minute, I don't say anything.

"Well, I'm not used to cut coke," I eventually manage to retort. I hate myself for being here in this limousine, doing this horrible, pointless drug.

"Fuck off! It's not cut," he snaps at me before adding, "Is it?"

The icy crystals numb my tongue and trickle bitterly into me. I listen to the leper outside whining, *"Baksheesh, baba. Ek rupiyah. Ek rupiyah."*

"How much did it cost?" I ask.

"About two hundred bucks," he says, bending down to do his second line. My mind races through the math. The beggar wants one rupee for food and I have just snorted a thousand rupees' worth of coke. I can't recall ever feeling more wretched. He comes up snorting, a couple of white flecks dripping onto the front of his shirt. "I'll kill that fucker Ajay if this is cut," he says in a voice that sounds like he has a cold. "Do you really think it's cut?" he asks, tapping me on the arm and presenting the bill again. I turn away from the pained expression pressing itself up against the window and look at Faizad.

"It's the shittiest coke I've ever had in my life," I say, stony-faced. Suddenly I realize that I am inches away from pummeling his face in with my fists, taking all his money, and giving it to the beggars. But something stops me. Perhaps I'm scared. "I'll pass, if you don't mind."

He sneers at me. "If you're gonna hang out with me tonight, you won't."

I close my eyes and try to block out the pathetic tapping sound on all the windows. Then, as I take the bill, I realize why I'm not beating Faizad up. It isn't fear. It's self-interest. Or, as my father would call it, single-mindedness of purpose.

I bend over and slam the drug into my system. I come up quickly then, the adrenaline pumping, the bowels rolling. I feel a rush of power. The coke only enhances my bitter mood but makes me feel superhuman strength within it. My ego inflates and floats, big and bold and overbearing. I lick my lips. They are sticky and dry. My mouth is numb but I can sense texture—sticky, like a white putty paste.

Then, as we eventually pull free from the driveway, everything slows down like a 45 rpm record quickly flicked onto the wrong speed. My inner mechanism lurches forward on the pace change. The ego zeppelin hisses and is collapsing with depression. I need another line.

MEHMET MAHMOOD

In the end it's worth it. Three parties, a bottle of rum, and a lot of cocaine later, Faizad confides in me. With the information I gleaned from Rumana earlier in the day, it isn't difficult to get him to confess. When you know which buttons to push, people will tell you their deepest, darkest secrets. He doesn't even seem to remember that I am meant to be a journalist. Or maybe he believes that his threat of the previous night will keep him in the clear.

We are sitting on Chowpatty Beach at the end of Marine Drive. Faizad says it's a good place to chill and have a smoke. I can't imagine why he thinks so. Street kids keep asking us if we want special massages and the lights that line the bay are bright enough for us to see the litter churning in the waves like soiled underwear in a washing machine. There's a smell of fish. Chowpatty Beach is a dump, filled with rusting cans and pedophiles. Still, I don't haul him up on it. He could be a pedophile himself for all I know.

"Do you mind if I ask you something, Faizad?" I don't wait for him to answer. "You see, there's something that's confusing me. I can't understand why it is that twenty-four hours ago you were beating me up and now, tonight, you've done nothing but take me to parties, fill me with drugs and booze, and introduce me to everyone as your friend. I mean, it's not as if you're short of friends, is it? From everything I've seen so far, you're a total player. Why the change of heart?"

"I like you, Josh," he says, a little falsely. "What's so wrong with that?"

"Nothing, I'm flattered. But you don't even know me."

"I don't know. I feel like we have something in common. I think that in some ways, you and I are very similar."

"Really? In what way?"

"I dunno, mate. Just the way you insisted we meet for a drink. You know. Pushy. Just kinda reminded me of myself once, not so long ago." It's hard to place his accent. It's partly American, or New York, but there are tinges of Australian mixed in—especially when he says "mate." "And besides, you shouldn't take the punch I gave you too seriously. I didn't mean to really hurt you. I just get a little emotional, well, you know, whenever people ask me about my films."

"Why? Because of what Mehmet Mahmood did to you?"

"Oh, so you know about that."

"Well, you wouldn't expect a journalist not to do his research, would you?" I say wryly. He responds with a small, smiling snort and an ironic nod of the head. "So what exactly did happen between you two? I mean, if you don't mind telling me. All I know is that he pulled the funding for your film and since then you haven't made another."

I watch the smile fade from his lips. "That cunt ruined my career." I don't say anything and for what seems like a very long time we just sit listening to the vague pumping sound of beggar boys giving men special massages at the other end of the beach. I am finding it hard to keep the image of what they are having to do to survive out of my mind. Eventually, he says, "You know, when I arrived in New York I had nothing. I literally just showed up. No visa, no income, no place to live—nothing. And I made it, man. I'm telling you, I worked my way up from nothing. Three years ago I was a Big Movie Director," he says with suitable pomp.

"So what went wrong?"

"I've been asking myself that same question for a long time. I guess it went wrong long before things actually changed for me. It's funny, but you can never truly understand the consequences of your actions. I mean, if I was to trace it all back I would say that my life was destined to fail before it had even begun."

"How so?"

Like Rumana, Faizad has difficulty editing his own stuff. He can't see the wood for the trees when it comes to telling his life story and he tends to overfill all the gaps with chronological detail. I find myself arranging his soliloquy down into the mock article I supposedly could be writing for the imaginary London paper I claim to be working for.

DOG EAT DOG

MUMBAI, India, 25 October, 1999—Five years ago Faizad Gerstad was a promising young talent, recently graduated from the New York Film School under the expert guidance of Chester Morris, the famous resident tutor who has nurtured new names like Scratch Lee and Nel Suriel.

With two small feature films under his belt and a few script ideas in his mind, Gerstad returned to his hometown of Bombay—now known as Mumbai—to embark on a film-directing career in the garish world of Bollywood. He flourished.

"I always knew Faizad would make it," remembers Chester

Morris in a telephone interview. "He was hungry. To do anything really worthwhile in this life, you've got to be hungry."

It wasn't long before word of Gerstad's films, which included mammoth box-office hits in India like *Killer Kali* and *The Love Bandit,* filtered through into the international film circuit. After just two years, Gerstad, now 32, got the call he was waiting for.

"I couldn't believe it when Mehmet Mahmood at Channel 4 called me and asked to buy the rights to my latest script," recalls a darkly handsome Gerstad. "It was a dream come true."

But while Gerstad didn't know it at the time, Mehmet's call turned out to be a poisoned chalice, and one that would ruin his career forever. Initially, the film was given an enormous budget and Gerstad went on a public-relations spree, hiring hundreds and boasting that he was India's big new director.

"The script was called *Bombay Boys,*" continues Gerstad. "I'll admit I was immature. I touted it as the next best thing since sliced bread and told all my friends and contacts in Bollywood that this was their chance to make it on the international film circuit."

In that sense, Gerstad sowed the seeds of his own undoing. Three days before shooting was due to commence, Gerstad received a telegram from London, ordering him to attend an urgent meeting at Channel 4's head office.

"It's funny, but when you get bad news, you can't admit to yourself that it's really happening," a morose Gerstad explains. "Deep down you know that you're in trouble, but you keep believing that everything is going to be okay."

That meeting turned out to be the worst hour of Gerstad's life.

"Mehmet insisted on a script change," he says. "And when I say script change I mean a complete rewrite. The only thing left on the script that was still mine was the title." Artistically vain and too immature to compromise, Gerstad then made what he calls the biggest mistake of his career. "I told Mehmet to f**k off and shove it up his a**. I then got on the next flight back to Mumbai and told everyone the film was off. I sacked three hundred people in one day, some of them the most important people in the industry. I remember, no one even believed me. All the big shots were calling Mehmet up. Most of them knew him personally. He told them that it was my decision to scrap the film. And that was that: my career—finished."

But friends and industry experts say that there was nothing Gerstad could have done. "Mehmet played Faizad like a fiddle," says Chester Morris. "He knew that Faizad would be too proud to accept such a dramatic rewrite. He just wanted to get his muggy little fingers all over it. I'm proud of what Faizad did. He stood up for his artistic integrity. Otherwise he would have just been another of Mehmet's lackeys, no better than a whipping boy."

"The only good thing to come out of the entire experience is that it taught me the most valuable lesson there is," Gerstad says. "You're nothing if you don't have power. Talent, creativity, ability . . . none of that counts for anything if somebody else is calling the shots. And the only way to be powerful is to be rich. You're nothing without money. If you're going to do what you really want to do in this life, then you'd better be rich. It's the only way. As far as I'm concerned it's a dog-eat-dog world out there, and I'm going to fatten up before I get made a fool of ever again. My motto? Screw the world before it screws you."

Mehmet Mahmood did not return repeated calls for comment by press time.

There it is again. That expression. Screw the world before it screws you. Just like the Brazilian said. And that's when it hits me.

Faizad is the bad guy I've been looking for.

His story, and the way he tells it, explains a lot. He had everything once. The sweet girlfriend, the successful career, friends. Yes, I realize it now, that's how Sanjay knows Faizad. They used to be friends, good friends.

But now?

I replay the evening over in my mind and remember second time around the way people approached him—wary, at arm's length. It's as if Faizad doesn't have any real friends. Not anymore. Not since he got burned, not since he went to the dark side. He's a good guy gone bad. A victim of his own ambition. He's lonely.

He's like my father in so many ways. The failed artist, ambitious and bitter and proud, he's sold out to make money, with the vague promise in the back of his mind to return one day to his dreams. Dad was lonely too. I remember that now. Maybe that's what you get for abandoning your dreams—loneliness.

Faizad is tailor-made for the role I've chosen for him. His story will be my story. His character will be my father's character. After all, Dad never qualified the role he might play in the Bestseller. He never specified whether he should be a good guy or a bad man.

He just said he wanted a significant part. And here it is. If I'm honest, maybe I always knew that Dad had to be the bad guy. After all, he did really piss me off with his suicide note. And, of course, me being who I am means that, really, I have to be the hero. It's so hard for me to think of myself any other way. There's a Bestseller in Faizad Gerstad, I know it. Whichever way I look at him, Faizad is worth several million bucks. Either I rip him off and make millions, or I use him as a character in a novel, posing as my father. It's sure to sell. Faizad is sure to sell. Faizad is my man.

I wonder if that's why I like him, because he's like Dad, because he's the bad guy I've been looking for. Because he's my golden ticket.

Hmm. That's a tricky one, but I don't think so, somehow.

As I sit here, looking at him, I realize, and I know this sounds weird, but . . . I genuinely like Faizad. Twenty-five hours after he's beating me up, and I really, genuinely, like him. Why? I don't know. Why does anyone like anyone? Maybe it's because I've re-alized that underneath his wide-boy persona, Faizad's actually funny and interesting, even when he's not trying to be.

I'm finding it surprisingly easy to let my hair down with him. I've spent most of the night getting lost in the moment. I laughed. I got drunk. I got high. After I'd spent all that time in the Green, constantly on my guard and distant while trying to infiltrate the secret travelers' network, it was refreshing to let go for once.

Because, if truth be told, I'm lonely myself. I've been lonely for a long time—ever since Dad died, really. Almost two years ago to the day. And, I don't know, as soon as Faizad started opening his doors, I just started to like him. In spite of myself and in spite of everything, I couldn't remain distant with him even if I tried.

He broke down my defenses. He made me give him some of me tonight, the real me. And it wasn't just an act.

I try telling myself that none of that matters. What matters is that I can see a way in, a way to earn his trust. Faizad's loneliness is my way in, I can see that now. I get the feeling Faizad shows up at parties with strangers a lot. I saw the way people looked at me tonight. Almost with pity, like I'm his next victim or something. Strangers are probably the only people prepared to be friends with him. They soon distance themselves, though, once they find out who he is, what he does.

I won't, though. I won't be like all his other one-night stands. I'll give Faizad my loyalty and he'll be surprised by it. I won't be a fly-by-night friend. I won't abandon him. After all, that's how I'm going to earn his trust.

I can feel the twinges of guilt lurking, I'll admit it. Like I say, I'm fond of Faizad, and it isn't because he fulfills all my ulterior motives in one fell swoop. There's more to him than that. He's a bad guy with a good side. This bad guy isn't all bad and the good guy in me isn't all good. This isn't Hollywood, this isn't fiction. This is reality.

But I tell myself, I'm not allowed to feel for him. Not genuinely. Only genuinely enough to make him trust me. Only genuinely enough to get him in a position where I can screw him. Be careful, I tell myself. Tread the line but take it easy. Don't get carried away.

"Why you are telling me all this?" I say.

"Why do you think?"

"Is it because you want me to write some nasty things about Mr. Mehmet?"

"Not just a pretty face, are you, Josh baby?" he says, smiling a little grimly at me.

I smile back at him. First light is casting a strange pall around us. Odd shapes are emerging out of the darkness to reveal themselves for what they are. I can finally see that the big dinosaur at the end of the beach is actually a merry-go-round and a slide in a fairground. It's still too early for things to have color. The world looks a lackluster blue and Faizad's face has gone a chalky gray. The pedophiles are slowly leaving, one by one but almost together.

"I think I'll make a move home now, Faizad, if you don't mind," I say, getting up on my feet and brushing cold sand from my backside. "It's been quite an evening. Thank you."

"Sure," he says, getting up next to me. "I enjoyed it. Let's get together again sometime." He hands me a visitor card. "Call me."

"You film types never change, do you?" I joke.

"No, guess not," he snorts. We start walking toward the road in search of a cab, the limo long gone. Then, looking at the ground, he says: "It's not just because I want you to write about Mehmet, Josh." He pauses. "I mean, I enjoyed myself tonight, I . . . like you. I feel as if we have . . . a connection."

That's the word I've been looking for. It's true. Faizad and I do connect.

"Thanks. I like you too."

"So call me. I mean it. We should hang out."

"Yeah, sure, I will." We look at each other. We've reached the end of the beach now and two cabs are conveniently driving toward us. Faizad hails them.

Before they reach us I find myself saying, "Incidentally"—like the detective asking "one last question" before letting the murderer go—"what do you do for a living these days if you're not making films anymore? I mean, how are you going to make all this money that you talk about?"

He doesn't reply.

The cabs pull up beside us. "I guess your not answering means that I have to go and do some more research?" I say, backing out of it, trying to lighten the moment before the good note that was ending the evening stops ringing completely.

He just looks at me, one hand on the door of his cab, and says chillingly, "Don't push it, Josh. If you don't want to get burned," before bending his head into the car, "then you shouldn't play with fire." His words keep replaying in my mind all the way back to the Shiv Niketan.

THE FEAR

I have a confession to make. Back in Delhi, just after Yasmin flew back to Amsterdam, I very nearly backed out of this whole Big Con thing. It was after I went to visit James in jail. Or rather I should say, tried to visit James in jail. I never actually made it past the prison walls. I chickened out at the last minute. When I got there—I don't know, I just got the Fear, really bad.

It came over me in an instant. Standing in front of those windowless walls crowned with barbed wire and parading prison wardens—maybe it was too much reality. Maybe it was simply some reality, any amount of reality, staring me in the face for the first time—at the very least for the first time in this escapade, perhaps even my entire life. I suddenly realized—in phantasmagoric detail—how bad things could get, well, if things got bad.

In the few moments that I stood there—outside those imposing circular walls caught between the desert nowhere and a suburban almost somewhere—I could picture myself in a tiny cell, no light, feces on the floor, getting fucked in the ass and beaten.

I could almost hear the going-mad screams of my fellow inmates. I could see the shaved heads and the baggy pajama outfits as we traipsed the corridors. I ate the terrible food and I caught all the appalling diseases. I suffered the inescapable tyrannies and the merciless tortures. I saw the rats and the insects and the bars.

I tasted my sweat—a rancid, cheesy sweat oozed by something fermenting in a hot container. And I saw an image of myself repeatedly flashing between all of these thoughts, like a slide shot against the wide screen of my mind, doubled over and grimacing as I got fucked in the ass, fucked in the ass, fucked in the ass.

The downside wasn't open to debate anymore. This wasn't like one of those chats with Sanjay—weighing up the pros and cons. These were walls, real stone walls that would trap and encase me and bury me alive along with all the other convict zombies. I was looking at a mass grave—a living, breathing, ulcerating mass grave. You can't argue with walls. You can't argue with prison. And you certainly can't argue with getting fucked in the ass.

It was then that I knew I could never do time. Not serious time. "Ten years, Mr. King, ten years," I could hear the judge with the pickled plum in his mouth saying over and over and over again in my mind. Now, *that* would kill me. Ten years would be my death sentence. Not sudden, but slow. That poor bastard James. He must be dying in there, I thought.

And that's when a guard came up from behind and told me that visitors should check in this way and that I should have my passport ready if I wanted to register. My about-face was sudden then, like a cheap revelation. He had handed me the perfect excuse to leave and, in the same breath, the perfect excuse to abandon everything. I knew that I couldn't go ahead with the plan anymore, and now I was effectively being told, in some uncertain terms, not to do so.

I mumbled my excuses and turned my back on the horror. I decided that I would return to Pahar Ganj and get myself a fake passport. I'd get Mani to help me. He'd help me get out of the country, wouldn't he? I'd write to Yasmin and tell her I was sorry. I wouldn't need to tell her why I was backing out. I'd start with something along the lines of: "On deeper reflection . . ." She'd understand. Surely? I knew Sanjay would. He'd been making noises about getting out since the very first moment he'd implicated himself with his rather reckless admission that he knew who Baba was.

And that, strangely, was what I turned my mind to on the return rickshaw ride home. As the desert suburbs slowly turned leafy around me, I found myself abandoning the image of being doubled over and pumped and instead started obsessing about Sanjay and his admission and what it had subsequently done to change the chemistry between all of us, but most especially between Yasmin and him. I should probably say started *re*-obsessing.

The fact is that my prison excursion—even if it did include some rather unsavory images—had been a welcome distraction from my thoughts about Sanjay and Yasmin and the way that they had shamelessly flirted with each other after he had fessed up to knowing Baba. Maybe that's why, subconsciously, I had taken the day trip to the jail in the first place—anything to distract me from my jealousy.

And now that it was over I found myself returning to the subject afresh. For a short while, it seemed I had pulled myself out of the thoughts that had kept replaying for days—circular and cacophonic, like a scratched groove in my head—and it felt as if the prison break had done me good. At least I could hear the music now.

My conclusion now became that Sanjay admitted to knowing Baba to show off. He'd been wanting to get one over on me ever since he'd first started noticing Yasmin and me getting close. It was a knee-jerk reaction to the pang of jealousy I saw flash across his eyes when I announced that Yasmin had come up with the idea to rip off the Mob. He probably didn't even mean to say it.

It had just come out, like one of his terrible chat-up lines. After all, that would have been *so* Sanjay.

I had to hand it to him, though. On this occasion, bizarrely and for once, it actually worked. Yasmin *was* nicer to him after that—much nicer. I tried not to blame her for being so tactile. Even *I* was being kind to Sanjay at the time, so I didn't really feel I could blame Yasmin. She understood the situation. At least that's what I told myself. We needed Sanjay. We couldn't alienate him with our overt displays of affection. It was more important to keep things cool between us and let Sanjay be the one to feel wanted.

Still, there were times when it stung. Like the time I saw her hook a finger down the top of his jeans as they walked along Pahar Ganj—actually touching his ass. The worst part was that she looked so hot when she did it too.

And it was because I started thinking about all of that stuff again that I never did end up writing that letter to Yasmin explaining why I wanted out. By the time I did eventually get back to my new guest house (the Green had kind of lost its adventurous appeal), the record had got stuck again and that image . . .

ARRRGH!

. . . that horrible picture of them walking together . . .

(Which I wasn't actually meant to see, but it was only because the shop I'd popped into had run out of Chestertons, and so I'd come out earlier than I should have.)

. . . and that's when I saw them—going ahead like that—with her finger down his pants . . .

Jesus, I was going to go mad with it.

So, instead of writing to say I wanted out, I found myself writing her my first love letter (in what later turned out to be a series extending over a six-week period). It wasn't easy—balancing the words between our brief intimacy and the terror of my obsession. Still, it was a hell of a lot easier than saying I planned to abandon the plan, which, I figured, would have been a surefire slingshot hurling her straight into Sanjay's arms. With me out of the way and James in prison, he'd have free rein to pluck Yasmin like a flower buffeted by the wind and plant her firmly in his own pot.

No, I was never going to allow that to happen. So I forgot about getting fucked up the ass and refocused on the task at hand. Getting on with the plan, earning Baba's trust, doing the suitcase switches, and, most important of all, fighting to make Yasmin mine.

And that's why, when I go to the post office and discover that there is a letter for me (finally!) I'm a little nervous. The man behind the counter gets a bit upset when I tell him I don't have my passport, but a hundred rupees soon takes care of that. This is the moment when I find out if I have been successful, I tell myself as he hands me the disappointingly thin envelope, post-marked "Nederland." This is the moment when I find out if Yasmin really loves me, or if she's just playing.

My darling Joshua,

Thank you, thank you, thank you for all your lovely letters and sorry it's taken me so long to write back. You write so beautifully. I wish I could write like that. Maybe you'll learn Dutch one day so I can explain to you the way I feel. Or maybe my English will get better! Of course, I miss you too—very much. And I really am sorry that it's taken me so long to write. But wow, I've been so busy! The gemology course is going really well. Most people say that you have to spend at least a year learning all the proper tests, but I've managed to convince my teacher to help me concentrate on just diamonds, rubies, sapphires, and emeralds since we agreed that Baba is dealing mainly in those. Some of it is really hard work. You wouldn't believe how complicated it gets. There are so many synthetic stones that are really well made, it's hard to tell them from the real thing. And the tricks people have come up with, you wouldn't believe! Like you can pack bad sapphires in mud mixed with titanium oxide to make them blue again. Just putting them in the microwave helps! And I watched this video the other day with these military scientists growing synthetic diamonds in petri dishes. They were coating the windowpanes on fighter jets so they wouldn't scratch when they flew low in the desert during the Gulf War. Isn't it mad? Some say that there is the technology to grow individual synthetic diamonds now, but I think it is still very expensive. We will be better off using fakes, as planned. Of course, they'll have to be very good quality fakes. You were clever to point out that we don't want Baba figuring out we've switched the stones before we've managed to get out of the country. Now that would be a disaster. By the way, I've heard that Bangkok is a better place than Amsterdam to sell the stones. Apparently they don't ask so many questions and more of the black market goes through there. As soon as Baba trusts you completely, we should book tickets.

How's Sanjay? Is he still talking in his funny accent? And how are you coping in your guest house? It sounds awful—even worse than the Green, if that's possible. And the Cellar! If I'd known you'd have to spend as much time there as you do just to get Faizad's trust, then I don't think I could have asked you to get involved. You poor thing. We'll have to go raving together in Amsterdam one day. The nightclubs here are amazing. It'll be my treat.

I got a letter from James the other day. He doesn't sound too well. He told me that you mustn't ever visit him if you are in Delhi. Meeting outsiders only makes him more depressed. Poor James. I am so scared for him. I hope he can keep his sanity together in that hellhole. Still, maybe it will all be worth it when this is over. If your calculations are right there will be more than enough to get him out of jail. With each day that goes by, I find myself believing more and more that we will be successful. Desert island happiness, here we come!

Oh, Josh, I wish you were here with me now. Sometimes I wake up in the night feeling so lonely. There's no one here I can talk to. My parents do not want to know and James's parents are blaming me—

don't ask me why. You always seemed to know how to make me feel better whenever I got scared or down. What a mess! I miss you so much. The only things that keep me going are your letters. You have been such a good friend to me. I feel like flying over and getting one of your hugs. All I want is for someone to hold me for a bit. Promise me you will look after me when I get back. Not long now. That's what I keep telling myself.

Write to me again soon.

Love,

Yasmin

P.S.: The guy who is arranging the fake money for us tells me that there's a company in Russia that makes excellent-quality synthetic rubies and sapphires. Do you want me to get some or should we get them in Jaipur as previously planned?

THE NOVELTY OF POVERTY

I am starting to wonder why I keep getting letters without any money in them. Not that the two necessarily go together, but I had been relying on Yasmin to send me more cash. It's all very well to tell me I write beautiful love letters—and I think I'm glad with the tone, seems I'm making *some* progress at least—but I now realize that I would rather have received word of a money transfer than a few "I miss yous." I had thought I was making my increasingly impoverished condition clear. Well, at least she's having a good time, raving in Amsterdam by the sounds of things. Christ. I don't want to admit it, but Yasmin is starting to strike me as just a little selfish.

I sit down on a light oak cricket bench and weigh up my options. A vague sense of anxiety starts brewing in the pit of my stomach as I slowly start to realize I don't have any options. Sanjay says he's broke and I've borrowed twice from his mum already. I have an eerie sense of foreboding, as if I can see the stars aligning before me—mapping out some dreaded yet entirely unavoidable destiny.

The post office spreads out in front of me, a strange mix of Gothic colonial architecture and blue mosquelike domes and marble pillars. Time travel. The clicking of horses' hooves on the cobbled roads echoes behind me, mixed with the sashaying of

Victorian dresses and the flapping of frilly parasols to help keep shade in the sun. A screaming horn teleports me back to the Now and I can't feel the history anymore. Just the white satellite dishes and the billboards advertising giant toothpaste tubes. Modern madness overruns, like creeper vines, all the ancient monuments in this urban jungle.

Then it hits me. There's only one place left for me to turn. I'll have to ring Mani and ask him a) why he didn't cover for me, and b) if he still has my 25 Gs. I know Yasmin thinks it's a risk, but frankly I can't really see why it should be. And besides, she hasn't exactly left me with many other choices.

I take a single-deck bus back to the Shiv Niketan, which thankfully isn't too packed. Normally, these journeys are like hot-dog sandwiches. One dick up the ass while mine is pressed into another. I've felt erections brewing up my bum on several occasions. There's no escaping. You just have to passively accept the rape. Apparently there's a word for it, *fraterous*—as in people who fraternize in public places, though I've never found it in the dictionary. I find an empty seat near the back. The rivets fastening the bus together have come undone, like poor patchwork, and a razor-sharp sheet of aluminum rattles and flaps next to me.

We pass Victoria Terminus, which has a new name I can't pronounce and no one ever remembers, then take Mohammed Ali Road, past the seventies-style mosque and through the Muslim district into Byculla. Hundreds, thousands, millions of people milling. I love to watch them. Maybe it's the color, I'm not sure. All I know is, when I see all of these people, I don't feel insignificant the same way I do when I'm in London.

When I'm at home and I look at all the gray suits commuting to their gray lives I can't help feeling like just another ant in the anthill. Maybe it's because I'm in my context, maybe it's because

I can relate to *being* one of them. It feels different here, though. Here all the different people—they feel like a celebration. Everyone looks different, without even having to try. They just are. Millions of people deeply, broadly different.

Three streets later and the aluminum sheet swings loose, exposing my legs to the outside world, just as the bus lurches to a halt outside the Shiv Niketan. It feels like my trousers have fallen down. I leap off eagerly while the driver jumps out to staple things back together. I wonder if I'll have enough time to grab the last of my money and jump back on it, catching a lift all the way to the telephone booths near Bombay Central without having to pay extra.

But events take over. As soon as I walk into the reception area I see my bag in the corner, hastily packed and loosely fastened by one plastic buckle. After a brief moment of confusion, I realize that I am being evicted. I become drugged with indignation.

"Just what on earth is going on here?" I exclaim, storming up to the desk and pointing at my bag. I can feel my own red face, hot, against the stuffy reception air.

The woman behind the counter doesn't look up from the blue book she is filling in with red numbers and screams, "SAM! SAM! Room 103 is here." Then she flips the page, scans down one column, finds my name, and inks it out in front of me. Erased. I wonder how long she has been waiting to do that.

A kindly-looking man with a full head of gray hair, a large, hairy pair of ears, and a nose that has decided to start regrowing in old age (why do they do that?), appears from some unknown back room. He offers me a Christian smile.

"Ah, Room 103, yes, yes, let me see now, Mr. Joshua, am I correct?"

I nod back at him, choosing silence as the weapon of my displeasure.

"Yes, Mr. Joshua. How do you do? My name is Sam." He extends his hand. I can't help but take it. "Yes, so now we are acquainted. Very good. Now tell me, Mr. Joshua . . . very nice name, Joshua, hmm." A brief smacking of the lips and gathering of thoughts fills the gaps. "Yes, as I say, my name is Sam, here, you may like to have one of my cards." He reaches into one of the drawers near the nasty woman, who tuts, and pulls out a visitor's card. He hands it to me. "See, there you are, that's me."

I study the card.

SAM PEREIRA.
Jesuit.
(But don't blame me!)

I can't help but smile and look up to see him beaming broadly at me. "Do you like it?"

"Yes, it's very good, I was baptized a Catholic myself."

"Really," Sam says, clapping his hands together. "Did you hear that, Rose? Our Mr. Joshua is one of us. Well, almost," he adds at the end, chuckling.

"Fascinating," Rose mutters into her blue-and-red book.

"Oh, come on, Rose, cheer up. Not much left of life to go." Then he says with deliberate volume, "For you anyway," barely containing his own guffaws. Rose ignores him and he shuffles and shrugs excitedly behind her at his own joke. I can't help but smile back. "Now, Mr. Joshua, I believe you are in need of some accommodation."

"Well, I wasn't until—"

"Until you failed to pay your bill," Rose finishes. She is looking up at me now. Her face is fattish but beautiful, hard and protective, with deep dark eyes and a small birthmark above her eyebrow. "And we still haven't received your passport details as you promised."

"I have paid my—"

"And you've been here more than a month," she interrupts.

"So?"

"Ah, Mr. Joshua." Sam steps in. "We don't usually take guests for more than two weeks at a time, it's a policy of ours."

I knew there had to be a catch to the cheap rent. "What? So you're just going to throw me out?" They look at me with "well, yes" expressions. "That's not very Christian of you," I add quickly. Rose lets out a labored sigh, as if she's had that said to her a million times before. I change tack. "Is there no way I can stay, just for a few days longer, until I find somewhere else?"

Sam looks at me with a question-mark face, then bends down to Rose's ear, which prickles against the brush of his lips. After a few moments she gives a small nod. "Mr. Joshua, we have decided to let you stay, for a few more days at least."

"Great," I gush with relief.

"On one condition." Sam cuts me off before I get a chance to say my thank-yous.

"What condition?"

"You will have to do some work for the local community."

"What kind of work?"

"Teaching English to the street kids and the hijras."

"The lady men! No way."

"Ah, please, Mr. Joshua, they are not ladies. They are eunuchs, and believe me, they have led very hard lives."

"I don't care. I'm not going anywhere near those freaks."

For the first time since I've seen it, Sam's face hardens. I suddenly realize that he is made of more resolve than most, possibly even Rose. "Hmm, very well. Then I must agree with my wife. Perhaps it *is* time you left."

Shit. I rush to recover the situation. "How often?"

"Two hours, three times a week," Sam says, quickly and forgivingly. "We give classes under the overpass. It would be marvelous to have a real expert."

"Okay, I'll do it."

"Wonderful," Sam exclaims as Rose softens into a big white smile.

OKAY, OKAY?

"I've got a job."

Sanjay's face is so full of expectation after he says it, I feel customarily obliged to give him lots of enthusiasm in return. "Really, that's great. Really great. What is it? How did you get it? Tell me everything."

We're sitting in Trishna, a reputedly excellent restaurant but really just another place in Mumbai to be seen in. With the odd exceptional beard, wealth can be gauged in here by the distinct lack of facial hair. Everyone looks very smooth. Even the waiters shave their mustaches and they have all the attitude to go with it. Personally, I would have been just as happy catching a couple of lamb kabobs and a Roomali roti from the street vendor behind the Taj, but Sanjay insisted. Now that he's in Bollywood it's more important than ever that he go to all the right places, get spotted by the right people. But I'm not really complaining. Sanjay says it's his treat, which means his mum is paying.

"Satyajit Chopra's doing a new movie called *Theek hai, Theek hai*."

"What? As in *Okay, Okay*? Bit weird, isn't it?"

"It's a cultural thing," Sanjay says. "You wouldn't understand."

I don't press him on it. I don't want to irritate him. After all, he is paying. A waiter comes up and pours our Kingfishers, which basically involves turning the bottles upside down in the glass and generating as much froth as possible. It makes sense. In a couple of minutes there won't be any fizz at all and the beer just won't seem quite like beer without a clean, white head. Best to start off with something resembling a Don King haircut and work our way down than run out of steam prematurely. We gulp them down quickly.

"Ahhhh," Sanjay gasps, smacking his lips together like the guy in the ad. "That's good."

I smile at him. "Carry on, then. What's the role? Who will you be playing? Are you a hero or a bad guy?"

Sanjay pauses for a moment. "Neither," he says eventually. "I'm not actually *in* this one. Not as a main part, anyway. I mean, I'll probably be doing some work as an extra now and again, but it's not really an acting job."

"What kind of job is it, then?"

"More of a running job."

"Oh," I say, trying not to let my surprise show. "What does that involve?" I ask, even though I know. Runners are the equivalent of whipping boys on a movie set. They are the peons, the lowest of the low, practically Untouchable.

"Lots of early mornings and late nights, basically."

"I see." I pause. I want to ask him all sorts of other questions like if that's what he really wants to do, but I feel I should probably stick with an excited mood. I don't want to spoil the occasion. After all, I get the feeling that Sanjay thinks this is his moment. Like he's finally made it or something. "So how did you get it? Is the pay good?"

"Pay's not great but I got the job on my own. Saw an ad in one of the trade mags and applied. Simple, really. Mum didn't help or anything, which I'm glad about, to be honest, 'cos she wasn't getting very far and I just felt dependent. It was unhealthy."

We look at each other. We both know his mum got him the job. She was probably just waiting for Sanjay to lower his sights. Runner on a new movie she could do, lead role in the next Bollywood blockbuster she couldn't. Still, I have to give her points for denying it. At least, Sanjay can claim a victory of sorts now, which I suppose partly explains his enthusiasm for it.

"I mean, you've got to start somewhere, haven't you?" he says eventually, as if he's reading my thoughts and coming back with the next defense.

"No, you're quite right," I reply. I'm not about to take the achievement away from him. He seems happy. I don't want to ruin it. "Chopra is huge, man. It's great that you got this job. As soon as he sees your face he'll want you in his next one, no doubt. You're right. This is just the foot in the door you need. It's really, really great. Cheers," I say, holding up my glass. We chink and gulp, then pour. More froth please.

"Thanks, Josh. You're a mate."

"No, I'm pleased for you. Really, I am. It's great."

"I mean that whole fucking mad shit we were thinking about up in Delhi. Jesus," he says, throwing his head back and half laughing. "What were we thinking? Ripping off Faizad just because we couldn't get the jobs we wanted. Seems so silly now, doesn't it? There we were wasting our time hatching some stupid scheme, when all we really needed to do was grow up and get a life. We were so arrogant to think we could just start at the top. We've got to work our way up from the bottom just like everybody else, haven't we?"

He doesn't look at me the whole way through his speech. I mean, he's looking at me but not *at* me. He's sort of focusing on the mid-distance between us, if you can call it that. I'd be surprised if he can actually see anything. He looks cross-eyed. But I don't think he wants to see me. I think he just wants to say it. Get his case across without getting distracted by my facial reaction. He knows he's pulling a fast one, and when the waiter arrives to present our food in five kidney-shaped metal bowls, he seizes the opportunity desperately, overjoyed, as if the longer he can stop me from saying anything the more likely it is I won't argue with him. Or maybe he just wants to enjoy the moment for as long as possible. The moment when he's told me that he's pulling out altogether and I haven't had a chance to make him feel bad about it. I just look at him as the dishes get presented and he blathers on, "Wow, wow, wow. Look at these prawns, Josh. Aren't they the biggest prawns you ever saw? Juicy, juicy. I'm telling you, the food here is great. Best in all Mumbai. You're gonna love it. I guarantee. Mmmm, mmm."

Even the waiter thinks he's weird. He eventually leaves us with a frown and a vague, "Enjoy your meal, gentlemen," which he slips in somewhere between Sanjay's inane banter. Sanjay throws food on our plates, all the time talking. Then he starts eating, far too fast, and he has to spit a steaming orange prawn back out onto his plate because he's burned his mouth. Even that doesn't stop his running commentary. "Hoh, oh, oh, my God that's hot. Wooo. Come on, Josh," he says, finally acknowledging my presence. "You're not eating."

"I've lost my appetite," I say.

That stops him but he tries not to let it. "Don't be silly," he says, still bending over his plate, not wanting to look up.

"If you wanted to pull out why didn't you just say so?"

"What do you mean?" he tries, finally allowing himself to catch my stare as he swigs on his Kingfisher. I can see him tonguing the roof of his mouth, feeling out the smooth, numbing area that he knows will eventually turn into a blister, then burst, then hurt. He's got a grim expression on as he does it. Nothing like a burned mouth to ruin a meal. Serves the traitor right.

"I suppose that's why you brought me here, isn't it?" I launch. "Thought you could just fob me off with a fancy meal and a couple of beers. Thought you could just turn your back on us. Let us down like that. Jesus, you're a wanker."

It seems harsh as I say it, but I'm a little wound up. Maybe it's the surprise. Maybe it's his fast-talking tactics that have gotten to me. I don't know. I just want to come back at him, hard, like he's come at me, blindside.

Sanjay's reaction is immediate. It might have been the "wanker" that did it, or it could be the burned mouth that breaks him, but Sanjay lets it all out then. He's careful not to talk too loudly—wouldn't want to cause a scene in Trishna—but his face says it all, blistering and red like the inside of his mouth. It's controlled rage.

"I never let you down, you prick," he says urgently, lips purple. "If anything it's you that let me down. Getting me involved in a stupid thing like this. This is my fucking town, man. This is where I live. I can't go around pissing off people like Faizad. I've gotta live here, for God sakes. And anyway, I've done nothing but help you and that stupid bitch you've got the hots for."

My turn then. "Call Yasmin a bitch again and I'll kick the shit out of you."

"You want to kick the shit out of me? Well, fine, go ahead. But when are you going to figure it out, Josh? She's just fucking using you, man. She's using you to get the money so *she* can get *her* boyfriend out of jail. What's in it for you? That's what I want to know. What's in it for me? I don't know what I was thinking, getting involved."

"Oh, I see, so that's what this is all about. Yasmin. You're pissed off 'cos Yasmin likes me and not you. Now there's something, isn't there? Josh gets the girl and Sanjay is jealous. Hmm? Admit it. You fancied her and now that you know she's not interested you want out. Jesus. You're even more pathetic than I thought."

"Yeah, all right, I'll admit it. I fancied her. Fanc-*eeeed,* being the operative tense. But, no, it's got nothing to do with you *getting her.* Because frankly, Josh, and I hate to be the one to point this out to you, but you haven't *got* anything. She's got a fucking boyfriend. She's not interested. Not in either of us. And even if she were, I wouldn't bloody well go messing with Faizad just to get in her knickers. She's not worth that. No one is."

"Would it make any difference if I told you that this has nothing to do with her?" I half lie. "It's about making the money so we can live our dreams, Sanjay. Remember? Our *dreams.* Like wanting to be an actor. The reason we're doing this is so you don't have to work your way up from the bottom. It's so you don't have to be some fucking peon on a movie set. It's about beating the system, conning the norm, having the money to make our lives different, significant, something, anything, just not the fucking mediocre crap everyone else tolerates on the way to their dreams and finds themselves stuck in twenty years later."

He doesn't say anything then. I can see that I've hurt his feelings. Despite all my best intentions at the beginning of the conversation, I've let my true opinion slip. I'm too honest. I'm socially clumsy. No. It's not that. I'm just bloody vindictive. I just wanted to get back at him. Tit for tat. He dumped me, so I hurt him. I've robbed him of his job glory, the one thing that's making him

feel good about himself. God, I hate myself then. What a bastard
I can be. Only pleasant when things are going my way. Otherwise
I can be a really nasty little character. Say all the things other
people might think, but have the sensitivity never to say. I can
never hold that stuff back. I lack the filter, the filter that makes
people pleasant. I'm a defective cog in the machinery that makes
society work. I fight social grace. I can't even be kind to my friends.
I'm evil.

The food is starting to congeal in front of us and I am vaguely
aware of the man at the table behind me tuning his ear back into
his own conversation and away from ours. I wonder how many
people have been listening. I wonder how loud our voices got. I
wonder if anyone heard us mention Faizad's name and whether it
would matter if they did. Sanjay looks really upset, like he's going
to cry or something. I feel for him then, a great welling from
within.

"Look," I say after a while, more calmly, a little quieter, leaning
forward over the table, "I understand why you don't want to be
involved anymore. You're right, this is your town, and don't get
me wrong, the job, it's great, I'm happy for you, really I am. I'm
sure things will go well for you. And you're right. You have done
a lot to help us. I've no right to ask you to do anything more. And
I'm not. I was never going to. You've done your bit. You introduced me, remember? You don't have to do anything else. Just let
us take care of the rest and we'll look after you—rescue you from
all that hard work you seem so keen to do. Call us your Plan B,
okay? Sanj? Come on, buddy, talk to me."

He's looking down at his food again. I hope he isn't crying.
Poor bastard. I love him, I think to myself then. He's pretty much
one of the few friends I've got, real friends I mean. Despite all our
up and downs, he's withstood the test of time, the only one fool

enough to stick around. He's always been there for me, for as long as we've known each other, which is a lot more than can be said for most people. After all, it's time that makes a friendship, isn't it? Not shared interests, exciting times, or even "connections." And if there's one thing Sanjay and I definitely have between us, something that's ours and only ours, it's time. And you can't get more precious than that.

He breathes before he speaks. "You don't understand," he says eventually, looking up at me. He's not crying. Doesn't even look close. He just looks serious. "It's not just about me pulling out. That's not enough."

"Not enough? What do you mean not enough?"

"You have to stop, Josh."

"I'm sorry."

"You can't do this anymore. You can't go chasing around after Faizad anymore."

"What do you mean, I *can't*?"

"Just that. I'm telling you to stop."

"Well, I'm sorry," I say, laughing a little bitterly, "I can't do that." I don't like people telling me what to do. Don't like them even going near the vaguest suggestion that they might be able to boss me around. I'm far too arrogant for that.

"Why not?"

"You know why. You may want to do your running thing, but I don't. I'm going ahead with this. And it isn't for Yasmin or James or you or anyone. It's for me."

"God, you're selfish! Can't you see that if you go ahead with this, nothing good can come of it? Not for me, anyway. If you succeed, I lose, if you fail, I lose. Either way, you screw things for me here. You destroy any chance I've got to make it in Mumbai."

"Why?"

"Open your eyes. Who introduced you? Who knows you? Who are you? You're Sanjay's fucking mate from England. That's who you are, and everything you do comes back on me."

"You're being dramatic."

"NO, I'M NOT!" he shouts, and then stops himself as two sets of heads turn. "No, I'm not," he whispers. "Mumbai is small, small, small. Everyone knows one another and they know that you're with me. Okay? So just stop. I was a fucking idiot to get involved in the first place. I don't know what I was thinking. I'm sorry, but basically you and that . . ." I can see he wants to say "bitch" again. "You and Yasmin bullied me. You press-ganged me into it. I was an idiot. I was showing off, I was thinking about all sorts of other things, and now . . . I'm sorry, but now this has to stop."

I look at him and weigh up everything he's saying. Measured against the mass of my own agenda, it all seems a little light. But I give him a chance to add to what he's got, a chance to convince me if he can, even though, deep down, I know he can't. But I extend him the chance. It's the least I can do. After all he is my mate. "Well, what am I meant to go and do if I drop all this, then? Where am I going to go? You forget, I don't have a passport and I'm wanted by the Delhi police for drugs."

He reaches into his pocket then and pulls out what looks disturbingly like a British passport and a plane ticket. "Here," he says. "These are mine. Take them." He hands them to me as a package. I flick through the details. He's right. They are his. I'm holding his passport, his return ticket to England.

"Are you serious?" I say. "It's never going to work and you know it."

" 'Course it will. You said it yourself. All those travelers in the Green sell their passports so that other people can use them. You can do the same thing. Just razor-blade my picture out, or even better, find someone who does it professionally and I'll pay."

"It's too risky, man. And anyway, I hardly look like a Sanjay, do I?"

"Don't worry. The name in there is my English one. Quentin Jones. How 'bout that? You'll be me now. Something you've always wanted," he says, trying to lighten the conversation, woo a laugh, make it look like we're having a good time in front of the all-important Trishna crowd.

"Very funny," I sneer. Then I pause. I suppose it's not entirely out of the question. But I'm kind of struck by how extreme Sanjay is being. I mean, giving me his passport and return ticket home. It might seem generous if it were coming from anyone other than Sanj. But somehow, this just seems desperate. Maybe he really is scared. Maybe I've been underestimating him, underestimating all of this. At what point do I trust good sense over my imagination? I mean it's been weird enough to have discovered that Baba really does exist, that my loose string of facts actually bore fruit, harbored a reality. How much of my imaginings will turn out to be true? How many of them do I want, really want, to turn out to be true? Is Sanjay right? Is Faizad right? Am I playing with fire? Am I going to get burned? Shouldn't I lean a little more toward self-preservation? It's not enough of a cushion anymore to tell myself, like some subclause to the text, that none of this is really real, that it's not actually happening, that I'm just acting out a story. I have certain facts now that make it all too real:

1. Baba exists.
2. Mumbai is small.
3. Sanjay is scared.

How much longer can I keep telling myself it's just a game, a make-believe, a fantasy?

But what if Sanjay's plan doesn't work? What if I get caught going through passport control? I suppose I've got to do it one day. Might be better if I'm doing it without a suitcase full of diamonds and cash. But then, after that, what am I going to do? Even if I get home safely, where does it leave me? Back at square one. Worse, back at square one minus a dream, minus a life, minus several long months, and minus all the cash I ever had. Oh yeah, and minus Yasmin. Which is what seals the deal, really. Sanjay can say whatever he likes about her and her motives and her boyfriend. But he doesn't know everything. He doesn't have all the facts at his disposal. He never looked into her eyes, through the door that opened, into the soul inside. He doesn't know Yasmin. Not like I do. It may all be make-believe or it may be real. Either way, it doesn't really matter anymore. This is a path that fulfills the needs I have in my life. The alternative holds nothing for me—even if it is more sensible.

"Sorry, mate, can't accept," I say, handing back the package.

Sanjay doesn't say anything for a few seconds. He just looks at me. I look back at him. I eventually drop the passport and ticket on his end of the table and then he looks at me again.

"I was really hoping it wouldn't come to this." He sighs.

"I'm sorry too," I say, not really knowing what he's talking about, just going with the rejection flow. He's sorry, I'm sorry, we're all sorry—an agree-to-disagree type thing.

"Well, that's it, then."

"Guess so." I'm quite enjoying the resignation of it all. He's out, I'm in, there's nothing we can do. It's just the way things are. It's reality.

Then he says, without drama, "You and I, we're over."

I feel my face screw up a little quizzically then. "Sorry?" What's he talking about, "over"? I'm a little upset that he's managed to up the ante like this, raise the stakes on our emotional volley. I was with him up until that last sentence, sending back everything he threw at me. Now I feel as if he has the advantage somehow.

"Listen to me carefully, Josh, because what I'm about to say, I mean . . ." He pauses. He's working the drama a little now, making the most of his lead. "From now on, I don't want to talk to you, I don't want to see you, I don't know you, and if anyone asks me, I'll say that I only just met you." I grit my teeth to choke the lump suddenly in my throat. This hurts. "You're nothing to me now. You've left me with no choice. I have to disown you, it's the only way. And it's not just for now, it's not just for a few months. This is forever. Otherwise, I'll never be able to do anything in this town without looking over my shoulder and waiting for your future here to catch up with me like it's my past."

"That's very poetic," I try.

"Well, call it my farewell speech. 'Cos this is good-bye."

Things happen quickly then. I can see that he's played all this out in his mind already, rehearsed the scene well. He gets up, throws down five hundred rupees, and picks up his passport and plane ticket. I sit there looking up at him as he does it. He's caught me totally off guard. "What about your cut?" I manage to splutter.

"Keep it," he snorts. "It's only air anyway."

Then, and I have to hand it to him because he does this very coolly, he slides out from the table, turns, and leaves, head high, no turn-backs, and then he's gone. I'm shell-shocked. I can't believe that we're over. Fifteen years of friendship, finished just like that. But something terrible inside me tells me that it has. It really has. Just like that. Just. Like. That.

WHAT WOULD YOU DO IF
I SANG OUT OF TUNE?

My first lesson begins badly. For starters, no one shows up. It's just Sam and me and another guy, a doctor with a wispy beard who works for an AIDS charity and says he wants to take blood samples from the hijras.

We wait for nearly two hours under the overpass, breathing the rush-hour fumes and trying to clear beggars and trash from the triangular paved area that Sam has designated as the "classroom." There are two enormous concrete pillars with red political graffiti—hammers and sickles mainly, and the odd reference to Thal Backeray, the local Hindu fundamentalist—framing the scene. It stinks of piss. I wonder how on earth we're meant to teach anything with all the noise around us.

"So how long have you been doing this, Sam?" I say as the darkness descends and the lights from the highway start leaking orange neon.

"Oh, many years, yes," he says.

"And who shows up? I mean, when do they show up? It's too dark to teach now, surely?"

"Oh no, no, certainly no. Many people come, you will see."

"But how will they see the blackboard?" I say, pointing at the concrete block holding up the overpass.

"No problem. Do not worry, Joshua. Everything is very good."

I look at the doctor, who just looks back at me. This is starting to seem like a complete waste of time, but I'm grateful for the distraction. Ever since Sanjay left me I've been feeling very sorry for myself, very lonely. I blame myself for his rejection. I can't help thinking the real reason he dumped me like he did is that I was so rude to him about his job. I don't think it had anything to do with me chasing Faizad or any of that stuff. I think I just really pissed him off and he decided, there and then and in an instant, that he didn't like me anymore.

I know that's silly but I can't help thinking it. Maybe it's the loneliness twisting my thoughts. Whatever the reason for Sanjay abandoning me, the result is the same. I'm here, all alone in a strange city. I don't know anyone, I don't have anyone, there's nowhere I can go. I find myself being super-nice to people I don't really know, like Sam, just to have them, anyone, be nice back to me, just to see if they will. I find it hard to believe that anyone might be nice to me. It's a wonder when they are. I'm obviously not very likable. I'd have more people in my life if I were.

Now who have I got? Dad's dead, Mani's betrayed me, Yasmin's in Amsterdam, Sanjay's ostracized me. I'm alone, really alone. I try telling myself that loneliness is a symptom of being a "traveler." Always on the move like I am, always in India, always in search of freedom—there's a price to pay for all that. I try to console myself: we're born alone, we die alone. That's just the way that it is. Get used to it, I tell myself.

But it's no good. Sometimes I cry, into my pillow so no one can hear me, or so I can hear my own despair that little bit better, really immerse myself in it. It just gets overwhelming sometimes. Because here's the thing, right—people aren't born alone, are they? We're born into our mothers' arms. As soon as we're born, we're with someone. That's what it is to be born, that's what it is to live. I mean, if we're talking spiritual, then sure, you could argue the whole "born alone, die alone" line. But life's not all like that, is it? Life's not all spiritual. It's corporeal, it's social, it's emotional, it's a lot of things. And in this life, people don't try to be alone. They try to be with other people. Because it feels good. Because alone isn't nice. And sometimes it's hard because it can be difficult to get along. But people do it. Because they're working toward something they want. Society. But I don't work for it. I don't put in the effort. I'm antisocial. I'm just not nice. No wonder no one likes me. No wonder I'm alone.

Sam suddenly throws his long arms and huge hands in the air and starts waving and shouting at two kids who happen to be walking by. I see their faces react with panic as if they've been caught smoking in the toilets, but they quickly seem to resign themselves to their fate. He's calling their names now and has managed to dodge his way through the traffic to their side of the road. They wait for him, huddling close to each other for protection.

Five minutes later and they're reluctantly trailing him, Sam beaming broadly with accomplishment. He starts calling at me from the middle of the road, cars veering to avoid him as he strides his way confidently across like a blind man unaware of the danger.

"You see, Joshua, I told you they would come. This is Pankash and Anoop, two very, very good pupils of mine. Yes, you will see, they like to practice their English very much. Don't you, children?" he says, looking down around him.

They are standing next to him now, drawn in and more intrigued that they've spotted a white man under the overpass. One of them, Pankash I think, is wearing a T-shirt that used to be white but now looks closer to a shade of shit. I can still make out the faded Nike logo on the front. The other one, Anoop, is only wearing a pair of torn trousers and one flip-flop. I can see the dirt against his brown skin. It makes it black, in patches.

"Children, this is Mr. Joshua," Sam says, resting one hand on Pankash's shoulder. "He is your new English teacher."

They both beam at me then, white teeth shining brilliantly in the darkness. "Hello, Mr. Joshua," they say simultaneously. Then, less so, "It is very pleased to be meeting you."

"No children, not like that," Sam tuts. "*I am very pleased to meet you.* That is what you say." Sam smiles apologetically at me. "I am very sorry, Joshua. They are out of practice."

"That's all right," I say, trying to sound teacherlike. The responsibility feels very uncomfortable. "Well, do you think we should start, or will there be more turning up?"

"Oh, we should start, we should start," Sam says eagerly, shooing the kids forward with a gentle push of their shoulders. "It is getting late," he finally admits.

"Yes, quite," I say. The kids walk toward me slowly, or it could just be reluctantly. "It's all right, boys, no need to be shy," I encourage them. They hover uncertainly, like animals. "I've got sweets." I reach into my pocket and pull out a Dairy Milk bar. They run forward and snatch it out of my hand. "Now be sure to share," I say as I feel Sam looking on, a little disapprovingly.

We manage forty-five minutes. Or rather I do. They don't say anything the whole time, except to repeat my words as I struggle through the names of things we can see from the street. Teaching English turns out to be much harder than I had anticipated.

Still, I manage and the kids seem to stay awake. At least they sit cross-legged and staring at me for the whole forty-five, heads held in their hands, barely blinking. Sam watches benevolently while the doctor sighs irritatingly and scans his fingernails. I end the class with a challenge for them to remember five of the new words I've taught them for next time.

"There will be a next time, won't there, Pankash?" I say, looking at filthy Nike boy. He just stares at me. "Anoop?" No word. I look at Sam. He looks back at me before suddenly shaking himself to, as if out of a trance, and beams back at me.

"Okay, children," he says, rushing toward them. "That's it for today. Thank your teacher Mr. Joshua, and we will see you here tomorrow, okay?" They get up casually, not thinking to brush the dust off their bottoms. But then why would they? "Try not to be late next time and tell the others to come," he says. I can't help feeling he's being ironic.

Anoop turns to leave but then Pankash comes up to me, hands outstretched, and says, "*Choccalate*, mister."

Sam starts speaking gruffly to him in Hindi and moves toward him. Pankash cowers against my leg for protection. "It's okay, Sam," I say, holding up a palm. "*Ne choccalate*, Pankash. *Choccalate* all gone," I say, looking down at him.

"*Finis?*" he says.

"*Finis*," I repeat back at him.

Pankash looks at Anoop then, who's hovering nervously, then at Sam, before back at me. He grins a big grin then, full of cheek and life, thrusting his hand out once again at me. "*Ek rupiyah*, mister?"

I look at Sam, who seems to be going off his head with outrage, and laugh. "*Ek rupiyah?*" I exclaim back at Pankash. "*Ek rupiyah!* I'll give you *ek rupiyah*," I say, and I grab him under the shoulders and start tickling his armpits until he starts laughing a marvelous giggle.

I see Anoop laughing then and Sam too, and even the doctor is smiling. It's Pankash's laugh—it's infectious. After a minute or so I let him wriggle himself free and he breaks, running toward Anoop, and then they both take off together laughing and shouting back at me as they dodge their way through the traffic, "*Ek rupiyah,* mister, *ek rupiyah, ek ruuuuupiyaaaahhh!*"

Sam sighs and shakes his head and tuts slightly as if to say, "What will I do with those boys?" until he looks up and sees me smiling. Then he smiles back and we look at each other and I know we both feel good and warm, because if nothing else, we managed to entertain the kids for nearly an hour. And an hour away from their lives is something, a big something, and I know I would like to do it again.

I don't feel quite so lonely anymore. I feel as if I have some people in my life. Dad, Mani, Yasmin, Sanjay—they may be gone. But I have new friends now, don't I? There's Sam and Pankash and Anoop and, oh yeah, I nearly forgot—Faizad.

FOSSIL FUELS

I follow him blindly, up the broad wooden stairs that creak as we climb the five flights. I can just make out the banisters and the odd broken floorboard. An old lady peers out suspiciously from behind her door, a weak stream of yellow light trickling through the crack, running true through the dim darkness. She closes it slightly as we pass, an inch within an inch.

Faizad says "Boo!" and she slams it shut, an instant of night, before opening it again after only a second passes, but only slightly, even less than before. Faizad laughs and says, "Come on."

I can hear the party thumping above us. Nearly there now. My lungs hurt. The flights are long ones, the stairs are steep. They must have been fitter in the old days, when they built this building. Or maybe there was just less pollution, it was easier to breathe. I can hear the traffic constantly honking its way through the intersection outside. We pass a set of French shutters in the next corridor, some slats gaping like missing teeth.

The woman, the dust, the crumbling plaster, the broken floorboards, the gummy shutters—everything is old. The building is old. The people in it are old. They're the only people that can afford to live here, in downtown Mumbai. They're the people who moved in when it was cheap. Just after the British left. Like the

Parsis did. And they never left. They're still here, getting old in this old building. Fossilizing.

It's hard to imagine there's a room full of young people upstairs.

Faizad, breathing and cursing, finally finds the door and fingers for the bell. Bass is thumping through the walls. I wonder if the fossil can take it, if it won't collapse tonight and claim me, young blood sucked down and down and down, by the living dead. We wait. And wait.

Faizad rings the bell and then just holds it down until someone answers. The door flies open with a *whoosh* and there's a rush of light and sound and people talking and glass bottles clinking and music bouncing and a girl, young, smiling, dark hair flowing, eyes tight but still round, like an Egyptian's.

" 'Allo, Faizad," she coos. She sounds French. She peers around him, and smiles at me, full of life and enthusiasm and freshness and innocence, and young, young, young. " 'Allo," she says to me. No more than eighteen, nineteen tops. She's pretty in an exotic way, but there's something wrong with her face, it's slightly distorted. I can't tell with her back to the light.

"Gungla," Faizad says, leaning forward to kiss her on two cheeks. "This is Josh. He's from England."

"Hi," I say.

"Hi again," she says. "Why don't you come in?"

She turns and we follow her. First through a kitchen where people mill and drink and eat and talk, then through some French windows into a bedroom where three girls and four guys lie on a double bed and smoke, then into a living room where people sit and dance and shout above the seventies sound system in the corner. Everyone young, everything old. It's a strange dichotomy, but somehow it works.

Another girl, very small, very young, with breasts that far exceed her frame, grabs Gungla's wrist and whispers in her ear. They giggle. Gungla turns to face me and that's when I can see that her face has had surgery, it's artificially smooth where it shouldn't be, and then I see her neck, which is wrinkled and raw with scar tissue. She looks half mannequin.

"Letta wants you to get things going," Gungla says to Faizad. She lacks self-consciousness. She's pleasant.

"Let me get a drink first," Faizad says.

"In the kitchen," Gungla says before turning. "Help yourselves."

Faizad walks toward a door, at right angles to the one we came in through. I follow him. We enter a corridor and it's only when I notice the kitchen at the end of it that I realize the apartment is circular. Faizad goes for the fridge while I attack the snacks. I'm starving. Haven't eaten all day. The money scene is getting tight, so I'm having to cut back on the odd meal. I tell myself it'll be okay as long as Faizad keeps bringing me to parties like these. I eat carrots and dips and pakoras and bhajis. Faizad prods me in the back with the bottom of a large Kingfisher.

"Easy, tiger, you'll make yourself ill," he says as I turn to face him, mouth stuffed. "It's a wonder you stay so skinny with an appetite like that."

"Seems like a good party," I mumble, grinning food at him.

"Students," he replies, as if that explains things.

"How can they afford a place like this?"

"Dunno. Five girls share it, I think. Rent it off some old dear."

"I see."

We don't say anything for a while. Faizad looks around, surveying the scene. Then he says after a few minutes, "I'll catch you later."

"Yeah," I say, turning back to the food. "Catch you later."

An hour or so later and I'm full. I'd like to eat more but I think my stomach has shrunk. I do feel a little ill now. I move toward the fridge for a fourth beer. Gungla, who's wearing a blue see-through silk scarf over the top of her head now, comes in. It makes her look even more exotic, like someone from the desert.

"Enjoying the food?" she says.

"Hmm." I nod.

"I cooked the pakoras myself."

"They're delicious," I reply. I have to do better than that, I tell myself. Haven't managed to talk to a single person so far. I don't know what's wrong with me. I think my lack of self-confidence is making me even more socially inept than usual. I realize then what a crutch Sanjay's friendship has been to me in India, and now I'm having trouble standing up on my own without it. "What happened to your face?" I blurt out without really knowing it. It must be a frontal-lobe thing. I'm just regurgitating the associations most recently impressed on my mind.

She raises an eyebrow at me. Maybe it's the only one that works. "I'm sorry?"

"I mean, you don't look Indian," I recover weakly. "Where are you from?"

"Nagaland. The northeast."

"I'd love to go there one day."

"You should. It's incredible." She says *encredebleu.* Her accent is sexy. Actually, come to think of it, she's quite sexy.

There's an awkward pause and then she says, "I ran into a kettle of boiling water when I was young."

"I'm sorry."

"You wanted to know what was wrong with my face."

I don't know what to say to that. But for some reason, I find her very attractive as she says the words. Maybe it's the youthful honesty. No games, just truth.

"What are you doing in Mumbai?" I restart.

"Studying."

"What?"

"Photography."

"What do you like to photograph?"

She doesn't say anything. She smiles and then her eyes flutter upward like she's having an inner convulsion of some sort. She grabs my hand and I take her fingers and she pulls me toward her and I feel my face drawn in and suddenly her tongue is in my mouth, soft and probing. I close my eyes and feel the warmth of her lips and I slide my hands over her hips and feel her breasts reaching my chest and she feels like a pillow, soft and warm and clean. And then she suddenly breaks with a "Pheww." I look down at her. Her face has gone into soft focus. Her eyes are glistening. She says, "Thanks." And then she's gone.

I stand there for a few seconds trying to figure out what just happened and then realize that I'm alone in the kitchen. I decide to follow her. I go in the direction she went, back through the bedroom. I see that the bed is packed now. Fifteen people at least lying on it, limbs twisted, hands stroking. The living room is still dancing, the music jumping. Then, like a trail of clues, I catch glimpses of the evidence, small flashes first out of my left eye, then out my right, then in front of me, and once I turn I see it all. The mirror, the rolled-up rupees, the eager grins, and the boy talking too loudly. The trail leads to Faizad and I spy him in a corner, behind Gungla's bum as she bends over. There's a guy next to Faizad dabbing. Faizad hands Gungla a small paper parcel. She gives him money. That's when he looks up and sees me staring. He looks at me. There's a moment. Then he nods, once and up, with his chin, just a vague acknowledgment. I don't know what to do. So I just stand there stupidly, and before I know what I'm really doing I find myself waving. Faizad grins at me then and I find myself smiling back. Fuck me, I think, Faizad really is a drug dealer.

I wonder if I can get a line.

ILL COMMUNICATION

The white plywood phone booth is carved to accommodate someone half my size, so when I swing the waist-high door open I have to turn and sort of fall into it, half crouched. A big green rotary phone sits on a small shelf by my elbow, and with each turn of the dial there is a deafening *clickety-clackety-click* until it returns to ground zero. After I dial just four of the seventeen numbers required to reach Mani in Delhi, a woman's creamy voice suddenly, mysteriously, and miraculously, comes on the line.

"What is number, please?"

"Hello, hello, is that the Mani Shankar Aiyer residence?"

"Hello, hello, what is number, please?"

"Hello, what?"

"Hello, this is operator. What is number you are reaching?"

"Errr."

"Hello, hello."

"Yes, can you hear me?"

"Yes. What is number?"

"Two-seven-two."

"Three-seven-three?"

"No, two-seven-two."

"Three-seven-three?"

"Nooohhh. Toooo-seven-tooooo."

Click.

"Fuck."

It takes me three more tries and forty-five minutes before I figure out that Indian English is the only way to make myself understood. Eventually, I manage to make the call. Ten minutes after that, the phone rings.

"Hello."

"Yes, hello." It's a woman's voice, scratchy.

"Hi, is Mani there?"

"Who's this?"

"It's Josh, I'm a work colleague."

Silence. A few radio waves, a couple of loud clicks, and the very, very distant sound of someone else's telephone conversation. I close my eyes for better concentration. Voices in the dark. It's like listening to space.

"Hello? Hello? Hello?"

"Yes."

"Can I speak to Mani?"

"He's not here."

"Oh." I can feel the receiver moving away from her ear. "Wait! Don't hang up."

"Yes?"

"Can I leave a message?"

"Yes."

"It's a very important message. Will you be sure to give it to him?"

"Tell me."

"Please tell Mani that I am in Mumbai and I need some money. Tell him I'm sorry I haven't been in touch sooner. I had to leave town unexpectedly and—"

"Wait, wait, you are talking too fast."

"Sorry." I wait for a second. "None of that matters now. Please, just tell him I'm in Mumbai and I need the money."

"Where are you staying? Where should he send the money?"

"Just tell him to arrange it so I can pick it up from the *Hindu Week* office here. Will you do that?"

"It will take time."

"Please just tell him it's urgent. Very urgent."

"Okay, Joshuaar, don't worry."

Something clicks, in my mind this time, not the line. Then everything goes dead. The man who runs the telephone shop is pointing at the clock. I compare it to the time on my Casio stopwatch. He's trying to charge me for ten seconds too many. Not that it makes much difference. I've only got fifty rupees left. The man mutters about the torn edges of the bill, but I shrug my shoulders at him. "It's the last one I've got. Take it or leave it." I turn and walk out into the street.

Suddenly the click in my mind connects. My heart sinks as I recognize the voice. It was Lyla. What was she doing at Mani's? They're probably having an affair. I hope she doesn't really hate me as much as I think she does. Mani is my only hope. Without his 25 Gs, I'm fucked. There's nowhere else for me to turn.

I've left it all too late, I know. I've been trying to get hold of him in the office for two weeks now, but of course he's never been there. It's taken me this long to find out his home number. Stupid of me. I knew, way back, when I got Yasmin's letter, that I had to contact Mani quickly. Guess I've been distracted. Had a lot on my plate, what with wooing Faizad and teaching the street kids, which has turned into a daily ritual. I never *really* tried to get hold of Mani. All those phone calls. They just seemed like such a waste of money. And now I'm stuck, well and truly.

I've no idea what I'm going to do about tonight. Faizad says there's a huge party on Manori Island, twenty or so kilometers north of the city center. I have to go. We've been getting on so well, I know I'm making progress. I can feel it. Trouble is, I'm starving. I've been spending the little I have left acting flash and trying to keep up. Faizad often offers to pay, but I can't accept all the time. He'll think I'm a leech. He might even get suspicious.

He says I look thinner each time he sees me, usually at some party or other he's selling at. At least I have some new clothes. He said I had to look vaguely respectable if I was going to hang with him so often. He's lent me some of his old things. They're small for me, but at least they're designer.

I've seen Sanjay around, at parties mainly, but true to his word he's ignoring me completely. I can't say it doesn't hurt each time, because it does. I tell myself to give him time. He'll come around. I just hope he doesn't pull the plug on the whole scam, tell Faizad who I really am, just to deflect any possible future embarrassment.

If Mani doesn't come through in the next couple of days, I'll have to start begging. Now that would be ironic. Jesus, I hope Lyla tells him. I hope she doesn't hate me that much.

The hunger is awful, worst in the morning. I spend all night trying not to think of it, craving sleep for the relief, and then, when I do sleep, I really just pass out for two, three hours at a time. I never make it to deep sleep. I wake up with a knot in my stomach and I usually have cramps for an hour before I can get out of bed. Parties are my only hope. I only ever get a decent meal when I go. And if there's nothing laid on, well, there's always the coke. That helps a bit.

I take a seat on the edge of a crumbling wall surrounding some office. Three street kids come up and ask me for money. I scrutinize their faces, to see if I recognize them from the class. I teach nearly thirty kids now and at least fifteen hijras. It was Pankash and Anoop who got the craze going. Told all the little urchins that there was free *choccalate* to be had. All they have to do is sit and watch this white guy point at things and go through the alphabet. They know most of this stuff already anyway. They just come for the *choccalate*. They know it. I know it. I try to balance their diet a little. I steal stuff from the parties when I can and keep it. It's savory and they don't like it as much, but I insist. I don't give them the *choccalate* until after. It's expensive and I can't afford it, but it's worth it, just to see their faces. They're my new friends now. I like to make them happy.

But these kids, they're not from the class. I pull my pockets inside out to show them just how little I have. They keep hassling me even though I keep telling them, *"Ne rupiyah, ne. Chalo."* It's because I'm white. They figure every white man has money. If only they knew.

And that's when one of them, a greasy-looking thing with a potbelly and a green birthmark on his arm, points at my Casio and says, "Hey, Uncle, digital clock, yes, I have? Yes?" And that's when I realize that I haven't lost everything, that I'm not completely broke. Not yet. All I have to do is pawn my watch.

MOCKNEY

I get two hundred rupees for the Casio, just enough for the train, bus, rickshaw, and then ferry to the island plus or minus a few drinks. I meet Faizad on the boat. I spot him as I get on board, before he sees me, talking loudly to a slim white girl with parted, short brown hair and a young open-faced Indian boy. He's laughing bombastically and I can hear his voice carrying over the water even though he's at the end of the boat, several meters away from me. He's saying how awesome the parties on Manori are, how long it's been since the last one, how good they used to be, legendary in fact, blah, blah, blah. They're probably new customers, I think to myself. Faizad has a nose for marketing. He always chats up likely lookers, and he almost always makes a sale at the end of it.

I vaguely hear the Indian guy ask him in a London accent who sorts everything out, and that's when Faizad sees me. He ignores the question as if he's storing an answer for later, when it's more appropriate, and shouts, "Josh, baby, yes! Yes! I knew you'd make it! Fucking awesome, man, come here and grab a seat quick before they're all gone," in a way that makes both of us look good.

I notice an Indian girl with too much makeup smiling at me as I clamber my way, clumsily of course, through the tightly packed legs and the wooden bench seats. I don't look back at her.

It's taking all my powers of concentration not to fall over someone as the boat rocks gently. I tread on someone's foot and they make no secret of it, a girl who squeals and then mutters something far too personal. I ignore her and blunder my way through.

Eventually I make it to where Faizad is. He grabs my hand in a tight, upright handshake, pulling me in and hugging me, our knuckles pressing painfully against each other's ribs as he does so. It's overplayed, but distancing myself in any way would be disrespectful, so I just grin and bear it. Out of the corner of my eye I can see the couple looking at us, smiling in anticipation of meeting me. Faizad quickly turns and does the honors.

"Josh, this is Nikki and Sumit." He pronounces the name *Shoomit.* "They just moved here from the UK." For some reason, I find myself liking them immediately, before they even say anything. It could just be that they're from England—it's not often you meet English people living in Mumbai—but I don't think so. They just have warm faces. "Sumit's a cameraman for Channel 4, would you believe?" Faizad says.

"Channel 4?" I smirk. "Well now, that's kinda wierd. Does he know Mahmood?"

"I dunno, I haven't asked him. Do you know Mehmet Mahmood, Sumit?"

"Nah. I mean I know of 'im but I'm not really a cameraman for Channel 4. I'm just freelancing for a documentary they're doin'." I half expect him to say, "Nah mean?" at the end, but he doesn't.

"What on?" I ask, squeezing in next to Faizad.

"The Kumbh Mela."

"Oh, that's that massif festival with all the *sadhus* innit?" I hear myself saying, instinctively feigning a Cockney accent to drown out the private school. I know it's sad but I figure being posh is a surefire way to get hated and I'm trying to make new friends. I hope he doesn't notice the change. I'm also hoping my knowledge of the holy men will impress him.

"Yeah," he says, forgivingly. "Watchya doin' out 'ere?"

"Josh is a journalist," Faizad says for me.

"Yeah?" Sumit says.

"Yeah," Faizad continues quickly. "He's doing an article all about what a wanker Mehmet Mahmood is, aren't you, mate?" He pronounces it *wonker.* It's a new word for him. He's picked it up because I use it so often, but it doesn't quite sit with his Australian/New York/Indian accent. He loves it, though. Uses it every chance he can get. In fact, I think the reason he's been talking for me is just so he could lay up that line and use his new word. We all start to laugh appropriately.

"I fink someone's already done that, 'aven't they?" Sumit offers, smiling with real pleasure.

We all laugh harder then, letting the joke travel on its own momentum. "Yeah," I add, giving it one last push as everyone snorts. "Several times."

The laughter manages a few more seconds before veering slowly into the hard shoulder. "No, seriously, though," Sumit picks up, before the conversation crashes, "what yer writing about?"

"The Indian film industry," I say, half smiling, taking things on seamlessly. The boat starts reversing then, the black sea lapping thickly like oil around us.

"Really?" Nikki and Sumit say together enthusiastically. "Nikki's doin' her fesis on Indian cinema," Sumit says, eyeing her proudly.

"That's interesting," I say. "What's the title?"

"*Indian Cinema and Its Effect on Popular Culture,*" Nikki says in a refreshingly normal accent.

"Wow," I say. "Where are you studying?"

"SOAS."

"Cool."

"I'd love to see your article, when it's finished, I mean," she says.

My heart sinks then. Somehow I knew the conversation would come to this. I've managed to avoid talking with Faizad about the article ever since our chat on Chowpatty. I was even hoping he'd forgotten about it.

"Yeah," Faizad suddenly pipes up. "When is your article coming out? You seem to have been working on it for ages."

"It's, er . . ." I feel very unprepared for this blindside. "I don't know, to be honest. I guess maybe in a couple more weeks," I add, realizing too late that I've let my wannabe Cockney accent slip. There's suddenly too much to think about and I'm finding myself having to juggle several balls to get myself through safely.

"Why's it taking so long?" Faizad presses.

"Er . . ."

"Have you finished it? When will I get to see what you've done?"

I avoid Faizad's eyes by looking out over the water. Three enormous pylons stand in the channel, electric wires hanging between them, over the water. That seems dangerous to me for some reason. The boat chugs. Little white horses dance. Mumbai throbs orange in the distance. The air seems much fresher out here.

"Yeah, I've finished it," I manage eventually.

"Well, when's it getting published?"

"It's not."

"Not what?"

"Not getting published," I say, letting my bullshitter's instinct take over.

"Why not?"

I notice that Nikki and Sumit have turned in toward themselves, tactfully excluding themselves from this conversation. I think they can sense the tension. They huddle together almost apologetically, as if they're partly responsible. They're very polite. I knew I had good reason to like them. I'm a good judge of character I think.

" 'Cos . . . well, I wasn't going to say anything . . ."

"What?" Faizad says, genuinely concerned.

"I lost my job." I say the words quickly, as if they're one word. Ilosmejob—you can find it in the dictionary under the letter *I*. It means: *redundant, fired, sacked, laid off.*

"What?" Faizad says now, incredulous. Even Sumit and Nikki open up their pose a little, their body language expressing sympathetic concern.

"Yep. About two weeks ago now," I say with matter-of-fact resignation, as if a distant relative has just died.

"Why didn't you tell me?"

"Not your problem," I say, happy to be regaining control of the situation. I even manage to inject some Cockney back into my voice.

"Well, what did you get fired for?"

"They didn't like the article I wrote," I say, the map of bullshit excuses suddenly unraveling before me, slowly and clearly showing me the way out of this latest situation.

"Why not?"

"My editor said it was slander."

"Slander?" Nikki says.

"Oh, Josh, you didn't really go and write a bunch of stuff

against Mehmet Mahmood, did you?" Faizad says, a little like a
proud parent, concerned for his silly little boy. "I was only kidding.
You must know that."

"But it was the truth. Like you told me, Mehmet Mahmood
has a monopoly on international Indian cinema and he acts like
a tyrant. Why shouldn't I write that?"

Faizad puts his head in his hand. "You idiot."

"You can't get fired for submitting an article your editor
doesn't like," Nikki says, meaning well, but really screwing things
up for me.

"Yeah," Faizad suddenly realizes. "You can't get fired for that."

"You can if you tell your editor to take it or shove it up his
ass."

I don't know where that comes from. Call it inspiration. I
know Faizad's going to identify enormously with it. I'm in the
zone. I'm fulfilling my role. I'm playacting to perfection. What
can I say? I'm on fire.

"You didn't," Faizad says.

"I did," I say with mock pride.

Nikki and Sumit smile nervously at me as if they want to carry
on liking me but everything I've said so far is making me come
across as a complete idiot. And that's not even counting the posh
accent and my pathetic effort to cover it up. But by now I don't
really care what they're thinking. I'm working Faizad brilliantly.
I can see his face twisting, pulling in all the associations and the
connections from the corners of his mind, drawing my experience
onto his, projecting his sense of victimization onto me, concluding
that now I too have been infected with the Mehmet virus. Poor
Josh, I can see him thinking, Mehmet Mahmood has fucked him
too, indirectly and in his own way. And the pride! Oh, the pride
he has in his eyes, for my telling my editor to fuck off. He loves

that. We are one, he is thinking. Josh and I, we're just like each other. I know I've got him then. Out of the blue and just like that. Who would have known that tonight would be my night?

"Fucking hell, man," he says, grinning and slapping me on the back. "You're a fucking nutter. I've gotta see this article you wrote. It sounds brilliant."

"I'll show it to you tomorrow," I say.

The boat is pulling in toward the dock now, one man running to catch a rope, the engines reversing, and water bubbling up behind us in an aggressive swell.

"There's just one problem," I dangle as people at the front of the boat start standing up, waiting to get off. Someone wolf whistles and whoops from the beach and we can hear the thump of techno music in the distance. I can see a row of rickshaws waiting to pick us up.

"What?" Faizad says, looking at me. I look back at him and into his eyes, for the first time this whole journey, preparing to tell him the first truth in a long time.

"I'm broke."

Faizad laughs, loud and affected and happy, almost holding his ribs as he does so. A couple of people look back at us. Nikki and Sumit are busy trying to see if anything in Nikki's bag has gotten wet. They'd put it under their legs near a puddle, it seems. Faizad looks at me and smiles broadly, "Don't you worry about a thing, mate. I'll take care of you. Tonight is my treat. Deal?"

"Deal," I say, trying to sound humble, noticing Miss Makeup look back at me briefly before reaching out for a hand to help herself off the boat. I smile at her, and after she makes it to the dock, she turns around and smiles back at me.

WORK TO DO

Faizad and I are sitting under a palm tree, the sand cold beneath our bums, techno music twisting all around us, the ocean pounding the shore in the distance. People turn and roll and rock on the balls of their feet, at times seeming to move as one, manipulated and molded by the music, as if it's choreographed. Improvized choreography, if there is such a thing. It could just be the bass.

It's a mixed crowd. Part local, part international, but all freaks—in their own way. I see corporate climbers and lost souls, Gucci outfits bouncing next to circus jesters, clean-cut buzz cuts and long hair in multicolored braids. God knows where all these people came from. There's a troupe visiting from Goa, I can figure that much, here for one last crazed drug fest before the flight back home.

The rest must be Mumbai, though I don't recognize a lot of them. Maybe it's because they're letting go. Some of the facial expressions are scary, grinning monsters the lot of them. They've all regressed to being infants with wind. It's the pills, apparently. Sumit tells me, "They're well rushy." He's bought three wraps from Faizad already and now he's going for it with Nikki over by one of the bass speakers. They seem to be having a great time.

Faizad and I are not indulging. I don't know why. Frankly it feels like a bit of a mistake. For some reason we've managed to get ourselves involved in a far-too-heated debate about the street kids and why I teach them English. Maybe it's too much booze, but Faizad's really pissing me off, trying to convince me that not only is teaching the street kids a waste of time, but also that I don't have the right.

"You're just giving them false hope," are his exact words as he takes two thousand roops from some sucker for another dodgy wrap.

I decide that if there is one thing I really don't like about Faizad, it's the way he treats the poor. It's hard to stop myself from blurting out to the lank-haired white guy that Faizad cuts his Charlie with Vim. I should know. I've snorted enough of it. But I stop myself. Partly because, to be fair, it's not just Faizad who has this attitude toward the poor. Practically every middle-class Indian I've met is just as bad, Sanjay included.

They all seem to talk about poverty in India like they have some inside information, some deeper understanding that they think entitles them to treat the poor like shit. I never see Faizad give to any of the beggars; he usually just shouts at them, and there's a bigoted disdain in his voice whenever the subject of the street kids come up. And it's not because he's a bad guy. It's because he's middle class. They all do it. They all treat the poor poorly.

Maybe it isn't to do with class. Maybe it's the caste system. As if things are the way they are because of karma, written in the stars, something I wouldn't understand, could never understand . . . because I'm not Indian.

As far as Faizad and Sanjay and Sanjay's mum and the girls I meet in the Cellar and even, in a strange inverted way, good, sweet, charitable Rumana are concerned, the poor are poor for a reason and there's no point fighting it. I watch Faizad dish out yet another wrap. I wonder if Rumana knows he sells coke to all her friends. I wonder if she'd mind. Probably not.

The thing that's weird about Rumana is that she does something about poverty in Mumbai. She constructively addresses the problem with soup kitchens and education workshops. Yet her attitude toward the poor is the same as Faizad's. I know. We talked about it that time by the swimming pool. I listened to her pontificate on random acts of charity like they're a pointless indulgence, a counterintuitive kindliness that only exacerbates the problem. She said that giving on an individual basis does nothing to solve the problem, it only turns people into beggars and thus begets itself. That's why I gave to the Akanksha Foundation. Anything to shut her up.

It was her attitude that threw me. She seemed to despise the poor almost as much as Faizad does, even though she does more than Faizad, or me for that matter, to help them.

It's all such a paradox. They're all paradoxical. Paradox is so common here it's a cliché. Rumana and her charity. Faizad and his coke. I mean, here he is, selling one of the world's most expensive drugs in a country racked by poverty. And he makes so much money doing it too. Coke comes from so far away, it's more expensive here than anywhere else. And the middle class pay here for it through the nose, quite literally. Why? I'll never know.

They're all the same, they're all peas in a pod. They live in India and none of their lives makes any sense to me. It's too extreme. Like that time Faizad had me in his limo, doing coke, with the beggars rapping on the windows. Or the time I saw a lipstick-red Lotus scream through the intersection outside the Shiv Niketan and nearly run over some kid selling newspapers at the lights. It's all the same sickness, something my sensibilities can't fathom. It's the margin, the distance between the poles, living together, all in the same space, interacting, happening, all of it in front of me: that's what I don't get.

I try to tell myself that this is the reason I came here. I try to tell myself that India is the only believable backdrop for my kind of narrative, that it's the perfect halfway house between my fantasyland and the real world. Remember . . .

. . . *Anything is possible, anything is possible* . . .

But it doesn't make any difference.

These anecdotes may make good fiction, but the reality of them is too much to stomach. Maybe I should give up the English lessons, or the parties, or both. I think the contrast between my two lives here is finally getting to me.

I tell myself not to push it. I tell myself not to blow everything on this stupid debate. I've made good progress tonight with Faizad. Don't ruin it now trying to pull him back up onto the moral high ground. That's not my job. My job isn't to make Faizad perfect. It isn't to make him "good." Because he's not good. He's a goddamn drug dealer, for God's sake. And I shouldn't try to change him. On the contrary, it's my job to go over to the dark side with him. I'm the one who has to change.

"Maybe you're right," I say, eventually managing to hide my hostility. "Maybe I am giving them false hope. I'm only really doing it so I can stay at the Shiv Niketan."

"I don't know why you stay there anyway," he says. "It's a shithole, that place, and Byculla, Jesus, that's about as bad as it gets."

"Where do you want me to stay? It's not as if I can afford to go anywhere else."

"What you need is a proper job."

"No shit, Sherlock."

"You could work for me," he says then, as if he's been working his way around to asking this ever since we sat down, ever since we started talking about the street kids.

"Doing what?"

"I dunno. Odd jobs. I've got some ideas."

"What sort of odd jobs?"

"We'll talk about it later."

"Come on. What kind of work could I possibly do for you?" I press.

"Listen, do you want a job or not?"

"Yes."

"Well, then, quit being a journalist and stop asking so many questions. You'll find out soon enough. All you have to do is do as you are told. And for now that means getting us six more drinks. Here's a hundred roops. Go take care of it."

"Yes, massa."

"And don't take the piss."

"Yes, sir, massa, sir," I say, grabbing the bill and hauling myself to my feet. He kicks me on the shins once I'm up and I nearly trip over myself as I take my first step.

"You're a clumsy fuck, did you know that?" he shouts as I step into the bass zone.

I stick my bum out and point a finger at the right cheek, mouthing the words "Kiss my ass," at him before leaving. I can feel him grinning behind me, and by the time I reach the bar I realize I am grinning too—very, very broadly. Fuck the street kids, I tell myself. Forget Pankash and Anoop. I'll quit the lessons. They've been a distraction. If the contrast is killing me, I'll quit the lessons. I need to stay focused on the task at hand. I don't need to make new friends. I need to maintain single-mindedness of purpose. I need to keep going to parties. Keep Faizad company and help him look cool as he sells coke on his own in the corner. Because I'm nearly there now, I think to myself. Oh so nearly there.

ARE YOU EXPERIENCED?

I'm in the Cellar, just sold my eighth sachet, not bad for 2 A.M. The latest customer is so preppie looking, a yellow sweater with the arms over his shoulders and crossed around his neck, it shocks me. After he's gone I look at that Oscar Wilde quote again across the room. "Experience is the name people give to their mistakes." It's become a favorite of mine since I started coming down here regularly.

"Boogie Oogie Oogie" by A Taste of Honey is playing, the wah-wah guitar testing the limits of the toilet-paper sound system.

Faizad never does actually confess to me that he's a drug dealer, not in words anyway. But I know and he knows I know and that seems good enough for both of us. I've seen him handing out packs at enough parties and he's made no effort to hide it. I think part of the reason he never actually talks about it is that he's a little scared I might yet react like all the other part-time friends he's made, might abandon him once it's said, once it becomes real, in tangible, said terms. Best just to leave it all tacitly understood, and we can continue going on, hanging out, being seen together, and acting like best buddies. And I don't say anything because I almost feel that if I do say something, I might even scare him off. I feel like maybe he'll reject *me* then, perhaps in anticipation of my turning my back on him, to preempt any potential rejection.

I guess what I'm trying to say is that the trust, the complete trust, it's not quite there yet. It's building slowly day by day, but it's not quite there yet. We're definitely operating on a new level now that I'm working for him. We've definitely graduated from being social acquaintances to being work colleagues, but we're not quite at the "friend friend" stage. Not yet. Maybe it just needs time.

At first, I ran around for him, like he suggested, simply doing odd jobs. Delivering packages mainly, a courier for the courier, if you will. Two weeks after that, he got me selling in the Cellar. I don't even remember how he bridged that divide. I think he just told me to hang around outside the toilets from 1 A.M. to 4 A.M. and to charge a thousand rupees for each little origami sachet I sold. Some sachets only cost a hundred roops. I think they're the ones with brown in them. I don't ask. I've stopped being a journalist. And besides, not much profit there. Faizad tells me to concentrate on the thousand-roop ones. Makes sense. Import-export. Better margins on the coke locally. The heroin business—I guess that's all international. Still, I get some requests for the brown, not many, but some.

I spot Sanjay squeezing his way through the crowd past me. I try to catch his glance but he doesn't see me. Or maybe he's just got better at acting like he hasn't seen me. I can't blame him. I think I understand where he was coming from now—that time he dumped me in Trishna. Word has got around that I'm Faizad's new right-hand man. Sanjay probably knows that I've started dealing in the Cellar. He may even be a little scared of me. Or that could just be an ego trip I'm having. He's with that tart he met that time we first came down. Seems like ages ago, all of that. Funny how things turn out, I think to myself then. I try to remember her name but I can't. I don't think I was ever really introduced. Who would have known that the next time we'd all be here together, in the Cellar, I'd be a drug dealer? I'm a little ashamed then and a little pleased Sanjay hasn't seen me. I back into the shadows just to make sure, make sure he won't yet have to act like he hasn't seen me. I wouldn't like that. Still can't handle the hurt.

"Walk This Way" by Run-DMC starts screaming.

"Experience is the name people give to their mistakes." On one level, Wilde is right to take the piss, of course. There's no point in dressing mistakes up—making out there's something good to come out of them. A mistake is a mistake is a mistake. It's something regrettable. Calling it "experience" doesn't make it any less regrettable. I mean, I think selling drugs in the Cellar is probably a mistake.

The worst thing about it is that I'm not even sure that it's getting me where I need to be. Selling coke in the Cellar seems all very well for the time being, but it's slow going when I think of where I've got to get to with Faizad. Jaisalmer, the international heroin ring, the suitcases and the switches, the "friend friend" level, it's all so far removed, a whole link in the chain away. And I don't get the sense that being Faizad's messenger boy/peon/dealer is necessarily getting me very far.

Sometimes it feels as if he's only employing me to keep me where he wants me, in Mumbai, by his side, friendly company when he needs it. If anything, I feel as if he's paying me to be his bitch. Perhaps that's harsh. I guess I'm just a little disillusioned with my career prospects, that's all. I feel like a local employee. I feel like a hack on the ambulance beat, when really I should be covering Afghanistan. I feel frustrated. I need to push things forward. Take things to a new level. Inspire more than Faizad's trust. I have to make him have Faith in me. Somehow I need to impress him. Maybe it will simply happen in time. Maybe not. When will Faizad really let me in?

The thing I have to do is make Faizad more money. Then, and only then, will he really believe that I can do this. That's the only way to make the transition to the next level, to get myself to Jaisalmer. He has to consider me a serious partner, see me work my way up through the ranks. I have to show some initiative. Boost profits, increase sales, cut costs. I have to make him do more than just trust me. He has to have Faith in me. I can't just leave it up to Time. That will take too long.

"You gotta have Faither, Faither, Faith . . ." George Michael blares.

And if I externalized my experience, made my mistakes mere fiction, I'd have something, one day, to show for it. I'd have chapters. Real chapters. I'd have actually achieved the consolation people look for when they label their mistakes "experience." I'd actually have something to show for my fuckups. And those chapters, they'd one day become my Bestseller. They say the best writing is based on real experience. Well, that's what this is. This is experience. I'm seeking out material. This isn't even a mistake. Nothing I do now can be a mistake. I can take things to the limit. After all, I'm doing something noble. I'm seeking out experience. I'm seeking out material. I'm becoming a writer. Fiction might be fiction but you can't just make it up, you know. You have to base it on experience, you have to live it, realize the fantasy. Sanjay was wrong and I was right. This story just wouldn't be believable if I wasn't actually living it, wasn't doing my research.

"Two, please," the girl asks. She's skinny. "Thanks." Her fingers touch mine as she passes me the wad of bills, all fifties. I don't count. She knows better than to shortchange me. After all, word has got around that I'm bad, Bad to the Bone. I believe that now. I'm Bad to the Bone. No, don't worry, that's not the next song.

And then it just comes. Just as the guitar in Frankie Goes to Hollywood screams "Na, Nah, Na . . . Relax, don't do it." I know how I'm going to do it. I know how I'm going to impress Faizad. I know how to boost profits, I know how to take things one step further. It's simple. Do the one thing all great capitalists do. Supply the demand. I've got the supply. I know where to find the demand. No point letting all that heroin go to waste, even if the margins aren't great. It's not a good thing to do. It's a bad thing to do. It will complete my migration. I'll become completely bad if I do it, just like Faizad. I won't be a hero. I'll be a bad guy. I won't like myself for it. I'll be ashamed. It won't make me happy. But that doesn't matter. If it gets me to where I've got to get to, then it doesn't matter if I'm happy, not happy, good or bad. It'll be an experience after all. It'll be an additional chapter for my Bestseller.

At least, that's how I justify the idea to sell the heroin to the street kids.

Faizad is walking out the door by the time I arrive at his place. "Josh! Wassup? I was just coming to find you. You're late today." He says it a little too loudly for my hangover.

"Yeah, sorry."

"No problem. None at all. You can be late as you like." I think Faizad is settling into his management role quite well. He's got a natural touch for admonishing and praising this employee in just the right measure, getting me to perform to the best of my abilities. I smile at him. "So," he dangles, eyes raised, "how did we do last night?"

"Good. Twenty big ones last time I counted."

"Twenty! Fucking hell."

"Would have been more if you boosted supply."

"Yeah, well, I've been meaning to talk to you about that." He's dressed all in white. Loose-fitting white combat trousers, a white cotton shirt, and white Adidas.

"Yeah?"

"Yeah." He pauses. I wonder if this might be it. Could this be the promotion I've been waiting for? "There's someone who wants to meet you."

"Who?"

Faizad purses his lips together. "My partner."

"Didn't know you had a partner. What's his name?"

"Yeah, you did. You just weren't paying attention. Ajay. He's the man in charge of supply, among other things, of course." Like selling diamonds, I think to myself. I smile at Faizad. "Yeah, he's impressed by you. We both are. Wants to meet you in person."

"Really? When?" This is it, I think to myself. I'm going to Jaisalmer. Should telephone Yasmin tonight. Tell her to get the next flight over. I've done it. At long last, I've got Faizad's trust. No, better than that. I've got his Faith. God, I'm looking forward to seeing her, I realize then. It's been nearly three months. And it's felt a lot longer. Finally, we're making progress.

"Now."

"Oh, right," I say, half looking down at my trousers to see if I'm appropriately dressed. "Where's he live?"

"Benson's, Colaba Causeway. Come on, we'll take the bike," he says, pointing at his Enfield, an enormous elephant of a motorbike, with British racing green mudguards and a gas tank the same color. The seats are wide and black. Faizad reaches under the mudguard and pulls out a set of keys. He flips them around his first finger, catching them in his palm as he straddles the bike proudly. Then he inserts a brass one in the ignition before pumping the kick-start. After a few tries, he pauses, then gives one big kick. The bike farts into life. "Get on," he says. I climb on the back.

It takes me about five seconds to realize that Faizad can't drive, which strangely makes him well equipped for driving in Mumbai. For the first ten minutes I am sure that we will tip over; he can't seem to control the bike with my extra weight on it. Somehow I think the weaving helps, though, because it keeps the other traffic veering out of our way and means we are able to negotiate a clear path.

But that only makes Faizad cocky, eager to go faster and show off his prowess. I cling to the bar on the back of the seat, wondering if I'll be able to jump off just before impact. I can't help staring at the ground, which rushes beneath us like a river. I get nauseous when Faizad decides he can drive and hold a conversation at the same time.

"Twenty Gs . . . amazing . . . Cellar . . . pay." The wind takes the words away on its own random terms.

"Whaaaatt?" I scream in his ear. Faizad flinches at the controls and there's a brief instant, a wobble, when we stand on the edge of the End. Somehow Faizad manages to pull us back from the abyss.

"Christ . . . have to . . . fucking shout."

"Sorry? What did you say?"

"Forget it."

We manage the rest of the journey in safer silence, and barring one incident with a truck too scary to recall, we make it to Colaba Causeway without a problem.

"What did you say to me on the bike?" I ask as I climb off.

"Oh, nothing. I was just wondering if we should increase the cut for the guys at the Cellar, with so much good business going through there. They deserve a bonus."

I don't say anything.

He props up the bike and starts walking toward the Benson Hotel. We're in tourist town now, just around the corner from the Taj. Compared to the six-lane highway and the Shiv Niketan, this is paradise. The streets are wide and woody and a lot of the buildings have spaced-out shutters shading large rooms with high ceilings and cool echoes. We are near the sea. "You should move here," Faizad suggests. "You're making enough money to afford it now."

"Yeah, maybe," I say, knowing that I can't. He pays me well but not that well, not well enough to move out of the Shiv Niketan. And besides, I'm still avoiding other travelers.

We walk into the reception area. A big wooden fan lolls lazily, the floor is checkered with black-and-white tiles. A man with grizzly black stubble and *pan*-stained teeth nods at Faizad as I push the chunky maroon button in the brown-carpeted wall. A five-floor elevator whirs into action on ancient mechanics.

After a few seconds the elevator arrives and I slide open the brass bar doors, a smaller version of the gates at the Shiv Niketan. We step inside. Faizad pushes the button for the third floor and then there's more whirring. We stand in silence. There's a royal red carpet on the ceiling. A bell rings and we suddenly lurch to a halt on the first floor. Faizad reaches to open the door.

"Why are we stopping here?"

"The elevator is bust. We have to walk the remaining two flights."

Is there any point to these episodes? Is there any need for all the Dr. Seussian nonsense, or is this just the *real* India? I tell myself it's just another quirk. Like Rumana and her charity, like doing coke in a limo covered in beggar barnacles—it's all just color, it's all just chapters for the novel. It is just this sort of ridiculous reality that makes an interesting and believable narrative. Far more effective than my fantastical imaginings. People can relate to stuff like this. We run up the remaining two flights, two steps at a time, and before I know it, we are outside the illustrious Mr. Ajay's room, Mumbai's big-time dealer. Faizad rings the bell.

Now, it's been a while since I last saw Yasmin and I know I've been having trouble remembering what she looks like, but when I see the girl who answers Ajay's door for the first time, all my perspectives on sex appeal go pear-shaped. I'm suddenly lost.

I mean, I had thought that I had Yasmin marked. Starting with the basics: I know that there is no such thing as a 10. Some models and really exceptional women, like Yasmin, are 9s. Beautiful women are 8s, pretty women are 7s, and so the scale goes, right down through to the bulldogs-chewing-wasps category in the 1s and 2s.

But there is definitely no such thing as a 10.

So how come this girl answering the door at Ajay's can be so stupendously, breathtakingly, stomach-wrenchingly attractive? I haven't even looked at her body yet, and as far as I'm concerned, even if she has the physique of a Sherman tank, her face alone is enough to cruise her easily into the 9s.

She looks half Indian, with the skin of a perfect tan. Long black hair, thin, tied up in itself loosely on the back of her head. Her eyes are huge, enormous in fact. Not staring or wild. But that's not really the thing about them anyway. It's their color. They're blue. No, aquamarine . . . turquoise . . . green. Jesus, they change depending on the light. It's freaky, haunting. Suddenly I know who she looks like. She looks like a grown-up version of that Afghan girl on the cover of *National Geographic*—the one that got all the awards. She is incredible. Long slender nose, fleshy slender lips, high cheekbones, lots of other perfect traits. But it's really the eyes that get me.

It can only mean one thing. There is such a thing as a 10.

Either that, or Yasmin's in line for a downgrade.

"Hey, Ayesha, Ajay in?" I can tell Faizad's trying to stay cool but I know he's staring. She doesn't say anything but steps away from the door and opens it to let us in. Faizad goes first. I trail weakly behind him.

"Hi," I say, shuffling past her.

"Hello," she replies, close enough for me to feel the warmth of her breath on my ear. She must be six feet tall! I find I have to stand up straight for my extra two inches. I realize I have stirrings in my loins. It's pathetic, or amazing, or both.

"Hi," I say again. I can't help it. She ends the conversation by gently pushing me out of the way of the door as she swings it shut. "Er, sorry," I customarily stammer. Why do beautiful women make me apologize?

Then, as she strides across the loosely fitted floorboards toward an archway leading into another room, it all gets too much. She's wearing a black cat suit with a plunging back that stops just short of two perfectly round buttocks. Above them I can see two enormous green eyes, tattooed at the base of her spine. It takes me a few seconds to click, but when I realize what they are for . . . oh boy.

I can only laugh.

Faizad looks at me acidly. "Be cool, bro."

"I am," I say, still smirking. "But, I mean, come on . . ."

"Hey, listen, dude," he whispers harshly. "That's Ajay's girl, so be cool, right?"

"Yeah, okay, whatever," I say, trying to gather my giggles like a schoolboy in class.

We follow Ayesha through the golden archway and into the main room. Ajay is lying on his back, propped up by opulent white poplin pillows, his chest hairy and bare, a pair of white combat trousers just like Faizad's riding up against his hairy dark legs. I recognize him instantly. He's a video jockey (VJ for those in the know) on Channel V, a talentless heartthrob. I can't help thinking that Ajay could so easily be a successful version of Sanjay, they even look alike, except Ajay's face is chunkier in the jawline, a bit more butch.

"Yo, my man!" Ajay says, stretching out his hand and propping himself up slightly on one elbow in token effort.

Faizad skips over to him and grabs his hand like a Brother. "Dude!"

"This him?" Ajay says then, pointing with a nod in my direction.

"Yup," Faizad says proudly.

"Hey," Ajay says, again nodding slightly at me.

"Hey." I nod back. I remember reading in some article somewhere that Ajay isn't really called Ajay and that he's a failed rock star who got talent-spotted in the streets of Mumbai for the Channel V job. I don't even think he's Indian. He's Canadian Asian or something.

There's an awkward pause, one that I usually don't have the tolerance for, the kind I tend to fill with some inane comment just to see the scene out socially, amicably, for the comfort of all involved. But for some reason, I'm able to ride this one out. I don't know why. Maybe it's because I'm in Ajay's place, Mumbai's big-time dealer. Best to keep quiet.

"Ayesha," Ajay says after a while. I feel her step up beside me. "Why don't you take Josh next door for a drink or something? I want to have a chat with Faizad for a few moments. That okay with you, Josh?" he says, overpolitely. I don't like the way he says it. It feels too chilly, too distant, not like he's about to promote me at all. He looks edgy. He keeps fingering his fingernails. His eyes have enormous black rings around them like ice-cream scoops hollowed out of his skull. He looks wired and tired—a nasty combination.

"Sure," I manage calmly.

Ayesha takes my hand and leads me through a door half stripped of green paint into a small sitting room.

"Get the door, buddy," I hear Ajay saying to Faizad, and then, as it shuts, his voice continues, muffled but there. I nervously try to stay tuned in.

Ayesha suggests that I take a seat on a cream-white sofa in the corner of the room. I tell myself to relax. Everything will be fine.

"What can I get you Josh? Whiskey? Beer? Wodka?" Her voice

is a little harsh, guttural like a Persian, and then, of course, there's the little lisp, or whatever it's called when someone can't pronounce their *R*s and *W*s or, in her case, *V*s. It manages to make her even more sexy. A ten and a half.

"I'm all right, thanks," I say, trying to stop my legs from shaking.

"Sure?"

"Yeah, sure."

"Where are you from?" she says, sitting down next to me, close.

"England," I reply, beaming.

"I gathered that much. Where in England?"

"Oh, right yeah, sorry. London." I'm nervous. I think she can tell.

"Where in London?" Maybe she's trying to distract me.

"Holland Park. But my parents only recently moved there, I mean parent . . . stepmother . . . oh forget it, it's too hard to explain." I can hear Faizad and Ajay talking through the door. I think I hear Faizad mention something about Rajasthan. I strain.

"Go on, I'm a good listener."

I don't answer her. Their voices sound like a radio turned down low.

"Is there something wrong?" Ayesha asks eventually.

"Wrong? No. Why should there be?" My legs are shaking again now.

"You seem distracted."

"What? No, of course not. No there's nothing wrong. I'm not distracted. I was just thinking, that's all."

"What about?"

"Well, if you must know, I was just thinking what lovely eyes you have," I say quickly.

"Oh, thank you. That's sweet of you."

"Both pairs," I try cheekily.

"Oh, you noticed those," she says, smiling. "I had them done a couple of months ago."

"They're neat."

"You think?"

"Definitely."

"I like the idea of being able to see what's behind me."

"Very clever."

"Especially useful for when I'm being fucked from behind," she says, straight-faced.

I almost choke. "That's nice." She smiles at me. I don't want to let the subject go but I can definitely hear Faizad mentioning my name. I think I hear him say Cynthia or something. Then I hear Ajay coming back at him, a little louder, more aggressive. I try squinting with my ears as I say to Ayesha, "It must be very nice for Ajay." There's a small pause. I drift back into the conversation next door.

"Why do you say that?" I hear Ayesha in the background. I'm not even looking at her. "Why?" Ayesha says again, touching my knee.

"What?"

"Why would it be nice for Ajay?"

"Well, because, I mean, aren't you two . . . ?"

"Aren't we what?"

"Well, I thought you were seeing each other."

"We might be. But it's not necessarily exclusive, you know."

"I'm sorry?"

Faizad clearly tells Ajay that he's being paranoid and then Ajay talks back at him in an indiscernibly loud voice. I wonder why I can hear Faizad better than Ajay. Maybe he's standing closer to the door or something.

"You heard me, and if you didn't," Ayesha says, smirking, "well, that's your loss." Another small pause. "Do you want a line?"

"Er, yuh, sure. Why not?" Anything to take my mind off the conversation next door. I know they're talking about me and I don't like it, I don't like it at all.

Ayesha gets up and walks toward a small table, also white, and bends over, lifting her ass toward me, flashing her eyes. It really does feel like she can see me. She pulls out a mirror with a rock of cocaine on it and then kneels down in front of a small coffee table across from me.

That's when the shouting next door really starts. Ayesha looks at me and then at the door, "Aye, yie. Those two. Always fighting, fighting," she says, before looking at me and smiling again. She's a real sex kitten, what with her green eyes and cat suit. I half expect her to start purring. She turns her attention back to the rock she's scraping. Tiny crystals pile up on her reflection like miniature salt mines. I wonder if it's her job to distract me. I wonder if that's why she's flirting and offering me coke. Making sure I don't listen to what's going on next door. Seems likely.

That's when I hear Ajay clearly scream, "IF YOU DON'T I WILL."

Suddenly the door slams open. Ayesha and I both jump. Ajay storms in. "YOU," he says, pointing at me. "UP!"

My bladder twitches instinctively. "I'm sorry?"

I can see Faizad hovering in the background, a helpless expression on his face. "You heard me," Ajay says, a little calmer now, standing over me. "I said up. Stand up and face the wall." I do as he says. He frisks me. Then when he's done, he says, "Turn around." I face him. For some reason, I realize with pride that I'm not wetting myself. That's got to be a first. "Who are you?"

"I'm sorry?"

"Who sent you?"

"Sent me?"

He slaps me, hard and full on the cheek, very fast, so it burns, red, raw and sore. I still manage to not wet my pants. "Start talking," he snarls. Faizad is biting his nails, looking at me, shaking his head. "Where's all the money coming from?"

"What?"

"The money. Where's it from?"

"Where do you think? The Cellar, of course."

He slaps me again and shakes me by the collar. "TALK, COP! Who are you working for? Interpol?"

"Cop?" I say with genuine surprise. I wasn't expecting that. "I'm not a cop."

"Yeah, come on, Ajay, you know he's not a cop," Faizad says, half laughing, quarter laughing really. "Just look at him, he couldn't be a cop if he tried, his feet are too flat."

Ajay's not impressed. "You can fucking shut up, Faizad, you traitor. You think just because I'm up here, at the top, I don't know what's going down in that shitty hole you crawl around in. You think I don't know what goes on in this town, you fuck."

"I don't know what you're talking about," Faizad tries.

Ajay's got one hand on my collar and is leaning against my breastbone as he talks, shouts really, now half turned at Faizad. "Nice try, buddy. Trying to cut me out. Even though I'm the one who got this whole business going, even though I'm the one who bailed your fucking ass when you were fucked. That's nice, real nice. And what's it got you? A fucking cop in on our operation. Good work, Faizad. Very good."

"You're being totally paranoid," Faizad says. "I never tried to cut you out."

"Oh, yeah? Well, we'll see about that. You," he says then,

turning back toward me, his face consuming my field of vision. I can see the blackheads in his nose. "How much did you make last night?" I try to find Faizad's eyes. I know this is a test. Ajay dodges in front of me. "Uh-uh. Don't look at him, cop boy. Just tell me. How much did you make?"

"Twenty."

I can see Ajay's face tighten. "Night before."

"Eighteen."

Ajay's breathing starts getting labored. His nostrils, which look raw around the edges, probably from the coke, flare. "Eighteen?" he says.

"Think so."

"Night before that?"

"Can't be sure." I know I'm giving all the wrong answers. I can feel Faizad tensing from the other side of the room.

"TELL ME!"

"I dunno, eighteen, I think, I can't remember."

Ajay lets go of me and storms toward Faizad and then past him, saying quite calmly, all things considered, "I knew you fucked me. I just knew."

Faizad says, "Ajay, wait, I can explain."

Ajay disappears completely from my view and I can hear him call, loud enough for everyone's benefit, "Good. I look forward to that. First, though, I'm gonna take care of the pig."

I can hear drawers slamming and doors banging. Faizad looks at me and nods urgently toward the door. I can see him mouthing words at me. I don't know what he's saying. There's the tinkle of coat hangers. Then Ajay shouts matter-of-factly, like he's going hunting, "Ayesha, darling, where's my fucking gun?"

I look at Faizad quizzically. He's joking, right? A gun? What's he going to do with a gun? Can you get guns in India? I mean gangster guns, revolvers, and shit. I wonder what type it is. I mean an AK in Kashmir I can picture, but a revolver in Mumbai? It just doesn't seem right. This isn't happening, I tell myself. But I know it is. And that's when I realize Sanjay was right when he said I didn't take the Mafia in India seriously enough. Why can't I picture guns in Mumbai? The Mafia shoot people here every month. And Ajay's one of them. Faizad's one of them. I thought maybe I was even one of them. I thought I was getting a promotion. It's all so unreal. This isn't happening. Faizad nods in the direction of the door again, but I still can't move. I half expect Ajay to come back in through the door yelling, "April Fool!"

But it's January.

Then, without any real warning, Faizad screams "RUN, JOSH! RUN!" and throws himself behind the doorway, presumably onto Ajay. I can hear the buttons on Faizad's shirt popping and tinkling lightly on the floorboards just moments before the two bodies crash together on the ground, the room rumbling as they tumble next door. Ayesha lets out a small scream, and though the doorway obscures my view, I can feel them scuffling around on the floor.

That's when a gunshot cracks.

Except for the faint tinkling sound of me pissing myself, there's only silence. Except for the ringing in my ears, there's only silence. Except for the creaking sound of floorboards as Ayesha runs next door, there's only silence.

Silence for several moments, before I find my feet.

I sprint for the front door. I don't look to see if Faizad's okay. I don't stop to see if he's dead. I just run. I run like he told me to run. I run out the door, down the stairs, through reception, out into the street, I turn one corner, then another, past a square, down a boulevard, along the seashore, back in another street, and I keep going. Running and running until, eventually, I run out of breath and realize that I don't know where I'm running to, that there's nowhere for me to run to, because I've got nowhere to go.

CHARACTER CONFUSION

I am looking at the sachet, delicately open on the sheetless mattress. The brown sits inside it in a rectangular slab. I'm nervous about trying it. I don't even know why I want to. Maybe I'm just bored.

I've been hiding in this windowless room for three days now. Pankash and Anoop brought me here. I found them after I ran away from Benson's, at the intersection outside the Shiv Niketan. It was only when I saw them that I realized that I'd been running to the Shiv Niketan the whole time, some subconscious homing instinct guiding me.

It was also then that I realized that I couldn't stay at the Shiv Niketan any more, that my homing instinct had led me to a place I couldn't even call *home*.

With Faizad out of the way, Ajay would come looking for me. Faizad must be dead, I'd decided, or very badly hurt at least. Scuffling around on the floor when the gun went off like that—he must have been hit. It wouldn't take Ajay long to find out where I'd been staying. He probably already knew.

So, when I saw Pankash and Anoop, I asked them for help. They said, "Yes," like they're asked for help all the time. They said the hijras would hide me, if I had money. I ran up to my room and found some, my cut from one week's work. I also took the smack—quite a lot of it. It was all I had left. The coke all sold, my other possessions—the designer clothes, the other stuff—worthless baggage.

They brought me to the Caged City, as they call it. This is where the whores and the lady men live, sitting behind barred windows soliciting passersby. I'm in a small room around the back. All day I listen to fat men fucking ten-year-old girls who have been stolen from the mountains and sold. After a while the girls give up crying. It's just the fat men fucking and grunting. That's all I hear.

Maybe that's why I want to do the smack—to drown out the sound and the smell and the stink of it all. Or maybe it's because I feel guilty. Guilty about selling smack to the street kids so I can continue to pay the hijras to hide me. Ruining their lives just so I can stay alive. Or maybe it's because I'm scared. Scared that Ajay is eventually going to find me. Scared that he'll eventually kill me. Scared that all this karma is going to come back on me. I may as well punish myself now, flirt with addiction before fate exacts some crueler justice.

Or maybe I'm just lost.

I've been in this town, all on my own, for so long now, doing all these things I normally wouldn't do—to get Faizad to trust me, to get Yasmin to love me, to get material for my Bestseller—that I've lost myself. I don't know who I am anymore. I've pulled down too many barriers, too many rules—like the rule that said I'd never do smack because I'm too pussy and too middle class and I've got too much to lose and I've seen all those eighties ads and I know it's a one-way road to hell. And yet here I am thinking about doing it.

IN THE BEGINNING

I have to get out of here. I am so homesick, I can't stop crying. I pity myself. The sadness feels like a warm blanket wrapped around my neck. It's getting tighter and tighter, but it's too comforting to take off, even though I know it's killing me. I just feel so sad. Everyone hates me. I have to get out of here.

I'm on the bottom bunk. Night-lights from the street collect in rigid rectangular puddles on the cold linoleum floor. Howie O'Neale creaks in the wire mesh above me. I wince every time he moves. I'm scared that he's coming for me.

He and Tommy Jones cornered me in the bathroom this morning. They ripped my towel off as I was brushing my teeth and whipped it wet at me. They called me names. They are older than me, much older. I am small. Then they forced me against the white tiles and rubbed themselves against me. I couldn't do anything, I felt so weak and they were so strong. Then Scallywag came in and told them to stop. When they left he smiled at me. Later Howie and Tommy said they'd get me. If Howie wakes up, I'll die. I want to die. I want this to end.

Alex Davis turns over in the bunk across the dormitory. He just got back. He had appendicitis. He nearly died because the doctors were watching the World Cup when the teachers first took him to the hospital and they said he was fine even though he wasn't. So they brought him back. I remember how he screamed that night and the nurse came and then Scallywag called the ambulance and then he was gone—four weeks, four whole weeks away from this hellhole of a school. Everyone's nice to him now. Even Tommy and Howie leave him alone.

That's when I get the idea.

I start moaning, gently at first, just like Alex Davis did. Then I hold my stomach and start clenching at the right side, pumping the pain and believing in it. That's the most important thing, I tell myself, believe in the pain. Howie's bed creaks again and I let myself moan louder. Someone tells me to "Fucking shut up," and I think about quitting.

But then I remember the morning and that tomorrow there'll be another one just like it, followed by another, another, and another, so I let myself carry on moaning until it eventually becomes a scream. I close my eyes and start rolling around in the bed, hyperventilating, and building up a sweat. Someone turns on the lights and I can hear Howie telling me if I don't shut up he'll really give me something to scream about.

I hear the door open and I scream louder and I know that behind my eyes everyone is awake now and maybe even worried. That's when I really do start to feel the pain and for a moment I'm worried that maybe I'm actually hurting myself in some way. But then I realize I'm just believing it and that it's working.

I'm a little scared when I hear Scallywag's deep voice and smell his stale coffee breath and the old furniture in his clothes. I think, if I don't pull this off, I'll be in serious trouble, maybe even get expelled and I'm only ten.

But then the nurse is there, big and soft with short parted red hair and freckly cheeks and a kind white smile, asking me, "What's wrong, what's wrong?"

I groan and hear Howie say, "I think he's got appendicitis, miss," as if he really cares, but I know he's only saying it because he's dormitory captain and he's at least meant to act like he cares.

Scallywag says he'll call the ambulance and then the nurse puts a thermometer in my mouth and climbs onto the bed with me and lets me writhe in the softness of her stomach and breasts, stroking my hair back and telling me to sssssshhhhhh.

When the ambulance men arrive, I hear her tell them that my temperature is 104 and I wonder how. Then I'm being put on the stretcher and I am being wheeled out of the dormitory and I see the boys gather at the window as I'm put in the ambulance and taken away, away, away from it all.

And then I'm in the hospital, lying on my side and being asked questions by the doctor. He looks like a Hollywood actor with dark stubble and a manly, handsome face and I wonder if I'll ever be a man. I know all the right answers to his questions, because Alex Davis told me everything.

Then the doctor puts a rubber glove on his right hand, picks up a jar of Vaseline, and tells me, "Everything's going to be all right, I just have to check inside to see if it's tender." Alex Davis hadn't told me about that bit, so I grip the nurse's hand hard when he puts his finger inside me and I wince as he reaches deep and presses around and down and asks me, "Is that tender?"

I say yes to everything.

They leave me then but I can hear the nurse and the doctor talking behind the curtain and the doctor is saying, "Better safe than sorry, don't you think? Especially after what happened last time."

And then the nurse says, "But two cases of appendicitis in two months. It's so unlikely." I hate her then. How could she betray me?

Luckily the doctor tells her, "I'd rather not take any chances. Call his parents. We'll get him prepped, then operate immediately."

"Yes, Doctor," the nurse says. Then the curtain whooshes and I remember to keep wincing and groaning as they wheel me down the corridor.

And then they wheel me into another room. I'm lying, still on my side, my bottom naked and cold and violated, sticking out from the back of a starched hospital gown. Then someone injects me in the bottom. At first it burns, like the cold can sometimes, and then it's just a little sore as the needle withdraws.

Then everything changes. My life melts away like ice in boiling water. The headache I have managed to give myself evaporates instantly and the air in my head clears and suddenly feels light and fresh like a cool spring breeze. So do my troubles. I don't feel sad anymore, I feel happy. I'm not even scared of Howie, and I wonder if we'll ever be friends. I feel a great peace emanate from within me and feel as if I have enough to share with everyone. For the first time since I have known it, life is beautiful.

I realize that faking appendicitis has been a mistake. I sit up in bed and try to tell everyone that I'm okay. The doctor comes in and he says, "How are you feeling now, Joshua?"

So I tell him how sorry I am for all the trouble I have caused because I feel much better, in fact, I never really felt ill at all, I was only faking it to get out of school.

He looks at me with steely, handsome eyes and has this stern, manly expression on his face before he pulls up the blue mask over his mouth and says to someone standing behind me, "He's ready."

And that's when they pull me down, back down onto the stretcher, and keep telling me that everything is going to be okay, even though I try and tell them over and over and over that I'm just a faker, I'm just a faker.

But after a while I give up. The panic doesn't last long. I can feel the rush inside me annihilate all my other emotions, flicking them out of my system like small playthings. I let myself give in completely.

I'm not even scared when I see the gas mask loom from out of the corner of my eye, hover briefly above me until there's a hiss, and then clamp onto my face. Nor do I worry when I feel the cold burn of another injection in my arm and then feel the icy liquid creep up my arm and across my chest. And when they ask me to count backward and think of my favorite food, I know with absolute certainty that these will be my last thoughts. But I don't mind. Ninety-nine, 98, 97 . . . and hamburgers, I like hamburgers. And then the darkness swells, from somewhere deep down in an unknown place in my mind, and it seems so large I believe it actually exists outside of me. That's when I know. I'll never wake again. But, like I say, I honestly don't mind.

JUST GOUCHING

I slip the coin in my mouth and stand it between my tongue and the soft fleshy part behind my teeth. I watch the brown hiss and bubble in the foil and then I vacuum the whiffs of smoke through the straw. I spit the coin out, laced with copper traces on the silver lining, and breathe in air to accelerate the rush. It feels strangely wholesome, like choosing brown bread instead of white. I feel high but pure. Then sick. The nausea is like the itching—nothing serious, not even uncomfortable. It's just a symptom, a mere and minor symptom of this blissful experience. When the vomiting comes it's an ablution, a purging of the excess. Afterward, I feel clean. That's when I really relax. With all my bodily functions taken care of, I have nothing left to worry about.

I realize now, as I do it, that I never needed to feel guilty about selling smack to the street kids. It's just like the morphine they gave me that time I faked appendicitis. Peace, contentment—an infinitely preferable alternative to the harsh reality of life.

No. I don't need to feel guilty. The street kids suffer. I know how they suffer. They're all runaways. Pankash and Anoop. All of them. Their mothers are dead and their fathers are alcoholics who beat them. They've told me their stories.

They'd rather come and live here in the shit than stay in those villages they came from—those arid backwaters of hell. They are trapped in purgatory. Condemned to starve. There's no hope of escaping the cycle. It's the new caste system. A whole new stratum, just below Untouchables. Street kids—destined to live and die in dirt. Why live like that? Why carry on hoping when there's no escape? Did you ever hear of a rags-to-riches tale in India? Faizad was right. Rumana was right. No point giving them false hope. Best to just give them relief. Best to just give them heroin.

I help kill their pain, ease their struggle. Now I understand. I finally understand—because suffering isn't relative. Nothing is relative. Everything is handed out in enormously disproportionate portions. I've suffered maybe a thousand days in my life. The girls, the ones who are forced to fuck in the room next door, have suffered five thousand already and I'm three times their age. Suffering isn't even the same for everyone. Some people suffer more than others. People start to go crazy. I've seen it on these streets. Crazy people feel more than the sane. They let down the barriers that keep the rest of us on the straight and narrow. They feel more of everything. Joy and sadness, pleasure and pain, sunshine and the rain. More pain, deeper, richer, and far more abundant—that's the truth for the kids on the streets and the girls next door.

But I never did see the logic of a life with pain. Not since that time they gave me morphine. Not since I saw how easy it is to cure suffering. After all, I was suffering. I was suffering so badly that I faked appendicitis just to get out of school. And it worked. I escaped. I found happiness. I was given morphine. I *should* give them heroin. I'm obligated. It's the right thing to do, because I can cure their suffering. Because I know how to, I've known for a long time.

That's when I realize I'm not lost. I'm found.

The brown-haired boy comes. He comes to the room, the one with no windows. Morning, night, I'm not sure. It feels like night. He talks at me. I'm too fucked up to care, to interact. When he walks through the door, it's like he's appearing out of a dream, or a waking state, his face—full in my view. Somewhere between my dreams and reality I know that he's there, but for some reason, it feels like I'm imagining him. Like his sudden appearance is simply too contrived to be true, something that is affected for the purposes of plot drive. Maybe it's the other way around. Maybe I am imagining him but he feels real. Does it matter? The fact is: I see him, I hear him. For a moment I think he's me. Young, hopeful, hair parted. It's like looking in a scratched mirror. It's hard to read his face. But then, when he touches me, I know he's just a young white otherperson. Not me at all. He says there's something I should know, something that will make it all different. He tells me it's important not to lose it. Tells me to hang on, for him. He says he needs me. He says they both need me. We love you, he says.

I watch him go through my pockets. I know he's doing it. I just let him do it. There's nothing to take. I'm down to my last wrap of smack. Eventually I try lifting my hands to stop him. It's humiliating to watch him going through my pockets like that, like I couldn't stop him if I wanted.

And I find that I can't. My hands feel heavy—heavy like eyelids in a waking-up dream. A dream within dreams. It's time to go to bed. He helps me lift my legs up. Says it will be okay. I should stay off the smack. It's no big deal, I say. I'm just trying it. No one ever got addicted just smoking the stuff.

He covers me gently in a blanket and then, just before he turns to leave, he says, "If you need money you should go see Mani."

FREDDIE'S DEAD

The *Hindu Week* office in Mumbai is in Nariman Point, among the skyscrapers and the rich City whiz kids. The streets are wide here, like Colaba Causeway, but there are no trees. Just a view of the sea and some albatross-sized seagulls feasting on the rubbish heaps in the rocks and the tide breakers.

I've washed and changed into some of my old things, laundered for less than a quarter of a wrap of smack. I'm all out now. No money, no smack, nowhere left to hide. I'm back out in the open. How long have I been gone? It's hard to say. I don't know the date. I haven't witnessed night and day passing. And the smack. It distorted my inner clock. I need to find a newspaper.

Now that I'm out in the open, the fact that I sold heroin to the street kids seems so unrealistic in the light of day. I wonder if I really would have gone through with the idea before, if only to boost profits, impress Faizad, earn an invitation to Jaisalmer? If I hadn't been driven to by my own desperation, wouldn't that have been just too out of hand, too far-fetched, even by my own fantastical standards? A middle-class white boy selling heroin to the street kids of Mumbai? I don't think so somehow. But once I became desperate? Once I had a motive? Did that make it believable?

I feel like I practically sought out my desperate condition now, on the run and hidden by the hijras, just so I could realize, justify really, this extreme act, this unbelievable idea.

Just imagine! You, Josh King, selling heroin to the street kids. What a story! Now justify it. Throw yourself deeper into desperation and hell to make it believable, make it real. It's not enough to just make this stuff up.

I feel like I'm losing my mind. I feel like I'm getting drawn deeper and deeper into my own mind game. What started out as an interest, a talent, a habit, has now become something bigger than me. Like that story about the chess genius who became so obsessed with the game, he saw chess pieces everywhere: knights, kings, castles . . . A tree became a queen. A rock was a pawn. And he played chess with everything, everywhere, all day. And then he went totally nuts.

Me? Is that me? Do I get a fantastical idea and then, before I know it, I'm realizing it, living it? Everything has reversed. I'm not using fantasy to excite reality. My fantasies are taking over; they're creating my reality.

Shit. I knew that smack would fuck me up.

There are two sets of elevators in the building, one for even floors, one for odd. I take the wrong one by mistake and end up having to walk down from the twenty-third floor to the twenty-second. Then I find that the fire escape is locked, so I have to trot down the remaining flights all the way back to the ground floor and start again. I am sweating heavily by the time I reach the office. Already, I've managed to make my clean clothes feel dirty.

A brass banner embossed with the words CHANDRA PATRIKA BAZAR is above the heavy wooden door. I walk in, half thinking about what I'll do if the fire alarm goes off while I'm here. No one is in the white reception area, so I wait around for a few minutes before deciding to take a look around. I can't hear anything. The place seems dead.

Behind reception, I find a long thin room that looks like it is really half of a big room, split down the middle with plywood walls. Papers and magazines are stacked in shelves along one side and there is an air-conditioning unit at the end. I stand next to it for a few minutes and cool off in the artificial chill.

Suddenly a door that I hadn't seen before swings out from the plywood wall behind me. I spin around on my heels. A woman with extremely frizzy black hair and deeply pockmarked fair skin stares at me impassively.

"You must be Josh," she says suddenly striding up to me and extending her hand, like she's been expecting me. Not cold, but definitely businesslike.

"Yes," I say taking hers, wondering how she knows me.

"I'm Savita . . . Savita Bavadam."

I recognize her byline.

"Oh right, hi."

"I'll just tell the others you're here."

Savita disappears back through the plywood wall. I decide to follow her. I was right about the room actually being half of one big one, but I am shocked to see how much activity is stuffed in the secret side. It's the noise that hits me first. Telephones, people talking, teacups clapping, and chairs on wheels rolling. I briefly wonder how such thin walls could be so well insulated.

It takes me a few seconds before I focus on Lyla and Mani at the end of the room. Lyla is sitting on one of the swivel chairs looking up at Mani, who is leaning against a desk, pressing down his hair. Savita is talking to them when they all turn to look at me. There's a moment when none of us seems to know what to do.

Amazingly, it's Lyla who jumps up and runs over to me to say hello. I get a horrible feeling that she is going to kiss me, but she stops herself at the last minute.

"Oh, Josh, thank God you're all right," she says, twitching her nose up and down, like a rat. "We were so worried about you."

"Really? Why?"

"Haven't you heard?"

"No. What?"

"Oh."

"What? What is it? What are you all doing here in Mumbai? Is it about my money?"

"Er. I think you'd better talk to Mani," she says, turning just as he arrives behind her—the perfect segue.

"Hi, Josh," Mani says, smiling gently. "How are you doing?"

"Fine."

"Sure?"

"Yuh. Why wouldn't I be?"

"Well, it's just that we've heard . . ."

"Heard what?" My bowels move. I hate the idea of anyone hearing anything about me without me knowing. It's embarrassing, if nothing else. I skip through my immediate past in my mind. My heart sinks. There's plenty for me to be ashamed of.

"Heard that you've been getting quite involved with your story." At least he has the decency to put it nicely.

"What's going on, Mani?"

"Josh . . ."

"What?"

"VJ Ajay is dead."

There's a lot of white noise in my head when he says it.

"Who's VJ Ajay?" I try lamely.

Mani tips his head and frowns at me. "It's okay, Josh, you

don't have to hide anything from us. We know about your connection with Ajay."

"What connection? What are you talking about?"

Lyla is looking up at Mani, gleaning interrogation techniques.

"Why don't you tell us what's been going on?"

I can't help staring into Mani's groomed beard. It's so perfect.
The hairs look like they've been strategically placed. Can you get
face wigs?

"Tell me how it happened first."

"He was found this morning on Juhu Beach—murdered."

"How?" I manage.

"He was shot in the face."

Nasty. In the face. That's harsh.

"Did you do it, Josh?" Savita says suddenly. Mani shoots a
glance at her, but Savita just keeps looking at me with black,
impenetrable eyes.

"What! No, of course I didn't."

Me? Why would she think I did it?

"The police are looking for you," Mani explains. "You'd better
tell us what's going on."

I'm starting to get a very bad feeling about all of this.

"What? Me? Why are the police looking for me?"

"Well, put it this way, Josh, you've made your associations
with Faizad Gerstad and VJ Ajay quite well-known round here.
Mumbai isn't such a big town. I was able to pretty much track
your movements from Delhi until a week or so ago when you just
fell off the face of the map. That's part of the reason I came down
here. To see if you were all right." I don't say anything. More
white noise. "Don't worry, I've spoken to the police. They don't
suspect you."

There's no relief when he says it. "Then why do they want to see me?"

"They just want to ask you a few questions."

"No way."

"I think you should cooperate."

"What? And let them throw me in jail for murder? No thanks."

"They won't do that. They know you're working for me."

"Fat lot of good that did last time."

"What do you mean by that?"

"Last time you said you'd cover for me I nearly got busted," I say bitterly.

"What?"

"The police came to arrest me the day after I saw you in Delhi that time."

"That's not possible."

"Well, it's true. They raided my room, took all my money, my passport, everything. That's half the reason I came down to Mumbai."

"I find that hard to believe."

"Why?"

"Because I had dinner with Police Commissioner Sanghvi that evening. I told him all about you and he gave me his personal assurance that you wouldn't be bothered."

None of anything makes sense. Why would the police raid my room if Mani had covered for me? Surely they wouldn't act on their own like that, without the express permission of the commissioner? Maybe they were just out to get me. Maybe it wasn't a police raid at all. Maybe Yasmin got it wrong. Maybe it was a robbery.

The only thing I do know is that I'm not going to walk into an Indian police station to take part in a murder inquiry in which

I'm associated with the victim; I'm a stranger in town, without
ID, and with the possibility that I'm also wanted by the police in
Delhi for drugs. Though maybe I'm not. I'm feeling confused.

Run, I hear Faizad's voice screaming.

Run. Run. Run. Runnnnnnnnnnnnn.

"I've gotta go," I say suddenly, getting up.

"What! No. You're not going anywhere, Josh." I start backing
away toward the door. "Josh, listen to me. Don't panic. Everything
is going to be fine."

"I'm sorry, Mani."

"Wait. You'll need some money," he says then. I pause, waiting
to see if he'll give it to me. "I'll give you all the money you need.
Just give me the story. Then I'll pay you."

Money. Better than money . . . Payment. I'd be a journalist
then. A real, undercover, investigative journalist. Maybe I should
take it. Put the Bestseller aside. Settle for second best. Journalist
is good, journalist is very good. At least it would be an end to all
this madness.

Mani's voice fades back in. "We're running a cover story on
Ajay's death. We want to go with an inside scoop. This is probably
the biggest story to hit Mumbai in years. Do you have any idea
how huge this is? Do you even know how big Ajay was in this
town? This is a huge scandal. You did it, Josh. This is your chance
to make it as a journalist. People will respect you. And we'll pay
you. We'll pay you very, very well. Just remember who looked
after you, Josh. Don't betray us now."

Mani is talking fast, like a salesman who doesn't want to give
me time to think, which, strangely, has exactly the opposite effect.

"You've got to be joking," I hear myself saying.

"Just think about it, Josh. It's the only way to get the police
off your back."

"Yeah, right, and the Mafia on it. They're going to want to get someone for Ajay's murder. I'm not going anywhere near it. I'm outta here."

"You're making a big mistake, Josh. If you run now, I can't cover for you. Just remember that. You're on your own."

I've been on my own for a long time already, I think to myself when he says that. A long time. And it's got me this far, if you can call "this" a place I'd want to be. Still, it's better than being dead. Still, it's better than walking into a police station, getting fucked in the ass, or taking an avenging bullet in the face.

"I'll take my chances," I say.

And, just to be on the safe side, I also take the stairs. You never know, they might be outside, right now, waiting to take me. Mani may even be calling them. Who knows whose side he's on? Who knows anything? I certainly don't. I don't know anything. Not anymore.

I don't bother taking the elevator at Benson's, and manage to sprint past reception unseen to Ajay's room. I've decided to go there first. Mainly because Colaba Causeway is nearer to Nariman Point than both Faizad's flat and the Cellar and they're the only places I can think of to go in search of leads. If I don't find Faizad fast I'm fucked.

The door is ajar. The loose floorboards crack noisily as I step inside. The place looks like it has been raped, stripped bare with some clothes strewn randomly.

Ayesha is lying naked facedown on the bed. The mattress has been torn half off it and hangs down heavily on one side. Good sense tells me to get out. I walk up to Ayesha, for some reason expecting to find her throat slit, drowning in her own blood.

She murmurs something muffled into the bedding.

"Ayesha?" I say, looking into her big green tattoos.

She lifts her head up, one side red and raw and imprinted with the texture of the mattress. Dribble shines stickily on her chin. She grins at me.

"Ohhhh, issssss you."

"Ayesha? Are you okay?" I say, touching the back of her shoulder.

"Issss youuuu," she says, smiling.

She's smacked out.

"Ayesha, listen to me," I say, sitting on the bed beside her and turning her to face me. The movement startles her briefly but then she slouches back heavily, her head lolling against the headboard. "Ayesha, listen, are you okay? Have the police been here? What did you tell them?"

She smiles at me through half-open eyes. "Fuck me."

"Ayesha, did you say anything to the police?" She nods off. "Ayesha? Wake up, wake up."

Ayesha opens her eyes and looks at me. "Fuck me, Ajay," she says, looking at me but not seeing. I haul her up. "Police have gone," she says suddenly, as if my question has only just filtered through—her brain working on heroin time delay.

I wonder what she told them. I wonder why they haven't arrested her. I wait for the next question, the one about what she has or hasn't told them, to worm its way into her consciousness. I have to know. I have to know if I'm going to take the fall for this. Then she nods, or tries to at least. Halfway into it she gives up and her head just rolls forward onto her shoulder. "What did you tell them?" I say. She manages to shake her head slightly. "Ayesha, what happened? What did you tell them?"

She points at the walk-in cupboard at the end of the room. I lay her back down on the bed and walk over to it. One side of the clothes rack has been ripped out of its fastening and there's a pile of shirts, trousers, and coat hangers slipping off the end of it. At the back of the cupboard is another door. It only opens when it's pulled out from the backing. I wouldn't have seen it, if it hadn't already been opened. It fits neatly, and in the darkness of the closet, the hairline cracks are invisible.

This must have been where they hid the drugs and money and diamonds. Excitement lurches inside me, like the feeling you get when a plane suddenly loses altitude in the turbulence. I'm getting closer to the action. I can feel it. I can almost taste it. I put my head inside and scrape along the dark edges with my fingers. It's empty.

It takes me ten more minutes to find out from Ayesha that the police just left. Reception buzzed up a special warning signal and she hid in the secret compartment. I realize then that that must have been how she found out that Ajay was dead. I feel sorry for her. Sitting, hiding in the secret compartment like that, listening to the police talk about her dead boyfriend. Can't blame her for wanting to get smacked out. Thank God she didn't tell them anything.

"Listen, Ayesha. Where's Faizad? I have to know. Where's Faizad? Have you seen him?"

The question gets lost somewhere. "Fuck me, Ajay . . ." Before I know what's going on, she slides two hands down, pressed against each other, palms outfacing, down between her thighs and starts grinding herself against her knuckles. I watch her do it. Her breasts stand firm and goose-pimpled in the air, pink nipples taut, her chest heaving. "Put your fingersssss inssside me."

Everything goes into slow motion. After what seems like a very long time, she pulls one hand from out of her thighs and reaches for my right hand, which is still resting on her shoulder. Then she pulls my hand down and starts kneading her left breast with it. I watch her slide two fingers into herself. I can smell her, sweet and tangy at the back of my throat. "Kissss meeee."

I can't move. As long as she is making the moves, I'm hypnotized. I can't act: I can't reject it, I can't accept it. I can't kiss her. I want to. But that would be me doing it to her. It's her doing it to me. I don't have the strength to say no, or yes.

She lets go of my hand and reaches into my groin, still kneading. She coaxes the swelling, massaging from the base to the tip. She rolls onto her side, pressing the weight of her legs against her own trapped hand and starts rolling her hips. She slides her head toward my groin, her mouth already half open, waiting, ready.

She fumbles with the zipper in my trousers. Practicality replaces the passion. In the brief lull, I find the strength to get a grip. "Ayesha, stop. Listen to me." I jump off the bed and start shaking her shoulders." She starts pawing for my groin. "Listen! Stop! LISTEN, GODDAMMIT!"

"Come back to me."

I see a half-drunk bottle of Limca on the bedside table. I grab it and pour it over her head. Then I pull her hand out from her groin and pin her arms to her side, holding her down against the bed. "Listen to me, Ayesha, you have to tell me where Faizad is. Ayesha? Ayesha?"

"Ajay? Ajay?"

"No, it isn't Ajay. It's Josh."

"Where's Ajay? Where is he?" I don't say anything. "He's gone, hasn't he?" Her mouth starts coiling downward. "Ajay's gone. THEY KILLLLED HIM." She screams. I clamp my hand over her mouth. She starts crying and writhing in my grip.

"Sssshhhh, Ayesha, sssshhh. Calm down, calm down. Who killed Ajay? Was it Faizad? Tell me."

She shakes her head.

"I don't know. Ajay's gone. I don't know."

"Think, Ayesha. Did Faizad come here?"

She nods. That could also explain the mess. Maybe Faizad came to get his cut, the diamonds, I don't know. Whatever was in the secret panel at the back of the cupboard, I guess.

"Did you see him?"

She nods. "Today."

"Today? When? This morning? When?" She loses interest and starts fumbling at me again. I stand up and hold her shoulders in both hands. "Ayesha, when did he come here? Where did he go? Tell me."

"Errchurchee Gate. Errchurcheee . . ."

"What?"

"S. Teshan."

"What?"

"Train. S. Teshan."

"Which train, Ayesha?"

"He told taxi, Churchee Gate S. Tation."

"When? Ayesha, when?"

She sinks into helpless sobs and she's gone. I try bringing her around, but after a few minutes I realize that it makes no difference when Faizad came or left. He's either at the station or he's not. And I have a pretty good idea which train he'll be catching. I grab a blanket curled up in the corner of the room and shake it over Ayesha into a floating canopy that embraces her. I wipe her hair out of her face, sticky with tears and Limca. "It's going to be all right, Ayesha. Just stay here. Everything's going to be fine." And as I run out of the room, Ayesha wailing mercilessly behind me, I can't help wondering why I find it so easy to tell people that, even when it's very clear that everything is not all right. In fact, it's all very fucked up.

The train is pulling out of the platform by the time I arrive. At least I think it's the right train. There's some confusion as to which platform the Jaisalmer express is supposed to be leaving from and then, of course, there's a chance that Faizad isn't going to Jaisalmer, or that he caught an earlier train.

For a few seconds I just stand there watching it leave. Polluted light filters smokily through filthy, thick Victorian glass archways above the station. Coir bundles pile up against themselves in the middle of the platform. Old men with metal trays and copper kettles hanging from their arms screech, *"Chai, chai,"* around the barred windows on the train. There are one or two outstretched hands exchanging coins for clay cups and other things.

Time is running out. I can't afford to make the wrong choice. It's pointless to ask anyone else. I know that in a tight situation, when they can see that you are desperate, getting advice from an Indian is utterly untrustworthy. Especially when you're white.

I suddenly have a brilliant idea. I sprint through the straggling crowds and last-minute merchants, with all the weaving skills of a Formula One racer, and leap onto the train. I scan the inside corridor but can't find what I'm looking for. I squeeze and excuse-me through one of the carriages. The train is picking up speed. I suddenly find the emergency cord, a thick red chain.

I yank it, bracing myself for the scream of the wheels and the sudden lurch forward. Nothing happens. The platform tapers away outside. I look at my hand, holding the red chain and the two frazzled pieces of string hanging off from either side. I notice two women looking up at me.

"Fuck." Train tracks dance and weave in ever decreasing patterns outside. Wind starts rushing through the carriage. Dusty, dirty caged fans start whirring.

"Nice try, Josh." I spin round. It's Faizad. For a second I think he's going to come at me and I find myself backing up against the inside of the carriage. "Why are you following me?"

"What?" I stammer. Faizad stares at me with the same shark eyes he had that time we met in the Taj. I find myself staring back, trying to see if he's a murderer, as if his face might say it. "I wasn't . . . I just . . ."

"DON'T FUCK WITH ME, JOSH!" The two women beside us jump a little and then I notice hundreds of black-lined eyes flashing and realize that we are in the Ladies Only compartment. I see Faizad notice them too. He gathers himself and hisses at me. "What are you? Was Ajay right? Are you really Interpol?"

"What? No, of course not."

"Then why the fuck are you following me? How did you find me?"

I try to change the subject. "Did you kill Ajay?"

Faizad sneers, "Fuck you."

"The police think you did."

"No shit."

"Why are you running if you didn't do it?"

"Why do you think?"

"I don't know."

"How did you find out about Ajay?"

My mind spins. I don't know what he's asking me. Is this a test? I have to bluff. "On the news, how do you think?"

"So then you'll know. The police have already told people that I'm a suspect."

"But if you didn't do it—"

"Oh, for God sakes, Josh, suspicion is guilt in this country. Haven't you figured that out yet?"

I don't say anything. So many questions, I've got frequency jam in my head. Just choose one, any one, I tell myself. "What happened that time, you know in Benson's, after I ran?"

"You mean after you abandoned me."

"Because you told me to run. He had a gun."

"Tell me about it. I'm fucking lucky he didn't kill me. He was completely off his head."

"What happened? Did you shoot him? Was it an accident? If it was an accident, the police will understand. Just explain. I'll back you up."

"No, I didn't shoot him. The gun just went off. The bullet hit the wall. It was fine."

"So what happened?"

"I don't know. After he saw you running out of the apartment, he calmed down. I think the shot helped, shocked him out of it. Ayesha helped as well. He was fine by the time I left his place."

"So who—"

"I don't know!" Faizad snaps at me. "I don't know who killed him. All I know is, it wasn't me. For a while, I thought it might have been you. I mean, where have you been the past week? Why haven't you contacted me?"

"I was scared. I thought you were dead."

"Jesus, what a fuckup," he says, shaking his head and looking out through the window. The sun catches his features and makes cubist shadows on his face.

"So what's next?"

"What do you think? Get the fuck out of town, that's what's next. I'm not sticking around to take the fall. I know when I'm being set up."

"Set up? Who's setting you up?"

"Dowdy. Mehmet. I don't know. Dowdy, probably. Maybe Mehmet set it up with Dowdy. Who knows? Doesn't matter much anyway. It all leads to the same place. I have to get out of Mumbai." There's a pause. "Come with me," he says then, suddenly looking at me. "Come with me to Jaisalmer."

There they are. The words I've been waiting for. All this time.

"I can't."

"Why not?"

Why not? Simple. I don't have any fake money, there's no fake diamonds, no Yasmin, no gem expert, no nothing. I've done everything to get the sting set up, and as soon as it's ready, I suddenly find that I'm not.

"I just can't . . ." I run through excuses in my mind and manage to cover a lot of distance before realizing that actually I don't have any. Not any I can use in any case.

"Josh, don't be stupid. The police are after you too, you know that? And if they catch you, it'll be bad."

"They won't catch me. I know where to hide."

The train lurches slightly as it slows up for the first of a series of local stops before hitting the express track. We both sneak a look outside the barred window and squint into the wind. I have to make a decision. I don't want to let this opportunity slip. If I let Faizad go now, I may never see him again. On the other hand, there isn't much point traveling to Jaisalmer empty-handed. After all, I've no idea how much Faizad might pay me—if at all—for joining him. The switch is still my best option for making big money.

The noise of the crowd sweeps down from the end of the carriage in a wave and then the platform filled with people blooms into view. The train lurches two more times and then stops. Faizad looks at me. I look back at him. Fuck it, I think to myself. Just go with him. Forget the switches. Forget the fake money. Forget Yasmin. Just go with Faizad. Trust him, like he trusts you. He's your only hope now.

A man in a thick blue jacket suddenly pokes a mustache through one of the bars beside us and starts shouting in Hindi. There's a woman in a purple sari behind him, three thick rolls of fat leaking at the seams along her midriff.

"What's he saying?"

"It's the stationmaster," Faizad says. I notice the brass buckles glint. "He wants to know what we are doing in the ladies' compartment." A hand enters through the bars, pointing and waving toward the end of the compartment. "That lady complained. He wants to see our tickets." She starts flapping her hand at us now, like a naked puppet. He's Punch and she's Judy.

Suddenly all the eyes that have been watching us look hostile. Each end of the compartment is flooded with limbs and bundles and yelling. There's nowhere to hide. We can see the conductor signaling a pair of policemen at the back of the platform crowd.

"Fuck," Faizad says. "Cops."

"I don't have a ticket."

"Really?"

I nod my head in reply.

"Shit." Faizad sighs. Then he looks at me, his eyebrows curling up, resigned. "Shit."

"I guess this is the end of the line," I say cheesily as the conductor starts to meet us at the door.

"Ticket, ticket!" the conductor barks. Faizad hands him his. The policemen are caught in the crush, halfway along the platform. The fat lady stares at me. I squeeze my way past her without waiting for the conductor to stop me, off the train and into the thickest part of the crowd I can find, away from the police.

"Meet me there," Faizad calls behind me.

I turn to answer. The crowd is consuming me. "Wait for me," I call back, but the conductor is blocking the view. I can see the policemen turning their heads, looking for me. I let the people digest me, heading for the station exit. I take one last look before I leave to see if Faizad can see me, if he heard me ask him to wait.

But all I can see is the fat lady wobbling angrily in the doorway as the train slowly starts to pull away.

PART THREE

REUNITED

Yasmin is back. She is standing in the doorway, looking at me. She looks different, more homely. A long dark blue dress and a tank top soften all the sexy edges she used to show off during our days in Delhi. Maybe it's because she just got off the plane. Had to dress sanely for customs. Or maybe it's for me—a sign that the madness is over. No more sexy chicks and crazy missions. I don't know. It could just be Sanjay's lecture still ringing in my ears. He hasn't stopped since I got here. A small part of me wonders why I came. I think it has something to do with my own perverted sense of fate.

It was only after fifteen minutes of fighting my way through the crowd that I realized the train had stopped at Charni Road, not far from Sanjay's place. It just made sense, I guess. I could have gone back to the Caged City, but the hijras probably wouldn't have put me up. After all, I had run out of money. And smack. And besides, the brown-haired boy knows I stayed there. I couldn't be sure he wouldn't grass me up to the pigs. And the Shiv Niketan was out of the question. I couldn't face Sam—not now, not ever.

Thankfully it was Sanjay who answered the bell, not his mum. When he opened the door he hugged me. Can't say I wasn't surprised. After all the chilly receptions he's been serving . . . Anyway, it felt good. Warm. A bit like coming home after a long, lonely time away. I felt as if he was forgiving me. Or saying he'd never really been upset with me. It had just been an act—to jolt me out of my behavior. It was as if he was saying we were friends again. Always had been. Always would be. I felt ashamed then, of everything. Felt I should say sorry. And I did. I whispered it in his ear. He said it was okay. Everything would be okay.

Then he started in on the lecture.

Of course the police had been around. Everyone has been looking for me. Where have I been? Now that was a good question. I generally avoided the interrogation. No sense in complicating matters with a complete confession. He didn't need to know the Truth, the whole Truth, and nothing but. He just needed to know that I was back, that I wasn't selling coke in the Cellar anymore, that I realized things had somehow gotten a little out of hand. And that I was sorry. Of course I was sorry.

He seemed to need to hear that more than once.

He told me about Yasmin. She'd just called from the airport, five minutes before I arrived. Weird, huh? Apparently, they'd last spoken two days ago. She rang out of the blue, asking for me. Said she hadn't heard from me in weeks. So Sanjay told her about me, the Cellar, the drugs, my disappearing act—all of it.

And that's why she decided to fly over. She was worried. Seems I have some friends after all. Funny. Didn't think anyone loved me. After all this time feeling alone, it's a warm feeling, friendship, affection. Even Sanjay's pedantry is charming, in its own, smothering mothering way.

Sanjay has just started saying something about how, now, all this really had to end when the doorbell rings.

His face somehow manages to say, "Saved by the bell" and "That's her" and "I'll get it," all in one expression. I follow him into the corridor. He opens the door. Then I see her, standing there like that, softly recognizable.

It's hard to read her face. For a second it's as if she doesn't know me. I can vaguely sense Sanjay looking between us, wondering if he should be breaking the tension. I don't let him. I want to be the one to announce myself, confirm that, yes, I really am here, alive, in front of her, after all these weeks.

"Hi," I begin.

She runs at me in three steps and throws her arms around me and kisses me half on the lips and hugs.

I watch Sanjay watching us, gauging his face for a reaction as she presses into me. He'd almost look happy if his eyes weren't so worried.

I have to admit, I'm not totally sold either. I try to fall into Yasmin's embrace, but something holds me back. You've been waiting for this moment for weeks, I try to tell myself. Let it be pure. I close my eyes but it doesn't help. Something's throwing me. I don't know what. I try to blame Sanjay. I can still feel him, on the other side of my eyelids, looking away now but still looking. But I know it's not him. It's something else.

Yasmin pulls back, her soft cheek sliding against mine, and looks at me, green eyes brilliant. Her face is miming emotion at me, a beautiful, beaming smile, fixed across her face like a ventriloquist's. "I love you," I can almost hear her saying, even though her lips aren't moving. "I love you, Josh."

I smile back at her, a smile that says nothing, a PR smile. Morag taught me how to do those.

Then Sanjay coughs and Yasmin half turns to face him, facing both of us, really.

"Happy to be back?" Sanjay asks.

"Hmmmm," Yasmin says, lips pursed. "Very," she says, beckoning him over with an outstretched arm. Sanjay moves toward us, into her hold. She slides her arm around his waist and kisses him on the cheek. "Very happy indeed."

GOOD SKILLS

Eventually, she draws me out. I don't know how. It's a talent. She sort of makes me feel that she's there, ready and waiting, with hugs and love and kisses—if I want them. But she doesn't paw. She doesn't beg. She doesn't ask what's wrong. She just waits. Waits for me to come around, like I'm a child who'll soon get bored of sulking. I don't know how she does it. I guess she's just stronger than me.

It happens while we're walking. Sanjay says we should get out of the flat for a few hours, just while he warms his mum up, tells her we're here to stay the night, and that we need her help. He says we can trust her. After all, she's known me since I was a kid.

We walk all the way to Mahalaxmi. The tide is coming in, cutting the Haji Ali mosque off from the rest of the world. Guys with beards shuffle along the rocky pier, the sea lapping at their feet. When the light catches it just right, it looks like they're walking on water. Walking on water on their way from heaven back down to earth.

I'm reaching the bit where I had to start teaching English to the street kids to pay the rent, leading up to my two-tone life—the one where I was going to all those flash parties with Faizad and starving in Byculla. It sounds a bit like a fairy tale in the retelling, like I'm Cinderella or something, having to get home before it all turns to pumpkins.

Yasmin doesn't say anything the whole time. She just listens.

"It was just after I got your letter," I say, to really drive home the point that she's partly responsible for my worsening condition in the tale, give it some relevance, to help her navigate her way through the events so she finds her part, understands the role she played in my disaster. After all, that's why I've been holding back. I've decided that I'm angry with her. And I want her to know it. I want her to explain why she abandoned me. Why didn't she send me any money when I asked, practically begged her, in all those letters I wrote? She could have at least written to me more often. She knew how lonely I was feeling.

"Which one?"

"There was only one," I say, in a "nice try" sort of way.

"You don't believe me."

"What's to believe? I only got one letter from you. I wrote to you every week. I told you I needed money. You never sent me anything."

"When was the last time you checked?"

I don't say anything. Now that I come to think of it, it has been a while. "So you're saying you did send me money?"

"Which letter did you get? What was the date?"

"October something." I know it's eleven, but I don't let on. Wouldn't want her to know that I've read it a thousand times, memorized every word.

"I put a hundred dollars in that letter. In fact, I put money in practically every letter I wrote. I also wrote you several letters telling you what an ungrateful shit you were for never even saying thank you. I've spent the last three months slaving it in a dive bar and sending you half my pay. After a while I figured the postman was stealing the money, so I wired it instead. I sent you three letters telling you to go to American Express. Don't tell me I never tried to help."

I don't say anything. I have to admit that I don't want to believe her. It would be easier to stick with my own version of reality, stay angry with her, make out that she was the one who abandoned me. Anything's better than admitting to myself that I've been a fool, that there's been money for me, all this time, after everything I've been through. All I had to do was ring.

"Why didn't you telephone?" she asks.

"I don't know." I really don't. There were reasons—no money, no time, it never occurred to me—but none of them seem decent enough justifications now. The truth is, I chose to believe she'd abandoned me. There was something in the idea, as I sat outside the post office feeling sorry for myself, that I found appealing. It became my reality and I lived it. Telephoning her was something that never fit into that frame.

Before I know it, I'm sort of saying sorry.

"Come on, Yasmin, it wasn't my fault. I genuinely believed you'd abandoned me. How was I to know that the post office would steal all of your letters?"

I say all this wondering when I'll get a chance to slip away and check. I mean, wouldn't American Express notify her if no one went to pick up the money? I don't know. I've never been in this situation before. I don't know how far a money-wiring service extends.

"You should have trusted me. You could have telephoned."

"I do trust you. I didn't have the money to telephone."

"You don't trust me."

"I do, of course I do, why wouldn't I trust you?"

She looks out over the ocean; the breeze catches her collar. It flaps in her whispering hair. I think I can see a tear brewing, but her expression is too hard to let it happen. I can see her tensing the muscles in her jaw, full of resolve, full of independence. I wish she wouldn't be so tough. I need her to need me.

"Yasmin, please, I'm sorry. Really. I am." I put my head on her shoulder. "I need you," I whine. "I can't go on. You just don't know how hard it's been. What it's been like. The things I've done. For fuck sakes, last week I was smoking smack. I don't know who I've been half the time. I lost myself. It was all that time alone. I changed. I don't know what I turned into, but I changed. I've been so lost. Lost and very confused. I mean, Jesus . . ."

She doesn't say anything. Even after that. She doesn't seem in the least bit impressed. This girl is made of sterner stuff than I. Somehow, she's taken control of me again. She's back and I'm looking at her and now I want her.

After a while she says, "Where's Faizad?"

"Jaisalmer," I reply obediently.

"Does he trust you yet?"

"Yes. I mean, I think so. Yes, he trusts me."

"Well, what are we waiting for, then?"

"What? You mean we should follow him?"

"Of course. What's all this been about?"

"Did you bring the money?"

"Hmm-mm."

"And the stones?"

"Yup."

"Wow. I didn't think, I mean I thought . . ." I want to say, "I thought you only came over to see if I was all right," but I resist. It would sound selfish and probably like I'm still having problems trusting her, insofar as I'm questioning her motives. "How did you do it?" I manage instead. "How did you get it all past customs?"

"I've got skills."

"That's true," I say, thinking of the way she's pulled me around.

She looks at me. I look at her. She looks lovely, really beautiful. I like homely. Or rather, I like a girl who can be sexy one time, homely another—depending on the situation. I mean, sexy is good. Sexy is great. But homely—you need that if you're going to introduce a girl to your mother. Not that I value Mum's opinion, necessarily. I mean, why would I? We've barely spoken since she left to start "her own family." Still, that's not really the point, is it? All I know is, I wouldn't even dream of introducing Ayesha to my mum. I could never handle those raised eyebrows. No way. But Yasmin. She can play it. She'd sweet her—no sweat.

"There's just one thing, Josh."

"What?"

"If we do this, you have to trust me. Do you understand?"

"I do trust you . . . it wasn't because of—"

"Sssssshhhhh," she says, putting a finger gently to my lips. "It's okay. I understand. But from now on, it's important, all right?"

I nod back at her. And that's when I decide. I'll never doubt Yasmin again. I won't even check up on her. I won't go to American Express. She's right. We have to trust each other. I want her back in my life. The past doesn't matter. The only thing that counts is the Now. I mean, she's here, isn't she? She flew all the way over, just to see if I was all right. I have been an idiot.

She smiles at me and then we kiss.

MATHAR

Yasmin certainly does have skills. Somehow she's managed to pack the fake diamonds and other stones, plus the fake money, all in a false-bottomed suitcase no bigger than a carry-on.

"That's amazing," I say, looking at the meticulous arrangement.

Sanjay's still next door with his mum. She says she doesn't want to see us. As long as she hasn't seen us, she can't lie to the police. That's her reasoning. I think she's really just furious and she doesn't want to let us see it. That would be rude, or unladylike, or something. I can hear her voice bubbling through the walls like a kettle that's about to come to the boil and scream. It's endless except for the vague resonance of Sanjay's single-syllable replies.

"The nuns at school loved neat and tidy girls. I was always neat and tidy. They made me head girl, you know."

"Really? I didn't know that."

"When do we leave?" she says, changing the subject. It's not the first time she's done that—changed the subject as soon as we get on to her past. It's like she lets these little nuggets slip out, then she quickly burrows them away again, as if she's hiding a vast treasure trove that she wants all for herself. She's been very evasive whenever I've pressed for details in Delhi. I guess she just doesn't like to talk about herself very much. I don't push it. I want us to carry on being friends.

"Tomorrow. There's a train in the morning. It's almost non-stop."

"How long will it take?"

"Twenty-four hours, not much more."

"A marathon train journey." Yasmin sighs. "Just what we need."

"All you've got to do is sleep. You must be exhausted, after the flight."

"Not really. I slept most of the way. I just want a shower."

"You should wait until Sanjay's mum has chilled. Sounds like she's still giving him a hard time."

"Why don't we just go somewhere else? A hotel?"

"A hotel will just mean passports and all that other stuff. It's too risky. We're safe here. It's only one night. Then we'll be gone."

"Will Sanjay be coming?"

I pause. "I don't know. I don't think so."

"Why? Did something happen between you two while I was gone?"

"I thought he told you all that, on the phone."

"He didn't say anything."

"Hmm." I pause for a second. Not like Sanjay to be so private, I think to myself. I wonder why he hasn't shared all our problems with Yasmin. I mean, I appreciate his tact, but what's he got to hide? "Oh, it's a long story," I stall. If he's got something to hide, then maybe I do too. Maybe I'll check with him first. "I'll tell you on the train."

"Does he want out?"

"Let's just say Sanjay would rather we were all out. He thinks this is the perfect opportunity for me to go home."

"Oh."

"I know," I say. "But let's face it, he was never that keen. I think he only helped because he wanted to impress you."

"Impress me? What do you mean?"

I raise my eyebrows at her. "You know what I mean. It's not as if you didn't milk it," I say, managing to keep it light, not sounding too bitter.

"I don't know what you're talking about."

"Oh, come on, Yasmin. You flirted and you know it."

"I didn't," she says, smiling.

"Yes, you did," I drawl, pinching her waist, teasing.

"Ow," she smarts. I can see it tickles. "That hurts." I do it again. "Stop it," she says, mock serious, trying not to giggle. So I attack her. She writhes in my grip and then falls on the bed, screaming, laughing, punching me on the shoulders, begging me to stop. I don't. I just keep going while she squirms under me, loving it. I like this new game we're playing—like Lovers Reunited.

Sanjay floods into the room. We're making too much noise. I can feel him stop, suddenly, behind me. We freeze. "Oh my God," he stammers. I turn my head to look at him. He's staring into the suitcase, at the diamonds, at the money. His mum's face drifts in behind his shoulder.

"Oh my God," she says.

"Oh my God," Sanjay says.

"Oh my God," his mum says again.

"Wait, Mrs. Dutt, I can explain," I say, clambering off Yasmin guiltily, like we're naked or something. I feel as if I have to cover myself up.

"Sanjay!" she suddenly squawks. "Joshua cannot stay here. They have to leave. Right now." Sanjay screws up his eyes and lifts a hand to his head, as if to block out the shrill of her voice. "Do you hear me? I will not have these people in my house!" He scrunches his hair in a fist. "Sanjay! Are you listening to me? Right now, I said."

Then, slowly, Sanjay opens his eyes and looks at me. He shakes his head slightly, his hand still in his hair, now relaxing. I look at him, vaguely hoping he doesn't hit me. Then something changes; it's in his walnut eyes, a small snap. Better than that, a release. I watch Sanjay's face let it all go. I can see it now. The pressure he's been under. It's been his mother. All this time, it's been his mother. It was her that made him dump me that time in Trishna. It's been her that's been fighting to keep me out of his life. He never wanted to abandon us, abandon me. Not really. Not like that.

And he's not going to let her overpower him again. He's not going to let her betray us. He pauses briefly and then he simply says, with calm resolve, "Oh, shut up, Mother," before taking a small step into the bedroom and gently closing the door behind him.

For a few seconds, we all listen to her screaming through the door, all pretense of ladylike behavior and English manners shot.

"I don't deserve . . . how can you . . . in my own home . . . after everything I've done . . ."

Eventually, he smiles at us. "Don't worry," he says with all the balance of a Buddha. "After a while, it just becomes background noise." Then, before we have a chance to ask him if he's sure he wants to do this, he claps his hands together, looks at the fake money, and says, "So, then. What's the plan?"

BRAIN WAVE

The general strike is consummate. All forms of public transport across the state cease. Something to do with wage revision and working conditions. I notice that the train conductors are asking for more money to pay for their uniforms. There will be a rally later in downtown Mumbai. Paramilitary police are erecting cordons across the city.

"They say it might last a week," I say, pulling down the morning paper to look at Sanjay and Yasmin.

"A week?" Yasmin asks.

"Maybe longer," I add calmly, like a doctor offering a grim prognosis. It's the cybercafé we're sitting in that's making me so detached. It's a different universe. Cappuccinos and café lattes, neon signs and mirrored metal surfaces, girls in miniskirts and guys in Levi's. A workers' union transport strike seems light-years away from where we are. Perhaps it just hasn't sunk in.

Sanjay looks depressed. It's taken him this long to come around to the whole idea, and now that he has, it seems he has to turn back. It is typical. I can see that he's dreading having to face his mother. It'll be like she's won now. Another moral victory for her to claim. Another vindication for her to use against him as leverage. Just so she can get him to do what she wants.

The worst part is that this isn't a victory for her at all. For the

PAPERBACK ORIGINAL **273**

first time, perhaps in his entire life, it was Sanjay who won. He made a stand. But he'll never tell her that. He played his ace and life just trumped him. It'll be too complicated to explain why he's returning to her. It'll just be easier to let her think she's won, to slip back into their old dynamic. She wouldn't understand even if he tried to explain. I feel sorry for him. I wish he could just stand up for himself without having to use us as his crutch. But I know he can't. His mum's too strong for him. She always wins.

"Sometimes life's easier when there aren't any choices," I say to him, for him, smiling.

He snorts gently at me.

"And there's no other way we can reach Jaisalmer?" Yasmin presses.

"The nearest airport is Jaipur and most of the flights will already be booked," Sanjay says sadly. Then, as if to confirm the hopelessness of the situation, he starts retroactively analyzing it, like it's a done deal. "We must be the last people in India to have heard about this strike."

I'm worried about Sanjay. For some reason, his situation seems worse than anyone's. "The station was like something out of *The Twilight Zone*," I say in sympathy.

"Well, that's that, then, is it?" Yasmin sighs, exasperated. She's finding it hard to believe that we're giving up so easily. But what else is there to do?

"That's that," Sanjay and I say together.

We all look at one another.

"We could hire a taxi," Yasmin offers.

"The roads will be packed," Sanjay says.

More silence.

"We just let Faizad slip away," Yasmin snaps with too much

irritation. I can't help feeling that she's directing it at me. It's not my fault.

None of us says anything. I rest my head against the coffee-tinted windows and look wistfully at the traffic outside. Then, for some reason, I let myself believe it's my fault. Self-pity seems like the only irresponsible option now. The window starts vibrating against my temples. Good. More pain for the headache I'm starting to feel. An Enfield streaks past, inside-taking all the traffic with precise daring.

"Faizad's Enfield," I say without thinking, my head still leaning against the window, my mind on automatic processing.

"What?" Yasmin says. Sanjay looks at me. He heard.

"Faizad's got a motorbike—an Enfield," I say, straightening up. "We could use that to get to Jaisalmer."

"What about the keys?" Sanjay scuppers.

"He keeps them under the mudguard."

THE SHORT STRAW

It takes Sanjay ten minutes to start the bike. He says he knows what he's doing and he keeps commenting on the amperes and the compression and generally bitching as he builds up more and more of a sweat. Yasmin and I keep looking at each other. We know that we are the only ones who can go. Sanjay keeps muttering to himself and I can't help feeling that he's justifying his own usefulness. A large cloud of black smoke and an unhappy roar bring the bike to life.

"There," Sanjay says, grinning and revving. "Told you I could get her going."

"Well done," Yasmin says, rubbing Sanjay's shoulder.

"Phew! It's hard work, though." Sanjay smiles. "You really have to know how to operate these babies."

"I think I can handle her," I presume.

Sanjay looks at me. "Have you ever ridden an Enfield before, Josh?"

"No, but I used to race bikes when I was a kid."

Sanjay snorts. "I'm afraid an Enfield is a little different from an 80cc Honda."

"Well, do you think *you* should drive it to Jaisalmer?" I cut to the chase.

"Maybe," Sanjay tries.

"Oh, come on, Sanj. You know it's got be Yasmin and me who go."

"Why?"

"You know why. And besides, I don't know why you're so keen to go chasing after Faizad all of a sudden. This time yesterday you wanted to call the whole thing off."

"No, I didn't."

"Yes, you did."

I notice that Sanjay keeps revving the engine each time I answer.

"All right, you two," Yasmin intercedes. "We choose short straws to see who goes."

"What?" I say. "No."

"It's the only fair way," she says.

I know that I am going to lose.

I do.

Sanjay looks at his straw and then at me.

"It's okay, Josh, you go. You're right, it should be you and Yasmin."

"Are you sure?"

I feel bad then. I've been harsh. This is even worse for Sanjay than before. Now the plan's back on and he *still* has to return home to his dragon-lady mother. Double jeopardy. I've only been so insistent because he was annoying me with his presumptuous attempt to remain in the game. But now that he's let it go, I feel doubly bad, triply bad.

"Yeah," he says softly. "I mean, it's you who Faizad trusts, isn't it? And Yasmin is the diamond expert. Not much point me going. I just didn't like the idea of being left behind, that's all."

I try to sound upbeat, no point indulging in his situation for him. There's the larger cause to worry about now. "We'll be back before you know it—celebrating," I say, smiling at him.

"You better be," he says, graciously accepting his own sacrifice. "Mum's going to drive me crazy. You have to rescue me before I'm institutionalized."

"We will. Now show me how to operate this thing."

Sanjay is right, the Enfield is completely different from any bike I have ridden before. The gears are back to front and on the wrong side. The mechanics are super-delicate and the bike weighs a ton.

"The main thing, of course, is not to skid," Sanjay warns. "You won't feel the weight once you pick up speed, but if you slide on one of these things, the tarmac will rip all the flesh off your leg in seconds."

Yasmin cringes and crosses her arms defensively against her chest. "Nice."

"How do we stop ourselves from skidding?" I ask.

"Simple. Don't do it. Don't ever travel at night; other drivers won't see you. Use your horn all the time. If you see a truck overtaking from the other way, get off the road. It'll just mow you down."

"Anything else I should know?"

"Yeah," Sanjay says, "it's going to be hot. Try and cover as much distance as possible at dawn and dusk when it's cooler and the roads are empty."

"How far do you reckon it is?"

"At least a thousand clicks. You want to average two hundred a day, otherwise you'll miss him."

"Let's pray he hasn't already done the deal by the time we get there," Yasmin says.

"I doubt it," I say. "There's a strong chance his journey got delayed because of the strike as well. Who knows? We might even overtake him."

"I wouldn't count on it," Sanjay says.

"Well, the sooner we get going the better," I conclude.

I practice briefly in the road outside Faizad's flat before deciding, a little too quickly, that I'm ready. Yasmin climbs on and we agree to meet Sanjay back at his place, which is only walking distance away, to pack, have lunch, and go. Somehow I manage to wobble our way there.

"Are you sure that you are up to this?" Yasmin checks, pale-faced, once we arrive. Sanjay is already there waiting for us when we pull up.

"It'll be fine," I say without looking at her.

Two hours later and we are on our way. Sanjay squeezes me very tightly when I say good-bye to him and shouts something just as we are leaving, but neither of us hears what he says and turning around seems too difficult.

The five-minute ride down Malabar Hill, past Breach Candy, Haji Ali mosque, and Mahalaxmi racecourse is easy and thrilling. On the road, skirting the ocean, sailing past the traffic, the wind in our hair—I can't stop singing the bass line to "Born to Be Wild." Yasmin warns me to concentrate, but I can already feel myself getting used to the bike. It's pure testosterone.

But by the time we hit Worli, the road turns inland and the traffic becomes harder to negotiate. Exhaust is everywhere. Engine heat bubbles like thick soup. There are several instances when I forget which side the brake is on and we nearly collide into the back of something. Five hours, thirty kilometers, twelve wrong turns, fifteen stops for directions, and a few frighteners later, the reality of the task ahead of us starts to dawn.

We eventually stop in a lonely fluorescent-lit hotel on the side of the road just beyond Dahisar. The room is less than basic. The bed doesn't have sheets and very large cockroaches mill around a drain in the bathroom and fill the broken sink. The light doesn't work, so we have to wash by flashlight. The dirt doesn't really come out anyway. It just sits ingrained in the skin like instant tan. Yasmin's hair sticks together in a stodgy wave. We don't say much to each other. We both know that we are the ones who have drawn the short straw. All we want to do now is get something to eat and go to bed. We are asleep in each other's arms by nine.

SECOND BEST

It doesn't matter that I only went to the toilet five minutes ago. I need to go again by the time I reach the starters' lineup. It's too late to go again. The only consolation is that in one more minute I know I won't be thinking about it anymore.

I jiggle and rock the bike, which is too tall for me, on the tips of my toes until I am in position, the front wheel just sticking out under the wire. The boy on my left has one of those helmets that wrap around the face and cover the mouth. I want one of those. They look really cool. I've just got a round one with a small visor buckled to the top. My goggles have a plastic face mask attached, but it's not the same. Daddy says he'll buy me a new helmet if I win this race. We both know I won't. Everyone knows that the winner will either be Jason O'Connor or Nick Reynolds. They always come first and second. Yamaha and Kawasaki sponsor them. The best I've ever come is eighth and that was because twelve racers got caught in a pileup on the first corner. Dad keeps telling me: "The first to the first corner wins the race. That's how Jason and Nick do it. They are always the first out of the first corner."

I can see him now, standing at the edge of the lineup. He's sticking his elbows out and poking his head forward. He's re-minding me to lean over my gas tank. It's an easy mistake. At least five racers will wheelie and flip out of the competition once the wire flies. I've done it several times myself. One time I even managed a full back somersault. Everyone thought I'd broken my neck, but Dad says I'm a tough one.

The clock is going now. There are different types of starters' orders. Sometimes there are flags, sometimes there are three lights. I like the clock best. You can see the "off" coming. The first thirty-five seconds is just a block of green and then there's a slice of red for the last ten.

Five seconds gone now and everyone is revving their engines. It starts off with short *vrmm*s—always in low-pitch pairs. *Vrmm-vrmm, vrmm-vrmm.* Then, as the clock passes fifteen seconds, they come in threes and fours, slightly faster, slightly higher.

I look to my right. Everyone is pitching over their handlebars. We look like American football players, with our shoulder pads, numbered colored shirts, and waists pulled tight in kidney belt corsets. I look to the left. I reckon that I'm roughly in the middle. I focus on the corner ahead. It's a hundred-meter dash before thirty of us have to squeeze our way through a tiny right angle.

"Don't forget to stick your leg out to ease your way through the turn," I can hear Dad saying. "Don't be scared."

"I won't be, Dad. I'll come first this time. Then will you buy me a new helmet?"

Twenty-five seconds now and the revving is getting faster and higher. The synchronization is lost and the *vrmm*s are everywhere, buzzing louder and more insistently. I look at the wire. It's shaking as bikers start letting out their clutches slightly. Front wheels brush up against it, pushing it, testing the barrier, ready to go.

Thirty seconds pass. The *vrrm*s fill the air like machine-gun fire, more staccato, faster. Left, right, the *vrmm*s are everywhere, faster and faster as the seconds build. White smoke melts into one long cloud behind us. The gas smells.

Thirty-five seconds and the frenetic *vrrm*s slip into one long scream, whistling through my helmet, into my ear, and piercing my brain like feedback. I hold my accelerator at three-quarters and shift forward on my tank another inch, my toes barely reaching the ground. I keep one eye on the wire, one eye on the clock. Forty seconds. The scream of the engines is constant. I edge out my clutch to biting point, the bike pulling underneath me like an eager dog on a leash. Forty-three, forty-four, don't flip, don't flip, don't . . . forrrrrttttteeee fi—

SNAP!

The steel wire whistles as it springs into the air and the *vrrm*s step up an impossible pitch as the front wheels bounce and the bikes hurl us forward into the mud and smoke and chaos. I think I notice the boy with the cool helmet flip, but I'm too busy trying to control the back wheel as it slips and kicks in the dirt and the ruts. I pull into control with an extra jerk on the accelerator and count the meters with the beat of my heart. Bikers veer in on me from all sides and it's hard to keep a straight line. I can see the rut on the first corner rising up out of the earth like a tidal wave. Don't forget to stick your foot out, Josh, don't forget, you have to surf it, surf it.

There's a yellow blur on my left and then a green one pressing in on my right. I can see it's a Kawasaki; it might be Nick Reynolds. I know that I'm in the front pack and that I had a good start. I could even be in the front five. The rut looms in front of us as we eat the meters, the chains chewing and spraying mud high into the air. I can see now—it is Reynolds! He suddenly veers in close enough for me to touch him and there are two bikes on my inside.

The corner sharpens the closer we get, but we hurtle toward it with suicide blood in our veins.

I can feel the air turning cold against the sweat on my face and then, before I know it, the corner is upon us. Reynolds quickly cuts a collision course for my front wheel and catches my mudguard. I feel my elbow give and the handlebar wobbles in the slick. Reynolds pushes his leg out and stakes his claim, inches in front of my wheel. I can see the grid on my tire snatch and growl at his thigh. We pile into the turn and my brain starts screaming.

"We're going too fast, we're going too fast, we're . . ." But I hold my wrist firm. "We have to brake, we have to brake . . . no, no . . . brake, brake now . . . no, no, nooOOOOWWWW!"

I haul in the clutch and stamp down on the back brake. My back wheel slips out under me before I regain control with a yank on the front brake. My body lurches forward and I let Reynolds pass. Then, as the corner catches me, I quickly remember to stick my leg out, but it's too late. I ride the rut high and it throws me down into the wash violently, forcing my bike to jump and then crash onto my foot. I can feel my ankle twist and churn between the wheels and the rocks and the hard inside wall of the turn. I know it's bad. The tears flush to my eyes.

But then, before I know it, I am out of the corner. And then I see. I am second. I am second, I am second. For the first time in my life I am second. Better than O'Connor, better than everyone—except madman Reynolds.

I keep racing.

With Reynolds just one wheel ahead, I sprint toward the first jump, a nice, high-flying three-quarter-size jump. Big build, steep drop, high air—great for looking good on. All I have to do now is not lean too far forward. If I go over the handlebars, the crash will be the last of my problems. I once saw a lead racer get crushed after he burned on a jump with the pack behind him. They tried to stop the race and the wardens tried to pull him off the track, but it was impossible. They just kept coming—one after the other, flying through the air and pounding on top of him. You could see the horror in the racers' eyes as they flew. The boy's body lying mangled and in their inevitable path, the parents screaming as his limbs flipped and twisted under each ripping wheel and sawing chain. He was dead before they even reached the hospital.

I pull on the accelerator full throttle as the mud lump looms. I feel myself rising up the ramp, good speed, the fronts of other tires tugging at the farthest back corners of my eyes. I climb and then see Reynolds sail, taking off high into the air and squatting tall on his foot pedals ready for the fall. He looks like a hero.

And then I'm in the air behind him and everything falls suddenly quiet. The air stops rushing and the scream of the bikes seems to float into the far distance as I soar over the crowd below. I feel in complete control. I appreciate the scenery. Everyone is looking at me. Perfectly balanced, perfectly serene—I am flying.

Before long, the ground starts to swell below me and I feel the gravity take hold. I squat and bend my knees, ready for the fall, and it's then, in the instant before I land, that I realize how stupid I have been. In that single moment when all the laws of time are betrayed, I can see what is happening before it actually occurs. My injured foot won't be able to take the landing.

But it's too late. My back wheel makes contact and throws the bike flat with a crash. The pain in my foot sears through my leg like a telegram, informing the rest of my body to crumble. I don't scream but I whimper. The pain flashes in front of me, blurred by a rush of tears. My lower lip quivers fatly. I slump into my seat and watch as my wrist limps involuntarily. Momentum peels off as the mud claws at the wheels. Five racers shoot past. Somehow

I manage to stop the throttle from falling away completely and limp my way to the next corner. The racers rush past in a stream of color. Reynolds is long gone.

By the time I approach the third corner I am last, barely holding myself above the handlebars as the pain in my ankle twists my stomach and makes every limb ache and burn. A warden waves an orange flag at me, telling me to stop, but I ignore him, determined to finish the race in which, once, for a few seconds, I was second just behind Nick Madman Reynolds. I can see spectators looking at me with creased brows and worried parental eyes.

I crawl up the main steep hill, each rock and bump thumping the spot with sadistic precision, and before I even reach the cusp, Reynolds laps me. Thoroughly demoralized as he disappears over the top, I can't stop the tears flowing. I want to quit then. I snail my way over the hill and am about to pull over when O'Connor cruises by and waves a karate-chop hand at me, impatiently signaling me to bow out. He's accusing me of blocking the race. Fuck you, I think. Fuck you, fuck you, fuck you. If I hadn't hurt myself I'd be beating you now, you fucker, and you know it.

My spine stiffens and I squeeze the pain with gritted teeth and sneering features into a little ball. I pull on the throttle and start accelerating down the hill, holding back the gap between O'Connor and me. I make the next corner, but after that there is another jump and my heart sinks. I can't bear to land on another jump. I let the throttle slip and watch as O'Connor zips away. As I gently creep my way over the mound, three more racers pass.

Eventually I complete the first lap, and as I approach the jump that destroyed me, I can see Reynolds on the sidelines, still sitting on his bike, shaking his long brown hair in the sun and guzzling victoriously from a bottle of water. I press on.

By the time I reach the top of the big hill, the whole course seems empty. I've got a bird's-eye view from here and I can already see bikes lining up for the next race by the starting wire. For a brief moment, I am worried that I will be caught up in the turmoil of the next event. The wardens have stopped waving orange flags at me. I might get a warning for holding up proceedings. For the second time, I agree with myself to quit at the bottom of this hill.

But then, just as I near the base, another motorcyclist streaks past. For a minute, I think it might be the leader from the following race and I panic that I've taken too long, but then I see: it's the boy with the wraparound helmet. He must have flipped at the starters' lineup. It's taken him this long to catch me. I'm not last, I'm second last.

And I'm not going to give it up.

I watch as he pulls ahead of me and sticks his leg out in preparation for the next corner. I squeeze on the accelerator and feel the bike power me toward him. I rear up into him and grit as his back wheel spits chunks of mud and rock at me. We turn the corner and accelerate into the straight.

I manage to pull up beside him. We look at each other as the final jump rises in front of us and then power on into it at full speed. I feel the earth inflate beneath me and pray to God to help ease the pain. We climb and climb and then we are in the air, side by side, neck and neck, the fronts of our wheels vying for inches of vital space and time. I am full of fear.

There's a lull in the lift and I feel the fall spread below me. I try to crouch and press as much weight on my good leg to soften the blow, but I know it's going to be bad. In less than a second, I'm going to come crashing down and my foot will snap and it will all be for nothing. I won't be able to hold it this time, I know it, and then Mr. Wraparound will be gone into the distance and I will finish last, if I finish at all.

But then, just as we're about to land, I see his front wheel tilt dangerously forward and his head wobble as it gets pulled over the handlebars. I see him crashing, his bike standing on its front wheel for a split instant, then flashing and smashing as it flips and flies—his body thrown forward in a maze of legs and arms that keeps changing.

Before I have time to smile, the pain bolts through me as I land a split second later, slamming my ankle and then my chest as my heart heaves and stutters with the shock. I scream then, high-pitched and animal-like from an unknown, primordial place within. My body quivers and shakes, but somehow I manage to hold on to the bike until, eventually, I crawl my way past the finish line—not second, not last, but second to last.

PEOPLE ARE STRANGE

I wake up. It's dark. It must still be early. Then I remember that there aren't any windows in the room. I decide to check the time. Then I remember I pawned my watch. I start to heave myself off the bed, but Yasmin curls into me and grips. I like the way she holds on to me, tight, like she doesn't want to let me go. I let myself fall back into her. Just for a few seconds. It's been so long since anyone held me. I stroke her hair, and smell her face, a vague trace of expensive perfume still lingering but mixing wonderfully now with the smell of skin. She smells of flowery flesh. I let my hand fall down to her waist and over her hips. I'm hard but I resist pressing. I don't want to molest her. I just want to feel her. I can feel the tip of her nose in my neck, one ear snapped in half against my shoulder. I kiss her eye. She wakes up with a sudden stretch.

"Shit," she says, still holding me, pulling against me as she yawns. "What time is it?"

"Dunno. I'll find out," I say, gently extricating myself. I feel the tips of her fingers briefly resist again, still gripping, needing, holding, before eventually relenting. I act casual, like I haven't noticed, like I don't care, like this is something we do all the time. Lie in each other's arms all night and wake up together and have to get up because there's Life to get on with even though we'd both rather just spend all day in bed together. It feels good—the intimacy of our acquaintance.

I open the door. Daylight and heat pour into the room. I squint against it and feel Yasmin throwing her arm up to protect her eyes. "Fuck," I say. "We've overslept. We should have gotten going two hours ago." Yasmin is on the edge of the bed now rubbing her eyes. I scramble into my clothes. She dresses like a zombie. "Come on," I say as I throw dirty clothes into a bag, pick up the carrying case with the money and the diamonds, ready to go.

"Leave me alone," she says.

"I'll go order breakfast. Pack the rest of the stuff and meet me at the restaurant. Don't take too long."

"Fascist."

I ignore her and stride into the day, half wondering what time it is exactly.

It's 8:30 when we start riding and the road is already busy. The only consolation is that we both got a good sleep. Yasmin is a bit cheerier after boiled eggs and coffee. She rests her head on my shoulder and wraps her arms round my waist as we drive. It feels good to be moving.

An hour later and we are completely clear of the city and the suburbs. We hit National Highway 8, heading north, skirting the coast—which we can't see. The road is open and I pull on the throttle. I try and keep us between 70 and 80 kph, but it strains the bike.

I want to reach Mahuva, the first major town on our route, by the end of the day. It is in the southern tip of Gujarat, two hundred and eighty kilometers from Mumbai. It's already starting to look unlikely. The air is getting hotter and the rush of the wind offers little relief. Fields stretch out on either side of us. We pass cows and carts, thirsty streams and lonely bridges. Dust billows in behind our sunglasses and stings our eyes. Every ten minutes we drive through a roadside town. They all look the same. All the time, the sun keeps rising.

"Can we stop?" Yasmin asks after three hours on the go.

"We've got to cover as much distance as possible before it gets too hot," I shout back at her.

"My bum aches."

So does mine. The hum of the engine has become a rubbing, friction-filled rattle and the soft leather seat feels hard and unforgiving. I wonder how we will manage five days of this. I tell myself to sit up straight, to support the weight of my upper body with my back, but it's hard. I keep slouching. Never could sit up straight. Remember, I tell myself, it's all in the stomach, sitting up straight . . . it's all in the stomach.

"Next town, we'll stop for a drink."

"Thank God," Yasmin says.

I rub her thigh. "Come on, Yasmin. We've got to be tough. This is just the beginning, you know."

She doesn't say anything. I can feel her face smiling against mine, but she's probably just wincing to fend off the blast of the air. We pull over, fifteen minutes later, in a roadside town. Getting off the bike is difficult. The muscles in our legs are already stiff. Yasmin touches her toes with a gasp. When she stands up her face falls. I turn to see what she is looking at. Eyes are gathering around us. Suddenly we seem to be the only white people in the world. We're used to being stared at, but this feels more like naked hostility than simple curiosity.

"Come on," I say nonchalantly. The best thing is to stay calm. "Let's get a drink."

I take Yasmin's hand and lead her through the crowd, which parts, to the nearest shop. Bottles of fizzy orange and dark cola are stacked up in crates outside. Garishly colored packets of potato chips hang from long strings of hooks. A red-and-gold billboard announces Gold Flake cigarettes in a stately font.

"*Panee,* boss," I order as we approach the open entrance with the crowd in tow.

The thinly dressed man sitting inside shakes his head. *"Ne panee."*

"Ne panee?" I say, incredulous. He looks at me as if to say he's told me once already, he's not going to tell me again. "Shit," I say, turning to Yasmin. Our audience, which is swelling into the hundreds now, looks at me for translation. They can see that this is a bad plot development.

"Well, what do they have?"

"Gold Spot, Limca, Thumbs Up," the proprietor calls, as if he heard her.

I shrug my shoulders at Yasmin. "Just give me a Gold Spot," she says.

"Do Gold Spot," I say to the proprietor. He takes two bottles from the top crate and flicks the tops off with a bottle opener. He hands them to us, spread-eagle between his front two fingers. They are warm and sickly sweet. Yasmin pays.

"I'm sure the next town will have bottled water," I say to Yasmin, wincing on the syrup. She sits down on a nearby bench.

"Hmm," she says, staring between her feet. Most of the eyes are boring into her now and I can see that she is feeling the pressure. She keeps one arm across her chest to hide the swell of her breasts as she drinks. I try to protect her from the attention by standing in front of her, but the crowd creeps around for a view from the wings. I want to tell them to fuck off, but I know it would be useless. We're barely a hundred kilometers from Mumbai, but many of these people have never seen white skin in the flesh before. Now that we are in the countryside, a lot of these places will be exactly the same. These are the kind of villages the street kids in Mumbai run away from—nondescript, stenciled, feudal places with ancient hierarchies and satellite TV.

After a few minutes Yasmin finishes her drink and says, "Let's get out of here."

I go to start the bike. Some of the crowd follows. She waits until I have started it before climbing on behind me. Thirty seconds later we are back in the blaze, the thirst taking hold again and our rear ends seizing up on the throb of the bike. Already, it's too hot to travel.

HORN PLEASE

Eventually we find an empty field with a stream to rest in. We wheel the bike off the road and, taking the bags, find a space shaded by an old-looking tree with sparse branches and small leaves. We wet our faces and necks and rub our forearms with the water. It's cool. We resist the temptation to drink it.

"We should have brought iodine tablets," Yasmin says, lying back in the shade with one wrist on her forehead.

"Don't worry," I say, arranging a towel to lie on beside her. "They'll have bottled water at the next town. They've got to."

"Let's hope so."

It's too hot to talk. We lie there, trying to ignore the glare of the sun as it beats back the leaves and burns us. We doze. An hour later, we have to move again. The tree's shadow has shifted and we are caught in the midday fire. We wet ourselves in the stream again, soaking our clothes this time, but within ten minutes we are dry. The heat is ruthless.

"Maybe we should try driving again," I say improbably.

"Don't be ridiculous."

The heat is exhausting. We doze some more. Time melts and swells. The sun keeps rising. Stretching higher and higher in a strategic arc, aimed with the singular purpose of baking us. We pant like dogs. We doze some more.

Three hours later and the mercury drops enough for us to make a move. Before we get on the bike, Yasmin has an idea.

"Let's soak our towels in water and use them as cushions. It will cool us down."

I also dunk an old top in the stream. I wrap it over my head and we fold the towels onto the seat. As soon as we start driving, the relief is immediate. Soon we are sitting in an envelope of fresh, cool air.

"That feels so good," Yasmin says, kissing my neck. "Doesn't it?"

Three hours later and it is getting dark. The road is getting busier as the night shift takes over. The trucks are turning their lights on. They seem to be set to shine directly in our eyes. Soon it will be too dark for sunglasses, but I can't take them off. They are the only protection against the dust. I'm already half guessing the lay of the road. If we hit a pothole at this speed, it will all be over.

We've had a couple of close calls. Like Sanjay said, the trucks overtake whenever they feel like it. If something is coming the other way, which it frequently is, there are only two options. Either the truck has to pass somehow (typically by running the other vehicles off the road), or they crash. We've passed several truck skeletons, lying on the side of the road or smashed in a field next to it.

Next to overtaking blindly, the most important thing is that everyone blows their horns as much as possible. Indian truck drivers are like three-year-olds just looking for an excuse to pound the squidgy button in the middle of their steering wheel. In some ways, suicide overtaking is just another justification to go, "*Beep, beep. Beep, beep.* Look, Mummy, no hands."

And when they see us—a white guy and a white chick on an

Enfield(!)—oh boy, they can hardly contain their excitement. This is more than just an excuse to blare the horn. This is a truck driver's wet dream. We can actually see their faces lighting up when they spot us. They point and grin and start bouncing in their reinforced spring seats. If something is in their way they hurtle into our lane, their overloading truck leaning heavily in the process, and just aim. If there isn't anything to overtake they simply veer in our direction anyway, as if to say hello, until we are run off the road.

Indian truck drivers are all psychos, there's no other way to put it, except to say that they have a Neanderthal, childlike quality to their psychoness, which makes them particularly frightening. It's that combination of stupidity, naïveté, and recklessness that makes them seem so evil. Like some mutant Giant Child, tearing up skyscrapers and crushing miniature people in a terrible B movie. Not only are they dangerous, they seem totally unaware of their recklessness. In short, they should all be shot.

Barring that, the best thing is to get off the road altogether whenever we see one coming.

"We're going to have to stop," I shout back at Yasmin, turning toward her slightly. For the last two hours, she has buried her head in my back, using me as a human shield against the blinding dust. She says she doesn't want to look at the barren landscape anymore—it's depressing.

"Thank Christ." She pauses. "Where are we?"

"It's not good," I say, the wind whipping around us. "We're not even halfway to Mahuvar."

"Are we in Gujarat?"

"No."

"Where are we going to stop?"

"I don't know. Next place we see." She doesn't say anything.

We haven't seen anywhere even vaguely hospitable since we hit the highway. This isn't exactly a well-trodden tourist route. "We'll find somewhere, don't worry," I try. Neither of us is convinced.

"Hey, what was that?" Yasmin shouts suddenly.

I hit the back brake and shift down a gear. "What was what?"

"That sign, I saw a sign."

"Was it a hotel?"

"Turn around."

The sun has already set and the light is fading fast. I stagger the bike into first. We pull a U-turn. Yasmin is right. There is a sign saying HOTEL—500 METERS, with a red arrow indicating a way to a concealed exit.

"Yasmin, I love you."

I can feel her grinning with relief. We find the road, a boulevard, curving its way west, toward the sea. I don't care that we're miles behind schedule. All I want to do is get off the road, wash, eat, and sleep. We can make a fresh start in the morning.

"Let's just pray it's better than the place we stayed in last night," Yasmin says. We turn a corner and there, in the fading light, it appears out of nowhere like a dream. "Oh my God," Yasmin says.

HOTEL CALIFORNIA

On the cusp of a gentle slope, an enormous pink mansion stretches across the horizon. It is a colonial relic, built in the style of the Renaissance, with sandstone pillars, arching doorways, and a thousand windowpanes. Another sign saying HOTEL confirms our best suspicions and we turn into the gates and drive up a gravel path. Grass lawns, filled with tall trees and thick shades, curve around us. We pass an old fountain filled with green water. An angel that has lost one of its wings trumpets on top of it. The gravel crackles under the wheels of the bike. A man comes trotting out to meet us.

"Hello and welly-come," he calls, waving.

Yasmin waves back. "This is incredible," she whispers as we pull up beside him. He is dressed in a white button-down coat and black trousers.

"Welly-come, welly-come," he says as I turn the bike off. I notice that he doesn't have a mustache. He almost looks naked without it. "Welly-come to the Grand Palace Hotel. Please, come, you are most welly-come." Yasmin clambers off the bike with a groan and a beaming smile. I jump off and pull the Enfield onto its stand. The man lures us in, turning occasionally to make sure we're still behind him. "Please, please."

We walk through the arched doorway and into an enormous

corridor. The ceilings are at least twenty feet tall. There are no lights. It is cool and dark inside. Our footsteps echo and creak across floorboards.

"What is this place?" I mutter to myself.

"Please, follow me, follow me," the man calls eerily. We turn a corner and walk into a room the size of a tennis court. Except for a single desk in the middle of the floor, a blossoming crystal chandelier hanging from the ceiling, and a few sets of strategically placed candles, the room is completely empty. "Please, you must check in," he says, shuffling toward the desk, his voice reverberating along the walls.

"Excuse me, but how much are the rooms?" I say in my finest English accent. I can't help it. It's the imperial ambience.

"Fifty rupees only!" the man calls ecstatically.

Yasmin and I look at each other. There has to be a catch. "Fifty rupees?" I say, squinting at him. "Why so little?"

"Special offer," the man says, clicking his fingers. "One time only!"

"Maybe it's haunted," Yasmin says.

"Would you care?"

"No."

The man has already shuffled his way behind the desk and is holding out a blue ballpoint for me to take. I notice that the guest book is empty. "Are we your first guests?" I ask.

"Yes, sir. My very first guests."

"You are alone here?" Yasmin asks.

"Yes, maddhum, all alone."

I print out my address.

"But do not worry," he adds quickly, "I will look after you very well. Anything you need."

"All I want is somewhere to wash," Yasmin says.

"Yes, yes. No problem. Please, I will show you to your room."

We follow him up a curving flight of stairs and down a very dark corridor to our bedroom. There is a four-poster double bed filled with pillows, a chaise longue covered in purple velvet, and a tall dressing table with an oval-shaped swivel mirror and a marble top. As the man shows Yasmin the en suite bathroom, I bounce on the bed. I have a feeling I am going to sleep very well. Yasmin comes out smiling.

"They have a bath," she says.

"This place is unbelievable."

"I know, isn't it?"

"I will bring you hot water. Dinner will be served in one hour," the man announces as he leaves. I follow him to get the bags.

By the time I get back, Yasmin is naked, her trousers and top crumpled and shapeless in a pile next to her feet. She looks at me before walking into the bathroom. I follow her. Inside, candles burn on white tiles and chipped shelves. The sound of water fills the room. A lead-framed window is open. Outside it is already very dark. An oval bath stands on four claws in the middle of the floor. Steam dances in circles. Yasmin points one foot into the bath and immediately steps in, seamlessly sinking down into the water. Her dark hair folds in on itself as she rests her head back, the end of the bath curving like a white thigh under her neck.

"This," she states to herself, "is my idea of heaven." She closes her eyes. I stand there, leaning against the sink, looking at her. She opens her eyes and reaches for a towel. She rubs her left breast and under her arm. "I haven't had a bath in . . . I don't know how long," she says, looking into the water. She sinks back down again. The top of her brow glistens slightly with the steam and the beginnings of sweat. "Aren't you coming in?" she asks with her eyes closed.

I undress.

She smiles at me as I step in, sliding up slightly to make room. The water burns at first. I gasp. She pulls me back against her. I can feel her breasts, slippery and soft, flatten against my back. She scoops water onto my chest and rubs my stomach. We lie there in silence. The trees rustle outside. The occasional breeze billows in, challenging the candles. They sweat wax in patterns. We lie there like that for a long time, letting the water prune us. There doesn't seem to be anything to say. I want to tell Yasmin that I love her. But I don't.

HAUNTED

Later, our skin humming with cleanliness, Yasmin and I are seated at a long table in another enormous candlelit room. There are frescoes on the wall. It's hard to see what they depict in the gloom. There are tall French windows opening out onto a terrace at the back of the estate. Yasmin is wearing a cream dress with golden borders. Her hair, which she washed three times, is still wet. She has it sleeked back.

The man serves us ladyfingers with dal and rice. His name is Ram. He tells us the room we are eating in used to be a ballroom. There were many balls here once, when the state prince still lived here. He points to a small alcove overlooking the floor.

"That is where the prince used to sit," he says. "Choosing the people from the crowd he wished to entertain him."

But those times ended long ago, he explains. The estate has been in steady decline for the last thirty years. Ram is the only servant left. The princely heir, who lives in London, tried to sell the house to a hotel company but failed. That is where Ram got the idea to rent rooms for his own upkeep. The heir stopped paying him and told him to "make do."

"But no one comes this way," Ram says sadly. "I try to keep things running, but as you can see, the house will soon be beyond repair. It is too big."

After dinner, when Ram has "retired," Yasmin and I play games. We fill the room with ghosts and imagine the rituals and the society events. We dance in huge circles across the floor and laugh. Everything echoes—the sound of our shoes against the wooden floors, the sound of our voices, even our smiles.

"Let's explore," Yasmin says at one point. I look at her. "Come on," she says, pulling me by the wrist, through a door, down a new corridor, up some unknown stairs. She squeals with excitement.

"Ssshhh," I say, "we don't want to wake Ram up."

"He can't hear us."

"Where are we going?"

"Come on."

When we reach the top of the stairs, she lets go of my hand and starts running. I chase after her. We turn one corner, left, and then another, right, and then down three steps and up five. The whole place is a maze. "Yasmin, wait. It might not be safe." She slows to a trot and then turns half around to face me, walking backward on the balls of her feet.

"Isn't it beautiful?" she says.

"It's dark."

"Do you really think it's haunted?"

"Maybe," I reply.

"I love it," she says. "I love everything about this place."

She stops at a door and looks at me briefly before turning the handle. I can hear her breathing. She opens it and walks slowly inside. I follow her. It's another bedroom, much bigger than ours. The bed is broken and a chest of drawers lies facedown on the ground. There are three enormous windows with long, heavy curtains. Yasmin draws one of them and coughs on the dust. Moonlight spills in.

"It's so beautiful," she says. The bedroom faces the front of the house, and we can see for miles over the gently rolling pastures. The neon glow of a distant town foams on the horizon. "I wish we could stay here forever."

"Me too," I say, sliding my arms around her waist and pressing her toward me. She covers my hands in hers and rests her head back on my shoulder.

"This will always be ours," she says as if she is thinking out loud. There is no self-consciousness in her voice. It's as if the house is overwhelming her and she's losing herself in it, in the moment that is the place. I don't say anything. I find I want her to say what's in her mind. I want her to speak without thinking. It will be like I'm reading her thoughts. She's breathing under me, inside my embrace. I can feel the rise and fall of her chest. She seems completely at ease, at home in my hold. I can feel her feeling for me. I know that I can make her happy.

And then, quite suddenly, there's a detectable tension. It's slight but there. She gulps and my heart starts. I try to block the sense out and stay where we just were. I close my eyes and feel her turning to face me. I keep my eyes closed but bite my upper lip to let her know that I'm listening, that I'm anxious to hear her say something. I can sense her calming as she looks at me, retaking control of the situation. Her hand strokes my face, brushing an eyelid. I open my eyes. She's smiling at me. I half smile back.

"Nothing can ever take this away from us," she says, looking right into my eyes. We both know it's a consolation statement, that it's the best she can come up with. I nod, very slightly, acknowledging her, but still hoping that she'll say more, that she'll let there be more to this than just a memory. I'm hoping that she might make this the foundation for a future, *our* future.

But she doesn't say anything else. She kisses me, and as I fall into her, I find myself forgetting. Forgetting all my hopes and all my dreams of what we could be together and accepting the only other alternative I have. Yasmin as she is, here and only now. Here . . . and only now.

DAWN

We wake up with first light, the day pouring in through the curtainless windows of our room. We want to stay but know we can't. The house will just have to stay buried, like a rare gem, in the mines of our minds. We leave Ram two hundred rupees on the bed. By the time we have the bike packed, the sun is only just rising. Mist sits on the surrounding lawns. The house looks much worse for wear in the cold light of day. Smashed windows and crumbling walls. It is still beautiful, though.

As we start driving, Yasmin sees Ram waving at us from one of the windows. She waves back at him for a long time. Eventually we reach the end of the drive and turn into the boulevard. The wind is cold and soon Yasmin is shivering behind me, so I ride more slowly. A golden-red sun winks at us through the trees. The highway is empty. We put on an extra layer of clothing and cruise at sixty.

After a few miles, Yasmin kisses me on the back of the neck. "Thank you," she says in my ear.

I smile in silence. Slowly, the sun rises and warms us.

ENIGMA

I don't know where the thought comes from. One minute I'm high on the tenderness Yasmin is showing toward me and feeling good about the progress we are making on the road; the next I'm suddenly depressed. It just hits me.

I realize that I have absolutely no idea who Yasmin is. I mean, I know who she *is,* in the sense that we've had enough conversations for me to summarize her. She is twenty-nine. Her father is a judge and her mother is an alcoholic socialite. They divorced when she was in her teens. She has one brother, a financial journalist in Hong Kong, and a sister, a housewife somewhere in Holland. She is a vegetarian but occasionally eats chicken. She studied political science at university and, at one point, thought about working for the UN. She can speak three languages. She's been to England twice. Can't cook, likes to swim, has never been to Africa.

But she's told me almost nothing about herself, in terms of how she sees things. How she feels about her parents' divorce, how she gets on with her brother, what it's like to cope with James in prison. I've tried prying her open, but unlike Faizad and most other people, she seems uninterested in telling her story. She rarely expresses an opinion or verbalizes an emotion. Maybe, I console myself, all that stuff was in the letters she sent, the ones I never received.

I feel as if I don't know her at all. Not really. I don't get the full picture. And even getting the bare facts has been hard. Single-sentence answers under a barrage of questions, usually. Sometimes, the odd thing slips out, like the head-girl mention, but rarely. I certainly never get the story. There's no narrative. She won't let me tune in to her inner voice so I can hear what's going on in her head.

What I'm trying to say is that her character eludes me. I seem to have so little to go on when it comes to figuring out *why* I like Yasmin so much. I tell myself it's a cultural gap. Different levels of communication perhaps or, like she said in her letter, her English isn't good enough to articulate her emotions. But I don't believe that. Her English has never failed to impress me. I wish I could describe her, what it is she has over me that Sanjay can't see.

Of course she's beautiful. She's also sexy and elusive. She seems intelligent and kind, in a hard, female sort of way. She displays mild moments of humor, though she has a tendency to laugh a little too hard at her own jokes. When she sleeps, the muscles in her face twitch and the corners of her mouth turn downward as if she is extremely displeased with the things going on in her mind.

But those things don't amount to much. To say that Yasmin is a certain person because of these things feels like I'm missing the point. There's something else about her, a whole other aspect that I have absolutely no knowledge or understanding of, like she's hiding something. Why do I think that with her?

Maybe it's the way she goes hot and cold. Like when we make love, and that door opens, I see fire, a real furnace within. Last night, she fucked me. She took pleasure from me, almost used me. I loved it. The way she made me feel, like an instrument of her pleasure. It was as if my only purpose was to feed her inner passion. It was base and beautiful. She made love to me the way a wild animal takes food. Like it was necessary to her survival. She ravaged me. She fell unconscious to the surrounding danger. Dangers like me. The danger that I pose, that I may see inside, that I may learn her, be able to hurt her, control her. She's usually so aware, so in control, of herself, of her emotions—making love like that, it made her seem so selfish and yet so wonderfully naive.

Maybe that's why she turns cold afterward. She goes chilly to ward me off the scent. Remind me that I'm not a permanent fixture. She doesn't need me all the time. Her entire existence doesn't depend on me, just her sexual one. Her desire is selfish. All desire is. I don't care about that. I just don't like the way she acts like I couldn't rip through her if I wanted. I hate the way she can fuck me so crucially then behave as if it wasn't so vital after all. I hate the way she can turn herself off.

That depresses me. Maybe that's how I came to be thinking about this in the first place. I think she might have stopped stroking my waist with her thumb, or something. A sudden cooling in her affections is enough to send me into a tailspin.

I simply cannot fathom why she plays me this way. Is it a trust thing? Wasn't she the one who said we had to trust each other? It's very frustrating. Either let me in or keep me out. Don't tease me. Don't fluctuate. It's too abrasive, like rubbing a raw patch of skin with a pumice stone because you have to get the filth out.

I don't know Yasmin. But I've known her. She has something—a lot of something very beautiful—to give. She's shown me. She's let me see it. She just isn't giving it to me.

Of course, it only makes me want her more.

But I'm fed up now. Why should she be the one to call the emotional shots? Why should she get to dictate when we can act like lovers and when we have to act like friends? I'm impatient for her true affections. And I don't care if I rock a good boat. I have to have whatever it is she has to give. Either that, or nothing at all. We're either going to be lovers or enemies. I don't care that this isn't a good time to have a fight. I need to break her. I want her to love me, goddammit.

TALK, TALK

"What are you thinking?" I start. We are lying under another tree. We have made good progress so far. We are past Mahuvar and we hope to make it to Vododara by tonight. It isn't as hot today. There is a breeze and the tree we are under has good shade. Maybe we just feel stronger. We ate an excellent lunch and we have enough water to last two days.

"Hmm, not much."

Yasmin is braiding three thin, bendy twigs. She has completed four sets already and is standing them, like soldiers in the dirt. I let her tie the knot on the one she is doing.

"Are you thinking about James?" It seems like a good way to get on to matters emotional.

"No."

"Are you thinking about him now?"

"I'm thinking," she says, raising her eyebrows at me. "Why are you asking?"

I pause for a moment and then say quickly, "What's he like?"

"James?"

"Yes, James."

"I don't know," she says, fiddling with her twigs. She starts as if to say something and then gives up, looking up at me instead and wincing as if in pain. "What do you want me to say?"

"Tell me what you like about him."

She pauses and thinks. After a few seconds, she curls her top lip and says, "Can't we talk about something else?"

"Why?" I say, genuinely perplexed.

"Because I don't really want to talk to you about my boyfriend."

"Why not?"

"Why, why, why . . . always questions. I'll tell you why. How about, why should I? It's none of your business."

"Have you told him about us?"

"No." She half laughs, incredulous.

"Why not?"

"Because that's none of *his* business."

"Oh, come on, Yasmin, give me a break. Don't you think he has a right to know?"

She looks at me violently. "Well, you are welcome to tell him anything you want after he gets out of jail. Somehow, I don't think the information would help him much at the moment."

"Okay, okay, chill out," I suddenly backtrack, asking myself how I could be so stupid to say something like that and beating myself up for the insensitivity at the same time. But deep down there's also a satisfaction. I know I'm trying to force a reaction. And, I just got one. "I didn't mean that you should upset him. I just, I don't know . . . I'm confused."

"What about?"

"About everything. About us. You and me. What are we doing?"

"Why do you have to analyze it?"

"I'm not analyzing it. I just . . . I've got feelings, you know."

She sits up then, moving back, defensive. I realize then that

I'm making a mistake, talking this way. "What do you mean, feelings?"

"Nothing. Forget it."

"No, go on, tell me, what do you mean you've got feelings?"

"I said forget it. Carry on fiddling with your twigs," I say, avoiding her look.

She doesn't say anything for a long while. She just looks at me. I close my eyes and pretend to be trying to get to sleep. The air feels full of scrutiny, like she's assessing the situation, assessing me.

Eventually, I hear words. They come slowly at first, like someone testing the water, making sure they want to dive into this. Then, after a few sentences, they flow freely. It just happens. Yasmin starts telling a story, the story of James and her. How it all began, what he means to her, why she will never leave him. Sometimes, most of the time, I don't even feel like she's talking to me. She's just remembering and reciting, like she's reading the text from the scenes in her mind. She's opening up. Which would be great, except she doesn't say anything that I find I want to hear.

They are one of those ideal couples. You know, the type of couple everyone loves, loves that they're in love. They are so suited to each other. It is fate. No one can touch their relationship. It's sacred.

Maybe it's because they start seeing each other so young. Fifteen. Before it gets confusing. When love is love. Theirs is pure. They're not together out of need or weakness. They're in love—happily, naively, beautifully in love. There are no ulterior motives at play. They love each other and they're beautiful. They're beautiful people.

In the beginning, love makes them adults. Children playing a grown-up game. Difference is, they're better at it. Real *Romeo and Juliet* stuff, but nothing like. Their love isn't outcast. Their love isn't forbidden. Quite the opposite, in fact. It's celebrated. It's publicized. It's adored. A society revolves around it.

James. One of the boys. Of course he is. Handsome. Cool. No one ever quite knows what he's feeling. He's charming, even when he's angry. Generous. Far too generous. Everyone likes him. He's crazy, wild. Loves to party. Every day is a party in James's life. One time he sticks his finger in the lighter socket in Yasmin's car. "It tickles." He giggles. Crazy guy. Wild, fun, lovely guy.

All the girls want him, in a "too good to touch" sort of way, like a boy-band pinup. No girl would dare go near James, even though he's gorgeous. Of course he is. No. They wouldn't because they've seen the way he looks at Yasmin. It's the only time people can really tell what he's feeling. Because it's so obvious that they adore each other. And besides, no one could look as good standing next to James as she does. The way they share each other's height, frame, and smile—they're like two halves of a puzzle. They almost look like each other but not so much as to make the mutual attraction seem narcissistic. No, it's not like that. It's only as and when they come together that people associate them in their minds and say: "Ahhhh. Now that makes sense."

After a while the sanctity of their love becomes a self-perpetuating myth that surrounds them. Half of their relationship is lived out in the public arena. When other couples argue the first thing they think of is James and Yasmin and would they fight this way, and they think: No, never. Not James and Yasmin.

So many of them split up because of that. Because they realize that they're not part of a James and Yasmin thing. But they want it. They want to be in a James and Yasmin thing so badly. They're jealous of what James and Yasmin have. So they leave a good thing, sometimes a great thing, in search of the best. It's only after several tries that they realize they'll never be part of a James and Yasmin thing. Because a James and Yasmin thing is special. It's rare. That sort of love doesn't happen to everyone. Only to the chosen few.

But while everyone around them tries on new partners for size, usually all from the same social scene as if trapped in some per-petual game of musical chairs, James and Yasmin go on. On and on. They never split up. Time passes and confirms what everyone has always known. James and Yasmin are destined to be together. Nothing can come between them. They're unbreakable. Even as they become adults, they still represent a childlike fantasy of what it is to fall in love. They've happened before everyone's eyes.

It's not true, though. It's not reality, the reality. James and Yasmin aren't the ideal couple. They may be superstar lovelings, but they're human like everyone else. Yasmin knows what it is to be in love with James—from the inside out, not the outside in. It isn't ideal. They argue. Of course they argue. They may be charming, always on the outside, forever charming, but on the inside, there are fights. Worse. There's unhappiness.

Part of it comes because she starts to feel claustrophobic. The way everyone watches their relationship like it's partly theirs. Policing it with eyes, and ears, and gossipy tongues. After a while, she rebels. She finds she longs for someone, anyone, a stranger to approach her. It isn't because of James. It isn't anything he's done. She's still in love with him. She just wants someone to brave the social judgment, penetrate the circle and the scene, to reach her, touch her—just for the sake of being reached, touched. Anything to feel that she's not totally cut off from the rest of the world.

But no one does. Of course they don't. James and Yasmin have come to represent something bigger than themselves. They represent the Dream of Love. Out of all the shit in this world, Yasmin and James are the one thing that's pure—even though they're not, even though it's a lie.

That's how the unspoken separation starts.

It happens after they go to the Osho ashram in Pune. It's Yasmin who insists they go. James isn't fussed. He's seen this stuff all his life. He practically grew up in India. His parents, both Dutch, met at the ashram. They even, so family folklore goes, conceived him at the ashram. He's spent every Christmas there since he was born. Playing and getting sick with all the other "little Buddhas," as their parents liked to call them. Sometimes his family would stay half the year before their money evaporated. Then his dad would return to Holland "for business" while his mum worked in the Amsterdam Healing Institute.

Secretly, James was pleased when his parents finally sent him to private school as a teenager. He never questioned how they could afford it, but somehow he felt that he belonged there, that he was among his own class for the first time. And he certainly loved the instant social status afforded him because his parents were flower power. Because they didn't mind drugs. Even advocated them.

And it was at private school, of course, that he and Yasmin met. At a dance, if you can believe it! She came from the sister school, a convent in a town ten miles from his. Yasmin remembers the nuns warning them on the coach: "No physical contact unless a sister is present." Even better, she remembers James's surprise—shock, really—as she thrust her hand down his trousers in the fifteen minutes that they managed to find for themselves, alone behind a bush. Even with all his liberal cool, she knew he'd never been touched there before. She was his first. And to think she only really did it to spite the nuns and all their hypocritical rules. Still, it impressed him. Still, it made him hers. None of the other girls could believe it. They were so jealous!

But seven years later Yasmin feels a void in her life. She hopes India and the ashram will fill it. Better than that, she hopes India will be a solution to the problem that James can provide. She wants James to be the one to fill the void, with something only he can provide. She wants it to be James who takes her to India. She wants James to introduce her to the mysticism, be her tour guide. God forbid that someone else fills the emptiness. Someone else or perhaps even herself. That would leave only one alternative—the unspeakable.

They are twenty-two. Maybe that's all it is—the seven-year itch.

They move in two directions almost as soon as they arrive. They take an overnight taxi from Bombay airport straight to Pune, a hundred and sixty kilometers north. She finds the place freaky. All the people in robes, maroon and white, affected laughter everywhere. The religion overruns the place. It's like a cult. James tells her he told her so. Knew she wouldn't like it. Give me a chance, she says. Really, she's saying, give yourself a chance—because there's nothing else out there that you can give me. If this doesn't work, then there's only one alternative.

It goes from bad to worse. Osho is still alive, still giving sessions. They go to one. They spend three hours "meditating" before he comes in. Everything is white. White floor, white robes, white room, white cushions, white skin. When Osho comes in, dark-robed and in soft focus, he sits in a chair that seems to refract light. Everything goes brilliant and the room starts to convulse.

"OSHO! OSHO! OSHO!" Some leap to their feet in ecstasy. "OSHO! OSHO! OSHO!" Yasmin is pinned to the floor in horror as she watches James leap and shout along with everyone else. "OSHO! OSHO! OSHO!"

She stares at him.

"Can you feel it?" he cries, looking at her, real tears. "Can you see it?" Brilliant, crazy, scary smile stretching his face into a shape she's never seen before. "OSHO! OSHO!"

She feels nothing. She sees nothing. Nothing but a silly little man with a long white beard grinning to the call of his name. Nothing but a bunch of confused middle-class Westerners paying to shout and scream and weep. She feels nothing. Nothing at all. Except panic.

"NOOOOOOO!" she screams at James, as if she's losing him. Then she runs out screaming and weeping all on her own.

The sannyasins tell her not to worry. A lot of people freak out when they see Osho. It can be very powerful. Any emotion is okay. It's great to let it out. We spend our whole lives bottling it all up. Long lectures. Even longer indoctrination sessions. James scowls at her. He's ashamed to be seen with her. He wears the robes. She says she just can't bring herself to. He spends most of the day at the ashram. She just can't bear to go back. So she spends most of the day alone. Wandering around town, trying to find India in all the madness.

That's how she meets Stefan, in the German bakery. He's a sannyasin but he's the opposite of James. Old, not young. Bearded, not fresh-faced. Private, not social. Raw, not polished. Rude, not charming. He's the one to open her mind. It all begins with one look, an instant connection.

While James spends all day at the ashram chopping vegetables and meditating, Yasmin sleeps with Stefan. He is the one who teaches her what it is to take pleasure. He is the one to fill the void in her life, and it's only after meeting him that she understands what the void has been. James has never really made her happy that way. They were so young when they started, she supposed.

In the end, it is Stefan who introduces her to the ashram, to Osho. He's the one to induct her. It is Stefan who convinces her to wear the robes. Not for him, but for herself. He initiates her. Enrolls her in the Sex and Spirituality course. It opens her. When James finds out, sees her in the complex, laughing like a wild flower child, he gets angry. She tries to encourage him to investigate her path, to take other lovers. He refuses. He leaves. She stays. With Stefan. There are others too. She explores her sexuality and she enjoys it.

It is only after they are back in Amsterdam, months later, that they start seeing each other again. James begs her back. So do all their friends. Everyone wants them to be together, just like always. It is too hard to fight it. She tells herself that the void has been filled. She's satisfied. She'll find satisfaction with James. They'll learn how to be together. She wants their life together to be dynamic, to be a journey.

Then his jealousy starts. Slowly at first, always private, always behind closed doors, never open, never threatening to destroy the public myth of the perfect couple, James becomes a jealous man. An angry, jealous man.

She never thought she would, but she enjoys it. The rages. The way he fucks her. He's not delicate anymore. It rips through them, like a paper cut. And she likes the feeling, the pain, the passion, the heat, and the danger. Nothing is comfortable anymore. Stefan has helped them. She's surprised to discover that, this way, she is satisfied with James. This works.

She likes it so much she doesn't attempt to reassure him. If anything, she aggravates it. She believes it's keeping them alive, preventing them from slipping back, back into their suffocating innocence. She leaves love letters from Stefan in places she knows James will see them. She disappears for hours at a time and won't explain where she's been. He goes half crazy with it. For a long time it works. The new dynamic. On the outside, everything is the same. On the inside, everything is different. Exciting and dangerous. It's a fantasy. She doesn't really betray James. Not anymore. That's over. And besides, Stefan is miles away. She doesn't take new lovers. She's happy with the one she's got. James. He's a great lover, when he's inspired. It's a game. That's all it is. A game.

Then something terrible happens.

Stefan is killed. Stabbed. Mysteriously, randomly. In a bar fight, in Vilingren, the Black Forest, his hometown. She reads about it in a newsletter distributed by the sannyasins. It shakes her. She grieves. She realizes then, too late, that part of her really loved Stefan. It feels terrible to lose someone like that—so permanently.

It affects James too. When Stefan dies, so does his jealousy. Gradually, he becomes his old self again. Charming, funny, carefree, calm, false.

And it affects them. Slowly, predictably, they become dull. Yasmin tries, sometimes, to play the old games, like her disappearing acts, but they don't work anymore. Without a Stefan, the danger doesn't feel real. James seems oblivious to her as a sexual entity. She is just his partner again. Lifelong. She flirts, but, of course, the inner social ring shields her. No man ever goes too close. After all, she's James's girl, and everyone loves James. Everyone seems happy, except her.

But she doesn't take another lover. She doesn't look for another Stefan. Even though they go back to Pune. Even though there are offers, opportunities. Without Stefan, none of it seems real. She's not the type to take casual lovers. It was a phase. Something unique that she went through, could only ever go through with one man, Stefan. And now that he's dead, she sees only pain there—in the fantasy. The fantasy only worked with Stefan. Now that he's gone, it's been neutralized. To live it would be to look for him in it. Then she'd remember—Stefan's gone, Stefan's dead. She doesn't ever want to lose anyone again. It hurts too much.

She doesn't want to let love go again, like that, whatever the cost. Losing Stefan, it makes her realize—she doesn't want to lose James. Even though they've gone back to the way they were, she doesn't ever want to lose James.

DISAFFECTED

It's only when she stops that I realize these aren't the words, the actual words, she uses. She could never tell her story that way. No one could. But they're the words I've heard. I've recognized some of the social scenarios, I've come across a jealous dynamic like the one she and James shared and I've imposed what I know on her story. It's perverted and projected, but somehow, it makes it more understandable. It helps me to see her story through my own eyes. It helps me to understand her.

Maybe it's just that I always have to be the narrator. It's a failing, I suppose.

After a while, she restarts, "I think what I'm trying to say is that James is a part of me. I believe we will always be together. Can you understand?"

"Yes, I understand," I say coldly. James is her boyfriend and I'm a Stefan—not even. I'm just an instrument to be used to help spice up her love life. Not to be fallen in love with. She's been there, done that—without me. Fine. If she wants a fuck, I'll fuck her.

Then she catches me off guard. "At least I used to believe . . ." She trails off and I find myself turning to face her. Her head is down. I think I can see a sadness in the shadow of her eye.

"You don't believe that you and James are destined to be together anymore?" I try, very softly, very coaxingly. I don't want to scare her off.

She sighs a big sigh, full of weight. "I don't know what to believe," she says quietly.

I wonder, I hope, I pray that it's my influence that's confusing her. I mean, how could I be another Stefan? James is in jail. And she's not telling James about me. Not in her letters, not during her visits—all three of them. She told James about Stefan, didn't she? But she doesn't want to tell James about me. She doesn't want to use me to make him jealous, make their relationship exciting. Could this be, at long last, an admission of her feelings for me? Is she trying to tell me that she and James were destined for each other until I came along? Is she telling me she loves me?

I tell myself to stay quiet, let her talk. But after several minutes of silence I can't hold off any longer. I have to seize the initiative. I can't let the conversation end here. "Do you feel guilty?" I blurt the words out and she smarts. I regret them immediately. Somehow they seem to betray all my selfish intentions. In four little words I've managed to show that I haven't been listening at all. I've simply been sifting through her sentences for clues that she wants me. I've revealed my Truth. That I believe this conversation is really about us, not about James and her. It's just the kind of sentence that says too much, that can screw up everything.

"Guilty?" she says.

Too late now, I think to myself. In for a penny, in for a pound. If I back out now, I'll just look weak. I may as well finish what I came into this conversation to do. I may as well press for answers. I may as well just admit that I'm only interested in James inasmuch as he's thoroughfare to the real issue at hand—what does Yasmin feel about me?

"Guilty about us."

"I don't understand."

I can't tell if she's deliberately making me spell it out, as if she's getting some sick pleasure from watching me squirm like this. I bite the bullet.

"I just thought that maybe it was us, you know, that was affecting your feelings for James."

"Us!" she snorts, half laughing. "No, Josh. It's got nothing to do with 'us.' "

I hear her stick the inverted commas around the "us"—making it quite clear she's quoting me. She refers to an "us" only inasmuch as it is an expression I would use. She says "us" for ease of understanding. She doesn't say "us" as if she believes in an "us" or as if she even knows what an "us" is.

"Then what's it got to do with?" I retort, hoping that my face isn't going too red. Not that it matters; she's not looking at me now anyway. We're back onto the subject that interests her, the one that doesn't interest me. We're talking about James again—James in and of himself. I can tell. It's the way she looks into the ground and then stares wistfully out over the horizon that tells me.

"Oh, I don't know," she says, fingering another set of twigs. "It's just that James, he's, he's . . . so different now."

James, James, James, James . . . blah, blah, blah. Who fucking cares about James?

"What do you mean?" I somehow manage.

"He's changed. He's changing."

Hardly surprising if he's getting fucked up the ass every day in that hellhole of a prison, I think to myself.

"Well, he's bound to change a little while he's in prison. It can't be easy for him." I say the words but I can't believe it's me talking. The last thing I want is to give James any benefit of the doubt. At the same time, perhaps there's a part of me that wants to make amends for my previous foolery. I feel as if I should present myself more nobly, having revealed my caddish side.

Yasmin looks surprised, which makes me feel instantly better for some reason. Maybe it's because I believe she's giving me my due—surprised, pleasantly surprised, that I'm defending him. Her face softens as if she's realizing something. "No, it's got nothing to do with prison, though he's gotten worse since he went there. No, he changed before all of that."

"How do you mean?"

"I don't know. He seems scared of something. I don't know what. Something I don't understand. He never tells me what it is. I've tried asking him, but he says there's nothing."

"Go on."

She smiles at me. She appreciates that. "Go on." Good words those. A lot better than "Do you feel guilty?"

"He . . . sometimes I think he . . . he can do terrible things."

"What sort of terrible things?"

Yasmin concentrates on balancing a new twig soldier, which seems determined to play dead.

"Just, terrible . . . He can be very violent."

"What?" I say, sitting up higher on my elbow so I can look more directly into her eyes. "Violent? With you? Has he ever hit you? Tell me, Yasmin."

"No, no, nothing like that. James loves me. He would never hurt me."

"Then violent in what way? I don't understand."

Yasmin shakes her head slightly then and stares as if she's trying to focus on the Here and Now, as if having just emerged from a dream. "Oh, nothing. Forget I said anything."

"What do you mean forget it? How can I forget it? Tell me, Yasmin. What are you scared of?"

"Nothing. I'm not scared of anything."

"Yes, you are, Yasmin. Now tell me."

Then she just explodes, suddenly and without reserve. I'm completely taken aback. "NO, I FUCKING WELL AM NOT. WHY CAN'T YOU JUST LEAVE IT? WHY DO YOU ALWAYS HAVE TO ASK SO MANY QUESTIONS? WHY CAN'T YOU JUST MIND YOUR OWN BUSINESS? WHY CAN'T YOU JUST LEAVE ME ALONE?"

She jumps to her feet, kicking up dust as she says the words, and delivers the last of them towering over me. I feel painfully small. I don't know what to say. I can feel my face looking shocked and surprised and there's nothing I can do to pull the expression back to normal. The muscles in my jaw and forehead are involuntarily tensing, forcing my chin to drop and my eyes to open wide. After a small delay I somehow find the wherewithal to affect bravado, leaping up to my own feet and shouting back: "WHY SHOULD I LEAVE YOU ALONE, YASMIN?" I don't know where I'm going with this. "YOU NEVER LEAVE ME ALONE." I don't even understand what I'm talking about.

"WHAT ARE YOU TALKING ABOUT?" she screams back.

Then the words just come—hot and utterly regrettable.

"I MEAN ALL YOUR HOT, COLD SHIT. ONE MOMENT YOU'RE ALL OVER ME, THE NEXT MOMENT YOU'RE NOT. I DON'T KNOW WHETHER I'M COMING OR GOING WITH YOU. I JUST WANT TO KNOW IF YOU LOVE ME."

She doesn't say anything. She stops and stares at me, scared almost. I frown. What's her problem? I think to myself. Why isn't she shouting at me anymore? What did I just say? Then I hear the words echoing somewhere in my synapses. Oh fuck. Fuck no, please don't let me have said what I think I just said.

She's still staring at me. This is going to ruin everything, I think to myself. I've done it again—like the clumsy klutz that I am. I've gone and put my foot in it and fucked everything up. Then, slowly, as if to help me realize that it really is happening, that I'm not just dreaming it, she extends her hand to touch mine. I stare at the ground. Big Mistake, Big Mistake, Big Mistake. I keep saying the words to myself, not wanting to admit to myself, believe that perhaps I haven't made a Big Mistake. Better to know it now. Better not to get my hopes up. Stay pessimistic. Avoid disappointment. It keeps going around and around in my mind. Not experience. Mistake. What I just said was a fucking Big Mistake.

"Josh," she says gently. I stay staring at the ground. "Josh," she says again. I look up at her. There's nowhere for me to hide. Time to face the music. I meet her eyes, her beautiful green going-to-make-us-rich-and-be-happy-for-the-rest-of-our-lives emerald eyes. And that's when, in a brief instant, I think I can see it—just like those glimpses I catch when we make love. Yes, now that I look deeper, I can definitely see it. Could it be? The Impossible. That she loves me?

"Yes." I cringe on the tone. I'm so begging for it and I'm so bad at hiding it, it's painful.

"You are a very beautiful person," she says. That's good, isn't it? Beautiful person is good. Except there's too much of a *but* in there for me to get comfortable quite yet. "I don't think I've ever known anyone like you before," she continues. Still no *but*. Still sounding good. "I know that I can be . . . difficult, sometimes. I'm sorry. I really am. Because I really, really like you. I'm not just saying that. I really do." Hmm, really, really like. Not sure about that one. Could be good. Could be bad. Could be very bad. "And I think it's amazing that you're doing all this." Doing? What am I doing? "Helping me get James out of prison, despite your feelings for me." Hey? What does she mean "despite"? Does she think I'm doing this so that she and James can ultimately be together? Is that what she's thinking? That I'm helping her get the money to get her boyfriend out of jail so that they can one day actually be together again? Is she crazy? Can't she see that I'm only doing this so that *we* can be together? Can't she see that all this is just an excuse to be near her? That I'm doing this for *us,* not *them.* That I'm doing this so that she will eventually fall in love with me? Can't she tell that one day she is going to fall in love with me? Isn't that obvious by now? "But . . ." Uh-oh, here we go. This is it. I can't believe it. She doesn't even consider a me and her. "I love James. I always have and I always will. I'm sorry. I love him."

The sentence punctures.

As she says the words, she closes her eyes, as if she's now shutting the door that's been letting me in whenever we've made love and that let me in just a few moments ago. She's shutting it now, sighing heavily as she does so, as if to emphasize the effort that it takes to close it and, even worse than that, implying the effort she's having to summon to keep it that way. The words she says and the way she says them—they're a package that comes, all wrapped and neatly delivered, like a home delivery product designed to make me feel very, very bitter. She says the words as if she is agreeing—finally—to tell me what she really feels about me. Forget the door, forget the lovemaking, forget the Grand Palace. If I want an honest answer, then this is the only one she can give me. "I love him." She says the words in a way that makes everything else untrue, everything about us and what we've shared untrue, in fact as if *we, us, me,* and *her* were never even there at all, merely an illusion, a fantasy, a fiction. In other words, she says the sentence in a way that can only really mean one thing: "I don't love you."

REPETITIVE STRAIN SYNDROME

I manage to sulk for the rest of the day. Yasmin tries everything from casual conversation—usually starting with a lame observation like, "Wow, look at that pretty bird," or "You're a really good driver"—to open confrontation. At one point, she insists I stop the bike so we can talk about "it." I ignore her, of course.

The truth is I'm relishing the attention too much to stop.

Eventually, she gives up. We ride in silence, still making good progress. We cover two hundred and twenty kilometers before dusk falls. My ass is killing me, so I know Yasmin is in pain. She doesn't say anything though. She is turning out to be quite stubborn. She's also taken to holding on to the silver bar at the back of the seat instead of on to me. I am of half a mind to accelerate suddenly to see if she falls off.

We make it to Vododara by six. There isn't much to see. We find a guest house, which is basic but clean. We take separate rooms. The sheets on the bed are blue. The water is cold. I notice that my left eye is very bloodshot. It must be the dust.

I tell her that I'm taking the bike to a mechanic for an oil change and that I'll probably find something to eat while I'm gone. She'd be better off having dinner without me. She just looks at me grimly and shrugs her shoulders.

I find a mechanic just around the corner from the hotel and

decide to leave the bike with him. I go in search of a restaurant where I can be on my own but run into Yasmin about five minutes later. She doesn't see me. For some reason, I don't know why, I decide to follow her. Maybe I figure that it's the best way to avoid each other. Vododara isn't exactly a big town. As long as I keep Yasmin in front of me, there can't be any surprise run-ins.

She seems to know exactly where she is going, walking straight past numerous eateries and ignoring hawkers. Eventually she finds a place to make telephone calls and walks in. There's a computer booth in the window with a sign saying E-MAIL over it. After talking briefly with a man inside, she sits at the computer and starts typing, very hard and very fast for a long time.

Now, who the fuck could she be writing to?

LOST

The potholes are steadily getting larger and more frequent. I am trying to maintain a decent pace but they are everywhere, springing out of the blind spots like booby traps. Every so often I have to slam on the brakes to avoid one. Yasmin has caught her chin on my shoulder on one of them and cut her lip quite badly. Oil has started leaking from the front suspension and I am worried that the mechanic did something to the bike overnight. The Enfield doesn't seem to be running as smoothly as before. I should have known better. Yasmin tells me I am going too fast. Eventually, I am reduced to weaving our way through the chaos at less than 10 kph.

"This is fucking ridiculous," I say, shaking my head.

"Are you sure this is the right road?"

I can't bear to admit that I might have taken a wrong turn. We've been riding for three hours. Turning around will essentially mean losing a whole day. But I also know that we've seen very little traffic and passed very few towns.

"It must be. Where could I have taken a wrong turn?"

"Maybe at the Vododara crossroads."

She's probably right. How could I have been so fucking stupid? I can't stand the idea of admitting it to myself. I try to tell myself that I was tired. I didn't sleep very well last night either. It's the beginning of an insomnia cycle, I can tell. My insomnia always comes in cycles, usually when I'm worried about something.

It begins because I am unable to stop my mind. I find I'm usually able to get to sleep at the beginning of the night, then some inner alarm clock goes off and I'm suddenly awake. I tell myself that I'm exhausted, but it never works. I just lie there and worry. I worry and worry, about nothing and everything. I've tried counting sheep, I've tried meditating, I've tried reading, I've tried masturbating. None of it works. The only thing that lets me get to sleep is dawn. It's only when I can see that gray light and realize with despair that I've been awake now for, yes, shit, for seven hours that my mind releases me.

In other words, I can only sleep when I've lost all hope. When I know that the race has been lost. Only when I've given up and I'm not trying anymore and I know that the hour and a half that's left of the night will never ever constitute a real sleep. Only as I lie there, 1,048 sheep later, sixty sessions of "Ohm" reverberating in my ears, 487 pages of a novel skimmed, and with a severe case of wankst—that special anxiety that can only come from too much masturbating.

And the only way to end the cycle is to get to the heart of whatever it is that's really bothering me. Until then, I'll spend night after night, my mind twisting and turning down avenues of thought, each of them—a dead end. It's only when I finally stop circling, when I finally work my way through the red-herring worries, that the insomnia will end. Insomnia is the process I go through to resolve my issues. Some people see shrinks. I lose sleep. It usually drives me mad. It depends how long it lasts. Sometimes it lasts for weeks.

"Well, we can either turn around or keep going until we hit the next town," I say. She doesn't say anything. It is starting to get hot and it's only nine. The landscape has turned sterile again and there are no streams in sight, so we can't have air-conditioning. We've also only got one bottle of water left. We hadn't anticipated getting lost. The wisest thing to do would be to turn back. But the thought of starting all over again sickens me. All those miles, all that time: for nothing. I'd rather press on. "I know that we are heading in roughly the right direction," I try.

"How?"

"The sun is still on our right, which means we must be going north." Actually that isn't completely true. The sun is very high already, and we are driving at a steep angle against it.

"Well, let's carry on going, then," she closes.

I try to seal the decision by picking up the pace again, but after a few minutes, we end up crashing into a deep pothole that almost throws us off the bike. It jars the front suspension badly and oil starts springing out in bubbles. I decide to stop at the next tree we find. I need a cigarette. Ten minutes later we find one, but it is too sparse for proper shade. I decide to stop anyway. When I get back on, the bike won't start.

AND FOUND

Yasmin says she just wants to be left alone. The water is finished. It is nearly 1 P.M. The air scorches our lungs when we breathe. We're leaning against the bike and trying to use the towels as a canopy, but they don't provide much relief. The sun just beats its way through them.

I know she blames me for stopping, probably for taking the wrong turn too. On top of the way I behaved yesterday, I can't help feeling guilty.

"It's going to be all right, Yasmin, I promise," I try as she curls up into the shade I'm making with her towel. She has her back to me.

"I'm getting really bored of hearing you say that."

Yasmin wants to abandon the bike in search of help. I tell her we stand a better chance of waiting for a vehicle to pass. So far, we haven't seen or heard a single one. It is too dangerous to venture out now anyway. We wouldn't last an hour in this heat, without water, without shade.

The only thing to do is wait and hope. Every so often I inspect the bike for clues, but I can't figure out what's wrong with it. I had hoped it was just flooded, but it isn't that. The engine just will not fire. Push-starting it is useless. The bike is too heavy and the road is too bad to be able to get enough speed to make it worthwhile. The spark plugs look clean. I keep telling Yasmin that it is just overheated. As soon as the sun sets a little, we'll be able to get going again. I know she doesn't believe me. We're both scared.

After a long silence I tell her I'm sorry. She says it's okay and turns in toward me. I gently pull a loose strand of hair and pin it in place behind her ear. Sleep comes. Some time passes.

I hear wheels squeaking. I see that Yasmin's legs have slipped their way into the sun and are very red. I shake her awake. She says something incoherent and jerks her head up off my lap. I notice a small wet patch on my shorts where she has been dribbling. Then I hear wheels squeaking again.

"What was that?" Yasmin says, looking up at me.

We both scramble to our feet. A young boy, with parted blue-black hair, black skin, and a dirty-white sleeveless vest, is riding a bike too tall for him toward us. He stands on one pedal, using the weight of his body to turn it, then he sits on the crossbar until the other pedal comes full circle. He catches it with his other foot and repeats the process, slowly making his way between the potholes.

He is about to pass us before we shout at him to stop. The front wheel wobbles dangerously as he looks at us, wide-eyed, running toward him, arms outstretched. He hits a pothole and falls off. He doesn't look very happy as we help him get up.

We both babble at him in broken Hindi for several minutes before it becomes clear that he doesn't understand a word we are saying. We use sign language and speak to him in staccato sentences.

"We. Need. Water," Yasmin says, pretending to drink from an imaginary bottle.

"Get. Help. Please," I say, pointing into the distance.

He ignores me and walks to the Enfield. He squats by the engine. I come up behind him. "Bike. Broken. Need. Help." He looks back and up at me, squinting. He has one of those infinitely wise faces you only see on young Indian kids—nine going on ninety. Then he climbs onto the bike, which I have lifted onto its kickstand, and turns on the ignition. "No. Bike. Broken," I stress.

He squeezes the compression lever, stands with two feet on the kick start, and slowly breathes air out of the engine. He sits on the seat and lets the kick start return to its normal position. He indicates for me to steady the bike. Then he bounces on the lever until suddenly, with a small jump, he snaps it down with a single jerk and leaps off the side, using the accelerator as a balance. On the third putt, the Enfield roars to life.

Yasmin and I look at each other. The boy grins at me. Then he points in the direction we are traveling and flashes five fingers at us five times.

"Twenty-five kilometers," I say, holding up ten fingers twice, and then an additional five to confirm.

He nods back at me. "Godhra."

"Godhra?" Yasmin says. "Where's that?"

"I don't know. Let's figure that out when we get there."

MIDDLE OF FUCKING NOWHERE

It is dark by the time we reach Godhra. Within minutes of arriving I can sense the hostility. There isn't a woman in sight and everyone is staring at us—a bad sign if you are traveling with a beautiful white girl. But we don't have a choice. It's too late to find somewhere else to stay and we can't risk it with the bike acting up. Eventually, we find a place that takes visitors.

It is a grim three-story building. They only have one room available. It has one window opening out onto the corridor that leads to the room. A thin wire mesh acts as security. It's depressing but it will do.

By the time we are ready to eat, all the restaurants are closed. A boy from reception says he knows somewhere. He has a nasty harelip and a vermillion daub on his forehead. He leads us down a dark alleyway and into a muddy enclosure several hundred meters off the main road. Inside, there are several tables packed with Indian men on long benches. They guzzle down lumpy brown food served from a large aluminum pot. They all have tar on their faces and in their hair. They are roadworkers. They take little notice of Yasmin and me. We sit down quietly in one corner and wait to be served. The food is surprisingly good.

Afterward, Yasmin says she wants to buy some fruit.

"Aren't you tired?" I try.

"No, I feel much better. Come on."

"I still think we should turn in." This town is making me very nervous. I haven't seen a single woman and we are definitely attracting aggressive looks.

"Stop being such a wimp." She's turning out to be not only stubborn, but willful too. I finally feel like I am getting a few holds on Yasmin's character on this journey. Impetuous, strong-minded, independent—I wonder what she's seen in her life to make her know so certainly what it is she wants. Maybe it's in the genes. I certainly don't have her resilience. Or confidence. She seems completely self-assured. She doesn't seem to care what people think of her. She only knows what she wants and she takes it, regardless of the consequences. It seems selfish but it's wonderfully attractive. It's so unlike me. I admire it. I wish I could be more like Yasmin. Less preoccupied with what people think. I wish I knew what I wanted and had the resolve and the self-confidence to take it. Life's too short for anything else. At least, that's the way it seems when I'm with her.

"Let's be quick, then," I concede.

Eventually we find a fruit stall manned by the only woman, if you can call her that, we've seen so far in the whole town. She looks like a crumpled old hag, with skin that's had the air taken out of it and a large mole on her nose sprouting three thick hairs. Yasmin inspects the bananas. They don't look very appetizing. A white halogen lamp burns brightly under a green umbrella. A man walks past. I distinctly hear him say "cunt" in Hindi. I edge my eyes right and left. It feels like there are people gathering behind us. I resist the temptation to turn around. Yasmin doesn't seem to be noticing any of this. It is obvious that the old lady is not appreciating Yasmin fingering her fruit. Another man walks past. "Whore," he says, again in Hindi. Suddenly Yasmin's resolve isn't seeming so admirable anymore. I'm scared. "Come on, Yasmin.

It's getting late." I try not to sound too agitated. Yasmin finally picks out two bananas.

"Kitna?"

"Dos rupiyah," the witch cackles.

"Dos rupiyah!" Yasmin exclaims. *"Ne, ne."*

I cannot believe she is haggling. Another man shouts "whore" at us. Yasmin holds out a green five-rupee note. *"Panche."*

Suddenly the hag leaps up, grabs her bananas, and stabs Yasmin in the shoulder with a gnarled finger. *"Ne. Dos. Chalo,"* she shouts.

Yasmin is too stunned to react for a moment, but I seize the opportunity to grab her arm and pull her away. She is so busy protesting and insisting we go back to take on the hag that she doesn't even notice the group of men that is following us.

We eventually make it back to the room. I padlock and bolt the door, close the windows, and turn off the light.

"What are you doing? I can't see anything."

"Sssshhhh."

I press my ear to the door and listen for footsteps.

"What's the matter?" Yasmin hisses.

"We're being followed."

"Oh, not that one again," Yasmin says in her normal voice.

"Ssshhh. Will you just be quiet for one second. Please."

"What's going on?" she whispers.

I explain about the men, but I don't tell her about the name-calling. Eventually, she agrees that it's time to go to bed.

We try sleeping but it is too hot.

After twenty minutes she whispers in my ear. "Do you think it's safe to open the window?" It's very dark. The air is sticky. We're both sweating against each other.

"It's just going to have to be. We'll never get any sleep like this."

The faintest of breezes wafts in from the corridor when she opens it, but it's enough for us to sail slowly into sleep on.

RAPE

"Josh, Josh, wake up." The words filter into my half sleep. "Josh, please." I open my eyes. It's dark at first but then I detect light coming in from the edge of my eye.

"What?"

"There's someone . . . someone out there," she hisses.

Strands of sleep and the darkness disorient me. I gather my bearings and realize that my face is buried in Yasmin's armpit. I move my head slightly until the horror of what is happening reveals itself. Yasmin is lying, in one of my T-shirts and a pair of knickers, rigid beside me. Light from a flashlight is scanning her. First it is on a breast, then it moves slowly down onto her stomach. It pauses, almost quivering, before moving, full of anticipation, over her sex, which rises from her outline. The light dwells on the crevices, moving back and forth, stroking. I squint into the blue where the light doesn't shine. I can make out three silhouettes. There is the faint sound of whispering, like flies buzzing against a windowpane. I can see an elbow moving.

I am suddenly filled with fury and blind courage. I leap out of bed and throw myself against the wire mesh, screaming. "GET THE FUCK OUT OF IT, YOU DIRTY CUNTS." I don't see their faces. I am attacking them with my eyes closed. Next thing I know they are running down the corridor giggling. The fear feels filthy. I turn around and see Yasmin, her knees pressed up into her chest. My heart is beating to a drum-and-bass track. My hands are shaking. I hate India. I feel guilty. Why have I brought us here? This is my fault. Yasmin is the real victim. I go to hold her. We're together again.

"Let's get out of here," I say after a few minutes. It's only three in the morning but we both know that neither of us is going to get back to sleep.

"Yeah."

We don't pay the bill and the black air feels cleansing.

The ability to just leave, to pack a bag and ride out of town, to have that freedom—it feels like a victory of sorts. A victory in the face of adversity. This moment, this specific moment, as we trace the night with the yellow light from the Enfield and cold air blows in our faces and the town, with all its horrors, shrinks on the horizon behind us; it's like standing at the top of a waterfall we've spent all day dangerously climbing.

And what do we want to do? We want to throw our hands in the air and whoop and scream. Some people call traveling escapism, and in many ways, I suppose it is. Whatever is left behind gets frozen in time and is there again, unchanged, having to be faced up to again upon return. If I am ever forced to return to Godhra, it will still be the same hellhole. Traveling isn't a solution. It's just a feeling. A feeling of self-determination, of retaking control. Retaking control of a life that somehow got too big.

CROSSING CROSS

We ride all day, only stopping for breakfast to celebrate getting back onto NH-8. We reach Ahmedabad by noon. At least we almost reach Ahmedabad. Ten kilometers short of the city limits there is an enormous traffic jam. We meander through the spluttering vehicles for several kilometers before eventually reaching the cause of the problem.

It is a railway crossing. The barriers are down but there isn't a train in sight. I realize that they must be running again, but I don't know if it's because the strike is over or because we're in a different state now. Cyclists and Bajaj scooter drivers are dismounting and tipping their bikes under the barrier to get through. The Enfield is too heavy and the barrier is too low for us to do the same. The only thing for us to do is wait.

I turn off the Enfield. Everyone else keeps their vehicles ticking over. We cook in the heat. Ten minutes creep by. I feel slightly faint. I can't help feeling annoyingly envious of all the vehicle-free pedestrians and cyclists who are managing to escape the gridlock. For some reason it doesn't seem fair. I keep turning over the idea of squeezing the Enfield through somehow, even though I've already decided that it isn't possible. It feels impossibly hot. Still no sign of any train. The lights on the barrier flash alternately, hypnotically.

"What the fuck is going on?" I say to no one in particular.

My sweat evaporates before it even has a chance to cool me. I start sneering at all the other drivers who haven't turned their engines off. Can't they tell how much worse they are making things? Why keep their engines on? It doesn't make any sense. We wait. Ten more minutes pass.

"This is a fucking joke," I continue with myself. Yasmin, who got off the bike almost as soon as we arrived, says she is going to find something to drink.

I smoke a cigarette. It burns.

In the distance, I can see the gleaming silver front of a freight train approaching. Everyone starts revving their engines even though it will be several more minutes before the train actually reaches the barrier. I try to tell the man in the truck next to me to stop flushing exhaust in my face, but he pretends not to understand.

When the train finally does arrive, I am amazed at how long it is. I count fifty-eight cars as they inch past at a geriatric pace. I tell myself that this nightmare will soon be over. We are minutes away from freedom. Then Yasmin and I can go and get some lunch and relax for a couple of hours. We deserve it. Maybe I'll rent a room so we can siesta. We've been on the move for eight hours today already. That's it, I decide. We'll have a cool shower, and a drink. Then see where we are. As the sixtieth car passes I turn the key in the ignition. There are only three cars left now. I pump the kick start a couple of times until the amperes reach the right level. I'm not even looking at the train now. All I can think about is what lies in store for Yasmin and me, half wondering where she might be. I assume she must be nearby and throw my weight down on the kick start.

There is a spine-chilling screech. For a second I think it is the bike and my heart leaps. But then, with the sound of tearing metal still echoing, I realize it is the train. It convulses to a halt. The last car stands proudly dead center in the intersection, the rest of the train snaking its way into a new horizon.

For a second, we all look at it and try to absorb what this means. I am one of the last to come to terms with this crushing development. Everyone stops revving their engines and imagined tuts and sighs seem to fill the air as I stare at the train, desperately trying to comprehend what has just happened. I am finding it very difficult to believe that the train has managed to break down at the final car. I'm finding it very hard to believe that any of us are here at all. The sun cannot be *this* hot. The situation cannot be *this* bad. *This, this . . . this* whole thing is too ridiculous to be real.

But it is real. The reality is there, standing stockstill in front of me. I am inches away from crying. I laugh instead. Short and bitter. I don't blink. I just stare at the train, meditating on my hot fury, welling in the midday inferno.

Yasmin returns.

"What's going on?"

"What does it look like?" I sneer without taking my eyes off the train.

I vaguely notice her looking at me strangely before wisely backing off. She finds a small square of shade just off the side of the road. Soon after that, wheels steam and engine-control men wave flags. The train starts moving. At last, forty-five minutes later, we seem to be getting somewhere. Then I look closer. Yes, the train is moving, but . . . I don't believe it. It's reversing.

"Please, this isn't happening," I say, throwing my head into my hands. For some reason, I am taking all this personally. Some-where along the line I have decided that this whole episode is designed to persecute me. With every car that repasses, I pile on the emotional distress. All they had to do was edge the train forward one car. Instead they are reversing their way through sixty. It doesn't make sense. I am letting this wind me up. Even though I know it is the worst thing to do in India, I am letting the madness get under my skin. I am playing a dangerous game.

But I can't help it. Even by India's standards, this stretches all reasonable bounds of farce. I count the carriages as they back up and eventually reach the final five. I take a deep breath and look for the light at the end of the tunnel. I tell myself that once they've got the train cleared from the crossing, they'll open the barriers and let the traffic pass while they fix the problem. It would be the only thing that made sense.

That's when the returning engine car, big and red with square edges, lurches to a halt—smack bang in the middle of the crossing. My left temple starts twitching. Anger blisters inside me. It just goes on. On and on and on. The train creeps forward one more time, breaking down at the final car once again before reversing all the way up to the engine car. Always, just inside the crossing.

An hour and a half after the episode began, the engineers finally garner enough sense to pull the train clear. With the train pulled back and broken down, they eventually lift the barrier. I am in a state of shock. My anger hasn't left me. I cannot get over the futility of it all. I want to know why this whole episode happened. There must be a purpose to it all.

There isn't the time to consider that now. The traffic starts edging into the crossing before the barrier is even clear. I turn on the ignition and start pumping the kick start. After five tries I look up to see that some vehicles have tried to pass in the middle of the crossing and now there is a new jam. I shake my head and concentrate on starting the bike. If they want to be stuck here the rest of their lives, that's their problem. That's why *we* have an Enfield. We will be out of this mess in a matter of minutes. At least we would be, except . . . the bike won't start.

METAMORPHOSIS

Something snaps. Maybe it's the heat, maybe it's the bike, maybe it's the train, maybe it's India, maybe it's Yasmin, maybe it's me. Maybe it's all of that. Maybe it's this whole misadventure. Why am I here? Do I really believe that I am about to make millions ripping off some drug-and-diamond courier for the Mumbai Mafia? Is that why I am here? I don't even believe that. That's just my story. Then why? Why am I going through this physical and mental hell? Yasmin? Is Yasmin the reason for my being here? She doesn't even love me.

Suddenly everything is pointless. I stop frenetically kick-starting the bike and simultaneously cursing. For a second I just sit. Then something happens to me. It feels physiological. At least, my sensory perception shifts, so I decide that it must be physiological. The honking cars and trucks and scooters sound suddenly muffled. The world turns matte instead of glossy. The heat is still there, but now there is an indeterminate line of separation between me and It. Even my body doesn't feel my own.

Everything seems different, distant, somehow elsewhere. I suppose that this could be an out-of-body experience of sorts. All I know is, I am not here anymore. I'm not in this situation. My body is, but I am not. I have stepped off the stage. Suddenly I am on the sidelines, invisible to the scene. It feels neither good nor bad. I don't feel relief or fear. I feel totally detached. I am emo-tionless, impartial to my surroundings. I see the screaming Indians and the broken-down train and it means nothing to me except a vaguely amusing anecdote. I turn and notice Yasmin, who is look-ing at the chaos, and all I see is a beautiful, slightly lost, and confused young woman.

And then I see myself, still propping up the bike between my thighs. I don't feel what my body is feeling. I no longer think what my brain and emotions are telling me. Somehow I have entered a new plane.

I decide to take a look around.

I am partly aware of the bike smashing to the ground as I climb off it, but it's only an observation really. There are none of the implications attached. I see people looking at me as I start stepping my way through all the madness, but their attention doesn't concern me. I am here now only as a witness. I stare into people's faces for character clues and consume the minutiae to flesh out the scene.

Wrinkles and wild eyes, sweating brows and worn hands, vapor-blue scooters and black exhaust, fierce gesticulations and desperate shouting. I push my body into the tightest corners for the closest look. I touch things, reading the texture in fingerprints. I listen, I look, I smell. Ahhhh—with one deep breath, the thick heat and terrible pollution. Everything is clear. I see as a Greek god sees. The world becomes an enormously complex play viewed from a lofty pantheon. I don't dictate the terms.

Yasmin's face suddenly appears in front of me. I watch her lips move in slow motion. Silk-thin saliva strands catch between the corners of her mouth before snapping and sinking while white teeth move. I watch the words as they waft toward me and say things for me to interpret.

"Are . . ."

The word sounds new, different—are, are, are—like staring at a word for a long time on a page until the spelling doesn't seem so certain and the whole thing looks strange.

"You . . .

"Okay . . .

"?"

A question. Yasmin is asking me a question. Am I okay?

I ask myself. "Are you okay, Josh?"

There seem to be numerous possible answers to that. The fact is, I don't feel myself at all—not in an ill way, but in an absence-of-the-ego way. For the first time in my life, I'm unaware of my needs. I don't have an agenda. I'm not looking at the world in terms of Me. I'm not interpreting events to see how they benefit me, affect me. I guess, in a sense, I am egoless. I vaguely wonder to myself if this is what enlightenment feels like. This sense of detachment. It's not that I don't care. I just feel much, much less involved.

There's nothing going on in my brain. No thought, no analysis, just . . . being. Just . . . watching. I feel spent. I don't want to talk. I don't want to answer Yasmin. I feel protective of this. I don't want to be sucked back into the Here and Now. I'm scared, in a dispassionate, nonattached, Buddha-like way, that speaking might make me aware of my senses again. As if speech will break the spell.

I just want to stand here and survey the world. It all seems so fantastically splendid. Being able to watch and observe like this, without emotion, without involvement. It's so liberating. Green is green, anger is anger, a truck is a truck. I'm not angry at this green truck because it's in my way. It's just there now.

Suddenly the world is full of possibilities. Every scene, every conversation, every character, every emotion—all stretch out before me in an endless stream of possible permutations. I feel as if I can truly narrate now. As if I have made some sort of transition. Deep, personal, something that's always been there, a potential within me, the narrator who, until now, has been in a cocoon, hibernating.

I feel, at last, as if this episode has been the point to my life, that this is the crossroads that my entire life has been leading to. That fine line, ever separating me gently from my fantasy, keeping me in reality—it's gone now. I have been under an illusion. The illusion of involvement. It's been the taking part that's confused me. The truth is I have to step out of it. Embrace and step into my own fantasy world. Escape and step out of reality to see it for what it really is. I am outside events. I can be removed from everything I do from now on. I can finally abandon the *I.* I can now see things on a whole new level. I have stepped into the novel. My life is suddenly, truly, fiction. And I am, dispassionately, its narrator.

THE HERO

"Come on, let's go," I say, grabbing Yasmin's wrist and pulling her out of the melee back toward the bike. She stumbles behind me. "Here, give me a hand," I say, signaling at the bike.

She takes the handlebars and together we manage to heave the Enfield upright. I pull it onto its stand and start unleashing the bags.

"What are you doing?"

I throw Yasmin her rucksack. "We're dumping the bike," I announce.

"Why?"

"Three reasons," I say, throwing the rest of the bags, including the money and the fake gems, to the side of the road. Yasmin gasps, waiting to see if any of the stuff spills out. I'm not worried. I don't care anymore about the precious cargo. I'm not involved anymore. I'm just acting as an agent in all of this. And besides, it is all fake. "One, it's broken," I say, working the gears into neutral. "Two, it's taking too long." I push the bike into a small, dusty space. "And three, we can catch a bus. We've already covered half the distance. We'll be in Jaisalmer by tomorrow morning." Then I pick up the bags and throw them over my shoulder.

Yasmin looks at me. "What about the strike?"

"It was only in Maharashtra. We're in a different state now.

Look," I say, pointing at the train. "The railroad is working here. If you can call it that. Chances are buses will be too."

"Are you sure this is a good idea? Leaving Faizad's bike like this?"

"Completely sure. We've got a story to get on with and this bit is taking too long."

"What?"

"Nothing." I point over the crossing. "We'll catch a rickshaw on the other side of this mess to the station. There'll probably be an afternoon coach."

THE BEAT

At the station, waiting for the bus, I see an article in the paper.

EXPRESS NEWS SERVICE

STONE-THROWING IN GODHRA

An altercation between a woman customer, identified by police as a certain Nalini Jaywant, and a banana vendor over the quality of fruit flared into an exchange of stones and other missiles between members of two communities in the Zahurpura vegetable market of Godhra town on Sunday evening.

According to the Godhra police control room, the vendor replied offensively when Mrs. Jaywant inquired about the price of the bananas. Her complaints reportedly had no effect, so she left and returned with her husband and some others. The vendor also had gathered some supporters. A verbal duel between the two groups escalated into a stone-throwing incident, the police said, adding that they dispersed when the police arrived.

I smile. The locals weren't swearing at us. They were swearing at the vendor. The women were probably cleared off the streets.

That's why there were only men around. That's why the town was so hostile—because of the riot earlier that day.

I smile to myself because the Truth was so far from my own take on events. Does it matter that I was *wrong,* that my self-obsessed perception of reality had absolutely no bearing on fact? After all, which story was the more interesting? Stone-throwing over the price of vegetables, or a near rape and hightailing it out of town?

I'm pretty sure it's the latter. Or maybe it's a combination of the two. Perhaps it's the contrast between them that makes the story. If I can put the two halves of the puzzle together, between what I see and what's really happening—maybe that's where the real treasure lies. Perhaps that's where my Bestseller rests. Between my inner narrative and the world outside, the one I've learned to observe. I'm starting to sense a novel with selling potential happening here.

PART FOUR

MOS EISLEY

Jaisalmer is like a scene out of *Star Wars*. It still has the medieval, *Arabian Nights* feel I remember from the last time I was here, but now there's a futuristic element that's making everything seem particularly surreal. Maybe it's the fighter jets we see sonic-booming their way over on the short journey from the bus stop into town. The rickshaw driver says that it's because of the tests. The army base is bigger nowadays. We pass a group of soldiers, marching like storm troopers, near the ancient fort. There are camels too. Lots of them, rocking their way around the streets like alien creatures.

The rickshaw wallah takes us to a cheap guest house of his choosing. We don't argue with him. The bus journey, which started in the afternoon and lasted all through the night with Hindi soundtracks blaring, means we're too tired for fighting. And besides, the place looks reasonable. It has a reception area that opens onto the street like a Mediterranean villa, with brown flowered tiles on the floor and whitewashed walls.

We check into separate rooms. Yasmin says she needs to get some sleep. I don't know if that's why she wants her own room or if it's just an excuse. There's a strange energy between us. I barely spoke to her on the bus journey—I was busy meditating on my newfound enlightenment, pondering what it all meant, bathing in the glory of my liberated soul.

I don't know what's on Yasmin's mind. It could be me, us, the journey, the scam, anything. All I know is, she's got her own distractions and she isn't letting on. Nothing new there. It's just that our mutual silence feels tense. It's like we're arguing again. The fact that we're in two different spaces, and we don't want to talk to each other about where we're coming from, feels like arguing, even though it's not—not really, not officially. I decide I don't want to enter it. I know where forcing Yasmin to talk leads to. It's just not worth it. This isn't the time. Let her get some sleep. In her own room.

I take a shower and then decide to attempt to track down Faizad. I want to touch base with him before it's too late. I've been feeling nervous that he'd go ahead without me ever since our first delay leaving Mumbai. It's been six days since we last saw each other on the train and I'm not even sure he knows I'm coming.

It doesn't take me long to find him. There is only one five-star hotel in Jaisalmer. Not like Faizad to stay anywhere less. The receptionist patches me through to his room. No answer. The receptionist comes back on the line and asks if I want to leave a message. I do.

I go back to my room and lie down, arms folded, with my hands tucked in under my armpits. The day is streaming into the room, making it nice and bright—just right for tackling my insomnia. Sleep starts to come, from the back of my mind, and I let myself fall into it, closing my eyes, not allowing myself to be aware that I'm nodding off—just letting it come and take me. I need this so badly.

Five minutes later and there's a knock on my door. Telephone call. My eyes are raw when I open them and I feel much worse, as if my body is exacting revenge for teasing it this way.

The telephone feels cold when I put it up to my ear.

"Josh?" I can sense nervousness in his voice.

"Faizad," I say it calmly. I don't want him to know how relieved I am to hear from him. "How are you?"

"Can we meet?" he says.

"Sure," I say, unintentionally letting all the casual pretense leak out. "You can shout me lunch at the fancy hotel you're staying in. Shit, man, you really know how to live it up, don't you? That place, what's it called, the Jaisalmer—"

"Can you meet me now?" he interrupts. I can't tell if it is my blustering on or his desperate tone that justifies it.

"Er . . ." The truth is I'd rather do it later. Now that I've tracked him down, I'd rather wait. I really am exhausted. "I guess so."

"Good."

I consider telling Yasmin where I'm going, but something stops me. I tell myself that I wouldn't want to disturb her. Not while she is sleeping. Not in her own room.

RENDEZVOUS

We meet in a restaurant on the west side of the fort. Faizad is already there by the time I arrive. When I offer to shake, he grips my hand and pulls me toward him. He gives me a couple of hearty back pats and then smiles as we break. Just like our days together in Mumbai. It's reassuring.

"Jesus, you look like shit," he says, scanning me.

I look down at my clothes and pull at the thighs of my trouser legs. "It's been a rough journey," I explain.

"Well, I'm glad you came," he says, looking back up at me, smiling into my eyes.

"Me too," I say, smiling back at him.

Faizad gets us an *haveli,* a kind of private balcony, overlooking the city below. A tall lattice shutter veils us from the afternoon sun. Outside, staircases run up the walls on each of the squat, flat-topped yellow buildings in the town below. They seem to weave and interconnect in an impossible maze. The whole town looks like it's grown out of the desert. And here we are, in the fort, sitting like miniature men in the sandcastle.

We order drinks. A jet fighter approaches from the distance. Faizad plugs his ears. It streaks across the sky, black and wings tipped, then disappears in the direction of Pakistan. Afterward, the sound cracks and explodes, as if it's breaking its way out of a glass jar. The world rumbles with the aftershocks.

"The fort will fucking fall down if they carry on like this much longer," Faizad says, unplugging his ears.

"I'm surprised it hasn't already," I say.

And that's how we begin the small talk. What the city is like, the seasonal changes, how's your hotel, not as nice as yours, etc., etc. It's a reasonable disguise for what I'm really thinking. Namely, how will Faizad's contact be able to smuggle drugs and diamonds across the border with all this military activity? If it hasn't already happened, of course.

Occasionally I wonder what Faizad's trying to hide behind the chitchat. He doesn't seem interested in my arrival, or how I got here—or at least he doesn't ask. I can tell that there's something on his mind, though. He keeps looking at the door as if he half expects someone to walk in at any moment. He spends a lot of time picking at the embroidered sausage cushion he's leaning against. He seems nervous.

Eventually we run out of nothings to say. I feel that we are at the edge of a "serious" conversation, yet neither of us seems prepared to make the first move. Time passes loudly in the silences.

"So, how are things?" I try one more time, for the third time, to fill the gaps.

"Okay, okay. Not bad," he answers, in the same way, for the third time.

I start getting fed up and show my impatience by sighing slightly and looking out the window. Faizad doesn't react. As I look outside I notice two beggars badgering tourists in the street below. I see one of them make a feeble attempt at pickpocketing.

One of the tourists swings around and some shouting ensues. Above them, a lime billboard explodes the word LIMCA at me.

"Do you want another drink?" I say absentmindedly. I need the caffeine.

"No, I'm okay."

"Are you sure?" He doesn't look at me. "Because I'm getting one." I groan as I get up.

No answer.

I pad out into the restaurant courtyard. A marble floor and high red walls spread coolly in front of me. The difference in temperature is noticeable. I breathe in the enclave air. I lean over the balcony and take a few moments for myself. I need to clear my head. I haven't felt this tired since . . .

And then I see him. Calm, confident, I can see the brown-haired boy. He's wearing baggy army-green trousers and a white V-neck T-shirt. There is the faintest sign of a goatee, blonder than the brown hair on his head. His cheeks are drawn against high, distinguished bones. He looks slightly smaller than me, more compact, but still tall.

For a few seconds I just watch him as he looks back at me. He's got that slight smile on his lips again, as if he knows something I don't. We simply watch each other. I want to say something to him, but I'm not sure what. Part of me feels that I should say thanks. For helping me in Mumbai, for telling me to get out of the Caged City, for reminding me to go see Mani.

And then it strikes me and that old fear, the fear I felt that time I saw him outside the Shiv Niketan, comes rushing back.

How come he knows about Mani?

I never really considered it at the time, too messed up to care, I guess, but now that I'm sober—it seems particularly strange.

Strange, like he-always-knows-how-to-find-me strange. For a

long time I've thought he was just doing a good job of following me. But now it seems as if things have been the other way around. As if he's always known where to find me and then met me there. Not like he's been following me at all. More like he's simply been making sure I am where I should be.

Like knowing that I'd be in Jaisalmer, here, in this *haveli,* today, how could he possibly have known that? And that smile, always that smug smile, as if he's sneering at me, as if he knows more than I do, as if he knows who I am, what's important to me.

I get a dreadful feeling then, a terrible new insight. Perhaps he's the narrator, the real author of this story, not me. He seems to know everything, and I know nothing. More importantly, if he's the narrator, then what does that make me? The hero, the villain, a minor player in some sidebar subplot? Is my version of events really what's going on here?

I think it's time to find out.

I move for the stairs, ready to trot down two, three at a time, ready to give chase—I know he's going to run. And he does. I am in the courtyard in less than five seconds. I spin on my heels, kicking up dust, and then make for the door leading out—out from the cool and into the glare outside. The heat hits me hard as soon as I step into the street. The scene burns silver white. I squint. Between my eyelashes I can make out spiderlike silhouettes. I can hear the tourists and the beggars still shouting. They seem very loud. I feel slightly sick. After a few seconds, I manage to open my eyes. I look left, then right, then left again. I can't see him anywhere. I look right and I think I see a pair of feet disappearing into an alleyway. It's him. I'm about to start running when I suddenly hear Faizad calling from the *haveli* above me.

"I said," he says as if he's tired of having to repeat himself, "what the fuck are you doing down there?" He stresses each word, to make sure I hear him properly this time. He doesn't need to. I heard him the first time around. I just needed a moment to come up with an excuse.

"Oh, nothing," I say, looking up at the hovering shadow. I feel I have to confess. It must be some subliminal Catholic thing in me, shadows behind lattice shutters. "I was just checking out the fight," I lie dutifully, pointing at the fracas. By now, one of the tourists is shaking a beggar by the scruff of his neck and calling out for the police. The beggar is also grabbing the tourist by the shirt and is shouting in a language I don't understand. A small audience is gathering.

"Well, forget that," Faizad says darkly. "Let's go get a shave."

That may seem like a random suggestion, but it's not. Barbers are one of the few treats in India, the only real pampering a man can get amid all the filth. And I need to freshen up after the journey I've just endured. Faizad's also got a thick crop of stubble that needs trimming. If anything, it seems like the most natural place for us to go next.

We find an empty barbershop on the path leading down from

the fort into the town. Two aging men whip red plastic seats and small towels to greet us.

"Please, boss," one of them, the one farther back, says, grinning at me. He has long graying stubble, which makes me nervous. I distrust barbers with haggard beards almost as much as hairdressers with bad haircuts. I take a seat and he whooshes me back into horizontal submission.

"New blade," I warn with one flat palm in the air.

"Yes, yes, of course. New blade, always new blade, sir." The barber turns his back to me and fiddles suspiciously around in the drawer and fixes the razor. I watch Faizad getting lathered up out of the corner of my eye. My barber swings around and sprays cool water from a plant gun on my face. He slaps the foam on in thick dollops and then clears my lips with a finger, like he's making a cake. A poster saying OHM SWEET OHM is tacked to the wall above the mirror. I close my eyes and tell myself to relax. Then I hear the blade scratching as he pulls sections of my face tight against the grain.

"Josh?" Faizad's voice sounds muffled.

"Yeah."

"I need to tell you something." I open my eyes slightly. The barber is swishing the blade across my face with elaborate elbow gestures, like a musical conductor. I try not to grip the armrests too hard. "I'm pretty sure now that it was Dowdy that killed Ajay."

"Yeah?" I say between swipes of the blade.

"Yeah. He's the only one who could have allowed it. Ajay was too high up for anyone else to get away with it."

"But why?" I pick up seamlessly, as if we're simply continuing the conversation we started on the train all those days and all those kilometers ago. I'm secretly happy to finally be broaching real matters at hand, happy enough, at least, to leave the brown-haired boy, and all that he implies, behind me. "Just to set you up? Why would he want to do that?"

"No. It was because Ajay was getting too big for his boots. You saw him that time in Benson's. The bloke was losing it. He was doing far too much coke and letting that L.A. porn star take care of everything." So that explains the tattoos. "And the amount of business we were doing on the side. I kept telling him we needed to cool things down, but he just wouldn't listen." He's talking fast, like a guilty child blaming his brother.

I don't say anything. Is this really what Faizad needs to tell me? Is this what's been on his mind? I thought we already knew all this. Then he starts explaining. It's clear we're no longer operating on a need-to-know basis. We're clearly operating on a "friend-friend" level now. I've made the migration. By traveling to Jaisalmer, I've arrived at the point where I need to be. Faizad starts telling me his story, the story he nearly told me on Chowpatty Beach, the story of his life—the life he began after Mehmet screwed him.

The barber keeps pinching the skin around my chin to keep my face taut.

"It was Ajay who introduced me to Dowdy Ibrahim. He helped me get back on my feet. He told me that Dowdy could help me get back into Bollywood. That he had connections. I thought he was helping me because he liked me. Looking back on it, I think he was just trying to get set up on his own. Recruiting me was his first step toward independence, toward becoming a boss. Anyway, I started out small, just running the Cellar and stuff. Then I came up with the idea to start selling drugs there. Ajay had a source for coke, and after I pitched the plan to Dowdy, customs took care of getting the stuff into the country. Dowdy had the connections.

It was easy. Everyone was happy. Dowdy got his share, Ajay got promoted, and I was making good money for the first time in a long time. It was good. Later, Dowdy told Ajay about the Jaisalmer connection. Said he wanted Ajay to take care of things, oversee a new operation. It was another promotion for Ajay. Ajay was ecstatic. Told me he wanted me as his right-hand man. It was too good an offer to refuse. The money was great."

He's not talking like that time we were on Chowpatty. Everything is edited. Just the facts. No need for color, no need for detail. Like he's running out of time. Like he's scared. Of what? I wonder.

"What Jaisalmer connection?" I say, playing dumb. "I don't understand."

"Dowdy wanted to smuggle heroin in through the Pakistan border. Ajay and I were put in charge."

"Heroin? Wow." I say it only because I feel that anything short of a show of surprise might come across as suspicious.

"Yeah, so what?" Faizad says, suitably indignant. "What difference does it make?"

"I don't know, Faizad, it's just that selling coke in the Cellar and smuggling smack across the border seem like two different kettles of fish. That's all."

"Well, it was. That's why we were getting paid so well."

"I see. Carry on."

"Well, after a while, Ajay came up with this idea to start selling on the side."

"What do you mean?"

"It was my fault, really. I'd been down to Goa and I'd seen so many Westerners smoking brown that I mentioned it to Ajay one day and we agreed that it was crazy for Dowdy to smuggle heroin out of India, when there was an international marketplace right on our own front doorstep."

"Very astute of you."

The barber keeps wiping the excess foam off the blade onto the back of his hand and now there's several wobbling dollops, inches from my nose.

"Thanks," Faizad says a little sarcastically. "Anyway. Ajay got a thing about it. Said we should start doing business on the side. Told me to go down to Goa and see how it went. It didn't take me long to figure out that we'd struck gold. I shifted a kilo in a week."

"A kilo!"

"Yup."

"Fuck me."

"I know."

"Didn't Dowdy notice?"

"No. After all, Ajay and I were in charge. Dowdy didn't need to know the details, he was just watching the bottom line and we made sure that stayed steady. Anyway, I soon realized that selling wraps in Goa was a long way around things, and after dealing with the same people consistently for a few months, we agreed to start selling in bulk, let them take care of the dirty work. And that's how we got set up in Pushkar."

"Pushkar?" I say. Part of me is reveling in the way my story is coming together, the way the facts are playing themselves out to fit my fiction. Another part of me is incredulous—I'm incredibly surprised to discover that all this time, there's been Truth (far more than I could ever have hoped for or imagined) in my fantasy. Is it luck? Or have I just been shortchanging myself on my fact-finding abilities? Maybe I've simply misunderstood the nature of stories, the nature of life. You only need a few facts, it seems, to form a reality. I can feel my sense of enlightenment growing with each moment, each sentence that's written as it occurs.

"Yeah, it was easier for everyone. The people we were dealing with usually came through Delhi, and it was much closer to Jaisalmer . . . so it just made sense."

"That's a pretty interesting setup."

"Yeah, well. It was. Until Ajay started losing it."

He pauses then, perhaps to let me absorb the information. Or maybe his barber just has a razor blade to his throat. My barber has finished the first round and is now lathering me up again for a second attack. Already my cheeks are burning and I know I'll get a rash when he's finished, but I don't stop him. Don't ask me why, it's a male bravado thing, I guess. I take the opportunity to restart the conversation.

"Was it true, then, what Ajay said, that time we were in his place?"

"What? About me cutting him out?"

"Yeah."

"Of course. I was sick of running around for Ajay just so he could get made. He wasn't doing anything to help me get back into Bollywood. Ajay was using me. So I used him. After all, like I told you, you've got to screw the world before it screws you. I knew Ajay would dump me once he got to where he needed to go, so I decided to make some money, real money of my own, before he did."

"And that's why you gave me those wraps of smack to sell?"

"Yeah. I wanted to check out the domestic market. See if I couldn't get something set up there."

"So you used me, just like Ajay used you," I say, a little hurt, genuinely a little insulted. "You hired me to do your dirty work so you could set up on your own."

"Don't act so innocent, Josh. It's not as if you weren't willing. You'd been trying to get in on my act ever since we first met."

"What do you mean?"

"Do you think I'm stupid? I know why you wanted to hang with me. There are lots of people who would have fallen over themselves for the job I gave you. I just needed to see if I could trust you."

"I was broke, I thought you wanted to help me."

"Funny, those were the exact same words I said to Ajay once."

I'm a little taken aback by all this. I thought Faizad and I were being honest with each other. At least, I thought he was being honest with me. After all the effort I put into earning his trust, I feel I deserve that much. I certainly never figured that he might have his own agenda. But I don't say anything. I guess there's just a small part of me that feels like I've failed. I thought I was the one playing Faizad, not the other way around. There are some things, at least, that I haven't perceived, that I've missed amid my fictionalizing. Like, for example, the idea that a character might have his own agenda, his own motives.

The barber uses less foam this time, just a thin layer, but he spreads it all over—under my eyes, my entire neck, even the tips of my ears.

After a few moments Faizad says, "To be perfectly honest, I never really thought it would take off. Heroin isn't exactly a club drug. I still don't know how you shifted the stuff."

"I sold it to the street kids I was teaching," I say, more as a comeback, a touché, than anything else, even though it's not true, not strictly. I only started selling heroin when I was in hiding. We know that now. Don't ask me why my profits were so strong in the Cellar. Maybe it was the marketing gimmick, an appropriate paradox: a middle-class white boy selling coke to the Indians in the Cellar. Just the sort of thing to attract business, most likely. Why should he be the one to spring all the surprises?

"You what?"

"Them and the hijras."

Faizad starts laughing then, loud and bombastic and painfully. Both barbers stop shaving till he stops. The room is practically vibrating. "Fucking hell, man, you never cease to amaze me. I knew I made the right choice when I hired you."

After what seems like a very long time, he calms down.

"So why did you take me up to Ajay's, I mean, if you were keeping me on the side?" I say eventually. "Surely you would have wanted to keep me a secret?"

"He found out. It's not as if word of a white boy selling coke in the Cellar doesn't get around. Even Dowdy knows about you."

"He does?"

"Of course. Mumbai's not such a big town, you know."

"So people keep telling me," I say.

Dowdy knows about me. That's not good. That's a little too much reality for my liking. I try not to let my anxiety show.

"Well, how did Ajay know that you were making money on the side?"

"I don't know," Faizad says, and sighs. "Lucky guess, I suppose. The guy was so fucking paranoid, he would have been hard-pressed not to have stumbled across some betrayal or other that would have been true. I mean, two weeks earlier, he was threatening to kill me because he thought I was shagging Ayesha."

"And were you?" I ask, half joking.

"Yes. But that's not the point. He didn't know. He couldn't have."

Poor Ajay, I think to myself, enjoying the irony. Suffering from the same delusional truths as me. Totally paranoid and totally right. Maybe it's a sixth sense we all have. If you imagine something, it's probably true. Or maybe imagining it makes it true. Who knows?

I don't say anything while the barber concentrates. He seems determined to shave every hair off my face; he's shaved the baby hairs just below my eyes and now he's making a move for my earlobes. After this, I think he's going to start on my forehead.

"Why are you telling me all this?" I say eventually.

"I need your help."

"What for?"

"I'm going to do another deal, this time to make enough to break out for good. If this deal comes off, I'll never have to work for Dowdy again. In fact, I'll never have to work for anyone again. And, if you help me, neither will you."

Maybe I should just go with Faizad, I realize as he says this. Trust him. Forget the scam. Ditch Sanjay, ditch James, ditch Yasmin. After all, he is promising to set me up for life. Isn't that all I really want out of this? My dropout money? Hmm. Well, it's definitely worth consideration.

"Go on," I say.

"I want you to come with me to the border."

"Why?"

He pauses. I get a feeling Faizad is finally getting to whatever it is that's been on his mind, what's been worrying him. I don't say anything. I just wait. I just listen. "I think someone's following me."

I can't help gulping then. Just as the barber reaches my Adam's apple too. The nick bites.

Is it him? The brown-haired boy? The omniscient one. Could he be following Faizad?

The cut is bad, I can tell. The old man is busy clotting it, with a camphor block, but I can feel a warm trickle. I glare at him. He just grins black teeth at me and wipes my throat clean with a flannel bib. The blood tickles.

"Who?" I ask eventually, heart thumping. Please don't let it be the brown-haired boy, I hear myself wishing, please no. The guy is starting to seem invincible.

"I haven't seen him yet." My heart breathes a sigh of relief and sheds fifty beats in the process. "But I think I know who it is— one of Dowdy's men."

"Why would Dowdy send someone to follow you?" I say, a little calmer.

"I think Dowdy tried to set me up for Ajay's murder. In fact, I'm sure of it. He never figured I'd make it out of town. It was only because I happened to be at Ajay's place when the police came that I found out early and got the chance to escape."

"You were there?"

"Ayesha had said Ajay would be out of town for a couple of days. That's when he got shot. The police found him and came straight to Ajay's place for clues. It was just lucky that I'd paid the receptionist that month. Ayesha set that warning system up to stop us from getting caught messing around. I cannot tell you how many times I've had to hide in that fucking cupboard. Anyway, that's how I got a head start out of town. I was just lucky." He pauses. "Which is why I was so surprised that you found me on the train. I still don't know how you found out so quick."

My brain whirs with "ers," but I silence them. "It was on the news, like I said."

Faizad snorts. "That's weird." He pauses. "Amazing the police didn't search the train."

"Well, I guess the police aren't as quick as the media," I say, wondering how Mani could have found out about Ajay so fast. Maybe he does have Mafia connections after all. Was he setting me up to take the fall in Mumbai? Was he lying about covering for me, in Delhi? Was it a police raid after all? Is Mani my enemy?

You and me and this whole game we're playing with your life . . .

I realize that I still don't know anything, which wouldn't bother me so much if I didn't feel so convinced that the brown-haired boy knows everything. It feels like he's controlling me. Like he's the narrator.

The barber sticks a wad of tissue on the cut to stop the bleeding. He tries to shave me again before I stop him with a shake of the head. He wipes what's left of the foam off my face and starts rubbing greasy pink cream into my cheeks for the massage.

"What do you want me to do?" I say finally.

"I need you to watch my back. I think Dowdy wants me out of the picture. He's trying to sever all connections with Ajay. He knows I've got to do another deal before I can leave the country. He's going to try and take care of me, I just know it."

I also realize that things are not going according to plan. Not even close. I can't switch the money if there's even the smallest chance that Faizad's contact might check. If Faizad's contact checks the cash, Faizad's a dead man. And if I'm there too, at the border, so will I be. Fuck. The whole point was that the Pakistanis wouldn't check. The whole plan assumed an element of trust. That Faizad would trust me, that the Pakistanis would trust him. Now that Ajay's dead, the trust is all gone. This is the problem with basing madcap schemes in far-fetched fantasies. Truth and reality can quickly seep in and unravel everything. It's all over. I feel faintly sick.

The barber uses a vibrating machine that rattles loudly and wobbles my cheeks violently, making it too difficult to talk. So I don't.

"I'm not saying it's going to be easy, Josh. I have to admit, I *am* nervous about this next deal. My contact may have heard about Ajay's murder, he may know that I'm not protected anymore. Plus, this deal is much, much bigger than usual. It's going to be risky. Chances are, you'll just be a show of strength more than anything else. If my contact sees you, then he'll know I have other options outside of Ibrahim. That's really why I need you there. Just a show of strength. Just to be sure."

The barber is wiping the last of the cream from around my mouth, so I don't have time to ask Faizad how he can know that, how he can be so certain. If I'm just a show of strength, is there a chance, a solid chance, that things will pass off smoothly, that the Pakistanis won't check? It's probably a good thing I don't get a chance to ask. It might all fall out, all my questions, all my secrets, if I'm not careful, if I don't check my desperation. The barber threatens to splash cheap aftershave on me. I stop him just in time.

"Look, Josh," Faizad restarts, "a lot of things have happened in the last few months, a lot of things I don't understand. I don't know who I can trust anymore. I'm ninety percent sure that everything will be fine. But I need someone I can trust, someone outside of this whole mess, who has nothing to do with Dowdy and the people I'm dealing with. Once it's all over, I swear, I'll make it very worth your while."

I breathe for a few moments. Maybe I should just forget the suitcase switches. Maybe I should trust my instincts, the ones I heard calling me on the train. After all, I am working for Faizad now. He does trust me. And I trust him, inasmuch as I believe he'd pay me well for helping him. I wonder just how much we're talking here. Enough for me and my plans? What about Yasmin? What about Sanjay? Should he benefit? After all, he never *actually* introduced me to Faizad. I'm the one who's done all the work, the real work. Maybe I should settle for this, get paid for making friends with a drug courier. It's not the jackpot but it is something. It doesn't make me Robin Hood but it does mean I'll beat the system. I'll never have to work again.

I see then that Faizad is suddenly standing over me. I look up at him. He looks different: young, fresh-faced—kind, even. He's shaved off his sideburns. He's looking at me with an expression that wants answers. "I'm not sure," I eventually manage with a difficult smile. "I've never done anything like this before."

"All I'm asking is that you think about it," he says gently.

"Okay," I say. It seems like the only fair response.

"Meet me at the hotel tomorrow, around nine, for breakfast, if you're interested."

"Okay," I say, then add, "Faizad?"

"Yeah?"

"There's just one thing I don't understand."

"What?"

"If Dowdy wants you out of the picture, why hasn't he done it already?"

"I stick to crowded places and hotels with good security. I screen my calls. I'm careful." So that's why he didn't answer his phone in the hotel. "Dowdy's man won't want a scene. He'll make his move when it's quiet. When no one will notice. He'll probably do it when I'm out in the desert. He knows I'll be vulnerable then."

Images of feet being hacked off suddenly spring into my mind. I realize then, instantly and completely, just like that time I stood outside the prison in Delhi, that I want no part of this madness. Not for any amount of money. Not for anything. Not even for my Bestseller; least of all for that, in fact.

But before I have a chance to say anything, Faizad pays both the barbers and is gone. It's like he knows that I need time to think, that my greed needs time to convince me that this is a good idea. Even when I know, and he knows, he of all people knows, that this isn't a good idea, not a good idea at all. But he's going to go ahead and do it anyway. The question is: Am I?

DAZED AND CONFUSED

The walk back to the guest house is a disorientating one. My exhaustion, the heat, and Faizad's words all conspire to confuse me. I wander through the dusty alleyways and turn festering corners, hoping that I'm heading in vaguely the right direction. I feel so tired. I pass an old man smoking a hookah, the wooden mouthpiece slotting perfectly between two missing teeth. There's a large mole on his right cheekbone and he wears a twirling Rajasthani mustache. His eyes are murky like dishwater, glaucoma or some other such affliction turning a pair of black eyes a poisoned blue.

Most of the time it feels like I am wandering in circles, doublebacking on myself and creeping under the same clotheslines until, eventually, I find where I am and exit the maze onto the main road leading home. I pass some tourists—phototypes with big lenses and camel-colored camera cases. They walk past in a group, grabbing the moment, snapping the scene, the women wearing wide-brimmed hats against the midafternoon sun. An alien camel plods past, dragging a large cart that rocks in time with it. Everything is so yellow. The air is dry and burning.

Fifteen minutes later I am walking the dark, tiled corridor back to my room, counting the seconds before I can crash. I put the key in the lock and enter, starting to strip my shirt off over my head before the door even closes behind me. Then there's a noise and I see a shadow looming toward me. Before I get a chance to defend myself, it's on top of me. I crumble back against the door and fall to the floor. I don't even have the time to call out for help.

SO CLOSE AND YET...

Yasmin can't stop giggling after I finally stop struggling with my shirt, which somehow managed to grow endlessly twisting sleeves the harder I tried to rip it off.

"Jesus, you scared the living shit out of me," I say, gasping.

She cups her mouth. "I'm sorry." She can't stop the laughter seeping out from the seams of her palm. Tears form. "But you jumped, you actually jumped in the air. It was so funny." She doesn't even try to contain the laughter then. It just pours out over me, her face shaking above mine.

I lie on the cold floor looking up at her as she straddles me. She looks more beautiful than ever. Her face lost in joy, her chest heaving with happiness. I can't help feeling pleased that she is being loving, but I fight it. It makes me suspicious. Why now? She's got this look about her, like a sulking child who's finally gotten her way and now she's being extra pleasant—to make up for her previous bad behavior. It's like she's admitting that she's the one who's been in the wrong. About what, I'm not exactly sure.

Whatever the reason for her sunnier mood, I decide I'm too tired now for her emotional tides. I push her off and manage to get up onto my feet. She suddenly stops laughing then, slumping against the wall by the door.

"What's wrong?" she asks.

"That was really fucking stupid, Yasmin. What were you thinking, attacking me like that? I might have hit you or something."

She can't stop another small giggle from surfacing. "I think you were too busy with your shirt to hurt me."

"It's not funny," I snap. "How would you like it if someone came out of nowhere and jumped on top of you?" Yasmin pulls her knees up near her chest and rests her arms, crossed, on top of them. She is wearing a pair of thin white cotton trousers with blue flowers embroidered on the bottom and a navy-blue sleeveless top. She is barefoot. "How did you get in here, anyway?"

"The receptionist gave me a key."

"Nice to know how the security works in the place." I sneer.

Yasmin frowns. "Are you all right?"

"What?"

She pulls herself up, using the wall as support, and starts walking toward me. "Is something wrong?" she says gently, her face slowly consuming my field of vision. She *is* beautiful. Her green eyes still sparkle with mirth.

"No." I can't help softening. It's her eyes. They're hypnotic. "You just gave me a fright. That's all."

She smiles slightly, revealing the tips of white teeth, then her face suddenly shifts and spreads with concern. "What happened to your neck?" she says, still moving toward me.

"It's nothing. The barber cut me, that's all."

She stops, inches away now. We're close enough to feel each other's gravitational pull.

"It looks sore," she says, touching the side of it with a brush of her thumb. "Let me clean it." She looks up at me. I look down. Her mouth is slightly open. There's no way we can't collide. I edge closer, and let my eyes close so I can just fall into the warmth blindly. But then, as I move to meet her, there's just empty space. I open my eyes.

Yasmin is past the bed, on the other side of the room.

DECISIONS, DECISIONS

"What do you mean you're not sure anymore?" Yasmin has climbed off the bed and is looking at me, a bloody alcohol-swabbed gauze in her fingertips.

"Just that. I'm not sure if it's safe to go through with it."

"After all this, you want to back out?" Yasmin flicks the gauze into the bin with disgust and is now pinning her hair back hurriedly and pouting at me.

"No, I didn't say that. I just said that it might not be safe. Faizad wants me to come with him on the deal. We never figured that he would ask me to do that." I realize then that I have done my job *too* well. I was only meant to earn Faizad's trust enough to sneak in a simple suitcase switch. I wasn't meant to become his new partner.

"So?" I've never seen Yasmin pissed off like this before. She's a little frightening.

"Well, he's told me that the Pakistani couriers are getting shifty. I'm worried that they might check the money."

"But you said that they almost certainly wouldn't check the money. You said that Faizad has been dealing with these people for years. You said that all we had to do was get Faizad's trust, then we could rip off the Pakistanis. You said it would take ages before they found out that the money was fake. You said—"

"I know what I said, Yasmin!" I snap back in my own defense. "But things are different now, aren't they? We didn't expect Faizad's partner to get murdered and for him to be on the run from the police and the Mafia. He's scared, Yasmin." I don't have the integrity to admit that I might have got things wrong. I don't have the guts to admit that I made up most of the so-called Baba-run.

"Oh, boo-hoo." She sneers. "Look, when we came up with this plan, we didn't even know Faizad had a partner. So I really don't see how his death has anything to do with what we're trying to do."

"It has everything to do with it," I say, allowing my bullshitter instincts to cover the tracks. At least I'm able to do that. Think quick on my feet when I need to remanipulate reality, make out like the fiction *is* the Truth, even when the facts make it abundantly clear that it can't be, that there was no way it ever could be. Above all else, my story must stay true, even though, deep down, I believe it is a lie.

"Why?"

"I've already told you why. Faizad isn't protected anymore, which means we're not protected anymore. If I go with him, I'll very likely end up dead."

"So don't go with him."

"What?"

"Do the switch and don't go on the deal."

"But then . . . what about Faizad?"

"I'm sorry?"

"What will happen to Faizad if we switch the money and they check?"

"What do you care? He's a fucking heroin dealer, for God's sake."

I draw myself off the bed and walk toward Yasmin, standing tall and looking down at her, meeting her stare.

"You don't mean that," I say menacingly. After all, Faizad may be a heroin dealer, but he's also my friend now. I won't be responsible for his death and I want her to know it. I want her to know that she can't go near that kind of suggestion again.

Her eyes shift coldly across my face in small movements. Her jaw is set and hard. She sucks air through her nose then lets it out quickly. "Fine," she huffs. "Have it your way. Let's just forget the whole thing. I'll catch a train to Delhi tomorrow and give James the good news." I shake my head at her. Does she really think I care about James? "After tomorrow, you'll never have to see me again."

But she does know I care about that.

I grab her shoulders just as she is turning away. "Listen, Yasmin. Take it easy, okay? Just give me some time to think. There've got to be other options."

Slowly, eventually, she nods. Relieved, I collapse onto the bed and fall back, my legs right-angling off the end. I'm so fucking exhausted. My eyelids are burning again.

I feel her climb onto the bed beside me. I turn and open my eyes, meeting her horizontal face. For a minute we lie there looking at each other. The fan squeaks. I put one hand on her hip and try to draw her near me. She closes her eyes and rolls over, her back to me.

"Do you mind if we just rest?" she says. Her voice sounds hollow when she's facing away from me. I try not to sigh too loudly. I let my hand fall to my side and look at the ceiling.

LET'S CRASH

There's four of us in the car. Me in the front passenger seat, my girlfriend, Kate, in the back with another bloke. His name is Phil. The guy driving is called Rob. He's driving fast. He's showing off. His father used to be a rally-car driver. Taught him how to drive. And he knows these roads well. Grew up here. With Kate. And Phil. They're all old friends. I'm the stranger in town. Just here for a visit. Just here to visit Kate.

I keep catching her looking at Rob every time I look in the sideview mirror.

But he drives well. He knows just how to negotiate the corners, braking early, then rebuilding his way up through the gears so that he can accelerate out of the bends without skidding. I can appreciate his ability. That's why I'm sitting up front, instead of in the back with Kate. I want to enjoy his driving skills. After all, I did race motorbikes, before I quit, before I lost my nerve. I think about mentioning my racing history and then decide against it. This is his turf, after all. Let him have his glory.

I watch him smile at Kate in his rearview mirror.

We're drunk, of course. I mean, what do you expect? We've just turned eighteen. All these things that we've been waiting for have suddenly arrived in our lives. For free. Without us doing anything. We're suddenly eligible. So we do everything. Drink.

Drive. Preferably at the same time. You would too if you could. If you could go back to the day when you were suddenly allowed. Just because you became twenty-four hours older.

Phil says something and we all laugh.

I love Kate. At least I think I do. Maybe I'm just more in love with the idea of being in love. Maybe it's just another one of those things that I seem suddenly eligible for. I'm eighteen, I can be in love now. So . . . I am. She's pretty. Not beautiful. But she's got a lovely laugh. And, I can tell, she's got a good heart. She's innocent. At least, I like to believe that she is.

Full-beam headlights loom on the distant horizon.

We've been going out for a year and a half now. We've kind of reached a junction. An unknown point where neither of us knows what happens next. She's a year younger and still at school. I'm about to go on my year off. I've worked since September and saved. On Dad's double-wage program, of course. I'm going away, for nine months, around the world. Neither of us knows what happens next.

Rob flicks the beam on and off at the oncoming car, and then drives faster.

Maybe she'll end up with Rob. After all, they've flirted shamelessly with each other all evening, pretending it's because they've known each other for such a long time, that it's perfectly innocent, like it's some sibling thing. I wonder what he's got that I don't have. Is it because he drives fast? It would seem logical. It was Kate who told me all about Rob's dad being a rally-car driver and how he was ten when he learned to drive. It was Kate who told me all about that, blue eyes flashing. I have to admit, it's all quite impressive. When you're eighteen, when it's all new—being able to drive like Rob drives—it's pretty cool.

But the car coming the other way doesn't turn off its full beam.

I suppose, had I kept up the motorbike racing, I'd be able to drive as well as Rob drives. It's all the same principle. And half of it has to do with having the guts to know that hitting a corner at sixty as you're accelerating won't send you into a skid. The trick is to be accelerating. And to have the conviction, the courage. That's all it is. I understand the technique. It's the courage element that eludes me now. I just get nervous, driving fast, taking on corners—ever since the motorbike race, the one where I tore my Achilles. Ever since then, that's been my weak spot.

Rob flashes again at the other car, more urgently this time.

Maybe it's not just the driving. Maybe Rob's got something, something broader, that I've lost. There's a part of me that feels like Life has gotten the better of me. I mean, I came onto this stage—the stage of Life—blazing. Then shit happened. Character attrition, I call it. Nasty experiences, nasty people. Like the Divorce. Like school. It happens. I was different and then Life happened to me and I learned to be not so different, not so . . . individual. It's called social assimilation. The process of wearing down the different. Smoothing out the rough edges. It happens to everyone, sooner or later. At least, that's what I believe. For me, it was sooner. For Rob—it will have to be later. Because he shows no signs of Life wearing him down. Not yet. He's larger than it. He still believes in himself. That's why he's able to drive so fast.

There's only one corner separating the two cars now, full beam, full brightness.

And that's probably what Kate sees in him. He burns brighter. I've let myself get dulled. I've let myself drive more carefully. I'm more interested in living longer than living now. It's all about self-preservation. It's got nothing to do with Life. It's just about seeing myself safely through the years. I'm scared. Scared of it, life, myself, my life. Already. At eighteen years of age, my whole life ahead of me, and I'm scared. Yes, that probably is what she sees in Rob. She's bored with scared. She's bored with safe. She's bored with me.

I glance at the speedometer. 95 mph.

You might say I'm just imagining all this, but I'm not. Kate as much as said so. She said the only reason I was going on a year off around the world was because everyone else was. Not because *I* wanted to. Well, she's right, of course, to a certain degree.

But there's another part, a part she doesn't know about, that wants to go away so that I can remember who I am, so that I can get back my bravery, so I can come back and get her. I need a life injection. I need to find myself again. Once I've got that, I'll get her again. I know it.

Everything goes white with light, like when you're blind. The steering wheel wobbles, then the wheels we're driving on.

If only she knew me beforehand, before Dad and Howie, before school and motorbike crashes. I mean, I was really enthusiastic. I used to be up for anything. The consequences never occurred to me. Not back then. I never even gave them a moment's thought.

For a second, Rob looks like he might pull us out of the beginnings of this spin.

I used to be able to drive fast. I only wish Kate could see that.

The car suddenly veers to the right, then left, then right, with ever-decreasing frequency and ever-increasing degrees.

We're spinning now.

And now we're crashing.

This is why I don't drive fast. I knew there were consequences, I should have told them. I should have explained. But it's too late now. Because we're crashing. We were driving too fast and now we're crashing. In the next five seconds, we're going to find out who lives and who dies.

Ninety-five mph.

We're crashing.

We're crashing. Everyone, we're crashing.

Ninety-five mph.

My stomach turns, like I'm on one of those fairground rides. The ones that go SCREEAAAAMMMMMM, IF YOU WANNNA GO FAAAAAASTER!

Stop. Stop. Stop. Stop. Please stop.

I don't know how many times we flip. It feels like we're falling. Different images flash. Green, black, metal. The car is coming in at me. I see the corner buckling toward my head. I throw my hands up to stop it and cower into my seat.

Stop, please stop.

I watch the car cut into my hand. Then we're suddenly upright, skidding through a field, the wind rushing because the windshield has smashed. It's cold. I remember now. It's winter. December. Frosty.

Still moving. Still not stopped. But slowing, slowing down now. Then *thud!* With a bump into a grass bank, the car mounts and then collapses.

It's over.

I'm still alive.

Rob's still alive. He's groaning. A big wooden pole fills his footwell. His legs are in my footwell. Or what's left of them. They're all smashed and mangled. The dashboard where the radio was, the bit between us, that's all just smashed plastic now.

I turn around to see if Kate and Phil are okay.

But they're not there.

?

???

That's what my brain says. A big ?

I tell myself: We've crashed. I'm a survivor. We've been in a car crash and I'm a survivor. I have responsibilities. I have to help the others. I mean this is what my experience has prepared me for, hasn't it? I've crashed before, I've been burned. I know how serious this is. I'm the one best equipped to deal with this situation. I'm alive. It's my job to save everyone. If only I could find them.

I feel like I have an audience. I feel like I have a role to play. Time to say my lines. I clamber out through the smashed windshield screaming.

"KATTTTIEEEE! KATTTTIEEEEE!"

For a while nothing. Then I see a silhouette stumbling through the winter mist.

"Kate?" I say, running up to it.

Male groan.

No. It's Phil. "Phil, Phil. Are you okay?" Groaning. "Where's Kate? Have you seen her?"

Head shaking. I'm scared now, really scared. Where could she be?

She might be dead. Kate might be dead. God, if only I'd said something to warn them. Life's not about being reckless. It's just not worth it. There's no point being stupid, driving fast, oblivious to the consequences. You have to be aware of the consequences. Life is too precious to risk.

Then I see her. Lying in the mud. Not moving.

I run and stumble to my knees beside her, calling her name. Her eyes are open but she's not moving. I talk to her. I tell her everything will be okay. I hear Phil calling. I take my jacket off and lay it on her, careful not to move her, careful just to keep her warm. I can see the fire coming now from the car—small flames but so orange against the night. Her mouth moves slightly. I tell her to stay awake, stay with me. Phil calls me. Says we've got to get Rob out of the car. The car is on fire. Help, he's calling. I turn and look and see that there's a car that's stopped on the road. I yell and wave my arms at it. I can hear Rob screaming as Phil starts pulling him from the car. Then her lips move and she says something.

"That's it, baby," I say, feeling the word against my lips. Haven't called many people "baby" in my life before. I'm still a baby. But I say it anyway because I'm in love and I've been in a car crash and I'm the survivor and it's my job to save my girlfriend and call her baby. She'll love me after this is over. She'll love me for calling her baby and for saving her. She won't love the danger after this is over. They'll all be jaded like me after this, they'll all be more careful and I'll be the one who looks good for being prescient, for knowing the Fear, for knowing that it's best not to be too dangerous, best to be careful, best for all concerned.

Her mouth moves and I bend down to hear what she's saying. "Cold," she says.

Phil yells for me.

"I know, my darling, I know."

I can almost feel the warmth from the car.

"Cold, I'm so cold," she says.

"I know, don't move, sweetheart. Stay with me. I won't leave you. Stay awake, don't go to sleep."

"Don't go," she says.

Phil screams for me now. I've got to help him. The car is on fire. Rob is trapped. I have to help.

"I won't, my love. I'll never leave you."

"Don't leave me," she says.

"I won't."

"Don't leave me, Rob, don't ever leave me."

The explosion throws me forward onto her and the rush of hot air is like standing too close to an electric heater in a drafty house. My bones are still cold, but my skin burns. For a few seconds, I just lie there. I don't move. I don't want to move. I just want to be near her, just for a few seconds. While I'm still able to block out the words, block out his name.

But, eventually, naturally, with all the force of gravity, they sink back into my consciousness. Rob. She really does love Rob. Even though he crashed. Even though he burned. She loves him. Not me. Because I'm too careful. I don't drive fast. Not anymore. I've been too scared. Too scared to live, too scared to love. And that's why I've lost her. I know it now. Because I don't drive fast anymore.

The Jaisalmer Garden Hotel is straight out of a fairy tale. It has a long winding driveway and tall cast-iron gates. There are palm trees in tended green gardens, marble pillars, and lions carved in moonstone. There is a chandelier in reception and bellboys in red uniforms with stiff collars. It makes me think of the Grand in its heyday. A pretty receptionist in a gold sari smiles uncomfortably at me when I walk past. I am vaguely aware of my scruffy appearance. I haven't had time to get my clothes washed yet.

I find Faizad outside, eating breakfast by the pool. Green umbrellas and white tables stand in fours. I twist my way through them.

"Morning," I say, taking a plastic seat opposite him.

"Ah, here he is," Faizad announces a little bombastically. "The mysterious Mr. Joshua."

"Mysterious?"

Faizad grins at me. "Showing up out of the blue like that yesterday. I must say, you did surprise me." He seems a lot more relaxed. He's wearing yellow shorts and a blue-collared shirt—unbuttoned. Black hair sprawls evenly across his chest and tapers elegantly below. "What are you having?" he asks, nodding at the menu between us. I'm glad he doesn't ask me how or why I got here. For the first time in a long time, perhaps ever, I'm tired of making up stories.

"What do you recommend?"

"Cheese omelette."

"Sounds good."

Faizad beckons a waiter, who is hovering nearby with his arms pinned neatly behind his back.

"So have you made a decision?" Faizad suddenly asks.

"Yeah," I say as the waiter arrives. "Cheese omelette, please," I say, looking up at him. The waiter nods and about-faces. Then I look at Faizad, who is sipping orange juice, looking expectantly at me over the top of the glass. I try to tell myself that it's not too late to back out, even though I know it is.

"You can count me in," I say. The words feel so painless, so easy, when I say them. I'm going to the border with Faizad. What for? To help him? Become his wealthy accomplice? No, that's not why I'm going. I've made up my mind. The scam is still on. Quite aside from the fact that I never felt completely comfortable with the idea of abandoning my friends and only going to the border to make enough money for myself, I've realized that this adventure has become about something more than just making money. Getting the girl, getting the story, getting involved. That's what this is now. I haven't come this far for a half-cocked ending. It's all the way or no way. Simple as that. Thanks for the offer, Faizad, but I'm sorry—I'm still going to have to rip you off. Nothing personal. It's just the way this situation has got to be.

"I always knew I could depend on you, Josh," he says, beaming. I smile briefly back at him, wondering what I've let myself in for, what diseases I'll catch from all this casual conversation. I really should be more careful. I really should use protection. "We leave tonight."

"Right."

After a few minutes he leans over the side of the table and says: "What's the bag for?"

"What? Oh, that. It's just some clothes. Thought I should come prepared."

Yasmin packed it for me and everything. Just like my mum, before the divorce, seeing me off to school. I noticed that same sense of dread I used to get when a new term would start. I'd barely acquiesced and she'd packed my bags, all ready for me to go. So considerate of her.

"Have you got any swimming trunks?"

"Yes."

"Well, why don't you get changed and dive in?" he says, admiring the pool.

"Sounds like a good idea."

"Use my room," he says, reaching into his pocket. "Here's the key."

THE SWITCH

I skip up the stairs. Faizad is staying on the third floor. The corridors are carpeted. I find his room: 308. I slip the electronic key into the slit. The red light blinks briefly and then turns green. I walk in. There's a brief moment of anticipation as I sense out the scene. The room has a small corridor, with a door to the bathroom and a wardrobe on the right, before it turns into the bedroom. I can see light from a large window coming in from around the corner. I get the vague feeling that there's someone else in the room with me. I tell myself it's just Faizad's presense lingering. I stride in. The bed isn't made; a green quilt hangs off the end.

I check the window. It looks out onto the pool. I can just make out the ends of Faizad's legs, crossed and sticking out, from under the cover of the umbrella. The waiter is already serving my breakfast. I'll have to be quick.

I find the suitcase in the wardrobe, one of those big, old-school ones with the brass combination lock on top. I pull it out and put it on the bed. It feels heavy. I unzip a side pocket in my bag and pull out a penknife. I know how to work these things open from school. Another boy used to keep his candy in one just like it, and every Sunday, we'd pry it open and steal his chocolate bars. They're easy. I squeeze the blade into the lock and lever it, firmly but not with too much pressure, inching my way through the combination and feeling out the numbers as the lock slowly gives.

Two minutes later, I'm looking at the padlock flaps, slightly bent but open. I don't even notice what the combination is. I take a breath and undo the main zip on my bag. I vaguely see the ends of various denominations inside. I put my penknife back in the side pocket. Then, with two flicks of the thumb, I open the leather flaps of Faizad's suitcase.

A hollow nausea pulls on the corners of my mouth and adrenaline catches at the back of my teeth. I try gulping but my throat is suddenly dry. I blink and breathe, blink and breathe for a few moments as the situation slowly makes itself recognizable to me.

Eventually, I manage to swear. "Oh fuck."

The fat suitcase is filled, to the brim, with clean, crisp bills. White paper belts organize them into bundles. I flick my way through one of them. The notes sound like leaves rustling in the breeze. I stare at the money for a few more moments, desperately trying to inject proportion into the scene. There's no escaping. There's no dressing it up as a fantasy, an imagining, a game. This *is* reality. I can't step out of it. My heart just keeps screaming and my eyes sting and blur whenever I look at the sea of green before me.

Somewhere I find the will to plunge a hand into my suitcase, feeling out similar bundles of fake bills. Except for a small discrepancy in the belts they look identical. Hands shaking, I then pull out as many stacks of fake hundred-dollar denominations I can find from my bag and stack them on the bed. After that I start pulling the money out of Faizad's case and pile the bundles neatly next to the fake stuff.

There really is very little, on first appearances, to tell them apart. I decide to take a quick look to make sure Faizad is still sitting at our table. He's not.

And that's when I hear the lock to the door clicking open.

MOB MENTALITY

My favorite tea stall in Pahar Ganj was little more than a makeshift tent—a square of blue tarpaulin on bamboo poles and a few wooden benches parked by the side of the street. An old couple ran the place. I loved to watch them work, the way they'd pump their kerosene stoves in quick, every-so-often moments and keep the rainbow flames hissing viciously. They would pour and spill, add things to the pots and drain away, serve cups and take money from customers. Watching them was like watching two jugglers spin plates. Their tea was a wonderful sweet milky mix with cardamom and ginger, served in red clay cups with china saucers. The saucers they kept. The cups got thrown away. I used to go there a lot, almost every night. It was the best place to watch life go by in those slow months looking for Baba and the three Westerners he dealt with.

One night, around seven, I found myself at the stall watching two men attempt to start a car. It was an amusing scene and the kind that tended to attract the attention of the crowd. Watching other people with public problems was always a good way to waste time in India. The car was a white Volvo station wagon, which only improved the drama. Broken-down Volvo station wagons weren't exactly common in a country otherwise filled with Bajaj, Suzuki, and Tata. One of the men, the one in the driver's seat, was wearing a dark blue turban. They both looked young. They must be rich, I thought to myself, to own a Volvo. I wondered what two rich kids were doing in Pahar Ganj.

Several times they tried, and failed, to get the car going. The one pushing would get the thing rolling and then it would lurch and shiver as the turbaned boy tried to kick it into gear. No one got up to help. After a few goes, they had to turn the car around because of a rising slope in the street. The whole thing went on for fifteen minutes, maybe longer. After a while, it got boring. I finished my tea, paid the couple, and offered to help. The turbaned boy spoke immaculate English and seemed very grateful. I wasn't interested in his appreciation. I just wanted to get the car started and leave. It was late and the show had gone on long enough.

I took one side, the other boy took the other. Brake lights burned on my shirt as I pressed my weight against the flat-back trunk. Then the lights went out and the wheels started rolling, slowly at first and then more quickly. I shouted harder once or twice and tried to run in little steps. Soon the car was rolling along nicely. With one last shove, we shouted, "Now!" and the Volvo lurched and sighed once more before, to general surprise, roaring quite suddenly to life. We watched it heave for a hundred yards or so. I felt some satisfaction that my help had made the difference. The other pusher smiled at me. Then things went weird.

Instead of stopping, the Volvo, which I had thought was going a bit fast for a crowded street like Pahar Ganj, suddenly screeched and disappeared around the corner. Then, to aghast faces and captured ears, there was a loud crash, followed by a stomach-turning scream, another screech of the tires, and then some very loud wailing.

Everyone in the street stopped. We waited for more audible clues. The wailing was very high-pitched. A woman or a child had been hit. I started jogging with slow and nervous steps at first, toward the scene of the crime. Then, as people peeled into the street from all sides, I felt myself getting angry. Soon I was filled with indignation. I wanted to see the crime, hunt down and find the turbaned culprit, and then bring justice to bear. He wasn't going to get away with this.

Before I knew what was happening, I had suddenly become a member of a mob.

I witnessed events in still frames. When I turned the corner, I saw a wooden cart smashed and upturned. Three large urns spilled off-white milk into the street. A young boy lay on the ground next to them, one leg sticking out at an impossible angle. People were waving arms and shouting. A cracked telegraph pole leaned over, fresh yellow wood showing brightly. Black blood poured down a fat woman's forehead while two men held white handkerchiefs to her face.

The crowd I was in found a policeman at the corner of the next junction. Some people kept going, chasing the long-gone Volvo down an orange-lit dual carriageway. I stopped and watched men shouting at the young policeman, who looked back at them with complete bewilderment. He didn't have a radio. He only had his bamboo *lathi,* which I thought he might use in a moment of panic against the pressing swarm. Everyone shouted at him to do something. Someone told him to telephone headquarters. In my frustration, I found myself shouting: "I know where we can get the license-plate number, you can telephone in and report him."

I'd barely said the words when I realized my mistake. Suddenly the attention of the crowd was upon me. All that anger, all that hatred, all that energy was now, quite suddenly, focused on me. Fear quickly replaced the anger I had initially felt. I was no longer the hunter, now, I was the hunted. I knew where to find the license-plate number. I was going to solve the situation. I was going to do all this, or, or, or . . .

One of the leaders turned on me. "Where is this man? Where is this man that knows the license number?"

Intense eyes ravaged me. I tried to stay calm. "Back there. There was another man, he was pushing the car. We can ask him."

"You take us."

Suddenly, with hands gripping the tops of my two arms, the crowd picked me up and surged back to where it had all started— me, their only clue, held firmly in the middle. I noticed the policeman skulk off quietly. I was on my own. We skipped down the street like this for a few hundred yards, before another small crowd suddenly appeared from a different direction.

"What is happening?" our leader said, holding on to me.

"He's down there. They've found him. Come on."

The crowd discarded me like yesterday's news. As quickly as the nightmare had begun, I was safe. I breathed and looked around, lost for a few moments, while the crowd echoed its way down the carriageway. I didn't know what to do next. Helping the hurt never occurred to me. Nor did going home. I felt compelled to pursue the action. My little outburst had changed things. I no longer felt a part of the mob. I was disassociated from the madness. I found myself gingerly trailing them.

It didn't take me long to catch up with the crowd, but by the time I did, things had already turned ugly. The car was run up on a tall pavement a few hundred meters down the carriageway—its front wheel buckled, presumably from the impact. The crowd shifted and swelled in patches around it. Three of the windows had been smashed, the rear one cracked like a spiderweb. Inside, the turbaned boy was flashing glances left and right, like a trapped animal. I noticed three policemen standing nearby in a tight corner under a neon light.

The crowd went about things methodically. They smashed the driver's window and then dragged the boy out screaming through the broken glass. They surrounded him in turns and beat him and spat on him and kicked him in the head. I saw one man open the back door of the Volvo while two others dragged the Sikh around so that his head was propped up in the opening. They smashed the door against his head, once, twice, three times. I counted eight times before they stopped. The turban came loose and long swathes of hair were matted in more black and bloody pools on the pavement. Someone said something and they put him back in the car. His sandaled feet were sticking out the end. I remember watching his hand reach up to the window as the crowd edged back. I didn't see how they started the fire. I watched him burn for a few moments before turning away. The crowd cheered behind me.

The next day I walked into the *Hindu Week* office and wrote a story on it. Mani loved it. He told me to call the police station and verify a few facts. Turned out the Volvo had faulty brakes. The boy who helped push the car was the driver's best friend. The car belonged to his parents. They'd taken it down to Pahar Ganj to get a bended bumper mended on the cheap. The mechanic had stolen the brake pads and a few engine parts—thus, the disaster. Mani made my story part of a cover series he was doing on mob lynchings in the city. Over the previous two months, a lot of bus drivers had been lynched by angry mobs after running people down. Mani printed my story under the headline MOB MADNESS: WHAT'S IT LIKE TO BE A PART OF A MOB? It was the first story I ever got published. Well, if you can call it that. The printer laid it out wrong and it came out half upside down and back to front, so it wasn't exactly readable.

Nevertheless, after it came out, Mani congratulated me. He said that I had just learned the first rule in good journalism. "You have to make your own stories," he said. "You have to do more than just seek them out. You have to create them."

"What do you mean?"

"A journalist can never just be an impartial observer. Just by being there, he changes the story. You have an influence. Make it work to your advantage."

"You don't think my story was impartial."

"Do you?"

"Well, I tried."

"Well, if that was your intention, you failed. You were the one who got the car started. You were the one who followed the crowd, made suggestions, got everyone heated up. If it hadn't been for you, that Sikh boy would probably still be alive today."

"You're saying that that boy's death was my fault?"

"No." He smiled. "I'm saying you just got your first story. And you got it by obeying a journalist's rule. You took part in the action. If you don't get involved, you'll never have anything to write about."

"So how long have you been in India?" the woman asks. She's Norwegian—mid-to-late forties. Pretty, with fair hair and ice-blue eyes.

"Two years."

"Two years!" she exclaims, adjusting the strap on her swimsuit so that it sits more respectfully across her shoulder.

"More or less."

"What have you been doing in India for two years?"

"I'm a journalist."

I don't know why I say that.

"A journalist! Really? That's very interesting. Who do you work for?"

"Reuters." I rise to the occasion.

"Wow. I'm impressed." I smile back at her. "You look so young." I don't say anything. Water is still rolling down my arms and collecting in a puddle below my seat. I feel much, much better now—after that swim. I physically aged when that cleaner came in, waving her feather duster through the door like a standard. It didn't take me long to get rid of her, but I still don't know where Faizad has disappeared to. I don't remember how I got talking to this woman. She is sitting at the next-door table and that seems reason enough in her book. I think she mentioned something about my omelette getting cold. "So," she presses. "What are you doing in Jaisalmer?"

"I'm sorry?" I say a little too defensively.

"Well, are you writing a story?"

"Errr, yes. As a matter of fact I am." I can't think of any other reason to be here.

"What about?"

"Drug smuggling." It comes out seamlessly.

"Drug smuggling!" she says, suitably astonished.

"Yes," I say with suitable boredom.

"There are drug smugglers here?" she half whispers, as if it's our little secret.

"Of course. This is one of the major heroin routes between Pakistan and India. That and diamonds."

"Diamonds?!"

"Yes."

"But . . . well, that's very strange."

"What?"

"Oh, nothing. It's just that my husband and I were looking to buy a diamond in Jaipur, but we couldn't find any."

"Well, I'm not surprised. Everything in Jaipur is fake. You had a lucky escape," I say knowingly.

"Maybe," she says slowly. "But we were told that there are no diamonds left in the subcontinent."

"Who told you that?"

"We read about it in the *Crowded Planet* guidebook."

"You shouldn't believe everything you read," I say sardonically. "There are still hundreds of mines in Pakistan that haven't been fully exploited." I'm just making this up. I can't let myself down now.

"Well, I don't know about that. But I do know that a lot of diamonds come to India from Africa."

"Africa?"

"Yes," she says. "They are cut in Mumbai and then they are re-exported. After Jaisalmer, my husband and I are going to go see if we can buy any there."

"Hmm. I didn't know that."

"Well," she says, turning the tables, "it sounds like you should do some more research before you write your story."

"Yes, I suppose you're right," I say, wincing at her. "But like I say, the story isn't so much about diamonds. It's really about drugs." Her husband drips over from the pool at the tail end of my sentence and the woman has stopped listening. They talk in Norwegian for a few minutes before she finally gets up to leave.

"Well, it was very nice to meet you," she says, looking down at me. "Good luck with your story."

"Thanks," I say quietly. "Have a nice holiday."

"I'm sure we will," she says, smiling politely. Then, as an afterthought, she adds, "Be careful."

The husband acknowledges my existence with a slightly bemused nod and half smile before they both turn and leave.

TOUGH GUY

I meet Yasmin for lunch at the same restaurant Faizad and I were in the day before. I saw Faizad in the lobby after my swim—busy organizing the Jeep and making telephone calls—so it wasn't difficult to slip away. When I walk in, she jumps up and kisses me half on the lips.

"I was getting worried," she says. She's tied her hair up and a few dark strands curl and hang around the back of her neck. I check briefly outside the lattice shutter to see if I am being followed. There is no sign of the brown-haired boy or anyone else who could be considered vaguely suspicious. "Did everything go okay?" she asks as I turn back around to face her.

I notice a cup of tea steaming and her sunglasses on the low table. "Yes, everything was fine," I say, taking a seat opposite to where I can see she has been sitting. She comes and sits next to me, pulling her tea around before taking out two cigarettes. She lights both of them and hands one to me.

"He didn't suspect anything?"

"No."

"When do you leave?" she says, spitting out smoke.

"Tonight."

"What? So soon?" she says, resting one hand on the back of mine. I look at her. "I didn't expect it to be so soon." I don't say anything. There's a sense of manly pride in my departure. "A man's gotta do what a man's gotta do" martyr-to-the-cause type thing. "Are you all right?" she asks eventually.

"Yes."

"You know, you don't have to go."

"Faizad might not do the deal if I don't."

I can see that she doesn't agree, but she accepts the answer. I think she knows that I have my own reasons for going, reasons she wouldn't understand. Having balls, taking risks, seeking adventure, searching for material, getting involved, driving fast—how could she understand what it takes to get the girl, to get the story? And yet, for my part, I'm only just beginning to understand that this isn't a game, this isn't an exaggerated story. I'm really going to go and do this, eyes open and brave. Why? Because, because . . . it's about time I faced my fears. I've spent my whole life protecting myself with the idea that nothing is real, that I've only been making it up, that bad things never really happened to me. I just say they did and then make out like they were a whole lot worse. Impossibly worse—so that I could pretend to myself that they didn't really happen, not like *that* anyway.

The drowning, the bullying at school and the faking appendicitis, the divorce, the car crash . . . all these terrible things that have happened to me, I've exaggerated and fictionalized to distance myself from really feeling the trauma. Bullshit has been my protection. A cushion between me and life. But deep down, more subdued perhaps, less dramatic (definitely), I know that these awful things did happen. They really did. And I suffered because of them. It's time I stopped hiding from reality. It's time I stopped disguising the Truth as fiction. Even though I'm privileged, even though I've been given a lot, bad things have occurred.

Life's a bitch and then you die . . .

It's time I stopped being scared. Or at least try . . . and if not now, at least in the long term. I mean, if I have to pretend a little bit longer on this misadventure, I won't blame myself. After all, learning to swim and car crashes are one thing. Doing a dodgy drug deal with the Mafia on the Pakistani border is quite another. I think most people would rather pretend it wasn't happening if they ever found themselves in my shoes.

"Did we have the correct denominations?" she says, changing the subject.

"Yes."

"How much was there?"

"I didn't get a chance to count. A lot. Take a look if you like," I say, pointing at the duffel bag beside me.

She looks at it for a second and I can see that she's tempted. "No," she says quickly. "It's not safe."

"Put it this way," I say. "There's more than enough to get James out of prison."

Yasmin's mouth drops. "Really?"

"Yes, really."

She squeals then and throws her arms around me and we kiss, her tongue in my mouth. I don't want it to stop, but after a few moments, she pulls back. "Wait," she says, taking my face in her hands. "If there is really that much we should just call it quits, shouldn't we? I could take the money to get James out and you and Sanjay can keep the rest."

I smile softly at her. "No. We've come too far already. We should go the whole way."

"But we've got enough. It will be enough. We don't need to make millions, we can just take what we've got and leave. You're putting yourself in unnecessary danger. There's no need for you to go with Faizad. It's pointless. Don't you see, Josh? We've already won." Her eyes are flicking across my face as if she's searching for a door, a way in that might convince me not to go. I don't say anything. Her face breaks. "I don't want you to go, Josh," she says.

I almost agree to stay with her then.

But something stops me. I can hear Yasmin asking me not to go, but I don't hear her saying the words to make me stay. It would be easy to make me stay. She must know that. She only has to say what I've been waiting to hear ever since that very first moment I smelled her at the Green. That's all it would take. But she doesn't say them. She doesn't say them because she doesn't really love me. She only pretends to. I know that now. It hurts to know it, but at least I finally know it.

"I have to go," I say. "I'll be back by this time tomorrow." Yasmin's mouth shifts with resignation before she eventually moves to kiss me again. And I let myself fall in—just one last time. At the very least, the hero deserves that.

THE DEAL

We leave at seven. There is a driver, Kamal, for the Jeep. He is a very ordinary-looking man—fairish skin, mustache, parted hair (slightly hennaed), serious expression. Apart from our introduction, we don't say anything to each other the whole journey. I assume he's busy concentrating. The road is bumpy and dust billows up in brake-lit crimson clouds behind us. He drives at a fierce pace, swinging his hands around the steering wheel like an actor in a black-and-white movie.

Faizad sits up front, resting one hand on top of the open windshield for balance, his suitcase firmly between his feet. I am sitting in the back wearing a black turban, shielding my face from the whipping wind. I try to get some sleep (it's been six days now since I had a decent kip), but it's no use. I'm too tired to sleep. I've passed the point of no return.

I spend a lot of time fingering the gun that Faizad has given me. I've never held a real gun before. It feels strange, much heavier than I'd imagined—weighty. I spend a lot of time looking up at the sky. There is no moon and the stars are out in force. I spot several satellites. I wonder if they can see us.

The meeting is scheduled for one o'clock. We reach the rendezvous point early, so we sit in the Jeep for a few minutes not saying anything, just waiting. There's not much to see, just a collection of crumbling mud huts on a small rising. I've no idea why there are houses all the way out here. There don't seem enough for them to be remnants of an extinct village. Perhaps they're all that's left of an old trading post or something. I can see the faint glow of the Indian army camp burning in the distance. The wind whistles and churns sand. It's bitterly cold now. My eyes feel as if they've collected half the desert on the journey, but I'm too pumped on adrenaline to really care.

After a few minutes Faizad says it's time. He tells Kamal to wait. We walk toward one of the houses, the sand slipping beneath our feet. It's pitch-black when we walk in, but I know someone is behind me as soon as I am in the doorway. I can sense him just as he grabs the top of my arm and spits harsh-sounding words into the back of my neck. A bright white light suddenly shines in my face and I can hear Faizad talking quickly in Urdu. I don't know what to do, so I just stand there blinking and squinting while a hand swims around my waist and thighs. It quickly finds the gun and removes it.

The flashlight goes out and for a brief second we all stand in the dark. Red and blue and yellow blotches waltz in the darkness as my eyes adjust. After a few seconds, the yellow glow from three lanterns quickly swells then floods the room. The scene reveals itself to me in sections.

There's a table, waist-high. Behind it, three men—all roughly the same height. They've all got beards and mustaches. They're all wearing open-face turbans. They've got machine guns slung over their shoulders. A tall, thin man with a long brown kurta and ankle-tight baggy brown trousers steps out from behind me and places my revolver gently on the table. Another man, stockier, steps out from behind Faizad and puts his gun next to mine. The five of them stand together looking at us, three behind the table, the two that disarmed us on the flanks.

The man in the middle starts talking. Faizad talks back in short, clipped sentences as if he's answering questions. Then, all of a sudden, there is a tangible easing in the tension. One of the men laughs briefly at something Faizad says, Faizad says something back, more laughter, then they all reach for their respective goods. Faizad swings his suitcase up and lets it crash onto the table with a small bloom of dust, all the time talking.

The Pakistanis are the ones replying in clipped sentences now and I get the feeling that they're old friends sharing news. There's a brief lull in the bonhomie when Faizad tries to open his suitcase and the locks jam. I notice him frowning at the combination and wonder if I remembered to return the numbers to their original position. He shakes his head with mild frustration before one of the Pakistanis hands him a knife, saying something pithy. Faizad laughs politely but I can tell that he's not amused. He levers the locks, which open, slightly bent, with a very unsatisfactory silence.

Meanwhile the Pakistanis are loading large cellophane-wrapped packets filled with white powder on the table. I count seventeen by the time Faizad's finished opening his suitcase. He opens the flaps and steps back very slightly so that the Pakistanis can get a good look inside. The middleman's eyes wrinkle as he smiles broadly then says something, which makes all the Pakistanis laugh but not Faizad.

The man on the right flank then picks up one of the packets and passes it to Faizad, who uses the knife he was given to open his suitcase to pierce the cellophane. He dips the end of the knife into the powder, shovels a small pile onto the end, presents it to his right nostril, and, with a pained expression, snorts the load. His eyelids seem to quiver heavily for a couple of seconds before he eventually smiles at the Pakistanis. Then he says something, which has everyone laughing very happily. Except me. There's only one thing on my mind, and as everyone gets down to business, it's the only thing I can think about: Where are the fucking diamonds?

Two of the Pakistanis, the ones on the left, pull out a large machine that looks like a Rolodex with a red digital number display on the front and start feeding bundles of cash into it with all the efficiency of a chain gang. I vaguely notice that Faizad is using some electronic scales to weigh the smack, but most of my attention is on the Pakistanis counting the cash. I see the middle one, whom I presume to be the leader, overseeing the operation. The Rolodex whirs and the bills flutter into a flurry of numbers on the digital screen. Still no sign of any diamonds.

Then the money-counting machine jams. There's a painful sound as the electric motor catches and whines. Everyone stops what they are doing. The middleman says something agitatedly and two of them lunge to turn it off. One by one they all gather around to see what's wrong. There's some fast talking and I see an elbow jerking while another one holds the machine steady. Then I see one of the Pakistanis holding up a torn bill and shouting. Everyone is looking at him as he spits and gurgles desperate words at the green paper in his hands. I notice Faizad turn to look at me. He looks worried. My eyes shift between him and the Pakistanis.

I'm not exactly sure what happens next. One moment I'm just standing there, watching the whole scene unfurl before me, worrying about the money, worrying about the shouting, worrying about the diamonds, the next thing I know, I've got both revolvers in my hands and I'm pointing them at the middleman. It's weird. I can't believe I'm doing it even as I pick them up. I really do feel like an actor now, just playing my part. And the part I am playing is Josh the Hero, the Josh I'm going to write about in my Bestseller. This isn't really me doing this. I'm just watching myself do it, an agent, listening to the inner voice narrate the events.

"Wh-what are you doing, Josh?" Faizad says slowly. I can feel him staring at me. I don't take my eyes off the middleman. All the AKs are pointing at me.

"Pack the stuff," I say assertively. I notice that the Pakistanis are all frowning with confusion and looking at my hands. They've only just figured that I'm white. I'd forgotten that I was wearing a turban.

"What?" Faizad says.

"I said, pack the stuff."

"Josh, why are you doing this?"

"Yes, Josh," the middleman suddenly says in accentless English. "Why are you doing this? We're not looking for problems."

"Then tell your men to put their guns down."

"You first."

"If your men don't drop their guns in the next five seconds, I'm going to shoot."

Time stops. The middleman stares at me. I stare back. It's a classic scene. Who'll back down? *That's one.* Will I get out of this alive? How can I? The odds are stacked against me. It's four against one. Things aren't looking good. And I know it. *That's two.* But I don't care. It was a risk I had to take. Deep down, I knew it was probably always going to come to this. I knew there wasn't any other way. *That's three.* Whatever happens next, I'll always know— there wasn't any other way. I had to come here. I had to play out this scene. For me, for my demons, for my story, for the girl. And every thriller has to have a climax. Is this it? Is this the climax? *That's four.* How's it all going to end?

The middleman says something in guttural-speak. There's a small pause and the AKs slip and then slide gently onto the floor. I smile under my turban. Nothing like a good showdown to sort the good guys out from the bad.

"Right, now hand over the diamonds."

"I'm sorry?"

"You heard me. The stones. Hand over the stones."

"You're mistaken."

I'm not sure if the bad guy notices me lift the gun slightly when I shoot, but it's enough to scare everyone. Even me. There's a lot of plaster and dust and shouting. Then some coughing. The middleman is shouting things I can't understand before eventually slipping back into English. "I don't know what you're fucking talking about, you crazy bastard. Who the fuck do you think you are? Faizad, do something."

"Josh, you're making a mistake. There are no diamonds," Faizad says.

"What?" I reply. "Of course there are. Don't lie to me, Faizad."

"Why would I lie to you?"

"There have to be diamonds."

"What for?"

"It's how you laundered the money."

"What are you talking about?"

"The profits from the drug deals. You and Ajay laundered the money with diamonds." There's a pause. "Didn't you?"

"No."

"But . . . but that doesn't make sense. There have to be diamonds. There have to be . . ."

Things are slipping away from me now. The story is slipping away. Without diamonds the plot can't hold together. There have to be diamonds for the second switch. That was the whole point.

The Smack-Pakis were meant to get fake money, Faizad-the-dodgy-dealer was meant to get his smack and the fake gems, and me and my pals were meant to get the diamonds and the cash. All in two simple suitcase switches. One before the deal, one after. Beautiful. That was what was so clever about the scam. Only the bad guys got hurt. Now it's all screwed up. Now I'm a fucking bad guy. This is a bloody heroin deal. The hero wasn't meant to be a heroin dealer. He wasn't even meant to go near the stuff. I wanted people to like me. I mean, don't all heroes have to be likable?

Got to stay with it, I tell my head. Mustn't show fear now. Stay tough. Drive fast. Remember. Pretend. This isn't really happening. If this were a story and I were writing it, what would have to happen next?

First, buy time.

"Pack the stuff, Faizad. We're leaving." Faizad looks at me. "DO IT!" He starts moving quickly, shoving the heroin into the duffel bags. The middleman stares dully back at me. I can see his mind working, staring through the turban, seeing the little boy beneath. I wait until Faizad has packed the smack. It only takes a few minutes. "Right. Good. Now go outside and wait for me in the Jeep."

"But—"

"Just . . . !" I snap.

Second, stay in character.

What's the one thing that defines me? I'm a bullshitter. Start talking.

I start backing away from the table. "Now, gentlemen. It seems I have made a mistake. Please accept my apologies . . ." I pause, trying to remember how this whole thing with the diamonds aspect started. "I was led to believe that we would be buying dia-

monds from you today." The middleman shifts on his feet. I can
tell that he is getting impatient. Come to think of it, the diamonds
never really made much sense. How can you launder dirty money
with dirty diamonds? I back one more step away, one step closer
to the door. "Which is why I have decided that you should keep
the money." The middleman gives a vague nod of agreement.
"There's no reason for anyone to get hurt today, is there?" I say.
Keep talking. Keep talking. "Especially over such a silly mistake.
There's no reason why everyone can't keep what they came here
for. The money is all there. You don't need to count it." If you're
going to launder money it has to go through something legitimate.
I understand that now. One step further, one step closer. Nearly
there. "And once again, please accept my sincerest apologies."

I can feel the air outside. I must be close enough. It's now or
never. They see me making my move and I see all four of them
simultaneously reaching for their AKs as I turn and sprint out into
the darkness, the middleman barking orders behind me. "GO!
GO! GO!" I scream at the Jeep, which already has its motor running by the time I reach it. I hurl myself into the back just as the
AKs start rattling. There's the sound of smashing glass and the
engine overrevving as it skids in the sand and then one of the wing
mirrors smashes and then the wheels catch and suddenly we're
speeding off down the road, the mud huts and the silhouettes
shrinking into the distance behind us.

Two hours later, when he's sure we've lost them, Faizad tells Kamal to stop the Jeep. It's fucking freezing now, first light hinting
on the horizon. He turns to face me, very serious.

"Josh," he starts. I'm still holding the guns, both of them hanging between my thighs, partly crossed like a coat of arms. "Josh,"
he says again. I lift my head to meet his look. "We made it," he
says, his eyes glistening slightly. That's when he starts to smile.
"We fucking made it, you genius!!" He starts laughing then,
throwing himself over the back of the seat and grabbing my neck
in a manly grip. "You were amazing in there! I never knew you
had it in you. Josh? Josh? Are you all right? Did you get hit? Jesus,
are you hurt?"

"No, I'm fine."

"Well, take that stupid turban off and let's see you smile. We're
fucking rich, you idiot, and it's all because of you. Jesus," he says,
shaking and turning his head alternately between Kamal and me.
"You were so incredible. I thought we were dead for sure when
we walked in and they were so heavily armed. Kamal, you should
have seen this guy, he was fantastic." I can see Kamal in the rearview mirror, grinning. "That line about the diamonds. That was
inspired. Bloody inspired. Where did you get that from? I couldn't
believe it. We'd never discussed that. Shit, man, you can be my

bodyguard anytime you like. Brains as well as balls. You're a hero, did you know that? A fucking hero! A fucking rich hero! Ajay couldn't have done a better job if he'd tried."

I smile beneath the turban and screw up my eyes just to please him. I don't want to take it off. I don't want him to see what I'm really thinking. So that's what it's come down to is it? I'm Ajay's replacement. Shit. Well, at least I'm one man's hero.

"What next?" I say.

"Pushkar, you idiot," Faizad says, smiling and shaking his head in continued disbelief. "Fucking Pushkar to make millions! Josh, I love you. You saved my life in there. I knew Dowdy was setting me up. I knew it was trouble when there were so many of them. There's never usually more than two on a deal. It was a rule. He must have told Akbar to take care of me. And he would have. If you hadn't been there, if you hadn't come up with all that diamond crap. You're a fucking genius," he says, again, grabbing my head. "I want to bear your children!"

"Easy."

Faizad laughs uproariously then. "Genius, genius," he keeps muttering. Then, as we get going again, Faizad spends the rest of the journey recounting the liaison in minute detail to Kamal, all the time exaggerating my cool. Kamal occasionally shakes his head in disbelieving appreciation. I don't really listen. I spend most of the time looking at the new dawn. The color is finally coming back in my vision. I'm starting to feel vaguely normal again. I feel exhausted, good exhausted, like I can sleep—for a week. The only part I do hear is the bit about the diamonds.

" 'Didn't you launder the money with diamonds?' That's what he said! Can you believe that? Right in front of Akbar. The cheek of it. Especially since all the money went through Benson's and the Cellar, which Akbar half owns with Dowdy. Can you fucking believe that?" He laughs again. "Who would have thought it? Nice little boy like Josh ripping off both Mafias at the same time. The bloke's a bloody genius, Kamal, a bloody genius. It's almost a pity that that was the last deal. Fucking Josh, hey? Who'd have believed it?"

A ROLLING STONE

I take a rickshaw back to the guest house from the Garden Hotel. I'm not in a hurry, but it's too hot to walk. And besides, it's not as if I'm short of cash. Faizad keeps throwing the stuff at me. Our car leaves for Pushkar at three. He warns me not to be late.

As usual, the reception area at the guest house is empty and the whole place seems abandoned when I get there. It doesn't matter. I still have my room key on me. As I walk the dark corridor, I get nervous. Or rather, I have a sense of anticipation. I don't know why. I know now that there's nothing to get excited about.

Still, I play out the scene in my mind. The one where I open the door and Yasmin leaps on me. I can see her, in the darkness, giggling above me. That all seems like such a long time ago. I can't believe, after everything that's happened, that I still harbor hope. But it's not impossible, is it? That she could, she might . . .

I push the key into the lock and feel the cogs twist as I turn the mechanism. The light is off but I can hear the fan whirring slightly. Maybe she's sleeping. She could be. You never know. I flick the switch and the fluorescent light hums before clicking and then flickering to life. Stark blue-white light fills the room—it makes the place look cold and empty. Which is exactly what it is.

Except for what's on the bed. Greens and blues and glinting

crystal—all sorts and shapes and sizes—spread out in a celebration of counterfeit color. I look at them and can't help a small snort. It's only then that the real absurdity of the whole adventure really hits me. Who were we fooling? Or rather, who was fooling me? Me, I guess.

Still, Yasmin must have known. Why else would she leave the gems? Is this some sort of ironic farewell? Maybe. Or maybe she figures that I still might not know. Might still not have figured out that she's been using me. All this time she's been using me. Just like Sanjay said she was. He could see when I was blind.

Even now I find it hard to believe. Because I saw something, I know I saw something. Even now I find it hard to believe that the love story was a lie. A figment of my imagination.

Maybe that's why Yasmin has left the fake gems. She knows I'll still believe, I'll always believe. I'll always believe in my own imagination, in *my* love story—more in that than in the reality. Even though the reality has been there standing, stock-still, in front of my face all this time.

Now that I think about it, she practically told me as much. She virtually warned me off. She knew the trouble I was getting myself into and, I think, that time we argued under the tree in the desert, she nearly told me so, nearly saved me from myself.

But I couldn't hear her. I was far, far too much of a fool. She saw that. And she knows that now. She thinks me so stupid. She knows I'll still swap the gems, hoping to find her again—in Push-kar, in a guest house in Delhi, back at Sanjay's place in Mumbai—so that we can pick up where we left off. So I can say, Mission Accomplished, and so she'll kiss me again and smile at me and flash brilliant green eyes at me. She knows that because she knows me. She knows me for the idiot that I am.

I finally feel a surge of anger then—at the humiliation of it.

All that time, she must have looked at me, when I was loving her, and thought me such an idiot. And I break, I finally break, ripping the sheet off the bed and screaming. The glass jewels smash against the wall and the fakes crack and tinkle and bounce on the floor as I collapse on the bed and throw my head into my hands. I want to cry but I can't. All I seem able to do is look at the rolling stones, bitterly remembering, remembering everything that's gone by.

In the white bubbly Ambassador, with its spring seats and wind-down windows, Faizad tries to cheer me up.

"Come on, Josh, why are you being so quiet? You haven't said a thing all day."

"I'm just thinking."

"What about?"

"Just stuff." I shrug.

"Like what to do with all the money you're about to make," Faizad says, beaming broadly.

"I'll believe it when I see it," I say a little too bitterly.

"Don't you worry about a thing, buddy. The hard part's over. The rest is easy. We meet these guys in a couple of days and then we're in the clear. It's all taken care of."

"How do you know they'll show?"

" 'Cos."

" 'Cos what?"

" 'Cos I've been dealing with them for years, that's how. Come on, Josh, fucking relax, man. It's all taken care of. What's the problem? Don't you trust me or something?"

"I don't trust anyone anymore."

I can feel Faizad frowning as I turn my head to stare out the window. "This isn't like you, Josh."

"What isn't like me?"

"This moroseness."

I want to tell Faizad that he doesn't have a clue what is and what isn't like me, but I pull back. The fact is, he's my only hope now. I should at least attempt to salvage some semblance of real profit from this wreck. And I'm in Faizad's hands. Whatever I get from this deal will largely come down to his goodwill.

"I'm sorry," I say eventually. "It's just . . . well, no offense, I just never had myself pinned as a heroin dealer."

I can feel Faizad wince at the words, but I'm pleased. It's a convincing response that I know he can relate to. Considerably better than: "I'm gutted because I met this beautiful girl and we wanted to rip you off, but now she's disappeared with the money."

After a while he says, "Well, me neither. But it's only this once. After this, we'll both be free to do whatever it is we like. Like I said before, I really am thinking about going back into film."

"Yeah?"

"Sure, why not?"

"What kind of a film would you make?"

"Oh, I don't know. Maybe one about a heroin dealer in India." I know he's smiling.

"Plenty of room for action," I say.

"That's right! And you could write the script. Perfect."

"What makes you think I'm a writer?"

"Well, you're a journalist, aren't you? At least you were before you started dealing smack," Faizad says, suddenly laughing.

"Yeah, I guess," I manage quietly between his guffaws.

"Well?" he says eventually.

"Well what?"

"Do you want to write the script for me?"

"I'm not sure that I would know how to. I've never written a screenplay."

"Do it as a book, then. Just make it fast-moving. Once I've made it into a film, it'll be a bestseller." I half laugh then. "What's so funny?" he says.

"Nothing, it's just ironic."

"What is?"

"Doesn't matter."

"I hope you're not being precious," Faizad says. "You must know that fiction's all about film rights these days."

PUSHKAR

The meeting is arranged for tomorrow night behind the temple on Tit Hill, as Faizad calls it. I couldn't imagine a better location for a climactic ending if I tried. Pushkar is a beautiful town, with whitewashed buildings lining a rusty lake, the desert stretching endlessly on one side, and a table-topped mountain separating it from the rest of the world on the other. And then, of course, there is Tit Hill itself, which rises out suddenly and surprisingly from the sand and frames the whole scene like a giant green punctuation mark. At night, lights line the cobbled path to the top like prophetic stars showing the way to heaven. Invariably, a crescent moon hangs perfectly in place above it, just for good measure.

At least, Pushkar *was* a beautiful town. After two days here, I discover that the lake isn't actually rusty, it's just turned brown with sewage. A lot of the old houses are now tourist shops and bargain-basement buffet restaurants and the temple is full of so-called Brahmins who terrorize visitors to do *puja,* a religious ceremony that involves paying a lot of money to throw rotting flowers in the lake. The whole place is stuffed with travelers, and tourists, and tourist-travelers and other combinations. The fact is, Pushkar is ruined, like a rare gem that has somehow turned fake with time.

Maybe it's just me—I'm starting to see the reality behind every illusion. I am sitting in a *bhang lassi* shop, drinking marijuana milk shakes, killing time. This is my third one for the day and I'm wasted. Getting stoned is the only way to stop thinking about Yasmin. Each morning I wake up feeling fine, but it only lasts a split instant before I suddenly realize where I am, and why I'm here, and then the day kicks in like a steel toe cap in the guts. Without the *lassis,* I probably wouldn't sleep at all. I can tell that Faizad's getting tired of me and my moods, so I'm trying to spend as little time in his company as possible. I'm afraid that he'll cotton on—or worse, that I might confess.

I stare aimlessly outside, vaguely aware that I am slouching across the table, my mouth lolling open. Street vendors and hotel hawkers are getting ready for the midafternoon bus, which I can see heaving and honking its way down from the flat-topped mountain that divides Pushkar from the rest of the desert. Waves of heat fizz from pores in the tarmac road.

Five minutes later and the whole world seems filled with belching fumes, frenzied voices, and outstretched arms. Plastic bangles that Rajasthani women wear from their wrists to their armpits click against one another as they swarm the bus and thrust their wares into the emptying windows. Elaborately mustachioed men dressed in *dhotis* clamber onto the roof and hurl cloth bundles randomly into the crowd below.

Amid all the confusion, it is the tourists who attract the most attention. Exhausted, excited, or both, they filter off the bus one by one, advertising themselves with *Crowded Planet* guidebooks and multicolored rucksacks. Rickshaw wallahs and hotel peons make every effort to single out the weak and unconfident, harassing them into a condition where they seem most likely to hand over the most money. I sneer at the new arrivals for being new.

The only one who doesn't look fazed is the brown-haired boy.

It's obvious that he's been here many times before. I watch him get off the bus and deliberately make his way through the crowd. He's wearing exactly the same clothes he had on in Jaisalmer, but he's shaved off his little goatee now. I could take him, I reckon. I could definitely take him. I'm not scared. Not of him, not anymore. I know who he is, and this time, I'm the one watching him. This time, I have the advantage.

Still, I can't be sure. Better play it safe, just in case. You can never be too sure, not when it comes to the Truth. You have to be able to see the Truth in black-and-white. It can't be a vague, gray suspicion. It can't be an imagining. No, it has to be black-and-white. Otherwise, how will I be able to write it?

"So what does he look like, this contact of yours?" I pant. The path leading up Tit Hill is much steeper than I had imagined and my thighs are already smarting.

"You'll find out soon enough," Faizad says.

The starlike lights show the way, mapping out my dreaded, yet entirely avoidable destiny at the top of the hill. The walk feels eerie. Trees claw at us in the night shadows and the temple looms above us like some monstrous House of Truth. Every so often, enormous foxlike bats swoop past, feasting on insects.

But Faizad doesn't seem nervous at all. He walks deliberately up the hill, even skipping a couple of steps every so often as if he's quite looking forward to this bit. He certainly seems much more enthusiastic than he was before the meeting outside Jaisalmer. I check the gun once more, which I've held on to since the border deal—to see if it's still in the bag. On this unusually humid night, even it's sweating.

Forty-five minutes later and we reach the top. There is only one light, a naked yellow bulb that pulses weakly in the bell tower. Other than that, there's just the light from the moon—a cold blue that makes everything look like it's been shot in negative film. I set down my bag and stretch.

I wander over to the temple door, acting casual, and notice

that it is locked. Then I wander around the back of the temple to see if anyone is coming. The hill falls away steeply and I have an unobstructed view of the path and the town below. Orange lights and building silhouettes shine in the lake. A strong gust hits me and I step away from the edge. A few pebbles slip down in a gravelly stream against the rocks below.

Then I hear voices.

I walk back around the temple and I can hear Faizad talking, but the wind makes it difficult to hear what he is saying. I wait— the corner of the temple shields me. Faizad says something else and then everything goes quiet. I listen to the wind, buffeting. I think about looking around the corner but decide against it. I stand there, pressed up against the temple wall, listening to gusts that howl and then the leaves as they rustle themselves back to calm. For a brief moment everything goes very quiet, deadly still.

And that's when I hear Yasmin say, "It's all there, you don't need to count it."

PAID IN FULL

I smile to myself then. It's a bitter smile but it's still a smile. The Truth hurts but at least I know now that I am right. I've been right for a long time. I don't know how long I've known exactly—maybe since the very beginning. I should be proud, I suppose. For once in my life, I managed to see the hard facts in the midst of all my fiction. I've made my first real step toward becoming a writer.

I step out into the light. The gravel crunches and I see Yasmin flash her eyes at me before I deliver the line I've spent the last five days preparing: "I wouldn't bother, Faizad. The money's fake." There. Said without a wobble. No cuts, no retakes. And Yasmin is double-taking perfectly. She really is beautiful, you know. Even now.

She doesn't say anything. They're both watching me. This is my moment, my "Columbo reveals all" scene. The wind blows. I realize something. I'm not scared anymore, not of anything. "I never switched the money, Yasmin," I say. She stares back at me, her hair dancing. "I changed my mind." Yasmin shows no emotion, her face a hard canvas. "It seemed a little reckless, you know, to go on the deal *and* switch the money." Still no sign of any emotion. What a heartless bitch. I might be dead now because of her. How could I not have seen? She doesn't care about me. She doesn't even care if I live or die. I walk behind her and pick up my bag, reaching in for the gun.

"What's going on?" Faizad says.

"You want to know, Faizad? You really want to know what's been going on?" I say agitatedly. I know—I'm a little worked up. But I can't help it. If there was ever a climax to this story it would be now. And Yasmin. It's really upsetting to see her again, now that I know the Truth. "It's really quite simple. Yasmin and I have been conspiring together for months, trying to rip you off." I move toward him, checking the gun. "The whole idea was for me to earn your trust, just enough for me to switch the money you were planning to use to buy the smack at the border. We figured you'd been dealing with Akbar for such a long time, he'd never check and it would be weeks before anyone figured out the scam. You've every right to be angry," I say as his face creases. "But trust me, Faizad, we—well, I—honestly thought everyone could get away safely. After Ajay's death, I knew it was your last deal, and I just figured the only real loser would be Akbar. I never thought he'd check the money till you told me. That's why I didn't do the switch in the end. Couldn't risk it."

"So this," Faizad says, screwing up the wad of bills in his hands, "is fake?"

I nod at him. "It wasn't meant to be fake. Was it, Yasmin?" She's not even looking at me now. She's just staring coldly into the night. "Oh no. That was the extra little twist I never considered. Yasmin wanted me to do the switch so she could buy the smack off you with your own money. Clever, huh? I guess she figured you'd be more suspicious than Akbar. Either that or you'd be dead . . . in which case, she'd have the real money anyway. Didn't quite work out like that did it, darling?" She still doesn't answer. "The only thing I don't understand is the whole diamond angle. What was the point of all that? If it wasn't true." She doesn't say anything. "Go on, my love. You can tell me now."

She still doesn't look at me, even as she speaks. "The diamonds were your idea, not mine," she says matter-of-factly. "I just let you carry on believing it. You wouldn't have done all this if you'd known it was only ever about dope."

It's hard to control myself then, hearing her speak, hearing her actually confess like that. For a moment I think I'm going to hit her and then Faizad surprises me because he does. He slaps her. Really, it's a half punch. It catches her in the eye and she reels to the ground. I'd always seen myself hitting Yasmin, but I never figured Faizad would do it. But now that he has, I don't feel good. I don't like to see her getting hurt. And Faizad's in a blind rage now, screaming at her and spitting and calling her a bloody bastard bitch. I have to hold him back from kicking her. He says he's going to kill her and he tries to grab my gun, so in the end, I have to point it at him.

"Just calm down, Faizad." He's looking at me, shivering with fury. I'm pointing it right in his face. "Just shut up and calm down, all right." Yasmin is holding her face and is curled up, fetuslike, on the ground.

"THAT FUCKING BITCH NEARLY GOT ME KILLED! AND YOU?! YOU FUCK—"

"I SAID SHUT IT!"

It's the first time I lose control. Up until then, everything had been going smoothly—or so I thought. I had been the cool, dispassionate observer throughout, quietly noting the surroundings and the people and the events, just as a good writer should. But it feels good now to get involved. Feels good to display some emotion, twist the scene with my own perspective. Because I'm just as, if not more, angry than Faizad. I've got good reason to be.

After all, I did . . . I still do . . . love Yasmin. I'm the one who should feel betrayed. But I still, even now, can't manage to hate her as I should. I bend down to see if she's all right and put one hand on her shoulder. She turns her head to face me and our eyes meet and I think I see, beneath all the fear, a flicker of the woman she really is, the woman I want, the one I'm in love with. She even vaguely smiles at me. And I think I smile back at her. But I can't be sure because that's when I get kicked in the ribs and the pain shoots through me like a javelin pitch and then there's a blow to the head and there's a noise in the bridge of my nose that sounds like wood splintering.

LIBERATION CONVERSATION

Looking down the barrel of a gun is a liberating experience. It doesn't leave much else to think about. By the time life gets boiled down to looking down the barrel of a gun, everything becomes pretty simple, really. I'm scared, of course; I just don't have the luxury of thinking about it. I can see the boy, his brown hair falling forward like a shroud over his face, looking down at me. He's smiling, of course. He's always smiling.

"Hello, James," I manage to gurgle. Blood catches in the back of my throat. Urrgh. I hate the taste of it. Smelled it too many times on this misadventure already.

"Hello, Josh." He smiles back. I can see Yasmin standing next to him, pointing a gun across me, presumably at Faizad. I move to get onto my feet, but James stops me with one foot on my chest. "Easy, tiger," he says. He has a very proper accent. I wonder why. I assumed that going to school in Amsterdam would make him sound Dutch. Or maybe he got the accent in India, during his parents' days at the ashram. Who knows? Do I really care?

"Lock Faizad up, Yasmin. I'll look after this one."

I watch Yasmin direct Faizad toward the chapel door with the end of the gun. She throws Faizad a key. "Open it," she says calmly. I can only see the backs of their legs now. I notice for the first time that she's wearing jeans. She looks funny in jeans—she looks together, more organized. Like she's going on an outdoor adventure of some sort. I suppose a drug deal on top of Tit Hill is an outdoor adventure. I hear the padlock clicking open. God knows how they got the key. Let's face it, they've been one step ahead the whole way.

I turn to look back up at James, his face slightly blurred against the foreground of the gun barrel. "What happens now?" I ask.

"Ssssshhh," he says very gently, as if he's calming a child to sleep, shaking his head very, very slightly. His gentleness is intimidating. It's as if he doesn't want to scare his prey.

I know then that this is bad. Reality starts biting like an angry bitch. I realize that I'm going to die here. I've been driving too fast and now I'm crashing. I wanted to get the girl, so I stepped on the gas and look where it's gotten me.

How the fuck did I get here, anyway—lying on the ground, in the dust, with a gun in my face? I sift through the events. If I had to tell this story—let's say at the Pearly Gates—where would I begin? Delhi? The *Hindu Week*? Meeting Yasmin maybe? Or getting raided by the "police"?

Yeah, that's a laugh. I see then how I blew my cover, all those months ago. I was so easily duped. Letting Yasmin into my room that night, that stormy first night when I smelled her. Was it all set up? Even the first raid? Probably. Clever way for them to check up on me. I suppose they must have picked up on me asking questions. They probably overheard my voice in the well. It's not as if I talk quietly. It's all part of my social ineptness, my general clumsiness. A loud voice that carries—it goes with the territory.

But they were clever. The way they went about it. They waited for a police raid and then led them to my room. Maybe they bribed the police to check me. That's probably why Ashok, the guesthouse owner, never warned me. He never knew. Then Yasmin came up and hid in my loo to see how I reacted. See if I was a traveler or a traitor. She found out. That night, that night when I thought I was being clever, was really the beginning of me being incredibly stupid.

And then there was the second *raid*. The one where Yasmin lured me away and James stole all my stuff. I see now why they had to do that. Why they had to trap me. If I was going to comply, if I was going to do all their dirty work, rip Faizad off for them, then I had to be desperate. I had to be trapped. If there was any other way out, then I would have taken it. Because, and they could probably see this, I was looking for every opportunity not to do any of this. Because I don't drive fast, not anymore, not since I lost my nerve. I sit on the fence. I don't participate in the story. I let it just happen to me. Or worse, I just make it up. I'm not the hero. I'm not the bad guy. I'm not even an agent. I'm just a victim. They could see all that. Just by looking at me. Just by listening. Am I really so obvious?

I wonder if Yasmin's sleeping with me was all part of their plan? I wonder how she managed it—if she despises me so much. Does it matter? Does it matter that she despises me, hates me, loathes me? Doesn't it all lead to the same point? That she doesn't love me? I knew that already.

So here I am. That's how I got here. In one way, at least. In another way, those things have really got nothing to do with anything. The events, even though they led to this point, even though they were one another's catalysts, the series of reactions ending in this result—they're really just incidental.

Because they're not really the story at all. Let's face it, I'm not in this predicament because of the events. I'm here because, as a person, I have absolutely no grip on reality. I'm in love with my own delusions. I go off on one. I lead myself up the garden path with my own fantasies.

The sexy girl, the drugs, the diamonds, the undercover-journalist role . . . I mean, I really believed in all those things. I really believed that I was a budding journalist, that there were diamonds, that Yasmin might love me, that this ridiculous plan might work. That's why I'm here—because I was in love with an illusion, I always have been.

Why am I like that? It's not even as if my illusions are that charming. They're certainly not worth dying for. I mean, Jesus, this whole episode has been little more than paperback formula. In fact, when I think about it, my whole life has been nothing but one big paperback novel. Wanting to be different, wanting to be original, has kept me rewriting the plot (life) and constantly casting myself as the hero. And this is just one more episode in that rather sad trend.

I really should read some better-quality literature. It might improve me.

I suppose the upside is that at least I know myself now. I know that, at heart, I probably *am* a paperback writer—over and above the challenge in my father's suicide note. Maybe Dad was right about me after all. Maybe all he was ever trying to do was do me right. Maybe I shouldn't feel so angry with him anymore.

Yeah, like I say, looking down, up really, the barrel of a gun is a liberating experience. I'm finally free of my illusions. I can finally see myself for who I am. I know now that if it came to it, I probably could write paperback novels for a living. And it wouldn't just be for the money. It would be because . . . I like it. Now, that's a novelty.

I've finally found something I'd like to do with my life.

Pity I'm about to die.

MY ONLY FRIEND, THE END

When Yasmin gets back, James tells her to pack up the dope.

"What about the money?" she says, very organized, very in-jeans like.

"We'll take that too. He's probably bluffing."

She doesn't look at me while she's getting everything ready. Soon this'll all be over.

"Can I ask you a question?" I say, looking at James. He doesn't say anything, but I think I notice a vague shrug of his shoulders. "Did you kill Ajay?" He still doesn't say anything. Silence is confession in my book.

He sighs slightly. "Come on, Yasmin," he says. "We don't have much time."

"I'm going as fast as I can," she says.

"I mean, was it an old score or something? Please, I have to know," I say. "It's for a story."

James laughs then. "You and your stories, Josh. They only ever got you into trouble."

Yes, of course. I was right that time I saw James spying on Faizad and me at the fort. He has been the narrator of this adventure, he has been the one with the broader perspective. How else could he understand that about me—*your stories only ever got you into trouble, Josh.* He must have seen me coming a mile off. And I've been walking blindly through his version of events ever since.

"Funny you should say that, I was just thinking the same thing."

"Then you shouldn't mess with things that aren't your concern," he says, almost like he cares, a bit like Harold Brisbane at Reuters. "If you hadn't been making a nuisance of yourself at the Green, asking all those silly questions, well, you wouldn't be here now, would you?"

"No, I suppose not," I say. There's a pause as the wind blows. "Still, I don't regret it," I add almost wistfully.

"That's good," James says.

"I mean, how could I regret all those nights Yasmin and I spent together?"

I see her pause then, out of the corner of my eye. James just shrugs his shoulders again. "I'm glad."

"So you know, then?" He doesn't say anything. "And you don't mind? It doesn't bother you? Even after Stefan?"

I watch him stiffen.

"You were just work, Josh. That's all."

"Really?" I press. "'Cos I have to say, I'm surprised. I mean, I'm really surprised. Is that really all I was to you, Yasmin? Just work?" She doesn't say anything. "Please, I'd like to know."

"Why?" she says, suddenly finishing the packing. "For *your story?*" She sounds particularly bitter then.

"No. I just, you know, I don't believe I was . . . *we* were nothing."

She is looking down at me now, her face next to James's. I feel pathetic, lying here looking up at them, like a wounded animal that needs to be put down—for its own sake.

"I'm ready," she says. "Let's lock him up."

"You go on," he says to her. "I'll take care of this one."

She looks at him then. "Are you sure?"

"Of course," he says. "Now go on. I'll be there in a minute."

They kiss.

When she's gone, James looks at me and says, "Thing is, Josh, you never truly appreciated the beauty of it all. Like Yasmin and me. I mean, we really love each other."

"I don't know how she could love a murderer."

"Ah well, that's just what I mean, you see. The things you don't know. I mean Ajay, shit, that guy really had it coming to him."

"So you did murder Ajay."

"Of course."

"But why?"

"Why d'you think? That fucker kept selling us dodgy smack. He was always screwing us. That's what I mean about the beauty of it all. Giving Ajay and Faizad a taste of their own medicine. Beautiful. And you! Oh, Josh, you were perfect. I mean, there you were just gagging to do all our dirty work for us. Like a little eager puppy, weren't you? Just dying for an adventure."

"So now you kill me."

"Obviously."

"But why? I never did anything to hurt you. Like you say, I did all your dirty work for you. I don't deserve to die."

"Of course you do."

"Why?"

He jumps down onto my chest then, his knees punching the air out of my lungs, one hand grabbing my throat, the other driving the gun up into one of my nostrils. He's sneering now, spitting, inches away from my face. "Think I'd let you live? After soiling my woman, you really think I'd let you live? Just like that bastard Stefan. I enjoyed killing him. He was my first, you know. I've Yasmin to thank for that. And I've Yasmin to thank for you."

. . . sometimes I think he can do terrible things . . .

"Does Yasmin know?" I say, my bladder twitching.

"I should have killed you in the beginning. I wanted to. At the Green, when you were sticking your nose all over the place. You piece of shit."

"Does Yasmin know you murdered Stefan?"

"I would have too if Yasmin hadn't come up with the idea to use you," he says, ignoring me. "She's the clever one, you know. She's always been the clever one."

"You need help."

His face creases up again. "It's just you and me now, isn't it?" He squeezes my throat tighter. "Just you and me now."

I try to scream for Yasmin, but before I get a chance he clamps a hand over my mouth and nose, pressing the gun into my eye until my head starts to throb. I can't breathe now. But I realize with surprise that I'm not pissing myself.

. . . real danger doesn't produce fear, it produces fearlessness . . .

I'm just looking at him as he does this to me. Looking at the gun he's drilling into my face. Watching my life flash before my eyes in words. Catchphrases and conversational titbits. So pulp. So paperback.

I wonder if he'll shoot me. I can see him smiling. Always smiling. I can feel consciousness slipping away from me like a delicate object. The harder I hang on to it, the further it slips away. Maybe that's been my problem all along. I've been holding on too hard. Maybe that's why life has always escaped me. Why I've been scared to live it. I've always held on too hard. I'm losing it now. Darkness is creeping in from the corners of my eyes. This story is at an end. The novel is finally coming to a close, the hero isn't going to make it. In fact, there is no novel. At long last, this is, really, THE END.

SHE LOVES ME, SHE LOVES ME NOT

"You said you wouldn't hurt him." It's Yasmin. She's back. James has released his grip and I'm choking air back into my lungs. My head hurts. James is sitting up now, the gun lolling to the side of my head, my eye still burning with its impression. "You said you wouldn't hurt him, James."

"What?" he says, half smiling like a naughty boy caught. "I wasn't."

I knew she wouldn't leave me.

"You killed Stefan."

I knew I wasn't nothing.

"What? No. No. You've got it wrong."

Yasmin has come back to save me.

"I heard you. I heard everything. You killed Stefan and Ajay too. Why?" She's crying now. Sobbing. It's all falling down. The illusion, the veneer, all of it is tumbling. "Why do you do these things?"

"Babe," he says, one hand upturned.

"No more. No more. It's got to stop."

He's getting up off me, the gun hanging to his side. "Sweetheart . . ."

"Please," she says. She's pointing the gun at him now. "Don't."

I knew she loved me.

"Baby," he says.

"Drop the gun, James." He takes one step toward her. "Please, James, drop the gun." Her shoulders are shaking. He takes another step toward her.

All this time, she really did love me.

And that's when the shot rings out. James's shoulder does a kind of little dance as it rolls with the shock of the bullet in its socket. I can't see his face. He just stands there for a second, rocking ever so slightly. The second shot hits him in the chest. He takes one step back. Then another, before collapsing on top of me. Yasmin is sobbing helplessly then. She drops the gun and falls to her knees, sobbing wretchedly. James is motionless on top of me, blood soaking into my trousers. I try to slide out from under him, but he's too heavy. My leg is trapped. Yasmin looks up and sees me trying to get out. I look at her.

"Yasmin," I call.

"Please," she says, her face stained with tears, like rain-splattered glass. "Don't."

"Yasmin."

"Stay away from me," she says.

I inch my way out from under James a little further. "Yasmin, please, wait a second."

"Don't," she says. "Please don't come any nearer." She points the gun at me. It's wobbling.

"Yasmin, listen to me."

She shakes her head violently from side to side and manages to get to her feet. I can see her knees shaking. She's still leveling the gun in my general direction. "Don't try to follow me," she says. "Just stay away from me."

"Yasmin, don't leave." She's turning now, reaching for the first step with her foot. I'm almost free. Just another inch. Almost free. "Yasmin," I say, turning to look at her. "I love you," I say.

But it's too late. She's gone.

SCOOP

HINDU WEEK EXCLUSIVE!

INTERNATIONAL UNDERCOVER DRUG-RUNNING RING EXPOSED!

ILLICIT OPERATION LINKED TO MAFIA KINGPIN DOWDY IBRAHIM!

MURDER OF VJ AJAY ALSO CONNECTED— BOLLYWOOD REELING WITH SHOCK!

It all started one muggy monsoon night in a seedy guest house on Pahar Ganj almost one year ago to the day. It was three o'clock in the morning and police were conducting a random search of the premises. Joshua King couldn't sleep. There was a knock on his door. He opened it. And that's how he met Yasmin Hoogland.

You might recall the name. Hoogland hit the headlines earlier this week after police launched a massive manhunt for her arrest following the murder of James Braxton, an Englishman whose body was discovered near the famous hill temple of Pushkar. Hoogland, an international drug smuggler well-known to the authorities, is believed to have shot Braxton—her longtime lover and business partner—in a dispute over heroin and drug money.

This week, in a very special edition of the *Hindu Week,* we can reveal the truth behind Braxton's murder and uncover the incredible trail that links both Hoogland and Braxton to an enormous multimillion-dollar international drug-smuggling network operated across the hypersensitive Indo-Pak border and which was ultimately controlled by none other than Mafia mogul Dowdy Ibrahim.

We also reveal how Hoogland and Braxton were the final link in a long chain of organized crime that connected the glamorous world of Bollywood with the underworld of Ibrahim's empire. The very same chain that resulted in the tragic murder of superstar VJ Ajay in Mumbai just three months ago.

It all sounds too incredible to be true, and if Joshua King, an investigative journalist special to the *Hindu Week,* hadn't been following the story from the very beginning, perhaps no one would have believed it. But call it chance, call it fate, call it what you like—Joshua King was there. He saw it all. He knows it's true.

And this is his story . . .

EPILOGUE

By the time I finally extricated myself from James's bleeding body, Yasmin was halfway down the hill. I stood behind the temple and watched her—running through the shadows and the pools of light, struggling with the two heavy suitcases. I briefly thought about chasing after her, but then I couldn't really see the point.

In a funny way, I felt as if I'd been enough trouble for Yasmin already, or rather, we'd been enough trouble for each other. Things were definitely at an end between us. It was time to stop kidding myself. There wasn't any future for us. There never had been. Things had been too screwed up between us from the start for us to have a future. Perhaps she'd always known that. Perhaps that's why she never really let herself love me. Or perhaps she was always just in it for the money.

Either way, as I watched her disappear into the night and from my life, I finally found myself letting go. I finally admitted to myself that I'd never really loved Yasmin. The truth was I'd never even known her, not really. All this time, I had been in love with a wraith, an illusion of her, someone my mind had conjured up. And now that ghost was gone. Yasmin was finally demystified.

And to the *real* Yasmin, the hard Dutch girl who was about to make millions on a major heroin deal—well, good luck to her. As far as I was concerned, I barely knew this person whose silhouette I could see melting into the night. From one stranger to another, that was how I felt. Good luck to her. Indeed, as much good luck to her as to all the heroin dealers and dodgy travelers out there. I may even have shouted it out, I can't honestly remember. She didn't turn around or stop or anything. But I meant it. Good luck. As Dad would have said—she was going to need it.

The only thing I do really remember was Faizad banging on the door of the temple begging to be let out. I used James's gun to smash the lock. He was pretty pissed off, as you can imagine. He didn't seem too concerned about the fact that I was still alive. He just came steaming out of the temple and spent the next five minutes kicking the shit out of James until he was quite convinced that he really was dead. That satisfaction was probably the only thing that stopped him from killing me.

The police arrested Faizad and me the following day, after they caught us trying to skip the fare on a bus out of town. They had found James's body. Mani was the first person I called. He said he could get us both out—for a price. The price being, of course, the story. So I told him. He came down to Pushkar and I told him everything, from the top. He couldn't stop grinning afterward. I think he knew, even then, what he had to do to make my story really newsworthy.

For the cover illustration he ran the police Wanted poster for Yasmin with the headline: WE KNOW THIS WOMAN. I never told him that it looked nothing like her, and for the first time, I found I was glad I'd never taken any pictures of her for the police to find. Apparently she's been slipping past customs for years now without them ever getting a solid fix on her. It must be the secret sannyasin world that shields her. I can only assume that's where she's hiding now, in some remote ashram, waiting for things to calm down before crossing the border to Nepal.

To be fair to Mani, though, he did pay me my 25 Gs in the end. He didn't have to. After all, getting Faizad and me out of prison was payment enough, considering the long list of charges and the stretch we were facing. But I don't think he thought that that was quite fair. The game we were playing with my life was over, and by his yardstick, I had won—in other words, I got the story. I think the way he saw it, I deserved to collect.

At least, that's how I've reasoned it.

I didn't stay in India for very long after that. Just a couple of weeks till the embassy could reissue me a temporary passport, and until I could find a flight for less than twenty-five thousand rupees—not an easy feat these days.

Two months after the *Hindu Week* story came out, I got a call from a publishing agent interested in my story. And, rather weirdly, at around the same time, the money I stole from Faizad's suitcase arrived at Morag's place. It wasn't much—fifty grand or so—certainly not the millions we were hoping for. But there was no way I could have risked taking too much, not if I was going to the border with Faizad. I was clever enough at least to know that stealing a lot would have been as stupid as stealing none at all. I sent the money to myself from Jaisalmer in a box, sewn up in white cloth by a tailor and then sealed with wax. It seemed like the safest way. After all, if there's one thing you can trust in India, it's a well-wrapped package in the postal system. I've always known that much. Lying about that was probably Yasmin's first big mistake.

It's been enough in any case to see me through the last year or so that it's taken me to write this.

The only people I really stay in touch with now are Sanjay and Faizad. They're both really excited about the book. Faizad is insisting I give him the rights to direct the film, and Sanjay says he's already down to play the bad guy. I think they're really just holding out for their cut. It took Sanjay all of about two minutes after we left the country to tell Faizad about my father's final challenge—and the £5 million should I succeed.

I keep telling them that it's got to be a Bestseller first. But they don't listen. They just pretend that they don't see how it could not be. After all, they say it's got all the elements—drugs, diamonds, exotic location, sexy girl, the plan that goes horribly wrong. It's tailor-made, apparently.

We'll see. Call it the final twist in the tale if you like. If you're reading this, then there's a small chance we've made it. All I can tell you is that Dad's lawyer hasn't called me with the good news yet.

And would you believe me if I was to say I don't care?

Not really. Not anymore. Because the really good part is that I feel much, much better. Somewhere along the line, somewhere between the fantasy and the reality, I've found a space where I'm comfortable. The bad dreams have stopped. I don't feel so lost. I don't feel so confused. I finally know what it is I'd like to do with my life. I'd like to write. And it won't necessarily be for the money.

Because the real reward from all of this has been *me*. The real story here hasn't been about drugs and diamonds and beautiful girls and double-crossing deals. The real story has been much, much simpler than that. It's really been about a guy who goes to India and finds himself. It's as wonderfully simple and cheesy as that. I went to India and found myself, *maaaaaan* (see Sanjay flashing peace sign).

After all, isn't that what going to India is all about?

Every writer dreams of producing a literary work that defines his or her generation. For J. D. Salinger, it was *The Catcher in the Rye*; for Alex Garland, *The Beach*. But for **Will Rhode**, it's, well, something like *The Beach*—but different. Born in London, Rhode has worked for Reuters in India and wrote financial journalism in Hong Kong. Moving to New York City with his wife and son, he worked as the editor of *Risk*, a financial magazine, until he worked up the courage to quit and write a paperback original. He now lives in London.